Stevie Davies comes from Mumbles, Swansea. She was a lecturer in English literature at Manchester University from 1971–84, leaving to become a full-time writer. She has published six volumes of literary criticism, including two studies of the revolutionary Milton, two books on Emily Brontë, one on Virginia Woolf and a feminist re-appraisal of Renaissance poetry.

Her first novel, the acclaimed *Boy Blue* (The Women's Press 1987), won the Fawcett Society Book Prize in 1989. Her second novel, *Primavera*, was published by The Women's Press in 1990.

Also by Stevie Davies from The Women's Press:

Boy Blue (1987)
Primavera (1990)

STEVIE DAVIES

arms and the girl
a novel

First published by The Women's Press Ltd 1992
A member of the Namara Group
34 Great Sutton Street, London EC1V 0DX

British Library Cataloguing in Publication Data
A catalogue record for this book is available from the
British Library

ISBN 0 7043 4309 6 pbk
     0 7043 5063 7 hbk

Phototypeset by Intype, London
Printed and bound in Great Britain by
BPCC Hazells Ltd.
Member of BPCC Ltd.

Acknowledgement

During the seven months' composition of this book, I lived in unnerving proximity to and even fear of implication in the evil of which I told. The darkness of this experience was alleviated by the steadying presence of my companion in the next room, in which the light was always on. I owe you thanks, Frank, for this keeping of vigil.

For Andrew
in continuing faith

Arma virumque cano, Troiae qui primus ab oris
Italiam fato profugus Laviniaque venit
litora — multum ille et terris iactatus et alto
vi superum, saevae memorem Iunonis ob iram,
multa quoque et bello passus, dum conderet urbem
inferretque deos Latio: genus unde Latinum
Albanique patres atque altae moenia Romae.

  Musa, mihi causas memora . . .

(Virgil, *Aeneid, I*)

The arms and the man I sing la la la whose
arms? Jesus? no it means armour guns and weapons
who First from land of Troy, driven by fate came to the
Lavinian shore by land and sea " by the powers
Above can't do the next bit Juno had it in for
him he had to suffer greatly by WAR till he
founded the city and something something
whence the Latin nations and the high walls
of Rome
o muse remind me of the causes
It means Aeneas traveled a lot over the map
not by his own choice he didn't like
being hounded no more than what we do he
Wondered WHY??? He were OK in the end he
founded the Roman Empire which come after
the Egiptian Emp. and the Mycinean Emp. and the
Greek Emp. and before Spanish and Turkish Emp.
+ some others which come before the BRITISH
EMPIRE which is where we are in the present
day and is all the result of the arms and the man

get a
bit of
blotting
paper
Morag??

(Schoolgirl translation [rough notebook], 1959)

1

The three-thonged leather strap – agent of discipline, extortionist of respect – hangs on its own special peg beside the blackboard on which a map of the world has been painstakingly drawn. A beam of sunlight burnishes the dull, war-weary leather to a matt, gold-tinged shine, which confirms it as an off-centre optical focus to the room. In the class-room at Kinleven Academy, Morayshire (where mixed-ability teaching is enforced by the smallness of the community together with its distance from civilisation), thirty-four children are filling in a map of the British Commonwealth and Dominions. While thirteen of the pupils are native Scots, twenty-one are Army children from the adjacent military camp.

'Colour in the British colonies red, the Protectorates pink, those countries which have been accorded Independence within the Commonwealth (as of today, 16 July, 1959) green. And do so neatly and without crayoning over the borders of your tracing paper into the next country – violating the boundaries, so to speak. *Do not*, whatever else you do, omit to provide a key on the bottom left-hand corner, boys and girruls.'

So instructs Miss Slorach of the electrifying red hair, spinning a globe in her left hand and wafting a foot-rule in her right, up there on the dais at the monumental desk,

1

looking down like majesty enthroned upon the hunched populace below. Scrapings of chairs, chesty coughs, the cry of gulls out there amongst the pines, shafts of sunlight like brilliant flying buttresses falling through the three high windows; Miss Slorach surveys the limits of her personal mandate, with its improbable mingling of itinerant rabble and indigenous patricians, an explosive brew compounded by religious schism – the followers of the True Faith sitting down (Heaven help us) next to the offspring of the Papal Antichrist.

'Begin!'

A fighter-plane from RAF Kinloss or RAF Lossiemouth Air-Sea-Rescue surges low overhead with a reverberant roar, as if it meant to fly in at one schoolroom window and out at another.

'I said, begin!'

Elderly nibs loaded from inkwells sunk in the desk-tops splutter names on pages, trailing uncontrollable blobs and inky spiders.

'Prudence Mary Xavier Cahill, Form 2,' writes Prue Cahill carefully, tongue between her lips, squinting through her inadequate lenses in concentration, face down close to the page as if hunting herself for errors. The image of her father punching and kicking her sister last night fades like a perishing electric light bulb under this intense focusing of energy.

Her sister January cannot oblige Miss Slorach with any account of the British Empire; she is out and away, truanting in the Housty Woods, hallooing to the squirrels in the Laird's forbidden trees.

Jacko Jackson, the most scrofulous and ragged of the Army boys, cannot oblige either, though nominally present in body. Despite having straddled the globe from Hong Kong to Aden, and having lent his part to the

British civilising of the world by pelting the native boys of both colonies with whatever weapons came to hand, from stones to broken bottles, his mind is innocent of the rationale of these acts, and liable to remain so. The cuffs of his dusky shirts are grimed and buttonless; his face is shrunk and blank like a little gnome's. Jacko's red crayon fills in the British Commonwealth and Dominions by random inspiration, laying claim to Poland, Czechoslovakia and most of the Soviet Union, as if to demonstrate the fictitiousness of the Iron Curtain; he then adds Texas and select portions of Mexico in green. These efforts complete, he sits back and picks his nose with one bony finger, ruminatively considering the strap on the front wall, of which he has felt too much by far in his year at Kinleven. At the primary school in Hong Kong they only tapped you with a slipper. When he's grown up he'll come back and give Miss Slorach a taste of that belt on her bare bum, only it won't be tapping and it won't be patting. He imagines this Day of Judgment at length and in technicolour.

Margaret Urquhart, the doctor's daughter, knows from her father, a vehement Scottish Nationalist, that Scotland is *de facto* though not *de jure* a colony of England. History demonstrates it and patriotic feeling deplores it, whatever Miss Slorach's official doctrine may dictate to pull the wool over native eyes and placate the invading Army of Sassenachs. Margaret, like most of the other Scots in the class, does not speak to the Sassenachs except on compulsion, and then in her snootiest, clipped voice. In accordance with these sentiments, Margaret Urquhart commences to colour in Scotland blood-red on her map. She is a bit vague about the rest of the world.

Isabel Gordon, the Rector's daughter, goes one better. This appalling prodigy scares Miss Slorach half to death,

3

though she conceals her lack of serenity behind polysyllabic fortifications. Isabel Gordon knows by rote and in alphabetical order the colonies, mandates, Protectorates and Zones of Influence of Great Britain, from Aden and Antigua through Cyprus, Fiji, Malta and Mauritius, to Singapore, Uganda and Zanzibar. She has further worked out that this great carve-up of the world between Empires is all the result of greed and violence, looting and plundering, genocide and repression on an almost unbelievable scale. Isabel, though even now only one month short of 13 years, laughed out loud at Eden's Suez fiasco three years back and suspects Archbishop Makarios (despite his cassock) of being a great liberator. She colours in her map with scrupulous exactitude, adding a comment in her best handwriting, to the effect that it is *all wrong*.

Paul Cox, much-travelled, cosmopolitan, son of a Warrant Officer, Class Two, can fill in all the places where he has set his nomadic foot, from the Rock of Gibraltar, Hildesheim in West Germany, and Singapore, to Ballykelly in Northern Ireland. He knows, because his father, who wants to buy himself out has told him, that British power is on the wane, and that the map of Britain is shrinking until in the end it will have deflated into that queer-shaped squiggle of the mother-country, leaving to independence or anarchy the continents we have infested. Paul Cox, who is well brought-up, has been forbidden to speak of nignogs, darkies, coons, Pakis or Black Sambo, and he hardly ever does. He cares little one way or the other. To Paul life is a great football match in which he hopes to play a defensive part in the winning team.

Bongo Smart draws Britannia with colossal boobs like balloons, cross-eyes, rabbit-teeth and a Hitler moustache. When Miss Slorach gets an eyeful of that, it would normally be the strap for him, but she won't clap eyes on him again till next term (for it's the last day of the summer term) and by that time Bongo will have made his get-away, posted to Malta – with any luck, if his father who's already over there, has found quarters for the family by then. He'll be sunning himself and swimming in the warm sea while old Slorrie boggles and fumes over his art-works. Taking up his red crayon, he draws a gigantic erect penis over his map of the world. Give her something to remember him by.

Isabel Gordon catches Prue Cahill's eye. She gives her a big friendly wink. Prue smiles back with that look of incredulous joy which she can never get over at the equality and friendship Isabel confers on her.

Margaret Urquhart registers the exchange of glances with disgust. *Goofy fat flat-footed goggle-eyed foreigner* is the gist of the message her eyes flash at Prue, who blushes and looks down at her map.

The ringing of the great hand-bell, with its vast brass clapper like a rude tongue thrust out; rustling of papers; chairs on tables; uproar of bird-winged girls taking off from the school yard into the clear, salty air of freedom.

★

In the high-walled garden of the Manse, the two Sassenach sisters, January and Prue, and the heretical daughter of the Rector, Isabel, are hanging by the legs from the bough of a beech. As they hang, they sing, and their green skirts bell down over their heads.

'Charlie is my darling – my darling – my darling . . .'

Their bodies rock gently; their fingertips trail the grass and lichen at the rooty base of the tree. Isabel's prodigious pigtails also hang down. The meridian sun casts spangling light and boisterous shadows over their bodies and over the warmly breezy upside-down world. In their luminous green tents they hang in delicious common solitude, like a line of washing, their bottle-green bloomers exposed to the air.

'The you – ung Chevalier,' they warble.

Prue hoists herself up on to the broad bough of the beech which is their lair. She gropes for her glasses which she had suspended from a handy twig.

'What's a Chevalier?' she wonders, replacing them on her nose with some relief. The world is safer behind her National Health lenses with their round, metal frames, though less strangely beautiful, and she sometimes takes them off to see it worse and hence see it better.

'Dunno,' says January.

'A Chevalier', says Isabel, part of whose alarming precocity is attributable to having been stuffed full of knowledge, some of it antiquarian and recondite, by a learned mother who is understood to mutter to herself in Latin over the stove, 'is a sort of aristocratic horseman.'

'What's aristocratic?'

'High-class.'

Charlie rides his high horse through Prue's imagination but not as proudly or as powerfully as she, Isabel and January master the bucking tree, whose warm flanks vault out across the great green dappled world. Sitting astride, she rests her eyes with satisfaction on the high wall of their fastness, over which mottled ivies, green and yellow, clamber on suckered feet and briar-roses wander, and against which giant rhododendron bushes grow in wild profusion. Within the extravagant rhododendron wilderness runs a system of dens and safe houses, with corridors between, like living catacombs.

> Oh there were mony beating hearts
> And mony a hope and fear

When Charlie came to our house
The you – ung Chevalier . . .

January's face bobs up. She heaves herself on to the back of the steed, her face beetroot-red. A villainous-looking child at the best of times, January has a hunted, mangy look, unlike her more kempt and couth younger sister. Mother-love and fatherly care have never come near her during her thirteen punishing years of global travel. From the beginning her father took against her; the beatings and sadistic punishments began at around the age of three. Her mother's indifference to her amongst the mass of other human burdens set hard into aversion as a result of the violence she seemed to unleash in her father. January was trouble. A bad girl, a black sheep. She brought it on herself, she brought it down upon them all (for if Hugh's fragile temper is lost, the hammer-blows rain down indiscriminately – they all have to watch out). Sometimes the child's face and legs are a mass of bruises or livid weals as if from claw-marks. She says she fell or fought a boy and somehow people believe, or affect to believe, or do not care to query these stories, so rough and hard does she make herself out to be. Her naturally sallow face, pitted with eczema scars, makes her appear perpetually grimy to the censorious adult eye, and she is frequently collared at school, propelled to the cloakroom and called upon to wash herself thoroughly behind the ears and under the arm-pits. Miss Slorach confides to Miss Peebles that she is well used to the savage Army children; they come from bad homes and have no finer understanding of Burns; but *this* one is a ne'er-do-well, the like of which she has never seen. Miss Peebles sighs and cannot but agree.

January is under-sized, the runt of the litter. She has no

flesh, only bones: she is all knee and face. And she does have face. She is a fighter and will take on a boy one-and-a-half times her size and mass. Perpetual defeat has brought no sense of caution to January, and Prue cannot protect her from herself. If Prue can't, and the privileged Isabel can't, then nobody else is likely to take a hand. They have, to date, a total of eight brothers and sisters living at home, two living away, and one dead, and the family has to be assigned double Married Quarters. Their mother runs in and out of the two front doors all day long and half the night, the Army having declined to knock a hole in the adjoining wall to unite the two domiciles. After all, when they have been posted away, the houses will be redeemed from their slum status and reallocated to two more normal families.

Yes, she is a fighter. She gets that from her dad, tough and punchy and never-say-die. As good as a boy any day, so her strutting walk told them, hands in trouser-pockets, kicking cans, whistling through the gap in her teeth. Good at conkers, good at tree- or lamp-post climbing, good at catapults, sprinting, vaulting, tackling, stone-throwing, anything you like. Though lately she has become tremblingly aware of changes, vulnerabilities opening up the sealed solitude of her body – tender little breasts, softening the thin rib-cage (and making it hurt more if she gets pummelled by Dad or whoever), the first shock of menstrual blood. A new feeling of uncertainty and strangeness, and the martens singing 'Who am I? Who am I?' under the eaves at morning-light, whose enquiry she ignores as best she can.

The Reverend Donald Gordon has forbidden January to come and play with Isabel, and Isabel to go into the camp to play with January. His unbending Protestant principles, fortified by the resurgent hell-fire Calvinism of his youth, theoretically rejected long ago, revolt against the thought of his clean-cuffed, neatly braided only daughter fraternising with the family of Antichrist. The Cahills are Liverpool Catholics by origin, as he surmises – 'Liverpool', a metropolis he has never visited, being a word replete with moral condemnation, in his lexicon. He tolds these views on religious grounds; on nationalistic grounds, as being English; on class grounds, as being low; and also on the medical grounds that he suspects the hair of January of providing a greasy breeding-ground for lice. Notwithstanding, the sister, owl-eyed, gentle Prudence – who has a virtuous name, has never been heard using profane language and was fleetingly a member of his wife's Brownie Pack (a Kelpie, just like Isabel) – is allowed to visit and is somehow exempt from the suspicion of harbouring fleas or germs.

Mrs Gordon, profoundly sombre and entirely kind, ignores her husband's dictates, knowing from her thoughtful reading of Scottish history the wilful wrongness of rectitude, and welcomes January to the garden and to the eating of secret apples in the attic at certain mutually agreed times when the Reverend Gordon is away visiting the sick or conferring with the elders and the deacons. The fact that this welcome is the outcome of her own inner struggle against tribal prejudice and class superiority makes her extension of warmth all the more decisive: the difficulty of love has never been hidden from her; the primacy of self-interest.

She now comes out with a plate of home-made toffee, a book and the labrador, Iain, who crashes through the undergrowth to Isabel and snuffles under her skirt where she still dangles from the beech, the tender skin behind her knees quite raw and the blood all having run to her head – with fortitude, outstaying time and outlasting the Sassenachs as did the Highland clans of old.

'Oh get away with you, you slobbering hound. Go on.'

Isabel somersaults down; then staggers giddily in the whirling world.

'Toffee for you, my bairns. It's still warm from the pan.'

'Thank you, Mrs Gordon,' says Prue, and nudges January.

'Thanks,' says January, grabbing the biggest chunk.

Prue blushes for her sister's snatch-and-grab tactics. She has discovered that you are better provided for if you smile nicely, but how is January to know this? Here comes January's foraging hand again, the first piece of toffee being stuffed in the recess of her cheek.

'Don't be so rude,' Prue whispers. 'Wait till you're offered.'

'Well, that's all right,' says Mrs Gordon, mingling faint reproof with strong reassurance. 'There's plenty to go round.' She is a tall, gaunt woman, with grey hair scraped back into a bun; darkly clad – her clothes seem all composed of shadows and clouds. Harsh and unforgiving with herself, she walks barefoot, the interior of a mind flinty as the ranges of her native Sutherland, like a penitent who must atone for the inhospitality of the world to all but the lucky few. In this way she accompanies these millions of the ill-shod or shoeless, shelterless, starving and supernumerary to whom this world is more of a concentration camp than a home. And then of course she must punish herself for the element of prideful complacency that taints this concern. And then, when she has conscientiously woven great swathes of useless anxiety and guilt, festooning her mind like ancient spiders' webs in a lightless attic, either she resolves it all in simple, downright acts of practicality or else, as now, the garden with its call of birds and children chasing through the dappled greenery awaken her to the fresh outdoors of keen enjoyment. She forgets herself, in sharing the life that is given.

'I didn't mean to be rude, Mrs Gordon,' January pipes up, her mouth full of toffee. 'Just, it's so good, what you make. We don't get nothing like this at home.'

That's not all we don't get, thinks January. We don't get: *There's plenty to go round.* What we do get is: *Keep your thieving hands off and a boot up your arse if you try it on.* She wipes her sticky mouth with a fraying sleeve of a green cardigan that came from a church jumble-sale, via Teresa who wore it into holes at the elbows, and passed it down, a disreputable inheritance. Do the Scotch ladies have *arses*, wonders January, do they sit on *bums* like we do? No, she is sure they descend to *bottoms*, they hide from their nether regions by translating them into foreign *derrières, posteriors*. They don't shit, they pass a motion, excrete, defecate, do their business, numbers one and two. The officers' children circumlocute their way around the world. It's a real pleasure to vomit dirty words over their prissy insolence, high-stepping over the muddy world. But the Scotch – some of them, not many – are rather different, hard to say how exactly. The austere, just Mrs Gordon with the plate of sweets, saying *There's enough to go round.* January is prepared to forgive that woman for not knowing she has an arse.

'Well, my lass, you enjoy it,' Mrs Gordon goes on. 'You don't look as if you get enough to eat. You're a wee stick-girl. I hope you eat your potatoes at dinner-time?'

'I *hate* mashed potatoes. School spuds is full of black bits like dead flies and lumps like gristle.' January steals sweets from the NAAFI; she doesn't go short and hasn't been caught yet.

11

'Oh but you must eat them up if you want to thrive. Many and many a time of famine, potatoes were all the poor folk of Scotland had – tatties and the occasional onion and carrot. We, thank God, live in better days. You and Isabel are never likely to starve.'

She looks doubtfully at the evidently perishing January. She has seen her legs severely bruised, her face and arms scarred. Once she saw blood seeping through the child's thin blouse; there was a great weal across her back, caused, January insisted, by a falling metal bar when she was playing down a workman's hole. Isla knows the child is always in a fight with some big boy or other, and concludes these to be the source of the bruises. Shouldn't the parents be told, the school spoken to? She suggested it once, to the child's evident terror. For 'Me dad would kill me,' she said. 'Promise you won't.'

Me dad would kill me. It rang in her mind for weeks after; that and the blank, hunted look in the child's staring eyes which seemed to code an SOS message – to code it and then to scramble it before Isla had a chance to construe. Some fugitive message of obscene damage, hurt, sealed-up misery was passed across. And then, 'I'm tough, I can look after myself,' said the girl's swaggering gait, and her mocking wink that said she saw through Isla but she liked the cake and fudge, and she'd come again for more. And then again, if the child was not loved and cared for, how unusual was that? As far as she could see, amongst the impoverished families of the camp, neglect was a norm.

And yet it has always been hard to believe that January and Prue came from the same family. In the summer garden, Prue with her pale, silky hair, is standing in sunlight, rosy, plump, the picture of health, sucking her toffee and making it last, hopping from foot to foot in ignorant

12

imitation of the elaborate steps of the sword-dance being executed by Isabel in the middle of the lawn, pigtails flying. Prue is decently attired in clean, darned clothes, her hair cropped short, parted at one side and tied with a red ribbon.

(And yet even with Prue one senses it . . . a vague feeling . . . of something not quite right . . . what was it? Behind the small, apologetic cough, the timidity and reticence, the poignant beauty of the trustful smile when you could elicit it . . . something withheld and suppressed, as if she asked herself 'Do I dare to, have I the right to, breathe, take up space, be me?' and walked with her stomach held in, taking quick, shallow breaths).

So vague and nebulous, it hardly counts as a thought. Prue is a well-cared-for child if ever there was one. Mrs Gordon looks from one to the other.

'The same person didn't bring up me and Prue,' says January uncannily.

'How do you mean exactly?'

'Well, the older ones look after the younger ones in our family because there's not enough parents to go round. Prue, she were lucky, she got brought up by Columba. But *I* got saddled with Malachi. Columba is soppy, she likes dolls and that, she spent a lot of time cooing over Prue when she were a kid, dressing her up and bathing her, she coddled her like a ruddy egg. But Malachi didn't fancy being a mother, he said. Malachi is a . . .'.

She was going to say shitface or turd. In lieu of a polite alternative, she shrugs her shoulders and looks frowningly at the toffee on the plate. The plate winks in the sun. Malachi's method of ensuring that she cleans her teeth and washes her hair is the disciplinary technique of dragging her into the bathroom by the hair and holding her head underwater until she chokes. When she cried in the night

13

as a very young child, he came in and administered a remedial punch. She prematurely dropped the habit of snivelling.

'That is a great misfortune for you, dear. But you are old enough now, you know, to look after *yourself* a bit. Have you thought of that? Wash your own hair, darn your socks, take a pride in yourself.'

January looks vacant. What would be the good of that? She is adjusted to being unwholesome. Unwholesomeness is not only a comfortable condition once you get used to it but a form of silent protest. They have to notice you if you smell. If you spit. Fart with vigour, pick your nose. It was Miss Slorach who pointed out that January was unwholesome; Miss Slorach with the flaming uncontrollable red hair that frizzed into an angry multitude of tight curls all over her head and shook excitably as she raised the righteous tawse to lash her, lash her, all in the name of God. 'Unwholesome girrul!' But January just sneered; the freckle-faced woman's easy blush was a blatant give-away. You could get to her, you could easily find her weak spot.

'Yes, Mrs Gordon,' January agrees, and tamely allows Isabel's mother to tie back her rough, dark hair in an elastic band, which Mrs Gordon extracts from a pocket filled with safety pins, paper-clips, odd buttons, hooks-and-eyes and other items of miscellaneous usefulness.

Speed bonny boat like a bird on the wing
Over the sea to Skye . . .

sing Isabel and Prue from the generous boughs of the beech with its ample arms acquiescent to all comers, maternally powerful. Prue supplies a beautiful impromptu descant to the song, and sometimes Isabel brings out her recorder, so that the tree itself makes music, vouchsafing the secret girls green refuge. Isla Gordon often hears the tree sing as she comes out of the Manse with Iain at her side and a basket over her arm.

> Carry the lad that's born to be king
> Over the sea to Skye . . .

Though the Charlie who was such a darling was (as she has gravely explained to Isabel) in general rather an over-rated bad boy and not of the True Religion, the tunes have been in her ever since she can remember. It is not enough, she has often reminded Isabel, to be bonny; one must have a thinking heart. Isabel, who after all is not bonny, finds it easy to agree. Her face is long and plain, but never dour; eager, heretical intelligence plays like a light over her features. She wants to know, and then to know more. To know better than Father and differently than Mother. She, unlike her mother, is sceptical of her cherished books, which harbour marginalia at once earnest and rebellious: 'I don't agree', 'Prove it', and 'Who says so anyway?' She crossed out several lines of *The Pilgrim's Progress* relating to the exclusion of poor Ignorance from Heaven, and wrote in the margin in tall capitals HE COULDN'T HELP IT COULD HE? Margaret Urquhart, the doctor's daughter, and Margaret Gillespie from the Grange, daughter of the Laird's estate manager, are her closest friends and likenesses: but in an unguarded moment she opened her heart illicitly to the gentle Prue from the Army camp, and along tagged January and she found she'd somehow let her in as well. And not out of pity or conde-scension, and not really out of mutiny against her father's prejudices (though that always adds salt) but with a real if restrained greeting, as underground fighters from different

15

ends of the earth declare common cause without a common language. Hardy and spartan herself, she particularly admires January's tree-climbing skills which outdare any cat, and in particular the way January will launch from a high bough of the difficult sycamore at the end of the garden to a rope suspended at a yard's distance, by means of which she makes an ululating flight to the next sycamore. She has often pointed out this prowess to Maggie U and Maggie G upon their commenting adversely on her keeping company with 'flat-footed Sassenachs'.

'And Prue may be English but she does *not* have flat feet,' she adds judiciously. 'She has unusually high arches. And in any case it's not her fault she's English, just her bad luck.'

In the tree-house, Isabel questions Prue about her sister's outlandish name.

'*January.* Why January? Not April or June?'

'They maybe ran out of saints' names,' suggests Prue reflectively. 'And she were born on January the first.' She is lying face-down along the stout back of the beech, clasping its warm body with both legs and both arms, at the point where it forks, and the forks stretch out almost horizontally. 'We was all named from saints, and prophets, and virtues and suchlike. There's Mary, Teresa, Catherine, Columba, Peter, Paul, Malachi and who have I missed out? – let's see – well, there's Charity, me Prudence – Francis, Damian and Noel.'

'That's too many names for the numbers.'

'Oh well, they aren't all at home. Mary is married, and Teresa is a Sister of the Sacred Heart, and Noel died of whooping cough. Father O'Brien said he saw our mam's bedside statue of Our Lady shed two real tears at the very moment Noel passed on, which were a comfort like to our mam.'

'Do you honestly believe that? *Honestly*, Prue?' Isabel has to restrain herself from shouting out 'Idolatry!' after the combustible manner of her father when he hears of such practices. Despite the impressive gravity of his daily manners and his many kind, though undemonstrative, ways, it is not only the Rector's granitic face which favours the physiognomy of John Knox.

'Oh yes,' says Prue, to whom the question has and can have no meaning. It is as much as to ask her, *Do you believe the grass is green, Prue? Do birds have wings and fly, in your private opinion?* 'Father O'Brien saw. And he heard the beating of angels' wings as they carried Noel's soul away.'

Prue, who had been standing outside in the garden at Mönchen Gladbach playing sevenses against the wall at the time of Noel's death, also heard the wings, and a kind of swishing-noise as the two-year-old soul was borne out of the house and out of the garden at great speed and out of Germany and into the immense gap in our understanding which lies beyond all we see or can fathom. Prue heard, but she never told. She keeps many things to herself, and sucks on them like old aniseed balls when nobody is present. And she won't say anything about it to Isabel, in that Isabel is a Proddie, and more of a Proddie than most in that her father's the Rector, and Isabel will go to Hell at the end of time unless she repents of her Proddieness.

Will she?

This thought of Isabel's body on fire, on fire forever, sizzling and hissing and spouting flame and pain, stabs Prue. Isabel's good feeling, Isabel's calm unchildlike fairness, can these be meant for the pit and the demons and the devils who turn you with pitchforks as you cook

17

amongst the charred embers of yourself? No no no no *no*.
God would be bad to hurt Isabel, and God is good. God
is good, and this is Paradise, thinks Prue, rubbing her
cheek against the grained bark of the tree and looking
down the glowing garden, the viridian grass white-flecked
with daisies and dappled with a commotion of shadows
from the ancient trees which mass around the ten-foot
walls.

Isabel scrutinises Prue's dreamy face, the high forehead,
snub nose, the reflection of the glare of light upon her
thick National Health lenses. When she isn't puzzling
other subjects of interest or controversy – Who made the
world? What is death? How long can I walk on my hands
without falling down? Wouldn't it have been better to
have been born a boy? How far away is the moon? – she
lets her mind squeeze around the resistant husk of Prue's
life, like a nut you need to crack. Each time, she pincers
the problem from a slightly different angle.

'Did your mother get very upset when your brother
died?' She means, *Weren't there eleven solid compensations
left her in the form of the extant Saints, Prophets and Virtues?*

'She still cries for him in the night,' lies Prue. Well, it's
true that her mother cries in the night, but a lie that she
mourns the loss of one in a family in which each is surplus
to requirements.

'Does she?'

'Yes. I hear her crying through the wall.' She also hears
blows and pounding noises, the crash of bedsprings and
drunken stumblings. Of these things she will never say a
word. Even in her private mind they are taboo. She will
not admit them consciously to herself. Isabel's questioning
and her own fabrications stir deep unease.

'Look – there's a magpie.'

'How do you know it's your brother she's crying for?'

18

'I don't know how I know, I just do.'

Isabel has never seen her mother weep; neither does she herself cry save on exceptional occasions, and never for a grazed knee or a poked eye. Prue's house is awash with outspoken, turbulent emotions, with people thumping each other, accusing, quarrelling, sobbing, shrieking with laughter and bellowing with outrage. There is no quiet space in that prison of crowded emotions. Even the toilet has no lock. One can't take one's knickers down without fear of invasion. Prue has made inconspicuous nests for herself in broom-cupboard and wardrobe, and cocoons herself there with book and filched torch. Where's our Prue got to? they occasionally spare time to wonder. Prue is the pause in the garrulity of the family's conversation, the comma in the sentence; what it has left unthought or unsaid.

Now they cartwheel round the lawn, three vehement, silent travellers, all whirling in the one clockwise direction. The world is spinning on its axis with dervish momentum. The clock-hands furiously retrace their business of yesterday and chase the tail of tomorrow.

The gravel crunches on the drive out of sight of the garden; Iain lollops toward a dark voice saying 'Hello boy, hello there', and 'Scat!' hiss Isabel and Prue. The forbidden January bolts towards the nearest rhododendron bush, and creeps up its collusive skirts. Two nice girls with their grey woollen socks pulled up to the knee and secured by elastic await the Rector on his lawn. The taboo girl pants crouched down in the fibrous interior of the Rector's bush.

Down the cool labyrinthine corridors of the rhododendron jungle she crawls and clambers, the waxen leaves on their branching lattice letting through very little sunlight, just the odd triangles, circles and strange geometrical rhomboids of brightness that fall on her hair and shoulders and black plimsolled feet. January hardly rustles a leaf or snaps a twig, not even when she begins to ascend the sycamore at the far end of the garden, right up to the point some way beneath the rookery, which is the highest safe access the tree affords. But January scales higher, beyond handholds and footholds, forty, fifty feet above the ground, her whole body knotted with effort, and sweating as she forces the reluctant tree's connivance. The rooks have all arisen, raving. Below her the pigmy people are exposed to her godlike view. The Rector is holding his hat in one hand and prodding a portion of the lawn lightly with his walking stick; the two girls are nodding their heads exaggeratedly, like the pistons of a machine, and 'Oh yes we do', they must be saying, and 'Yes thank you'.

All the time Donald affably questions Isabel and her friend about their day and how they propose to spend the seven holiday weeks; looking over the top of his glasses at the two bonny faces, poking daisies with his cane he is also feeling that he would like to get hold of his daughter and shape her as the potter does a piece of wet clay on the wheel. Bringing out the latent form; imposing his conception. With loving hands but coercively and definitively. For, proud though he is of her fine intelligence and much as he loves her, what a worry she is. She's never precisely as he'd have her be. Why can't she be *normal*? A normal girl is malleable and orthodox, feeding on the beliefs that are put out on the plate for her consumption. A boy would have been simpler. A boy would have been made in his image. There would never have been this embarrassment and complexity, the tender protectiveness that makes him long to bound her in his arms alongside the raw sense of threat that hits him when he gets up close and collides with that vertiginous freedom that inhabits her. The recoil then, the need to control and manage her life, is tempered by his involuntary respect for the bright thing she is, the earnest rightness of her wrongness on every issue. He jabs a daisy right in the eye with his cane, and advises Isabel not to neglect her Latin verbs for all it's summer. Wiping the perspiration from his forehead with a handkerchief, he smiles benignly and goes indoors.

'Amo amas amat amamus amatis amant,' sings out Isabel, spinning on the spot as if to unreel the spool of bonding that is also bondage. A shadow has got between herself and the sun, dulling the luminous garden and cancelling the shine from every leaf.

'Non serviam, non serviam, non serviam,' he hears her fluting, taunting voice from amongst the din of chaffinches and thrushes. As he goes in through the Manse door, the sun comes out again, as if someone up there winked.

High up in her eyrie above the green amphitheatre, January surveys it all and them all (the puny puppets bobbing around) and her heart soars in one of those rare fits of sheer joy that still arise in her despite all they can do to knock it out of her. Her hot palms rasp and blister on the tree-bark; taut muscles tremble; the toppling world drops away beneath her in a nightmare declivity; and there is elation in all that danger and effort. Just being alive is the thrill, just being herself, January Cahill up a tree up in the air up where you can't catch her and can't see her, buoyed in the here-and-now, with the world partitioned between dark-green shadow and sparkling flakes of light far below. She cocks a snook at the lot of them from her high-status altitude.

Then Prue skips off, waving, and her feet scrunch the gravel-path; January shins down the sycamore and scrambles over the wall.

2

The Manse, twinned to its dour grey stone church, lies at the north-eastern edge of the compact village of Kinleven, built around a crossroads; to the north-west runs the great river-estuary, separated from the mainland by a silted expanse of wetlands called the Carse. Prue looks round as they amble out of the gates on to the coast road with wonder as she always does; she can't get over the prodigious beauty of it. The love it calls from her is more the sort you'd give to a person rather than a place: her motherland to which she is bonded and belongs (even though it disowns her). The huge turquoise sky, filmed with a veil-like cloud-layer, sweeps away over the wide Carse to the pearly horizon.

'Let's go and mess about on the Curse,' suggests January.

'No, I don't want to.'

'Come on.'

'No, Jannie, no, I don't like it out there.'

The Curse, as the Army children call it, is a quaggy no-man's-land laced by burns and hidden quicksands; its green deliquescence forming the habitat for reeds and sedges, livid emerald and sulphur-coloured lichens and sphagnum mosses, hummocky grasses and cotton grass. It's out of bounds, and said to be haunted. Ghosts and ghoulies lurk there at twilight and pull children in to the peaty water by the ankle. Prue went there once but never again. She saw a nasty face in the queasy water, dead and staring from the sockets where its eyeballs should have been.

'Tame thing. Weedy weakling,' taunts the swaggerer.

'No, I'm just hungry.'

'Well have a toffee then. I nicked some when she weren't looking.' January produces three large slabs of toffee, stickily embedded with fluff from her pocket. 'Have a toffee and come out on the Curse.'

'Oh Jannie – you didn't ought of.' Prue is aghast that her sister would steal from the generous Mrs Gordon. She wants to take a toffee, but principle forbids.

'Why not, cock?'

'Because she's a kind lady to us – and she'll know it were us what took it – and she won't invite us again.'

'Balls. She's got plenty, she won't miss it. I nicked an orange too, and some nuts.'

'That's a tangerine.'

'Tangerine then. Want a bit?'

Prue shares the loot but she doesn't feel good about it. She doesn't share January's socialistic instinct that all property is theft so that you'd better join the thieves or feed on the starvation rations of your own daft honesty and don't complain.

'How many tangerines was there in the bowl?'

'A whole pile – eight or nine, I should have took more.'

Prue has never tasted a tangerine; she likes the taste of the exotic name as much as the delicate sweetness of the fruit which flushes her mouth with pleasure. They are walking along the coast-road which runs parallel with the estuary, past the sealed school-house just east of the Manse, built on sandy waste-ground dotted with occasional pines and Douglas firs. Turning into the Glebe meadow which runs between the Manse and the village and (to the south-east) the Army camp, they have a full view of the three miles of countryside leading to the Housty Estate, with its rich agricultural land and dairy herds and its dense forests of pine, birch and beech stretching as far as the eye can see.

This heart-gripping natural beauty, along with a sensitivity to its timeless antiquity and hereditary dignity, makes Prue ache with joy; the scope and freedom of it excite January's pulses. Yet these nomadic children, inhabiting the territory of their hearts' desire, can be in it but never of it. They appropriate nothing of what they see, however they strain to insinuate roots into the native soil. Wherever they go they encounter the earth's indifference and the indigenous people's aversion. In two-and-a-half years the foreigners will be aborted to some new posting and be seen and thought of no more. Their Mancunian, Birmingham or Cockney accents specify their difference from the tight-lipped Scottish community that tolerates them only because it must. Some of the older Scots resort to Gaelic in their presence, but they need not have bothered, for their language is in itself as impenetrable as Swahili to the Forces children. Even some of the teachers at the Academy are well-nigh incomprehensible to English pupils, who are therefore judged more moronic than they may actually be.

'Why don't they speak proper here anyway?'

'It's us what don't speak proper, Jannie – they get all their grammar right.'

'You're kidding! Hoots mon and up yer kiltie! Remember the other day when old Slorrie was at me for the date of the Battle of Bannock-bleeding-burn and *What is meant girrul by the word con-VAIN-ticle?*'

Prue giggles. ('Haven't the foggiest,' said January, asking for it.

'A Con-VAIN-ticle. Come along now, think think think. Any more impudence and it's the belt for you.'

'A sort of convent innit? For ticklers.'

'Stop that sniggering. Out here.'

'No, miss, I've thought.'

'Well?'

'A Conventicle were a kind of fried Scotch testicle, fried and eaten with haggis.'

'Out here. NOW. How dare you, girrul. Hand out.'

As January remarked, she did not give a monkey's. Nobody can make you learn. Nobody can force you to be what they want you to be.

I – whack – *am* – whack – *my* – whack – *self* – whack – *and conventicles to you!* There's not much they can do to her that would make her wince. She's been, after all, for just over thirteen years under strict military discipline from their brutal dad. She's in training.)

The long, shining grasses of the Glebe meadow swish around their calves as they wade through its soft cool sea. Prue's hand trails lazily over the seed-heads of oatgrass and rust-coloured dock. Tortoiseshell butterflies flicker in the haze and daddylonglegs and horse-flies are momentarily lustrous in the droning air. On the coast-road they have just left, a party of conscripts in vests and long khaki shorts sweats past on cross-country training, their feet thudding on the warm tarmac, encouraged on their way by the alsatian-like barking of their sergeant major.

'You put on a Scotch accent, you do. You want them to think you're one of them – not common like us.'

'I don't so,' exclaims Prue, stung. She's a bright, book-ish girl, and a good mimic. She is craftily picking up the Scots intonations and pronunciations, and gradually introducing them into her parlance. She has even invented a Scottish middle-name for herself – Fiona – to which she hopes unobtrusively to switch at some later date when she has been accepted – she knows it may take quite a long time – as an equal, or even a Scot by adoption. The accent is not as hard as the grammar, which she is working on, but the whole enterprise is compromised by the presence of her sister, whom such ingratiating artifice disgusts, and Prue can see why.

'You do.'

'I don't mean to. It just comes natural like, with keeping their company. I love it here, don't you – I don't never want to leave.'

'I'm not bothered.' January does mind, she deeply minds, but she shrugs it off. You may as well accept things you can't change, is her philosophy. It's all rather like a film, anyway, where they've been and where they'll be going to – a technicolour film of strange lands and stranger peoples, a celluloid phantasmagoria she has witnessed but never entered. And besides, at the centre of this scene of tranquillity and beauty is a node of secret violence: the bleeding stump of the cord that attaches her to the matrix of the world like the unborn baby to its womb-wall, that is constantly being scissored and constantly trying, with less and less success, to heal. And wherever they go it will make no difference. 'All places are much the same.'

'Paul Cox's dad is buying himself out.'

'Bully for him.'

'Do you think Britannia ought to rule the waves, Jannie?'

'Nah. But it's dog eat dog in this life, innit? If Britannia didn't rule the waves some other bugger would. Like them ancient bally Romans.'

Prue, who is learning Latin, does not sympathise with that axiomatic contempt for ancient Romans shared by January with the mass of her fellows designated pig-ignorant and relegated to the study of domestic science and technical drawing. '*Arma virumque cano* – The arms and the man I sing,' declared Virgil in the first line of the first Book of the *Aeneid* nearly two thousand years ago. And Prue, sitting with the élite minority of swotty·Scots lads and lasses adjudged fit to wrestle with the abstruseness of a dead language, opened her blue dog-eared copy with its pencilled crib down the margins in various childish hands, and read over this testament with a kind of reverence, not doubting that here was greatness and that she, Prudence Mary Xavier (Fiona) Cahill (with a flying start over the Proddies conferred by her familiarity with Church Latin) was in touch with the greatest of all subjects: arms and the man.

This first clause (unlike the coiled-up grammatical involutions that came later) had at least the virtue of being fairly comprehensible. So she paused to mull it over. *Arma virumque cano . . .*

Or was it comprehensible? For who was this unknown man and why were his arms advertised as being delivered separately from the rest of him? The more she puzzled over it, the more it got on her nerves. Why sing the arms before you sing the man? A spare pair of arms dangled on a string before Prue's musing mental eye. Ah no, it must mean Jesus – Jesus who lives for Prue as familiarly as any other resident of her world, given tactile, solid form in the little crucifix unpacked from its swaddling newspaper from the trunk with tender hands at every posting, made of dark wood and first thing up on the wall of every new billet. Jesus' outspread arms have been raised in blessing over Prue's troubled childhood as long as she

27

can remember. Arms of shelter and benediction over-arching like a tree. *Arma virumque cano . . .*

After a bit the penny dropped. It didn't mean that at all: arms, Army, armour, armature, armada, armed man. Virgil meant a weapon. *Of course.* Now she was at home, she knew where she was.

'*Arma virumque cano*,' she begins to chant to herself under her·breath, ducking under the wire fence which encloses the camp perimeter and gives them forbidden access to the pleasant compound of the Officers' Quarters.

Almost immediately a twanging female voice admonishes them: 'Orff, orff,' it seems to be shouting. 'Orff, go on, shoo.'

That officer's wife with the blue hair seems to have made a profession of prowling at her window while the char polishes the door-knocker, policing the area for incursions from the Other Ranks. Officers have detached houses of various design, with a garage and car; their gardens are planted with rose-bushes and ornamental shrubs, their children speak with a nasal twang and wear pleated skirts, white cardigans and Clarks or Kiltie fitted sandals. Prue hares off but January strolls, hands-in-pockets and dribbling a tin-can down the centre of the road, ignoring Blue-Hair who still gestures from her window in sign of agitation. A kind of apartheid operates between the Officers and the Other Ranks: even the public toilets in the camp are segregated. Prue waits at the edge of this quiet suburbia for her sister to catch her up, and they walk together towards their own Married Quarters – row upon row of identical red-brick semis thrown up in a hurry, with small bare patches of back garden, open-plan at the front. The roads are mostly named after famous blood-baths, as Isabel has pointed out – Oudenarde Crescent, Passchendaele Terrace, Waterloo Avenue – with occasional mass-murderers thrown in – Montgomery Way, Earl Haig Road, which abuts on to their own street. Where the sergeants and warrant officers reside, things are more couth and cultivated to some degree. They attempt to grow peas and beans in the back gardens and hang their own chintzy curtains at the windows. Their families are often small – one or two children – and looked after attentively.

The Cahills' area, at once the newest and the seediest, seethes with innumerable spawn of children. The houses are still surrounded by builders' rubble which nobody has bothered to clear away, and the paint on barge-boards and drainpipes, slapped on in the rain last summer, is already flaking. Every cup and plate in their house is regulation; every stick of furniture. Prue never minded that a bit until she visited the Manse, where everything, though basic and utilitarian, was odd and individual: the cups refused to match the saucers, the mats on the bare boards were woven by hand, the bed-quilts were resplendent patchworks of colourful odds and ends. Now the very doormat of her own dwelling offends her by its bristly matter-of-factness; the thick white china lip of the regulation cup meets her own lip with a weight of dreariness, and her eye is bored by the sterile walls on which you are only permitted to hang a small maximum of pictures – which in their family's case, of course, means crucifixes and pictured saints.

White, pink and khaki washing hangs still and lifeless in parallel rows of lines. The German woman from Number 4 is out beating a mat hung over a clothes-horse: the dust ascends into the sunlight with each relentless smack of the carpet-beater.

'Bloody *Kraut*,' comments January.

'*Sauerkraut*,' mutters Prue, but under her breath. She doesn't like to offend people: it's a sop to her companion and no more. She flinches back from the sight of pain – whose issue is anger, and their anger blights. She hates to tread on a worm; will pick her way fastidiously round a colony of ants. Her own existence she has for several years suspected of being unjustifiable.

'Hun! *Schweinhund*! Pigdog!' sings out January at the top of her voice. Mrs Gertrud Binny in a floral apron, hands on her hips, stares excoriated from under her coils of flaxen hair at the dirty English street-urchins. Taking a couple of paces forward, she waggles the carpet-beater in their direction with one muscular arm.

'*Bösen Kinder – gehen Sie hin!*'

She always means to speak in English, but rage and hurt don't easily translate.

'Eva Braun – Eva Braun – Eva Braun!' January sets up a chant, but she nips off smartly as the carpet-beater advances.

'Yah!' shouts Jacko Jackson as he catches them up at the corner of Winston Churchill Street, and again, 'Yah!' His fat tongue out, his thumbs in his ears, he dances at them in vast inanity. He is a weedy little boy with pimples and black hair on end like Smiffy in the comic. 'Catholic bitches! Yah yah yah!'

As January goes for him, he swerves and dodges behind a pair of dustbins, whose lids he clashes together in the manner of cymbals. Mentioning his suspicion that their father is a fucker and their mother has the clap, Jacko suddenly drops the lids and scarpers.

'Hey you Cahill girls, put those lids back on my dustbins this minute!'

'We didn't take them off, so why the hell should we put them back on?'

'Don't you give me that, my girl. Put them lids back on or . . .'

Prue replaces the lids quietly.

'Right now, clear off and don't let me catch you nosing round my property again.'

'It isn't your property anyway, it's the Army's, and we didn't touch your smelly bins, so there.'

'Rough children,' says Mrs Jones, shaking her head.

'Rough bleeding grown-ups,' replies January. She makes an obscene but original gesture, in which both little fingers are inserted, whilst rotating, into the nostrils. They walk off, heads in the air. The Catholic families, with their numerous offspring, are pariahs amongst their class, and lie under the related suspicion of being Irish, even if their accents indicate otherwise. To be Irish is not to be human. Prue, sensitive as she is, and reflective, can neither retaliate with robust ripostes nor reconcile herself to this alienation. She cannot elevate herself, as her mother can, to a martyrdom whose bitter-sweet compensations taste sickly on her tongue; neither has she the resource of an embattled aggression, but tries instead to understand and reason out within her mind why these things should be so, why she is to be counted amongst dregs and leavings. It is a knotty problem.

'Scum of the earth,' remarks January. 'She's got it coming to her, she has.' Her frown denotes malign relish.

'No, don't, Jan,' says Prue vaguely.

'No don't what?'

'Don't anything.'

January is unconvinced by these pusillanimous collaborator's tactics. Fair's fair. Mrs Jones won't like justice to be done and to be seen to be done in the form of a dustbinful of cinders, fish-bones, potato-peelings and sanitary towels tipped out for public display all over her lawn; and, as it turns out, she doesn't at all.

★

At home there are no books except the Missal Book and their mother's battered recipe book and knitting patterns. Prue sometimes gets so desperate for printed texts that she finds herself reading the labels on the tins and cornflake packets. Isabel has begun to lend her books, old leather-bound *Gulliver*s and *Robinson Crusoe*s and *Jane Eyre*s, which make the skin of Prue's spine prickle as she takes them in her hands.

'Are you sure, Isabel? I'll take great care.'

For these books she feels an aching reverence. She stores them under her pillow wrapped in two layers of paper bags, and looks for private times and places to get them out and open them on both knees, turning the dry, crackling pages with fastidious fingers. When someone approaches, her antennae are alert to intrusion before the person has had a chance to enter the room; she smartly shuts and hides the book so as to avoid violation.

'What are you reading?' are words she dreads to hear. 'Come on, give it here, let's see.' They whip the book from her lap and they thumb through the pages, scoffing mostly, though sometimes genuinely curious to know what keeps a healthy girl so still in cool, somnolent shadow through whole racing summer afternoons. But mostly they let the bookworm alone.

As Prue reads, the house rumbles and the twin front doors endlessly slam as children volley in and out, thunder up the carpetless stairs and squeak across the brown lino. Voices call from windows and there is miscellaneous crying. The toilet flushes and the cistern emits first a clanking, then an echoing grumble which goes on for the five minutes it takes to refill. From downstairs, where her mother is cleaning the grate with an angry riddling of the poker which broadcasts her griefs to the whole house, the wireless blares Mantovani. It is the silence at the Manse that Prue finds so precious. Isabel, as poor as she is in material possessions – no car, no refrigerator, washing machine or television – is yet rich in silence and space; can stand in the centre of bare-boarded, high-ceilinged rooms with abounding emptiness all round her; can stand there for hours if she so desires and hear the luxury of nothing at all.

Malachi acts as the family gong. He exhorts them to eat by standing astraddle at the bottom of the stairs and bawling, 'Tea!' He is a devastatingly handsome youth, after the style of the teddy boys. His mother's darling, he is dressed up to the nines in drainpipe trousers and a long jacket with velvet cuffs. Malachi, who has left school and works at the NAAFI, spends many hours at the bathroom mirror with his head at an angle perfecting his high-standing quiff with Brylcreem. Girls loiter, making bovine eyes at him where he works selling cigarettes behind the NAAFI counter; he struts like a turkeycock, his quiff quivering. As each sibling descends for tea, he thumps it playfully under the ribs at its approach and slaps it behind the head with the flat of his hand as it moves past.

In the midst of the usual pandemonium, Prue eats her hard-boiled egg, her corned beef, beetroot and slice of bread, and drinks her tea. Columba, Prue's carer when she was a little child, sits next to Prue.

'Where did you get to this morning? Mam wanted you and January to go shopping.'

'Oh just around and about.' Even to the trustworthy Columba, far more of a mother than the driven, over-burdened Mam has ever been, Prue is unwilling to confide the secret of her other world. Columba is a plump, soft, bosomy presence who wears a silver-plated cross at her neck and confesses herself to Father Friend every week, but she is business-like and practical as well as devout. Her red-gold wavy hair is tied in a pony-tail; her face is fair-skinned, freckled and homely.

'Hold your knife and fork proper and sit up straight,' she reminds Prue. 'And don't go round with January so much – you don't do her no good and she'll get you a bad name. And don't keep kicking your feet under the table like that, Prue, it isn't done, it's slovenly.'

'Don't go on at me, Columba.' Prue puts up a token resistance, but really she laps it up. To be nagged in a household where you are generally left to bring yourself up is a sign of unique grace – Prue knows it, and Columba knows it.

'I'm not keeping on for the sake of it – it's for your own good.' Columba has to speak at the top of her voice to surmount the din, and now pauses to jerk her head aside out of the trajectory of a Farley's rusk which has been hurled by the angry baby, Damian. Arching his back in his high-chair, he sticks his arms and legs out stiff and bellows from a beetroot-red face, winding himself up like a siren.

'Stuff that for a lark,' says Peter, who has been half-heartedly trying to feed him, in compliance with orders. He shoves his chair back gratingly with his bottom, crams his mouth with the remainder of his bread, and leaves his post, banging out of the front door.

Damian stops bellowing in order to look round and assess the effects of his performance up to the present; none being observable and his feeder having disappeared, he quietens in a sort of nervous shock, his chin a mass of dribble and egg-yolk. Then with renewed ferocity he bursts forth again and nobody takes the slightest notice.

'And Prue,' shouts Columba, 'you're to stop climbing trees or going through barbed wire or whatever it is gets your socks in ribbons.'

As a desperate last throw in his bid for attention, Damian successfully executes a projectile vomit, his speciality since his first intake of milk became a spectacular output and he had to be wooed to survive. His stomach contents shoot all over the table-cloth, spattering the islands of two children's plates, to the outrage and disgust of the users.

'Mam! He's at it again!'

'My dinner's ruined!'

'I'm not clearing that up!'

'Mam!'

Damian seems to decide to rest upon his laurels. He drums with his fists upon the apron of the high-chair.

'Now Prue, don't forget what I said.' Columba, still insanely hortatory, is now engaged in drearily hoisting the baby from the high-chair. The siren goes off again. This was not the end he had in view. He hangs in mid-air, pinned under her arm against her waist in a state of shock, to be removed to his cot and there dumped, still raving.

'What is it now?' asks Prue's mother, emerging from the kitchen and the mangling. Her face, once round and fresh, has long been sunken around nearly toothless gums, whose comfort she prefers to the ill-fitting dentures which restore her to a sad, grotesque echo of someone she half remembers being. The dentures chafe her upper palate and rub her lower jaw into a mass of sore places if she keeps them in too long. And her speech becomes a risible dialect of sucking and gargling noises, with high-pitched sibilants like a boiling kettle. She looks nearer 60 than 45. Only her blue-green eyes still startlingly recall the lively, talkative, gentle person Hugh Cahill courted in Salford thirteen children ago. When Mary meets her image in the mirror she persuades herself she doesn't care. Who looks at her anyway, who's bothered? – except the Blessed Virgin, who sympathises with all womanly sorrows, however trivial or undignified. As for her husband, he accepts her as she is and hardly looks at her; once or twice a week he comes home plastered and shoves his thing inside her under cover of the unmerciful dark. He works and grinds it in and out, hard and fast, panting like an animal. She doesn't like it; at one time she hated the regular beatings far less than the licensed rapes, but now she is philosophical. It doesn't go on long and if she lies still and fixes her mind on the shopping-list she hardly notices it. Men are like this; it's just a fact of life. And he doesn't kiss her mouth, so why should she need teeth?

'That sodding Damian again,' complains Paul. 'He wants thrashing, he does.'

'Language,' says Mother succinctly. 'Wash your mouth out with soap.' She begins to mop up the mess wearily. 'Get a bowl in, Prudence.'

'Much better idea.' Malachi, her bright-eyed boy, her first-born (the older girls don't count), the apple of her eye, can get away with anything. 'Clear, logical thinking. Just pick the whole lot up in the table-cloth and bung it in the sink.'

The great bundle of clanking, jangling crockery and cutlery is swept out of the dining-room door and into the kitchen. Prue and Columba are left to sort it out and wash up while Mam mangles on. Two cups are broken and three are chipped; several saucers are cracked. It will all have to go down on the inventory when they surrender the house. The inventory is always a worry, even when you first move in.

'You ought to be stricter with the boys,' Columba chides her mother.

'Oh boys . . . they're good boys.'

'Malachi is brutal,' says Columba.

'Malachi brings in some much-needed money to the household,' says Mary with aggrieved protectiveness, jerking the mangle-handle so that the whole contraption lurches. 'I couldn't manage without him. And don't you forget that, my girl. Malachi is a good son to his Mam.'

'Well, I bring in money too, Mam,' objects Columba, equally aggrieved. 'I give you more than he does in proportion. His all goes on his greasy hair. Thinks he's Elvis. He's a lout. His gang are louts.'

'Yes, well, you're a good girl, Columba, too. I don't complain of you. I'm not one for complaining, thank God, not that it would do me much good if I was.'

Prue thinks, as she stacks the washed and dried plates, how old her mother looks compared with Mrs Gordon; how old, and how low. She would not like the two to meet. She thinks that if they bumped into Isabel's mother coming up the street, she would explain Mam away afterwards (toothless Mam with a headful of curlers tied round with a scarf, wearing open sandals all weathers and no stockings, and a fag hanging out of her mouth) as an unhappy charwoman she happened to meet and took pity on, and whose basket she offered to carry. Prue thoughtfully contemplates Mam at the mangle and Columba at the sink. She alone can do this with impunity in a household whose occupants are wont to bellow, 'What the hell do you think you're gawping at, goofy?', by virtue of a kind of invisibility she seems to have acquired. So peaceful and so reticent is Prue that she can come and go like a little ghost, melting in and out of rooms, her presence like her absence restful and unnoted. Her footfalls are delicate and her breathing airy.

Only Columba is mindful of Prue; only in Columba does Prue touch home. She touches her often, wrapping her arms round her sister's firm, wide waist, laying her face against the spongily comfortable bosom that gives to the push of her head. Pell-mell they came careering out of Mam's striving body, like cascading windfalls from some dying but prodigiously bearing autumnal tree, and – if they were lucky, as Prue knows she was incredibly lucky – there was someone waiting beneath to catch them and break their fall. Seven-year-old Columba broke her little sister's fall. She did everything for her – warmed the milk in a pan to feed her; kept her nappies clean; bathed her in the washbasin, laboriously cradling the bald vulnerable head with its beating fontanelle in her left hand to guard against the tap; walked her out with more-than-maternal pride. Columba projected all her own crying need of nurture upon Prue and in proxy Prue fulfilled that need. She has depended on Prue and it will be hard to break the tie. But Columba feels stirrings and presentiments of a freer life; there is a local boy she likes, the newsagent's son, Duncan Macintosh, and cinematic vistas of a future less drab and drudging.

'Prue, I won't be here to say goodnight to you tonight.' Columba puts a confidential arm around Prue's shoulders.

'Oh won't you? Why?'

'I'm going out.'

'Where?'

'To a dance at the Youth Club.'

'Who with?'

'Duncan.'

'Oh.'

'What's the matter? Why are you sulking?'

'I'm not sulking.'

'Yes you are.'

'I'm not, I'm honestly not. But do you have to go?'

'I don't have to, I *want* to, silly.'

'Oh.'

Prue is fingering the cross Columba wears around her neck, which shows so dramatically against her black lambswool jumper; she has to resist the impulse to stick her thumb in her mouth and suck. She makes her face go expressionless, then she puts on a smile.

'I'll say "God bless" before I go.'

'Yes, that's all right, I don't mind.'

Prue skips off up the stairs with every appearance of light-heartedness, and contracts herself so thin and weightless as to slide down in between the pages of the book she is currently reading. They are calling for January but January is nowhere to be found. She wasn't there at dinner; hardly ever is, but lives by stealthy foraging like an alley-cat of infinite resource. Prue, finespun as a cobweb, goes outside-in, disappearing even from her own view as Crusoe, miraculous survivor of his shipwreck, makes inventory of his providential salvage.

*

Prue's dad comes in tight, late in the evening; staggers upstairs, still in his battle-dress and fetches his accordion. Standing with his back to the fire he flexes the instrument, dragging its tight lungs out, squeezing them in, running his fingers over the keys in a preparatory way. His eyes shine, the room swells with anticipation.

'Go on, Dad, play!'

'Are you ready?'

Huge, beaming bonhomie radiates from Hugh's

39

quixotic face. His pulse bounds. Ancestral music throbs in his heart. His children cluster adoringly round him.

'Play, Dad, go on, play!'

Dad will play. With a whoop and a skirl he begins, and five of his little darlings (three of whose names he remembers, the fourth being on the tip of his tongue, but can't be placed) take the cue at once and dance. Hugh laughs with tipsy indulgence at the tribe dancing to their Daddy and urges them to sing along. January alone fails to respond to the promiscuous invitation. She lolls in the door-frame chewing gum, examining the shining bald spot, egg-shaped and rosy, at the crown of his head. The children clog-dance to the accordion, a tradition they took with them from Hugh's native Lancashire to Ismaelia, via Rheindahlen and Ballykelly, and now to Kinleven. The lino screeches under pivoting soles and heels, and the plaster statues of King Jesus and Saint Sebastian stuck full of enjoyable arrows tremble on the clayey plinths to the crashing vibrations of the leaping, clapping, whooping Cahills.

You can hear them at it three blocks away. Even in this worst area of the camp, where all the big families and problem cases are ghettoed, the Cahills are anathema. *They should do something about it*, the neighbours complain; *It didn't ought to be allowed* – but of course nothing is done.

Prue's face appears behind that of January; she watches over her sister's shoulder. Her foot taps; her eyes are eager.

'Come on, girls! Don't be bashful – join in. *That's* the way!'

Prue is drawn into Hugh's magic circle, where the firelight and the glow from a disreputable standard lamp in the corner burnish limber young springing bodies and flash momentary pearls in the pupils of excited eyes. Prue leaps with them, hands at her side, her feet executing a version of the intricate steps of the mill-girls who were their parents' parents' parents. The music swells, Hugh's cheeks dimple as he sings, smiling like a winsome young lad in his heyday; the fingers of one hand nimble on the stops and of the other plangent on the throbbing keys and in and out, *in* and *out*, he works the instrument, in and out, drawing the easy sentimental tears from his own eyes.

Prue tugs January; January resists, with a flounce and a thrusting-out of her lower lip. She won't let go, won't join in. She refuses the lush, seductive coercion of the music and her father together. Then much against her better judgment, suddenly lets go and begins to bound on coiled springs, joy in her eyes. As Prue sails up, January bobs down. Their skirts float, hair wafts. Then in unison they beat out a rallentando.

'That's it for now!'

Hugh has had enough. His vagrant moods come and go, quite unpredictably, as if someone happened to turn him on at random, then switched him off. The children, hectic and wound up tight as alarms that have to be let to go off, won't and can't stop. They stomp on minus the music, determinedly, a roomful of bouncing anarchists.

'That's it, I said!' Hugh roars. 'Shut up. I said bloody shut up.'

From convivial he passes to evil-eyed, and the hands that caressed the yielding sides of the accordion are now looking for someone to whack. He gives the nearest child, Catherine, a shove, catching her off-balance, which sends her sprawling into Peter, who falls heavily with Charity against the wall. Both begin to cry. Hugh can't stand children crying. Never could. It really gets him. Wading through the throng, he grasps the heads of the two offending children and bangs their foreheads smartly together.

Prue flinches at the crack of the skulls. January spits on the back of his battle-dress and leaves. Peter and Charity stare at their father in stunned silence.

'That'll teach you,' Hugh informs them. 'I won't have it, do you hear?' but what it is that he won't have, he has forgotten or never knew.

Out in the kitchen, Hugh lurches round looking for his Guinness. Someone has hidden Hugh's Guinness. He is sure to God he had three or more bottles on the second shelf of the pantry but there's certainly nothing there now, apart from two cans of baked beans, one can of prunes, a plate of cold mince and an empty egg-crate. Hugh gets right into the pantry to make sure.

'Bottle,' murmurs Hugh to himself. 'Bottle, bottle, bottle.'

Baby wants his bottle, thinks January, observing the red bristling back of his neck which bulges somewhat above the collar of his battle-dress. *And Baby shall have his bottle.*

'Are you looking for this, Dad?'

Hugh shuffles backwards out of the pantry eagerly. January hands him a full milk-bottle.

'Mary Mother of God.' He takes it by the neck and dashes it to the floor. His boots wade through a spreading lake of milk. 'Bitch. You filthy little tyke – come back here, come here I said, you bastard.'

January has smartly evacuated the room.

'It's the belt for you,' he hollers through the door. But before the belt, it's the Guinness which must be found, the comforting, needful Guinness.

A whining, appeasing voice implores him to believe that 'You drank it all last night, Hugh, so you did.'

'Liar, filthy liar.' He aims a corrective punch at the treacherous source of this duplicity, his wife, who has made the mistake of appearing from the adjoining house,

and who now adroitly skips, ducks, and backs toward the
door, slipping on the milk.

'You did, Hughie, you did so, on my honour you
did . . .'

'You've hid it.'

'No.'

'You have. Where is it?'

'No, I haven't, why would I?'

'You hate me, that's why. You're all against me.'

'No, Hughie, no, we don't hate you, you drank it last
night – don't, don't hit me – for the love of God . . .'.
But she knows it's all up when he says they hate him. It
isn't a matter of whether he'll strike, but when.

'Where – is – it?'

'God is my witness . . .'

'And Peter and Paul and all the saints are *my* witness,
Mary, you've stolen – my – bottle. Give – me – my –
bottle.'

With every word a shake, her bony shoulders and
collar-bone a brittle nest of twigs in his grasp. Hardly a
woman but an aproned scarecrow whose ribs the wind
could whistle through. Hugh takes pity.

'I won't hurt you if you just tell me where it is. Not a
hair of your head. Come on now, Mary darling,' he
wheedles. The scarecrow shakes worse under his soft than
under his hard harangue. It looks at him helplessly, tears
in its rheumy, scared eyes, its voice clotted with catarrh.

'I haven't touched your bottle and that's God's own
truth,' she wails, and the tears form and drop: a bad
mistake, given Hugh's constitutional and moral objection
to snivelling.

The house is silent, bating its breath, all ears. No one
dares to intervene. Malachi might have, but he is out on
the razzle with his fellow teds, enlivening the evening of

the villagers of Fiddich by riding pillion up and down the main streets with his mates. Columba might have (ineffectually) but she's dancing in another world with callow Duncan at the Youth Club. Prue peering down through the bannisters, sees framed in the open doorway the shadow of her father's raised arm, then turns away at the sound of the impact and the gasp and high-pitched yelp abruptly terminated, which follows, and then a short storm of blows and shrieks.

One down; one to go.

Hugh pulls off his belt and wraps the webbed khaki round his right hand, brass buckle dangling. He shoots up the stairs three at a time; passes Prue cowering on the landing and enters the room she shares with January. Not there. A disappointment. He looks cursorily under the bed and throws open the wardrobe doors. Then without warning his lust slackens, he loses interest. The flaccid weapon resumes its function as support to his trousers.

'Make us a cup of tea,' he tells Prue in a pleasant, matter-of-fact voice. An agreeable torpor has set in. He wipes the sweat from his forehead and divests himself of his jacket. When he gets downstairs his wife is nowhere to be seen. A few minutes later, in an amiable frame of mind, he sits in his braces, toasting his socks at the fender, with a pile of digestive biscuits which he rhythmically dunks and sucks. Prue can hardly distinguish the scalding warmth of the fire from the warmth of relief that floods her with the onset of his good mood. She crouches at his feet on the hearth-mat, brushing up coal-dust on the hearth with fussy little motions. Unconsciously she blesses him for sparing the rest of them; smiles up at him from the complexity of her silence, seeing which he favours her with a big wink of his left eye, and she blinks back.

'You're a good girl, Charity,' he slurs. 'Not a hooligan like that other one. Your Daddy's darling girl.'

Prue, who does not think it politic to remind him that she is the one called Prudence rather than Charity, always gets an odd pang at her father's imperfect grasp as to who she is – and even at times whose she is. It's important to be somebody, surely. And yet it's also safe to be nobody; to glide through the clamorous mass of competing individuals like a dun-coloured bird interchangeable with its background, able to ride out the malignity of weather and fellow-creatures by remaining well-nigh invisible.

Dad is falling asleep. His head drops back on the chair-cover and his mouth lolls open. In the red well of his mouth, picked out by intrusive light, his flaccid tongue is a moist mass like a snake quiescent. Prue peers at her father and strains her mind to put the questions she has not yet the years nor the language to formulate. The questions flock to the fore of her mind and seethe there restlessly, without definition. She looks at his hairiness, the fuzz of dark hair on the backs of his hands, the grizzled, abundant hair of his head, the few hairs poking from his nose and ears. Once she came upon him padding naked from the bathroom to the parents' bedroom and he laughed then, raising his arms to terrify her in fun, and she ran, for she saw a man all hair, with a pelt like a gorilla. And it came as a queer shock, which was revived in her thoughts again and again, sometimes voluntarily, to see this black-tufted creature so foreign to the soft androgynous nudity of her familiar brothers. Then she cancelled the memory, razed it out (she can do this) until now it surfaces as she kneels by the fire peering inquisitively and rather guiltily into the orifice of his mouth. The whiplash tongue is dormant now. The butting, bulbous nose, purplish with drink, with its large, dark pores, is snoring. Prue's questions press upwards to the very surface of her mind, and there simmer like nudging bubbles in a pan that just fails to come to the boil.

January is already in bed when Prue comes upstairs. She is sucking a lolly.

'Where've you been?' asks Prue anxiously, putting on her nightgown.

'Out.'

'He went for her.'

'So tell me something I don't know.'

'He were after you.'

'Didn't find me though, did he.'

'What'll he do to you?'

'Lather me if he can catch me, if he's sober enough to see. But I don't give a sod.'

'Don't you? Don't you honestly?' Prue can never comprehend this Trojan attitude. They hear him thrashing January but they hardly ever hear her scream or cry out. Several times she's blacked out and once she was concussed and violently sick all night, but without a whimper.

'No, not bloody likely. I don't give him the satisfaction, the bugger.' She looks over at her sister superciliously. 'I don't give a damn about any of you. You're all the bloody same anyway.'

'No we're not.'

'Yes you are.'

'Not.'

'Are.'

'Well I'm not, anyway.'

'Oh, *you're* the worst of the lot. I hate you worse than him. Owl-eyes. Goggle-eyes. "Yes Daddy, no Daddy, three bags full Daddy." Nice little well-ironed, hard-boiled Prue. You make me want to heave. You and that lump of dough Columba.'

She holds her stomach graphically. Her collar-bones show prominently through the torn and grubby neck of her flannelette nightdress; her eyes stare; she looks emaciated, like something out of the death-camps Prue saw on a film and didn't believe. Prue turns away. She hates January. She wishes she shared a room with Damian and Paul; all they do to annoy you is cough and cry with bad dreams. They don't have baleful eyes and make you feel angry and guilty all at once.

January symmetrically turns her back on Prue. The sweet comfort of the lolly is gone, and she drops the stick on the floor amongst a welter of litter no one will bother to clear.

'I hate you, hate you, hate you,' she again confides, to keep the conversation going. She doesn't like the night. She hears creatures under her bed rustling, and severed hands claw their way like crabs up the curtains.

'Do then. I don't care,' mumbles Prue. She kneels at the foot of her bed and puts her hands together to say her prayers. Columba is not there to ensure her peace and safety through the night with her familiar benediction: 'Dear God, keep Prudence safe this night and may thy Guardian Angels watch over her and bring her safely through to morning.' Prue has to station the Guardians at the four corners of her bed by her own spiritual resources and it is a struggle. Columba spirits them there nightly with magical ease. And there they stand all night long, blessed, white-robed sentinels with moonlight glittering in their wide-awake eyes.

> Matthew Mark Luke and John
> Bless the bed that I lie on
> And if I die while I'm asleep
> I pray to God my soul to keep.

Prue gets the Apostle Matthew into position by her pillow after a considerable tussle. Matthew is grave and bearded, with long, crinkly hair like Jesus' in the icons. But Mark will not come at all, and Matthew himself is only a fitful presence which keeps dissolving into air the harder she stares and conjures.

'You don't think God actually listens to all your crappy, pious mumbo-jumbo, do you?' asks January with contempt. 'You probably make Him as sick as you make me. Sicker even – if that's possible.'

'Yes, He does,' affirms Prue. But Matthew vacates his post completely and won't come back. She turns off the light, takes off her glasses and gets into the unsafe, unhallowed bed, whose sheets are cold around her body. The Army mattress is in three 'biscuits' which part company with one another during the night unless you tuck the sheets well in. They have little ridges where they meet.

'How do you know?'

'I just do.'

January knows she knows far more than her moon-faced, credulous sister. She knows that nobody cares about anybody else in this world, whatever they affect and profess. People are out for themselves, for what they can get, and so is Prue, and so is she. She knows about words, which are more often than not lies people want to believe in. 'Love' is paper over a hole. The world is punched full of such holes like a colander. She knows she's been betrayed. It has been intimated to her that she's guilty of some astounding crime which brought down this betrayal upon her before her birth, too vile to be named. At the same time she knows she's perfectly innocent, the victim of slander. And she is outraged that this should be so – outraged and defenceless and impossibly burdened, all at the same time. She lies in her bed which smells frowstily of her sweat and her farts, and holds the place between her legs for comfort: the strange, fascinating area where tendrils of coarse hair have grown and where there is a button you can rub, and juice comes from you, and little darting sensations of tender pleasure like far-fetched echoes or rumours of some better life to come, beyond this loneliness of lying in the dark holding on to your self.

'Prue, are you awake?'

'Yes. Are you?'

'Have you got any licorice?'

'No. Have you?'

'No. Prue?'

'What?'

'Can I come in with you?'

January is already out of her own bed and hovering over Prue's; for she is certain not exactly of a welcome but of her sister's inability to refuse her solicitations.

'Come on then, Skinny Minny.'

'All right, Mealy Mouth, I'm coming. Shove over.'

Their little budding breasts lie together; warmth seeps symbiotically from one to another child. Prue's arms slacken round her sister's waist and as she begins to drift down into the couldn't-care-less of sleep, she feels January slip past her suddenly into a sleep of great finality, as if she had fallen down a trap-door. Prue registers a faint tremor and an eddy in the wake of that rushed departure. She turns over and falls down too.

3

Isabel wakes very early this Sunday morning
and knows, beyond the shadow of a doubt, that there is
no God. She is, at just short of 13 years of age, rather
young to have made this discovery, but she is an excep-
tionally thoughtful and honest child, and it has been
coming to her steadily over a period of time that things
are not exactly as her elders maintain they are and no
doubt themselves conscientiously believe. She pulls the
curtains of the tall sash-window and stands looking out.
Every tree and shrub throws a shadow several times its
length out across the emerald lawn; and all is quiet and
still out there except when a breeze scatters back the leaves
in a gently disputatious ripple, to reveal their silver-grey
under-sides. The leaves rise, the leaves fall. The clock
echoes in the great uncarpeted barn of a room. The world
is very beautiful and alive with promise. And there is no
God.

Isabel feels small distress at this recognition: on the
contrary it's rather a relief. The sky above the Manse is
no longer a giant blue or grey eye committing espionage
on Isabel's least thought; it's just a space on which such
thought might actively play. From earliest days there has
been the worry, bred by a Calvinistically inclined and
occasionally Apocalyptic father, as to whether one would

turn out a sheep or a goat. And although Isabel, rich in self-esteem, was generally persuaded that she belonged to the lucky flock, there always remained the doubt. Sheep to the right, goats to the left. God, like Hitler, had ovens for the goats, the unfit, the unrighteous. It seemed so unfair, and it was so unfair, and now she realises it was also untrue. There is no crematorium awaiting the unloved at the end of time, no glorious booty for the elect, there is just a turning over and a going to sleep. Yes, thinks Isabel, *yes*. Good. No Almighty Father. No angels. No hell. No heaven. Two thousand years of Christianity are abolished in the blinking of an eye.

She won't go to church, she won't, and that's flat. They'll have to carry her in bodily and chain her down to keep her there.

This thought is at once ecstatic and sharply scary. What happens to you when you go right out on a limb, when you break out from the guaranteed protection of your docile collusion and their authoritative assumptions? Can you live in the complete vacuum of dissidence – on your own and on the outside? Her father's disapproval she can cope with, but to court her mother's is endangering.

From the window, Isabel moves to the mirror. She watches herself cleaning her teeth, addressing the brush to the enamel in the approved manner preached by Mr Stuart the dentist, circular movements and one hundred times repeated. Her teeth are excellent as a result of the fastidious disciplines practised in the Gordon household, and the regular eating of apples, celery and carrots. She would hate to have January's front teeth, yellowish-brown and evidently rotting away. Doesn't she get the most awful toothache? She stares at her reflection. It stares back woodenly. She tries to make it smile; it smiles like Pinocchio. At the window the view was clear but in the mirror things are tarnished, vaguely troubled and uneasy, partly because of the antiquity of the mirror, with its mottlings and the show-through of its silver back, advertising that there is nothing there really, nobody out there real and solid. She inspects the image carefully. She cannot deny that it is an austerely plain face, with a high forehead which puckers slightly between the eyebrows and is prematurely rather lined; it is a long face, rather equine, with a long, straight nose, thin cheeks. The mask which has to be Isabel's, which she is stuck with, and doesn't much like, and yet *is* Isabel, so she tries to like it and hopes other people do, gives her a direct, rueful glance of commiseration. Her mother remonstrates if she finds Isabel looking in the mirror, thus reinforcing her constitutional shyness. Vanity is amongst the worst sins, according to Isla, for:

'When we think of the suffering in the world, Isabel, the *enormous* problems that have to be solved, the amount there is to *learn*, it seems a wickedness to be wasting time preening and prinking in the mirror.'

They don't have bodies in their house. They don't have gender. But Isabel admires and respects this rigour of her mother's, and the freedom that it grants to the mind, and the tomboyish run of the licit garden it accords.

Isabel has taken to breaking out in public on issues that strike her as crucial. She did it yesterday afternoon, quite without premeditation, but under the impulse of a powerful certainty that *they* were all wrong, badly wrong, and only *she* could see the truth. When her father vehemently enquired afterwards what in Heaven's name she meant by it? how she dared behave in that arrogant, shameful way? why she could not behave herself properly? she told him it was through the Inspiration of the Holy Spirit, which seemed to knock him sideways and silenced him for nearly a minute. He visibly reeled, and turned to her mother with a helpless gesture.

There had been a high-tea for a gathering of church folk. Mr Ross, Mr Harty, Mr Mackenzie, Dr Brodie and various womenfolk. Isabel had known them all since her earliest days and was entirely comfortable in their presence. She handed round cups of tea, then sat on the hearthrug with Iain, dividing her attention between the oat-cakes, malt-bread, fruit-cake and the conversation. The talk turned to the invasion of Cyprus and Archbishop Makarios.

Mr Harty remarked that Makarios was a mass-murderer who wanted shooting.

Shooting him was too good for him, so was hanging, as Mr Mackenzie observed.

Corpulent Mr Harty, red in the face and visibly swelling with wrath, pointed out that he had just been saying the same to Mrs Harty at home before they came out.

Mrs Harty agreed that he had.

'And you agreed with me,' said Mr Harty.

Mrs Harty agreed that she had agreed with every word he said.

'A churchman too!' shouted Mr Harty. 'He claims to murder in the name of God!'

Mr Ross opined that he was no churchman, Makarios. No, he was an agent of the devil, if not the devil himself.

'Why, what has he done?' Isabel wanted to know.

Outraged voices explained that he had caused the deaths of hundreds of British soldiers and airmen.

'Why are they there at all?' asked Isabel. 'Whose island is Cyprus?'

'Cyprus is an integral part of the British Empire,' explained Dr Brodie.

'You mean we stole it?'

'Well, really,' said Mrs Harty, looking significantly at Isabel's mother, who was contemplating her daughter with a sort of amused abstraction.

'You cannot condone murder', reasoned Dr Brodie, 'whatever the rights and wrongs may be.'

'I thought soldiers were paid to murder,' queried Isabel. She didn't really mean any affront. She just thought there was something obvious, glaringly obvious, which somehow adults missed seeing. 'Don't you think it would be a lot better if we all came home and left the place in peace?'

'What has the child been *reading*?' Mr Harty turned to Isla. 'The *Morning Star*, the *Daily Worker*?'

'It's nothing I've read,' said Isabel. 'I think for myself. Don't you?'

'Isabel!' thundered the Reverend Gordon, coming in with an armful of logs for the fire.

'What is it?' Isabel looked round at the horrified faces. 'I'm not trying to upset anyone. It's just I don't think people should be paid to kill others, and I don't think there should be a British Empire, and I can understand the Greeks wanting their own country – and I think it's all so simple if only people would realise.'

'Bless her,' said Mrs Brodie. 'She doesn't understand.'

'What have you put in this delicious fruit-cake, Isla?' enquired Mrs Mackenzie. 'Do I detect dates?'

'You do indeed. Sultanas, dates, currants and walnuts.'

'Most nutritious. And so light. You must give me the recipe.'

The brick-red Rector poked at the logs on the fire, which spat out resin and damp. Later on Isabel heard him exhorting her mother to keep her under better control; she must not become arrogant and opinionated on subjects about which she knew and could know nothing whatsoever.

'She was thinking aloud,' said Isla. 'She's growing up. Straight as a die. I'm proud of her. But it's true; she ought to be careful not to upset folk.'

So perhaps, thinks Isabel, staring into the mirror, she'll understand about there being no God. And anyway if she does or she doesn't, I'm not going to church; they can't make me.

★

Isabel undoes her pigtails which have been bound around her head for the night. Lavish hair, burnished copper under the sunlight from the high window, streams all over her shoulders, upper arms and chest, crinkled from its bondage in the braids. Here is another fugitive Isabel, from whom the rigid shyness entirely melts away. The cork comes off and the bottle transiently fizzes. Her fingers nimbly plait the hair into two braids. She passes away into comfortable invisibility from the blank eye of the mirror.

Downstairs Isabel sits at the scrubbed kitchen table eating porridge with brown sugar and salt. Her eye traces the familiar whorls and irregularities in the wood worn smooth by years of elbow-grease. Her mother in a grey woollen housecoat, hair drifting from its bun, is busy at the range.

'Well, what will you do with this lovely morning before church, dear? Will you take Iain for a walk?'

'Yes I will – but – I'm not going to the church.'

'Are you not feeling well?'

'No, I'm fine.'

There is a pause, in which Isabel continues to trace the patterned grain of the sunlit wood, and Isla glances over at her daughter with a puzzled frown. She notes that Isabel is wearing that kindled, suppressed look that commonly

55

prefigures some excess. One of the strangest things about having children, she mused, is that from the very first they show such a determination to grow into their own selves – yet why should that be strange?

'You see . . .' says Isabel, and can't go on. She feels nervous, and chary of giving offence, but truth is at stake, the truth she knows the Covenanters fought for, even though her truth is different from theirs. Although there is no God, as she still plainly sees – she keeps checking with herself, to make sure – there is God in her denial. There is something one would not barter without remorse.

Isla, pulling out a chair to sit opposite, is moved by the look of lambent intelligence in Isabel's face. Isabel, looking up from the cooling porridge which she has been churning with her spoon, is moved by a gaunt, washed-out look on her mother's pale face.

'Are you all right, Mother?'

'Oh yes – don't you worry. I'm a wee bit anaemic, that's all.'

She bleeds constantly; has done for well-nigh two years, but does not want what she calls the *bother* of visiting the doctor's surgery. There isn't time; too much to be done and thought about. And at the bottom of it lurks the painful embarrassment of discussing yourself, let alone showing the most intimate parts of yourself, to the doctor. There is at present no lady doctor at Kinleven.

The exhaustion some days is so profound that she can hardly bear to move her lead-heavy limbs to get out of bed in the morning. *Migraine*, she explains apologetically; *such a nuisance*. She lies for hours in black torpor, not perfectly asleep, not distinctly awake, her mouth open, weights on her eyes. Folk – Isabel, Donald, the little Cahill girl, friends – flit like bodiless shadows on the very verge of her consciousness: she hardly recognises them as having a bond with her or a call upon her. She forces herself to respond to their needs, feigns their reality and her attachment. Then she can begin to focus them again and warm to them; she seems to heave herself out of the constraining element that drags her down, and she comes up with a shock, snatching air into her lungs like someone all-but-drowned. She can be virtually normal, if tired, for days on end. Isla deludes herself into not recognising that the fatigue is gaining, the pain swelling. She is more loving and understanding with Isabel; indeed she is conscious of being in the process of changing her mind, shifting perspective, on many things. Nothing – except her unshakable faith in Christ, her abiding sense of his nearness, even in the dark – looks quite the same from where she now stands.

'So what's the problem about church?'

'I can't tell you,' says Isabel with mournful intransigence. 'But I won't go – no one can force me to go,' she adds in a high-pitched voice. Anne Askew, the Protestant martyr, was burned at the stake for keeping to her truth. She read her testament with pulsing excitement. She could have nerved herself to do what Anne Askew did. She is enamoured of such heroism. But they don't set fire to you these days, the powers-that-be; they just tug and drag mercilessly at the tendons of your heart by getting up from the table rather stiffly, turning away and in a quiet, even voice saying,

'No one shall force you to do anything against your will, Isabel. That would not be right.'

Isabel takes one of Isla's hands before she can move away. She holds it in both of her own. The wrist is thin and knobbly, the veins stand out, but it is a beautiful hand, one which has both worked and written, and never been raised to strike. Isabel chafes the hand, which is cooler than her own, on impulse drawing it to her lips and kissing it between the knuckle and the wedding ring. The deep, physical shyness which possesses the family is momentarily broken. They have hardly ever hugged or kissed. From the beginning an invisible boundary of respect has demarcated each individual, guaranteeing her space; too much space perhaps.

'Tell me about it, Isabel,' says Isla, sitting down again but gently disengaging her hand. She feels a transient relief succeeded by a surge of guilt and barrenness at being able to give herself – or willing to give herself, is it? – so inadequately. She wants to take up the slender young hand again but somehow that would be too conscious an act. 'Tell me anything,' she says in recompense, 'I'll try to understand, really I will.'

Isabel registers the pull of the ebb-tide against the flow-tide in her mother's behaviour. An angry pang that rejects the rejecter shoots through her. And yet she understands. She too is like that, a private self that would bruise with too much touching.

'You won't like it.'

'Maybe not, my bairn. But I can listen.'

'I have scruples.'

'Well, that's fine.' Isla nods. This is what she and Donald have taught Isabel from the first: to examine one's conscience, to read oneself like a book. 'But you also have doubts?' Doubts are legitimate, they also taught, for they are the shadow that proves the sun.

'Oh no,' says Isabel. 'No doubts. I *know*.'

'What do you know?'

'That there is no God,' sings out Isabel with the sort of joy she felt when the congregation burst out into one of the jollier psalms or the Magnificat, and the joy comes partly of the fact that to say this aloud is to test its reality, and the conviction holds. It holds fast. There is assuredly no God.

'What has brought you to think this?'

Isabel cannot tell her mother exactly. It is a knowledge kaleidoscopically composed out of a thousand coloured pieces of the world she's seen. From the way the cat Billy, who had just been fed, prowled the lawns where the birds were pecking up worms, and she saw him pause, trembling with lust, his jet coat sleeked by her own fondling hands minutes before, his body retracted, and he sprang like a missile, burying claws and canines in the creature's throat. Isabel watched Billy shake the bird's bloody body; she watched him savage the unlucky animal enjoyingly. He was not hungry. He liked to kill. She realised that. But it was not his fault. It was how he was programmed.

Later Isabel was sitting at her desk in her bedroom doing her homework – Euclid's theorems, with compass and set-square, her desk set out neatly as she liked it. She was filling her fountain pen and sharpening her pencils. The birds began to sing piercingly just outside her open window: a rich, throbbing recitative volleyed back and forth between two voices. *Oh those blackbirds*, she thought. She squeezed the pen, held it in the bottle of blue-black Quink for three seconds, and let the ink flood up; did it again. Wings beat by outside the window and beat back again. The throbbing vibrato went on and on. The beauty of the music through the twilight overwhelmed her with happiness. She put down the pen and listened, enthralled; then crossed to the window and there spied Billy at the far end of the lawn, one forepaw raised, his lynx-eyes looking back, another dead bird drooping from his jaws; and the wild beauty of the music which had given her such happiness turned out to be a by-product of the danger-calls of the parent-birds as again and again and again they swept past Isabel's window from the pine to the larch. She watched and listened, half-an-hour or more. The still girl on the darkened edge of the world was narrowed and intensified, so as to become no more than a pair of wide eyes and ears, alert to their unlimited distress. But Isabel could not share with the creatures her comprehension; she could not say, *I understand. It is like this for us, too.* For several hours the music continued with unalleviated urgency. Then, all of a sudden, it stopped dead. Isabel had finished and checked her geometry. In maths you could get everything exact and perfect – that pleased her. She ruled a line.

Billy slid round the door and rubbed his arched back against her legs. She put her hand down automatically and sleeked his forehead and ears over his delicate skull. All must be forgiven, with the exception of God, whose crimes she everywhere detected. The empty snail-shells by the smooth stone at the bottom of the garden testified against him; the pictures of sick and dying children in Africa; her Uncle Angus and his wheelchair; the bruise she saw on the thin skin of the inside of January Cahill's wrist after Miss Slorach beat her with the strap that time. Everyone cried when Miss Slorach gave the strap; she was so viciously moral and she liked to hurt. Even Jacko Jackson blubbered, and Peter Horner the bully had to have his arm held in place by Mrs James, co-opted in for this purpose, for he whipped it away at the last moment to avoid the blow. She whacked once; his face winced. She inspected the face. She wanted it to break. She whacked twice; it rang around the class-room. Thirty pairs of eyes were glued to the boy being belted, with uneasy sadism like covert sexual arousal, mingled with alarm and com-

60

passion. *Thank God it's him and not me*, their held and released breaths said. On the third stroke the tears spurted straight forwards from his eyes, and by the fourth he was writhing and crying. Complicity with, and hostility to, the teacher made the room a rancid brew of implicated emotion. Peter Horner dragged back to his desk, head bent, shoulders hunched, his wounded hand cradled in his pocket; then, wiping his eyes on his grubby shirt-cuff, he glared round at the rest. But his willpower and his dignity had been smashed, he could not disguise it. January was one of only two girls ever to be belted. Miss Slorach strained the muscles of her right arm trying to squeeze a tear out of her. 'Unregenerate girl!' she cried out, red-faced, on a rising cadence. 'Hardened reprobate!' Isabel thought January was an Ancient Roman: *I salute you*, her grave eyes said as the girl passed on her way back to her desk. The horrible bruise which ripened on January's wrist was, to Isabel, an image of the bruise on the Creation itself. It accorded with much of what she had already witnessed. It gave her pain to think that God would stoop to perpetrate such a universe. Better far to allow no God at all than one so cruel.

Isla has to hear an odd, disconnected tale of cats and blackbirds. The child thinks so much and feels too keenly, beyond her years. She questions things she is not equipped to ponder.

Or is that so? Is it she herself who has not thought simply and deeply enough? There is something in the painful earnestness of Isabel's face which calls her to account. It is often like looking in a mirror and finding, to one's considerable shock, that the reflection talks back.

'Let's talk more when we have more time,' she concludes, limply. 'And, well, maybe don't say anything to your father.'

Unhappily, the Reverend Gordon has overheard most of it from the doorway, hardly able to believe his own ears as the child of the Manse blurts blasphemies which the wife of the Rector appears complacently to condone. The devil's loose in his kitchen. His heels resound on the paved floor as he marches swiftly across to the table, to confront them toweringly.

'Kneel!' is all he says.

Finding no obedience, only stunned perplexity, he places his hand on Isabel's head and levers her down to her knees.

'Kneel – and beg the Lord's pardon for your – *iniquity*.'

'Oh Donald, really!'

'How dare you collaborate! How dare you!' His high rage shakes off her restraining hand from his arm like so much dust.

'Don't be ridiculous, Donald. You can't act like that in this day and age.'

'Oh, so I'm ridiculous – ridiculous, am I?'

As his pressure lightens, Isabel meditates an instant resurgence like a bounced ball or a coiled spring, but the far-off ceiling seems to have descended and to be pressing on Isabel's head.

'O Lord in thy mercy . . .' prays her father fervidly. Isabel observes the tassels of his shabby tartan dressing-gown, one hanging slightly higher than the other. She arranges them symmetrically in her mind's eye, '. . . and purge her heart of the Evil One . . .' His carpet slippers are dark brown and woollen, reaching high over the ankle. She mentally rubs out the worn patches and pulls off a stray thread, '. . . and remove her from all Evil influences . . .' She shifts her weight from one knee to the other on the cold slabbed floor, resists the giggles that keep welling up and having to be choked down.

'Now go to your room', he ends, 'and seek for Grace and Light.'

Up she comes. She looks him in the eye, thoughtfully, pityingly, and leaves the kitchen at a measured pace.

'Now Donald, you shouldn't, you really shouldn't!' Isla is remonstrating. 'She didn't mean any harm, she was just thinking aloud. Always such a sensitive lass. You do untold damage by coercion. You can't force her and you mustn't.'

He's such a kind man normally, caring and tender behind the wall of reserve and shyness, but there is this madness of fanaticism in him.

'You do see, don't you?' she pleads.

'I do see that, sensitive lass or no, we cannot allow rank blasphemy in our very kitchen. What were you thinking of, Isla, letting the child believe she has every right to be an atheist – a professed atheist?'

He looks into his wife's face but without confronting her eyes, focusing on the cheek-bones made prominent by the increasing gauntness and angularity of her frame. He concentrates on a small blemish on her left cheek. Only askance can one set oneself against a being so inexorably honest and invincibly right-minded.

'Well,' says Isla reflectively and with some pity. 'When you come down to it, I suppose she does have that right. In the last analysis, she must follow her own conscience.'

'And I suppose you go along with it, this free-thinking cant, this licensed spitting in the holy eye of God?' The more he feels himself to be humanly in the wrong, the more his religious indignation swells.

'No, Donald, I do not.'

Though his anger does not abate, his love suddenly rises and surpasses it. A shiver goes down his spine. She is so reserved, so untouchable. From the very first when he reached out with timid, clumsy fingers to try to take her to him and make her his, there was always this sense of apprehension at her chaste, fierce self-completeness. She stood there barefoot in her long, white nightgown, her unbraided hair all down her shoulders and back, defenceless and yet totally her own and sacrosanct. She has rarely resisted him but when she has, he has felt mastered. His theological expostulations are a skimpy fig-leaf over his personal nakedness, and all the more vehement for that. Isla sleeps on the remote island of her single bed, impregnably, her blankets tightly tucked in, topped by his mother's patchwork quilt. Isla is a good woman. Her very goodness exasperates. One cannot touch her.

'No, no, of course you don't. But Isabel is coming under thoroughly undesirable influences, you will agree with me, Isla. We must put a stop to it.'

He means the Papist Antichrist, the English invader, the hosts of the ungodly encamped around the tents of Israel. The Great Whore of Babylon has sent her armies to Scotland and God's Chosen People must hold fast against infiltration. No more of that Catholic Cahill girl, for instance. He points this out to Isla, who turns away without a word.

*

Babylon's daughter cruises the Rector's garden almost soundlessly in her plimsolls. Light glints on quartzy gravel; it lends a peaceful sheen to the long, waxen leaves of rhododendron and the rind of the holly. The dog never barks when January comes; he knows she's family. He bounces his huge feathery tail from side to side and licks her lavishly. But the dog isn't around – shame, she likes the dog.

She enters the shadow at the side of the house and pads

along to the nether regions. The roots of the red-brick house are mossed like trees and the soil is dank and moist from the heavy night-dew. Tentacular ivy swathes the wall, eating out the putty between the bricks; it is laced with tendrils of honeysuckle. The backside of the house is where you see a glimpse of something solid and common, evidence of the vulgar necessities to which the Manse disdains to admit itself condemned. An old rusted bucket without a bottom rests in a patch of nettles. A solitary galosh is beached on a pile of garden rubbish. There is a vegetable garden right at the back, well-stocked with lettuce, radish, peas and tatties. January unearths a crisp young lettuce and a handful of radishes, wipes them on her skirt and crunches. She retires with her spoils into the safe lee of the house and hunkers down to feed.

Her eyes stare out of her pinched face like polished hazelnuts, unblinkingly, at the washing-line just beyond the vegetable-garden. Propped with a high wooden stake which raises the line at a jaunty angle so as to fly its contents like bunting or flags, hangs an array of laundered combinations, bottle-green bloomers, a whole armoury of whale-bone underwear and neatly pegged grey socks.

Here then is Mrs Gordon's arse.

Here is the undeniable evidence that this high-class lot sweat, shit and piss like the rest. They are no different, no better than us. To January the washing-line bears mocking witness against the pretensions of the well-bred and the literate. In the same way, the window of the pantry, open on the second notch of the latch, is a token of the legitimate right of pilfer to one to whom not enough has been given. Climbing up the green drainpipe, January has on several occasions fiddled the latch open, reached down to unfasten the main window, and hence squeezed through, being a girl naturally nimble and adroit and also bonily narrow enough to penetrate sideways through a needle's eye. Flapjacks and scones in her pocket she scrambled out again, pondering the identity of two flea-bitten putrid corpses of birds hanging on the pantry wall. Dog-food perhaps.

January will not thieve this morning, but this has nothing to do with conscience. She sees nothing wrong in scavenging what you want from those who have enough, more than enough, even if they have been kind to you and let you eat apples in their loft. For in fact all such apparent generosity is strictly rationed, January knows. It goes so far and not an inch further. They never scant or stint themselves. You get their leavings, you are not a guest at their feast. These good people are just as bad as the others who give you a wide berth like a leper or an untouchable. They are buying a cheap ticket to Heaven in a ship full of Holy Joes. It doesn't impress her at all. January has not the words for this perception but it is part of her silent creed, her heterodox wisdom. On the whole she'd rather not be caught. Especially by Mrs Gordon, who is not just words, but toffee too, shortcake and fudge still warm from the pan, which melts on your tongue and floods for the time being the whole of your mouth with pleasure – and plenty of it. Food takes up most of the imaginative space in January's life. She is always thinking of how to cadge or nick it; she dreams of sensual eating, tables covered in jellies, banana custard, doughnuts and cream-cakes. When she gets hit, her eyes don't spout tears, her mouth waters. Only she knows that.

And yet for all the tooth-rotting sweets she packs away, she never puts on an ounce of fat. January's like a bean-stalk. Hasn't properly started her periods yet, though Prue who's ten months younger started ages ago, unsuccessfully trying to hide her blushful efforts to cope with the blood and pain from her sneering sister. January day-dreams she's a boy, not a girl. Unconsciously she mimes a boyish swagger, hands in pockets, whistling, and finds a strength amounting to immunity in that pretence.

She'll have a look in the kitchen window while she's reconnoitring the back of the house. From a perch on the drainpipe, she leans her head to the bottom corner of the high window; sees the mother's grey head sombre and bowed; the father in a demented attitude raising his face to the light in ardent prayer; and Isabel she does not see at all until, looking downwards she gets a view of a section of her head and torso kneeling at her father's feet. She knew the Proddies were bloody weird but she never knew before that they prayed to their own fathers. Catch January praying to her fucking father. She descends, landing light as a cat on the compacted soil of the path. Looting a bottle of milk from the front doorstep, January passes away into the crisp morning air.

*

'No, Prue dear, Isabel will not be playing today . . .' says Isla, trying not to notice and, when she has noticed, not to respond to, the subdued melancholy in the girl's eyes. '. . . and possibly not for some time to come,' she continues with a voice all iron and tinkling. 'Isabel must concentrate on her school work.'

'Oh. Right. Thank you,' says Prue, shrinking in to herself and turning to go. Then she turns back again and asks hesitantly, 'Do you think I could play in the garden for a bit, Mrs Gordon, even if Isabel can't come out?' Sometimes when Isabel was ill or at the dentist, Mrs Gordon has licensed this bliss.

'No, I don't think so, not today.'

It is not possible to say *not ever*, as Donald has insisted.

She shuts the door gently but decisively. Through the frosted pane she can see the downcast child's figure hovering there, and then wavering and blurring as it recedes.

Suddenly she finds herself re-opening the door. The nape of Prue's neck and the very hang of her long blue cardigan with its patchwork of darns are unbearably vulnerable, and hence imperative.

'Come tomorrow, instead,' she says.

The child's features relax into a huge, enchanting grin. The sun sails up into the meridian like a yellow balloon. She is off skipping down the drive.

The Whore of Babylon indeed, the Antichrist, thinks Isla, and wants to giggle. Her life has been on the whole rather threadbare in the area of humour. Her cast of mind is at once so literal and so seriously inclined that she would seldom 'get' a joke. It had to be anatomised and hence killed before she could see it. 'Yes, I see,' she would say, embarrassing others, embarrassing herself, and nod thoughtfully. Nowadays she finds she wants to laugh, more and more, at the preposterousness of human pretension – laugh indignant Swiftian mockery, laugh in mourning, or, as here, just burst out at the daftness of it. The daftness of Donald, forcing Isabel to her knees on the cold, stone floor; the daftness of history which consisted in precisely that, one group of self-righteous people pop-eyed with prejudice, forcing another group of people to their knees. Then that group bouncing up from their oppression and forcing the other lot to its knees.

'Oh don't be so daft,' she wanted to tell Donald this morning. 'Let the poor lass alone. Leave her be.'

Could a due perception of daftness then be the secret of arresting the remorseless repetition of the cycles of history? She sits down by the living-room fire, which has just been lit, and contemplates the sizzling effort of the flames to wring concession out of the resinous pine-logs, bleeding their pearls of sap which the fire aromatically boiled to vapour. The room seems full of the susurrations of the flame as it licks and flaps round the logs, and full, too, of the pungent fragrance that comes of the chemical meeting of living fire and living wood. She raises her beautiful hands to the flames and toasts them and her face. Always it is the simple, homely things that bless and satisfy – this fire now, and Iain the dog lying asleep at her feet; the hot bread, new-baked from the oven; the taking of a book in both hands (as now, reaching for a volume of Buchanan's sixteenth-century *History of Scotland*, which she reads in the original Latin). These things – fire, bread, books – reach right back to her girlhood in Sutherland, her father also a cleric, her mother a schoolteacher, a life at once hardy and nourishing. Buchanan in Bordeaux taught Montaigne, he survived the Inquisition, converted to Protestantism on returning to Scotland and denounced Mary Stuart and the murder of Darnley. The book in her hands is an early edition, as precious perhaps as the whole house over her head. When the book creaks open, and she spells the words over to herself, Buchanan springs alive into the room, she overhears the voice of a mind, speaking in the here-and-now, with all its biases, subterfuges, struggles and conflicts. *So, George Buchanan*, she challenges him, *What have you got to say to me?* It is all one long tale of antipathy and violence, the dog-fight of the murderous clans, the depravity of the English, the hell-fire theologies warring it out on the page; the voice of the historian, an implicated judge.

But where is my history and Isabel's? she wonders, raising her head from the book. The voiceless, nameless women bent in the fields, at the looms, gutting the herring at the docks, hanging over the cradles, seem to crowd the margin with acts for which there is neither testament nor memorial.

Isabel coming in to the living room sees her mother reading, stooped over the book, spectacles low on the bridge of her nose. Her haggard face is in repose, as always in company with a book. Books, she knows, are sacred in their house. Isabel precipitately ripped several pages out of her Bible this morning after the scene with Father, and now regrets it more than a little. She has glued them back in as well as she can. Only Barbarians deface or burn books. Vandals and Vizigoths, the Spanish Inquisition, people who don't know any better. And besides, she is in a state of acute muddle and stress. Things that were clear no longer seem obvious, or, if they do, they are skewed and darkened by a sense of shame and dread. In the very obliquity of her feelings there is a panic. It is as if the unweaned foal in the pasture had defied its parent, and crazily on tottering stick-legs made off before its time to suicidal autonomy. Isabel does not recant but she runs to her mother with burning face and buries her head in her lap.

*

'A most regrettable girrul,' observes Mrs Harty to Mrs Brodie over a cup of tea in the vestry. The eloquent rolling of her 'r's echoes through the coldly flagstoned space. The hanged man drooping from a peg on the door is the Rector's ministerial garb, ghostly in the murky light; the musty air is invaded by the carnation scent of the flowers the two ladies have been arranging. 'A deplorable girrul and positively a handicap to poor Donald. Did you *ever* hear *anything* like it, the outburst the other day?'

'Oh, she's a bright, canny lass – no harm in her.'

'Well, I must say,' Mrs Brodie bridles at this wicked

absence of malice. 'I must say, if *that's* what is to be expected of a child prodigy, give me the common average any time. I thank Heaven that my Geraldine is no genius. I go by the Book of Proverbs: a docile, biddable lass is worth more than rubies, I believe is what it says. So worrying and embarrassing for her mother, and as for the Rector . . . well. So opinionated, so frankly *arrogant* about matters on which she can have no knowledge and therefore should express no opinion.'

'And yet she's a gentle wee thing – quite shy really.'

'Shy! You call that shy! Well I do not. "God the Mother, God the Daughter and God the Holy Spirit" I heard her singing at Morning Service last week – yes, really – at the top of her not inconsiderable voice. "Shush," I said and I dug my elbow in her side.' Mrs Harty's censorious loquacity swells in proportion to Mrs Brodie's unworthy mildness. She cannot see why the black lamb should not be coerced into bleating the same tune as the rest of the flock. She meditates aloud on whether her upbringing has been at fault, too much freedom perhaps, running around like a heathen savage; she speculates on who will be found to marry such a lass; and prognosticates a bad end for Isabel. She pours herself another cup of tea.

'Oh no; she'll settle. I've known her since she was born.'

'That's as may be,' says Mrs Harty doubtfully and, shaking her head as one who has sucked all the juice out of a subject, concludes lamely, 'You mark my words.'

4

Hugh Cahill has ten days' leave to look forward to. He sprawls in the easy chair at his fireside with a pint in one hand and his socked feet resting pleasurably on the fender.

'This is the life, Mary, so it is.'

Mary has her teeth in and her curlers out. She is understood to be 'making an effort', which she periodically undertakes with the help of the Blessed Virgin, her name-sake – an intermediary she may badly need to fall back on during the period of Hugh's leave. When he's around there are so many incendiary possibilities he might hit upon. The children are explosive devices timed and set, and the whole place seems a mine-field. Somehow you learn to live on this hostile territory, this no-man's-land of eternally imminent catastrophe. At times Mary ceases to care where she treads. It's all the same anyway. At other times she 'makes an effort'.

'I'll be under your feet a bit, won't I?' he goes on with boyish winningness. 'But I'll give you a hand with the kids. If I can shift some of that builder's muck from the back garden, I might get round to digging it over. The lads can give me a hand. Give you a rest for a change.'

Poor old cow, he thinks, recalling what a fresh, sweet little thing she came to him, twenty-four years ago. He took her to the mess and she sat up very straight, all 5 foot 1 of her, with her Pimms Number One in her hand, sucking the cherry off the stick like a child. She crossed her legs in imitation of the film-stars and her hair was crimped like Carole Lombard's. The lads looked her up and down. *Nice bit of skirt, Hugh*, said Lofty Short. Hugh adored her. He worshipped her. The agony of jealousy if she so much as smiled at anyone else – the electric need to hit out conducted to his very fingertips, grinding his clenched fists in his pockets. Hard to believe this ageing, raddled woman, with her slipshod ways, her hangdog look, is that sweet, early Mary. She stopped looking after herself, of course, when the children came along; let herself go.

'What colour were your hair in them days?'

'When?'

'When we was courting. You told me you was Carole Lombard's sister when I first asked your name. Didn't half look like her, too.'

'Ash-blond, it were. Peroxide. Give you a right shock when it grew out dark brown.'

My hair were brown, my teeth were white, my figure were 34–19–36, and my name were Mary Murphy. She licks the Guinness froth from her upper lip and enjoys the memory. It is experienced as a mental film-reel, completely distinct from and unimplicated in the squalor of the present. She sits and gawps at it by the hour, as if on the back row of the ABC, nibbling popcorn.

'Here's to old times,' says Hugh benignly, stretching out his glass to hers. 'To the good old days. Come on, me darling girl, drink up and top up.'

The glasses chink, she drains the heavy silky liquid, ferrous and dark as tarn-water. The anaesthetic, soothing effect almost but not entirely relaxes the fibres of her vigilance, as does Hugh's placating tone. It took years to learn to resist the tears and the fondling entreaties, as Hugh begged pardon, purchased immunity with a kiss and a blandishment. She was a slow learner of the lesson that words meant nothing. Words were air. They were of the moment. Words were mere tricks, trade, unbacked currency.

'God help me, I'll never do it again, Mary.'

'I'm not worthy of you, Mary.'

'I swear it on the Holy Bible, Mary.'

He'd get down on his knees to her, he'd cry, his face buried in the folds of her skirts, authentic, copious tears which left a wet patch when he'd done. He was sorry, he was so sorry, honest-to-God, how could he have done that, how could he? He loved her, he'd die for her. He'd anoint her puffy, bruised eye or cheek or breast with witch-hazel and atoning kisses. He told her it was his mother's fault, he'd never had enough love, and she accepted this and pitied him, believing she was powerful and with the help of God could heal him. He crawled around on the floor vituperating himself, repeatedly assaulting his own head with his fist. He explained to her, in the intimate, relieved calm that came as the aftermath of the storm, that it was as if another person did these outrageous things and he, the real Hugh, looked on aghast but incapable of intervention. For a while she would be the victor, pure and whole and perfect, so that his every speech and act was a concession and nothing was too much trouble for him. Then one day he would awaken with a dead-eyed expression on his face. He'd go for her or for one of the children, especially January the child he hated and disowned, and she'd remind him of his promises and apologies, and he'd come back with:

74

'Did I say that? No, I never. You've made it up – liar, cunt, bitch, hag.'

As the years of steady drinking advanced, the violence repeated itself and slowly escalated, while Hugh's remorse became more perfunctory and finally disappeared. He seemed to get less of a kick out of his routine attacks, so that he'd stay mad for days and even weeks on end, looking for trouble, looking for satisfaction of his violent need like an animal desperate to rut.

Why was she gifted with such a good memory? It would be better, far better, to forget as he did, wiping the slate clean with every new day. Starting anew with each fresh morning, he stays relatively young. His rather greasy complexion is hardly wrinkled at all, shining there on the pillow when she switches on the light and hands him his tea in the morning. His baby-face looks guileless and innocent as Prue's now, or Teresa the nun (her pride and joy of all the girls) when she was an idolised only child. Mary's face in the mirror looks as if someone had put over it a web of wrinkles, defaced it with minuscule scratch-marks. It was written all over. If she powders it, the powder lodges in the cracks and makes it worse, so she has given that up. Her face some mornings is covered with his sins: blue-black, puffy swellings that turn green-yellow like meat that's gone off. Does she deserve to bear this testimony? She studies this problem and has put it obliquely to Father Friend, aptly named.

'Our Lord has a special tenderness for martyrs,' Father Friend assured Mary.

This comforted, if it could not satisfy, Mary. With each fresh blow the question repeated itself like a festering wound incapable of final healing. Do I deserve this?

'Our Blessed Saviour suffered humiliation on the cross for sinners. We, too, may go the way of the cross,' said

75

Father Friend. 'There are times when our loved ones pass on their pain to us and all we can do is to hold the pain and refuse to pass it on ourselves to others. This is our Gethsemane, our Calvary.'

Mary's salvation, her ego, sucks on this and is nourished and strengthened. She is greater and better than Hugh. She looks down upon him from the vast, vertiginous altitude of the cross to which he has given her a leg-up. She spreads her arms for the nails like mighty wings. She sees him for the worm he is, little, brutal, scared and impotent, peeping up the colossal height of her elevation. She forgives him.

In the practical realm, there is an urgent need for cash. If only they would promote him, but the Army keeps him stuck at the rank of corporal. His ungovernable rages apparently do not qualify as evidence of leadership-quality; she would have thought he could have kept his fits decently private within the sanctum of the home, but (more and more frequently) they spill out at work, and he goes for people who get under his skin – with his tongue rather than his fists, of course, but even so it is imprudent behaviour. His immediate superiors are now younger than himself; the boy-officers are children and the WRACs are jumped-up tarts. Now he's on leave, at least that irritant will be absent.

'Run along out, Peter, your father's home on leave . . . Off with you, Prue, take your sandwich with you, and don't come back till tea-time. Go on. I said, *go on*.'

She shuts the door on all but the babies. Where they are or what doing all day, she does not enquire. Malachi cadges a ten-bob note from her out of the house-keeping.

'Ta, Ma,' he says, and winks. He's a good boy. For the thousandth time she admires the long, curly eye-lashes dark around the knowing pale-blue eyes that are so heartmeltingly beautiful. She can refuse him nothing. But she cannot smile back at the lad. She is weary and sick. She had deduced from her symptoms that the blessing of the menopause was setting in; God knows, she has prayed for it, to God, his Mother and a variety of relevant saints. She prays that the nightmare of a life spent breeding, turning oneself inside-out like a gutted chicken, ridding oneself of one's contents in a scalding brew of pain and starting again, might have an ending. She might have peace. But now she's almost sure she mistook the signs. The fourteenth child ripples its fluent limbs inside her womb; it's waving to her in its sleep, and she already ponders, *Boy or girl?* and a medley of far-fetched names drifts through her mind, holy, venerable, safe-guarding names like benedictions – *Clement, Jerome, Benedict, Ignatius* – names to light the infant on its way.

Malachi struts out of the door, his thumbs stuck in his pockets, waggling his hips in their tight trousers.

'Ta ta, Ma,' he says. 'See ya.' He leaves the door wide open.

One or two of the children are still within earshot of the house. She shoos with her hands, calling, 'Go on and play. Go on, off you go, the lot of you.'

They sheer off, disappearing round the block. Mary returns to the business of making an effort.

*

Always from the beginning he was a fighter. He came butting out of the womb fist-first. Everything was in doubt except his pugnacity, and that was what helped him to survive in the overcrowded deprivation of Salford in the 1920s. Like a litter of piglets they squealed and scuffled over the teats of the mother, widowed and ill, stranded on her side as the many mouths drained her life into

77

themselves. During her stays in hospital with TB, the family looked after itself; ten-year-old Hughie Cahill roamed the streets looking for smaller Proddie or foreign girls or boys to punch. The blows were punishment, meted out to redress the injustice and the unlove. He hit back at his mother's desertion; her illness and her endless tears when she was at home were a crime against his need. For the rest of his life, he could never bear people, especially women, to be ill – it brought out all the latent cruelty in him. His childhood was one long tale of fisticuffs and gang brawls.

Fighters were the stuff of which Empire was made. Hugh joined up marginally before War broke out in 1939, at the age of 23, as a professional soldier eager to lay his talents at the disposal of King and Country. Those were the golden years of his life. He was one of the lads, accepted into the man's world of fraternal bondings and simplified emotions. He fought with the Eighth Army under Alexander and Montgomery against Rommel's Afrika Corps in the Western Desert; he was there at Alamein. After the War things declined. He seldom managed to get in on the action, not in Palestine, Korea, Malaya, Kenya, or Suez, those colonial theatres in which the British fought for and then conceded authority, leaving faction and despoliation in the wake of their withdrawal – only a frustrating few months in Cyprus. Hugh was disgusted at the ceding of independence to these wogs, these nignogs, these subhuman beings: they needed to be governed, these buggers, for their own sakes. He was very bitter about the existence of Pakis and blacks in the British Army, and often succeeded in getting into drunken fights with them. The one exception to this rule was the gallant Gurkha regiments – excellent fighting machines, as he

said, and loyal to the flag more than the average Eng-
lishman.

At work he did a menial job in the Equipment Stores;
at home he ruled his family with voice and fists. All men
who *are* men knock their women about a bit, everyone
knew that. It's just a fact of life. It's to show who's master,
who wears the pants. And he's not as bad as some men,
not by a long chalk, nothing like; he challenges anyone to
say he is and he'll knock their bloody block off.

Granted, he's got a bad temper. Granted, he drinks –
and then he's not responsible for his actions. But that's
not his fault, that's the way he is. They should try to get
round him more. But they insist on rubbing him up the
wrong way, riling him. They talk behind his back, he
knows they do, they leave him out, mock and reject him
– so they've got it coming.

Some days he smiles and dances to some raffish tune
that bubbles from his own head; other days there's a pent
up storm of anger in his head, belly and prick, black and
seething, and it *must* discharge its load of killing pain on
some other head or do violence to himself. He never
knows from one minute to the next how he's going to
be.

But at present, today, weather is fair, visibility clear.
He reclines in his chair with one leg lazily hanging over the
greasy arm, wearing his civvies and listening to Workers'
Playtime; he refills his glass, not a care in the world. He
whistles as he meditatively checks the scores against his
Pools Coupon: Sheffield Wednesday 2, Aston Villa 1;
Partick Thistle 1, Celtic 4. He'd have liked to be a football
player, that was his dream; soldiering's not so different
though, if you're actually in the fighting line, playing for
victory with your mates, the crowd roaring you on:
United Kingdom 10, Rest of the World NIL. But the end-

less practising for parades, sorting kit, filling forms, doing fatigues for being drunk on duty, that was not what he had in mind at all when he joined up. Still, he's on leave now, answerable to none, and he has the feeling his luck's in for a change. Stenhouse Muir 2, Queen of the South NIL.

*

Vairmeo rovano,
Vairmeo rovani,
Vairmeo ruoho,
Sad am I without thee.

Dreamily, Prue and Isabel sing the beautiful Eriskay love lilt, hanging on ropes from the great sycamore in the enclosed grove at the remotest end of the Manse garden. January tied the ropes to the bough at the beginning of the summer, shinning out with extraordinary agility and daring like a lemur along the branch and securing them one-handed. It was yet another feat which commended January to Isabel as a girl of Sparta. She herself could not have attempted it, as she freely admitted.

There are loops like nooses in the bottom of the ropes for your foot; you stand in the loop with one sandalled foot and spin or swing. It is a day of uncharacteristically intense and somnolent heat. Even here in the dappled shade the warmth acts like a drug, bringing lassitude and tranquil spirits. Bluebottles shine, jade and jet, on leaves or buzz about the margins of the song. Prue hangs out from her rope, her head flopping right back, and lets the upside-down world play its lights and shades on her lazy eye. A butterfly hovers around her scarlet ribbon, so still does she hang.

80

'I love the Scotch songs,' says Prue. 'I love how sad they are.'

They all seem to tell of something secret and beautiful we once had and now have lost and shall never have again – an exiled prince, a lover turned into a seal, someone overseas who can't be seen, only sung about.

'We do not say "Scotch". The right word is Scottish or Scots – never "Scotch". We are not whisky or sticky tape.'

'Sorry.' Prue is flustered. She has made this error before. Isabel is constantly correcting her vocabulary, but Prue doesn't resent this. She's a quick, conscientious pupil, who wants to learn. She wants to know the right words, to appropriate the magic lexicon which will qualify her as an equal in this northern world, so admirable compared with her own impoverished nomadism. Prue is making a gradual but systematic importation of what she discerns as key Scottish words into her speech-patterns, as well as copying the accent and inflections.

'Isabel,' she says. 'Do you think I could ever become a Scot?'

'Well, you'd either have to have been born here or have Scots ancestors – which I doubt.'

'But if I lived here a long time? If I sort-of transplanted?'

'It would take a long, long while,' Isabel warns doubtfully. Her loyalties are tribal and exclusive, in a way she scarcely comprehends herself. It's one thing to tolerate the foreigner, another to accept him into the clan.

'I could marry in,' says Prue, rather desperately. She is greedy to claim the sharing of this space, this garden and this first real friendship of her life, as of right.

Isabel stares reflectively. She sees something about Prue. That she doesn't want to be herself: she wants to be someone else. That's alien and sad. Isabel's a rooted tree; Prue's flotsam.

'I would marry you, if I was a boy . . .', she says kindly. Prue's eyes glow. '. . . but I'm not,' she goes on crushingly. 'In any case I don't intend to marry. I want to go to the university.'

She spins on her line.

'Oh so do I,' says Prue, spinning too. She hadn't thought of it before but now it becomes her chief ambition.

'You could, you're brainy enough, even though you are . . .'

'Are what?'

Isabel was going to say '. . . an Army child' but substitutes '. . . not Scottish. Edinburgh, St Andrews, Dundee or Glasgow, those are the places I might go. My father went to Edinburgh.'

'Isabel,' says Prue, who has been told a peculiar story by January about Isabel being on her knees in the kitchen on Sunday. 'Is it true that Protestants worship their fathers?'

'*God* the Father certainly.'

'No, I mean Dad the Father.'

'Certainly not,' says Isabel. 'At least as far as I know. Shall I tell you a secret? Promise not to tell?'

Prue crosses her heart and hopes to die. 'No I won't, honestly I won't.'

Isabel dismounts from her rope and Prue follows her. In the shimmering heat-haze the dappled ropes hang like twin nooses. A bee meanders on a flight-path straight through one. The thick, resin-scented air pours round their bare arms and legs like a warm bath.

'I found out something. There's no God at all. People have just been imagining him, Prue.'

'Oh *Isabel*, don't be silly, of course there is! I can show him to you.'

'Of course you can't.'

'I can.'

'You can't.'

'I can so, Isabel.'

'Where is he then? Show him to me.'

She gestures with her arm, a wide arc encompassing the quilted light slanting out on the encirclement of evergreens, plucking out of the prevailing dark shadow scrolls of bark, knots of root, shining pine needles and the veined, translucent leaves of the beech.

'If you are there, God, come out and strike me dead!'

Prue claps both hands over her mouth, as though the challenge had burst out inadvertently from herself and she must stopper up her own mouth against further blasphemy.

'You see, he hasn't come. He isn't there.'

'Oh Isabel, you mustn't tempt him. It's dangerous.' She crosses herself surreptitiously. She doesn't want to get mixed up in this heathenism. She hopes proximity won't be taken for connivance.

'Now I've denied him twice', says Isabel, with evident satisfaction, 'and I've not been turned into a pillar of salt.'

'Come with me,' says Prue. 'I'll show you Jesus, his Real Presence. In person. Then you'll see.'

*

'There,' whispers Prue, having genuflected. 'There he is. There's God.'

In the Nissen Hut which houses the Church of the Holy Name at RAC Kinleven, the curtains are closed to obtain the dim mood most beneficial for prayer. Rows of utility chairs as in the school hall stand before a statue of a startled-looking Jesus bearing his bleeding heart, which he tenders to the spectator with white, dainty fingers, and a corresponding statue of the Madonna and Child in white, blue and flaking gold. Above the altar, Christ Crucified ascends. There is a complex odour of incense, snuffed candles, summer flowers, hair-grease and wax polish.

'Where?' whispers Isabel. 'I can't see him. Do you mean that statue?' The statue looks down at Isabel with its eyebrows raised, wearing an expression of pained surprise.

'No, of course not. Over there.'

'Shush,' hisses a kneeling woman in a headscarf, who has been telling the beads of a rosary with an incantatory mutter. 'This is a church, not a playground.'

A rival woman opposite is also telling her rosary, very rapidly, and appears to have gained ground and overtaken her competitor during the interruption. The admonitory woman, after emitting a fierce 'Tut!' launches off again, gabbling the prayer as if it were one helter-skelter word of infinite longevity, 'HailMaryfullofgracetheLordis-withtheeblessedartthouamongstwomen . . .'

'Sorry,' murmurs Prue. They approach the altar rail. 'In there. In that tabernacle is where God is. His Real Presence,' she says reverently.

Isabel can see on the altar a sort of silvery breadbin, about three feet high and made of silver metal, with doors that have been left wide open. Beside each door stands a lit candle in a red plastic container, and inside the breadbin is a silver plate with a wafer.

'On the Feast of Corpus Christi and lots of other days like today', Prue goes on, eyes fixed on the tabernacle, 'in the morning the priest performs the Exposition of the Blessed Sacrament. People can come in any time to visit Jesus. And that there *is* Jesus.'

'But there's nothing there,' whispers Isabel. 'Just a tin and a piece of bread.'

'There is, there really is, if you believe and know he's there; Jesus is there, you can see him.'

'Can you see him now?'

'Oh yes.'

'What does he look like?'

Prue can't say. She shrugs. It's not with her bodily eyes but with the eyes of her heart that she comes equipped to see a person where Isabel can only see an empty breadbin. The candle-light glimmers red on her spectacles. This is home and comfort, even more reassuring than Columba, and somehow associated with Columba though in a different way. These beautiful rituals on special, set days of the year so that you know what to expect and when to expect it. The gentle lights, sweet fragrances, the consecrated vessels and chalices, the censors and candles, the skirted priests like women, all these are home to Prue as home never was. Coming in here is like opening an oven-door when the waft of freshly-baked pastry rushes out at you and gives you a lovely shock. Prue often comes in and sits in a special seat which she has secretly chosen to call her own, near to the remembrance candles, and is quiet with herself. She folds her hands in her lap, crosses her feet, stares at the candle-flames and thinks of nothing. She comes in empty and she goes out filled. This is how she knows that Jesus is here. Prue is alarmed at Isabel's myopia. But she reflects that heathens and atheists are less wicked than Proddies, the priest has said. They burn on a slow heat low down in the oven of Hell, whereas the Proddies are sausages spitting and sizzling by a naked flame.

'It's a mystery,' she whispers to Isabel. 'You aren't supposed to understand.'

'I see,' says Isabel.

She holds her peace, will say no more. She likes the candles. Their flames stand constant and motionless, contenting the eye with gentle light. Otherwise it is all as foreign and other as Babylon or the tomb of Tutankhamun; and inclines her to take a more lenient view of her father's ways and notions, which seem rather sensible beside Prue's inheritance. She hears his voice now in her mind, stertorously sermonising, *The gewgaws and the gaudy cant of Rome*, and sees the hats of the elderly women in the front pew nodding approval. She went home that day singing to herself as she hopped, skipped and jumped, *The gew – gaws – and – the gaud – y – cant*. She looked up gewgaws in the dictionary and found it meant toys, frippery, playthings, knickknacks for show.

And yet, for Prue, God was there among the breadbins and the gewgaws. How is this?

She studies Prue's face as they emerge into the dazzling, bleaching sunlight; and Prue can feel herself being looked at – a habit of Isabel's she doesn't much care for. The interrogative, straight look makes her feel shy and distressed, fearful that she will ultimately be seen through and discarded. That would be unbearable, to lose this privilege of access to the Manse and the affection that goes with it, from Isabel, from her mother, from Iain the dog, from the very trees that take her weight and give her space. In sad hours, when Dad has been thrashing Mam or January or Paul, or when there has only been bread-and-dripping at every meal for two days, or when she sees herself in her mind's eye, a girl with a fat round common face and National Health specs, dressed in the remnants of a jumble sale, she knows it cannot go on. She will be seen through and got rid of; the dwarf's fraternisation with giants will be over forever. Prue cannot judge the Gordons. All they are and do is the best that can be imagined. And in any case she will have to move on when the posting comes. But that seems very far away. Posted like re-addressed letters no one could possibly want to read to the desolation of some new camp, faceless and barren, where there will be no Manse, and no chance to count as her self, Prue, but she must be shunned as one of them hooligan Cahill slobs.

Perhaps it was wrong to have brought Isabel here. She couldn't possibly understand.

But she won't give up Jesus, even to secure Isabel Gordon's approval. Jesus is bedrock real, Jesus is Prue's friend and related to her, Jesus and his Mother Mary. She carries her head a fraction higher, and the hangdog look passes away.

They stroll out of the camp, between the barracks with their corrugated iron roofs, black wooden walls and green-painted doors. To Isabel the military environment is unfamiliar and, in a different way, as bizarre as the church: the predominant maleness, a community minus the female, as if they bred by parthenogenesis and came out fully developed service personnel, each one in his maker's regulation image. A contingent of conscripts marches past; their boots clump and they swing their rigid arms exaggeratedly. One poor lad is hopelessly out of step. Blushfully, he shuffles his feet to get back in time with his stamping comrades, but now something seems to have gone dreadfully wrong with his arms. The sergeant major moves up on the inside and begins to bawl at the young man in a foghorning voice, an unintelligible volley of vituperation which he delivers at point-blank range from a red, irascible physiognomy. The soldier's nerves have completely unstrung; his unco-ordinated arms and legs jerk, the muscles round his eyes spasm. He is a fair-haired, lightly built boy, with freckles and thin wrists. Isabel and Prue trotting alongside the squad at a little distance note the trembling of his lip. Evidently he is on the verge of tears.

The sergeant major bawls again. The conscript is condemned as a poufter and a bleeding nancy-boy, the conscript's mother is accused of sexual irregularities with the milkman. The squad is halted and, after a few more imprecations, and the nancy-boy being directed to march ten yards up the road by himself and back again, he is re-inserted into the squad.

'BY – the RIGHT – QUICK – MARCH, one-two, one-two . . .'

The machine starts up again and crashes up the road on its hundred-and-twenty boots as one man.

'At least he didn't cry,' says Isabel.

'No, he didn't. He nearly did though.'

'They come in human beings, and they are converted into killing machines, that's what my Uncle David says. They humiliate them on purpose, to break their spirits.'

'Why do they?'

'Because they want to rule the world. They send them all over the globe to keep the natives from speaking their own languages and wanting independence. Aden, Singapore, Cyprus, Ireland.'

'But those are all English places.'

'*Are* they?'

Prue has always somehow thought of England as a scattered place, with outposts everywhere, given to us by God and nature, which we are duty-bound to go and protect. We look after the poor ignorant natives who haven't the power to do it for themselves and are grateful to us for our sheltering benevolence – all except the bad natives, that is, whose ingratitude takes the form of bombs and lynchings, and who have to be ruthlessly put down for the general good.

'Thank God we can't be called up,' says Isabel. 'Just think, there are 300,000 of those national servicemen, all having their spirits broken – but not us. We'll be free. It must be awful when people bawl and bellow at you and you can't reply.'

'Yes, it must.' Prue keeps private the fact that she has never known a different state than being bawled and bellowed at, without right of reply. Before she came to the Manse she thought all negotiations in families were carried out at the top of people's voices, right down through the hierarchy, Dad bawling out Malachi, who bawled out Catherine, who bawled out Peter, and so on. She was amazed to hear the quiet, civil voices at the Manse. 'I'd hate it, I would.'

'What if he *had* cried?' Isabel goes on. 'He'd have been so humiliated he could never have held up his head again. Margaret Gillespie says men can't cry. She says they have an anatomical defect in their tear-ducts which prevents it. Her father's a doctor, so she should know.'

'Jacko Jackson cries', says Prue, 'when he's belted, and so does my brother Paul. I don't think there's anything wrong with their tear-ducts – just they're told Boys Don't Cry and so they don't.'

'Come to that', says Isabel. '*I* don't cry, and my mother doesn't either.'

'Nor me,' lies Prue hesitantly. Her easy tears have often sodden the pillow at night when the light's turned out and January is asleep, and the gush of salt water brings healing; she pours out the full bottle of her pain and is eased of its astringency. 'Well, not much anyhow.' Maybe Isabel has nothing to cry about.

'Marching is ridiculous,' announces Isabel. 'Look at them now.'

The squad has right-wheeled and about-turned, and is returning the way it came, to a bark of 'EFT – EFT – EFT – IGHT – EFT'. They cross the road to ascertain the condition of the fair-haired young man. His arms and legs swing stiffly as if his whole body were strung on wire. His face is furrowed with concentration, his green beret perched on a mass of wrinkles. He seems to be doing better now; to have faded into the marching mass, becoming less of a person and more of a unit.

'He's all right now,' says Prue. She knows that feeling of blanking yourself off. You merge in with the others, losing yourself in the corporate identity. You go quite still and hide your face. Nobody picks you out. You are safe. It's a principle in nature, she has seen it before: earth-coloured toads and tree-coloured fledgling birds. Sometimes, of course, it misfires and they get stepped on.

'*Heil Hitler.*'

'*Achtung.*'

'*Donner und Blitzen.*'

'Fascist *Schwein.*'

Sandals and short white socks stepping out, Prue and Isabel frog-march, goose-step behind the crashing column of men, giggling in complicit mockery.

The sixty young men who can't cry veer off to the right until the thudding of their boots becomes more subdued than the drone of insects in the sultry air.

5

Columba Cahill and Duncan Macintosh are necking in the second-to-back row of the ABC Cinema in Elgin, along with several dozen other couples coiled in the smoky darkness in postures of uncomfortable abandon. Flickering cowboys discharge guns from behind giant cactuses. Two classes of Indian – noble savages helpful to the white man on an individual basis and scalp-hunting, ululating barbarians full of cunning dirty tricks – meet their respective just deserts. Back at the old corral gun-happy outlaws meet point-blank deaths at the hands of the sheriff's posse. All is as it should be on the flickering screen and no one watches. Hands slither from knees to thighs and linger at the bulge of bare skin between stocking-top and pantie, negotiating the cumbrous girdle for a blind foretaste of bliss to come, but not today. Suspender-belt fastenings pop like pods. To the rhythm of heavy-breathing, fingers grope the cups and straps of bras; the more practised gain some sort of limited access while the gauche fiddle in embarrassment at the complex contraptions of whalebone and plastic that elevate the pointed cones which fashion currently dictates as breast-plates. Each couple maintains a fiction of privacy in the sweaty dark. Here and there a lighted cigarette glows as couples take a breather, or where the odd, isolated individual has come in expressly to watch the film, and stares imperturbably at the screen amidst the sea of churning flesh.

Duncan Macintosh takes no liberties with Columba Cahill's person, let alone infiltrating her underwear. He is a bashful young man who knows that she is a thoroughly nice, respectable girl. He has progressed from kissing her modestly, reverently, and uncertainly, with little pecks, to kissing with open mouth, touching her tongue with his. Her arms and shoulders are plump and warm in their sleeveless cotton blouse; she gives beautifully to his touch. Her eyes are closed as she lies against his tweed shoulder. He looks at her shut eyes, the long curling lashes, the eyebrow like a beautiful sloping wing. He feels her breath on his cheek as he draws his face away. He sees the reflection of the black-and-white film playing excitedly upon the pupil of her newly opened eyes. She smiles into his face, so close. A great joyous, gentle, maternal smile.

He must have her always.

His own, for himself.

No one else must have her. He's 17, she's 19, why shouldn't they?

'Columba, will you marry me?' he whispers recklessly.

'Yes,' she sighs. 'Yes, yes, Duncan.'

'Tomorrow? Next week?' She must not get away. He might never get another chance, a shrimp like him and a great, soft piece of Heaven like herself. He's working his apprenticeship at Findlays' the butcher; she's hair-dressing – they could live with his parents.

'Yes,' breathes Columba, as if half-asleep. And then she remembers, sitting up, 'I can't.'

'Columba, *Columba*,' he mourns. He knew it. It was just a dream that he could have her, like the film that rewards the mangy underdog with the voluptuous, expensive star. 'You don't love me.'

'Oh yes I do, of course I do,' she whispers. 'It's not that. It's just that you're not of the Faith.'

'Och is that all? – That's nae problem, Columba. I'll take the Faith. What do I have to do?'

'You have to be instructed,' explains Columba. The girl selling ice-cream and cigarettes wobbles up the aisle on stiletto heels with her torch. Bad Cherokees ambush the intrepid posse at the base of a gully, amidst noisy gunfire. 'Instructed by the priest,' Columba goes on during a pause in operations. 'You have to really and truly believe though, Duncan, not just pretend.'

'I will believe it,' he can assure her without a qualm, and without cynicism. If she who is without blemish can believe something, it must be worth believing. Two thousand years of religious wars come down to this – this laying down of conscience to love. 'Oh I will. Nae problem.'

Columba leaves the ABC an engaged woman and Duncan a Catholic-to-be. It is as simple as that. Neither household puts up any sustained objection to the match, save for the antagonistic opinion expressed in Prue's getting in to her wardrobe, curling up amongst the mothballs and the old shoes, and refusing to come out.

Columba exchanges Prue for Duncan blithely, lightly, and Prue will never forget nor forgive the defection. No one now enquires as to whether Prue has cleaned her teeth or washes her hair twice weekly, no one puts the Guardian Angels in place and blesses Prue for the night ahead. Prue has been abandoned in the heap of dereliction, tossed away with the rest of the refuse.

Columba denies it. She points out that Prue is a big girl now, almost a teenager. That she, Columba, has a right to a life of her own. That she still loves Prue in a special way and that does not come to an end, does it, Prue? Just because Columba has grown up, as she had to do, in the nature of things. Does Columba not notice, wonders Prue, excoriated, Duncan's sallow, spotty complexion, his low stature and the way his toes turn in when he walks? She sees them walking along together hand in hand, conspicuously admiring Columba's engagement ring, £2 2/6 from Daw and McInnes, the corner jeweller and watchmaker. A foolish spectacle, Prue feels. Columba is like a big strapping bouncing mother-hen, brooding over her gawky chick as if he were the eighth wonder of the world.

After the first shock of betrayal, Prue retires into a more total silence than that she preserved before. She sits amongst the boisterous throng of eaters and drinkers and throwers of missiles at table in a deep stillness like one of the becalmed, dispassionate saints on the side-board. She eats tidily, not tasting the Spam or the brown-skinned rice-pudding Mam ladles into their plates, but eating because it is necessary to eat, and because when you have eaten, the plate is satisfactorily cleared. Columba's influence still lingers, though Columba has all but taken wing. Prue still automatically combs her hair and ties it in a bow; she cleans her shoes and places them at the bottom of the bed each night. She puts her hands together and squeezes her eyelids shut, rigidly kneeling for the customary period in token of prayer.

*

Dad's temper breaks like a storm long pent and building, foretellable by any meteorologist of merely average competence as a piece of classic weather-behaviour. He beats January for giving him the evil eye. At white heat, with an electric storm exploding in his brain, he lifts her bodily into the air and dashes her to the ground. She curls in a foetal ball as he kicks her back, backside and thighs, then scoops her up, sets her on her feet and begins to slap her face, left-to-right, right-to-left. He then pummels her torso with a boxer's jabs, going especially for her delicate, tender breasts, the sight of which seems to excite him to higher and higher fury. Finally he knees her in the groin.

Then he gathers her up in his arms and crams her down into the coal-hole.

There is a deafening silence.

He breaks it by informing his family that January is a bastard anyway, not his daughter; he only brought her up out of pity and goodwill; if anyone wants to know who January's father is let them ask their Mam, their Mam is a tart as the whole of Aldershot and Ismaelia knew and had it off with every fucker in trousers; that January is in the coal-hole until further notice to teach her a lesson, not that she is teachable, the trash, and that if anyone presumes to let her out of that hole without his say-so they will feel the sole of this shoe – see this shoe? – on their arse, and they'll be so sore they won't be able to sit down for a week; he won't have insubordination is that understood?

The silent listeners all nod, blank-faced.

'And damn well cheer up or I'll cheer you up, you moping dish-cloths.'

Their faces grin like skulls, in response to his imperious glare.

'Don't crack your faces, will you?' He chucks Damian under the chin. 'There's my lad. There's his Daddy's boy.'

Damian flinches at the touch of his father's hands, hoisting him up under the arms.

'UP in the air! – And down! – UP! – and down! UP!'

Damian bawls in terror, frantically bucking with his whole body and making a cross out of his arms.

'Get down then, you ungrateful brat.'

Damian scuttles out of the room and flees, screaming up the stairs.

'Go on, skiddaddle, bugger off,' says the father to the remaining group of stock-still silences. 'I'm off to the mess. And don't you dare touch that coal-hole if you want to keep your skins on your backs.'

Prue wonders how many people her father killed in the War with those hands, just before she was born. She knows he has killed because he boasts about it. Wops, Eyeties, wogs, Japs, nignogs, darkies, coons, A-rabs, they were not human, 'them' not 'us', just as January is not human to him, not family, not equal, and neither somehow is Mam. If he had not killed all those natives, they would understandably have killed him, and she would not be at all, and January would not now be buried in the coal-hole.

The knocking has been going on for half an hour when Prue plucks up courage to go down to the entrance to the bunker. The lid is a trap-door made of grey-painted wood ingrained with coal-dust, situated just under the kitchen window. January is coughing violently, and retching.

Prue kneels down beside the bunker and knocks back.

'Jan. It's Prue.'

'Prue. Prue. Let me out.'

'I dursen't.'

'Prue – Prue – I can't breathe Prue – I'm going to die – don't go away for pity's sake – Prue I'm so frightened . . .'

The sobbing voice is coming from right up against the lid. There isn't much room in there, as the coalman came this Wednesday.

'You'll just have to sit quiet-like and wait. He'll calm down and let you out.'

'I can't breathe I can't stop coughing – it's the dust –

it's so dark. Open the lid, Prue – for God's sake give us some *air*.'

Prue feels at the side for the catch. There's no choice but to let her out if January is going to die, however terrified she feels herself at what he'll do to her.

'Oh Jan! He's padlocked it!'

'Oh God, oh God!' January's voice rises to a keening wail. 'Get our Mam, get our Mam! Mam – Mam! Let me out of here – Mam Mam!'

Prue sprints for Mother, who won't come. She's ironing their father's uniform under a wet tea-cloth. Steam spouts and hisses with every thrust of the iron. The creases will be as sharp as knives when she's finished. Her advice to Prue is to keep out of trouble, and her opinion of January is that the child is a lost cause who has never from the day she was born brought anything but trouble, trouble, trouble, and has got what was coming to her.

'But Mam, Mam, she's choking; she can't breathe, honest-to-God,' shrieks Prue. 'You'll be had up for murder,' and she catches hold of her mother's skirt and pulls. She whips the plug out of the socket.

'Stop that,' says Mam. But she does reluctantly consent to come to the coal-hole, still holding the hot iron, and tells January to calm down and pray to God to forgive her sins.

January, coughing, sobbing, retching, implores her mother to intercede.

'The Blessed Virgin wouldn't let Jan stay down that coal-hole,' mutters Prue.

Mary kneels by the lid. 'Look, you'll be all right,' she says in a weary, helpless voice. 'You'll be *all right*. Just calm right down. Your Dad will be home for his dinner. He'll let you out when the time is right. Be a good girl, now.'

97

She vacillates a few moments, wavering between the coal-hole and the back door. *Hugh shouldn't . . . He shouldn't really . . . He's like a wild beast. He's not like a man. His eyes go mad and staring when he turns. There's nothing anyone can do then. What can she do? Nothing. Nothing at all.* She goes back to the hole. January is silent.

'Now then; now then,' she croons. 'You're feeling better now aren't you?'

'*Mam!*' The unseen voice shrieks out like a ghost in torment. 'Don't leave me underground – get me out, get me out of here!' She begins to pound on the lid with both fists.

Sighing, with a helpless shrug of her shoulders, Mary goes indoors and resumes the ironing.

Prue runs next door to Corporal Smithers' house.

'My sister's got accidentally shut in the coal-hole,' she says to the Smithers' teenage son. 'Are you any good at smashing locks?'

The Smithers, who have had nothing but bother from the Cahills, whom they recurrently report to the camp authorities on the grounds of noise, vandalism and constituting a risk to public hygiene (and of course nothing is done about them) look upon their neighbours as a rampant kind of vermin.

'Pull the other one – it's got bells on.' The son slams the door in Prue's face.

She runs up the street to where Sauerkraut lives, the German woman; bangs on the side door. Sauerkraut's face peers out fleetingly between the net curtains, flashing Prue a look at once stricken and suspicious. Then it vanishes. Prue bangs on the sitting room window.

'Missus!'

Prue hears an irate foreign sentence shouted at her which includes the word *Polizei*. Prue withdraws.

Malachi shoots round the corner on a borrowed motor-bike, which he rides right up on the grass verge to the very door, inches from where January is sealed.

'Malachi, he's shut Jan in the coal-hole.'

'So?' He dismounts, removes his crash-helmet and slicks his hair back.

'Will you get her out?'

Malachi casually squats and listens in to his sister's coughing and shouting. He seems vaguely amused.

'She's putting it on,' he finally concludes, straightening up.

'No she isn't – she'll die. She will, Malachi.'

Malachi fetches a hammer and smashes the lock. He raises the lid. January rises up, swaying slightly from her crouched position in the impossibly confined space her body had occupied between the coal and the lid.

'Proper little chimney-sweep. Black as a nigger,' observes Malachi. 'Look at you.'

January's knees seem to crumble; they launch her forward on to the lawn where she kneels, apparently half-fainting, her eyes closed, then capsizes sideways on to her left hip and shoulder. Her face, hair, and the palms of her hands are black with soot. Prue crouches down by her and lays one hand hesitantly on her arm. She feels she ought to put her arms round her but doesn't want to dirty her clean, white cardigan.

'It's you what bring it on yourself,' Malachi explains to January. 'You talk back to him like and get him all worked up; I think it gives you a thrill. What do you expect? Keep your bloody gob sewn up from now on and keep out of his way. He'll kill you one day, he will. He hates the sight of you. Get what I'm saying?'

In response to this counsel, January begins to scream. Her body goes rigid, fists clenched, splayed out on the grass; her screams come in regular spasms, like those of a new-born baby, but deafening.

'Is she having a fit?' asks Prue.

'Nah. Is she heck. She's just trying it on, buggering about. I know this one from a long way back.' Malachi, who was appointed January's carer in his own love-hungry snotty-nosed youth, speaks with that fatigued cynicism observable in many parents of recalcitrant children. 'Shut up, shit-face, no one's listening,' he remonstrates, poking at her heaving body with his winkle-picker.

On and on January screams, her lungs pumping out the hysterical panic and anguish of, it seems, years. When her mother, alarmed and vaguely remorseful, tries to calm her, January staggers up and points her coal-stained, bleeding index finger at her.

'Leave me alone, you. Leave me *alone*. You're the one wouldn't get me out. Don't you come creeping round me now, don't come anywhere near me. You let him do this to me. So it's you – it's *you* – what done it.'

Mary backs off; January staggers, squinting round incoherently, her eyes screwed up as if unaccustomed to the alien light. The patchy grass at the front of the quarters is on a slight incline so that she lurches down to the bottom, her dark, shaggy form like that of a drunken beggar. A knot of curious children has gathered and offers derisive opinions on the spectacle, together with helpful tips on washing methods. January looks round once, then lopes away from them; looks back again; begins hob-blingly but with gathering momentum to run. Prue pelts after her. She has a terrible, wordless feeling that she must not let her sister go. Her white and yellow figure pursues its blackened counterpart, as if she chased her own shadow and must re-attach it to source to remain a bona fide part of the solid, sunlit world. But Prue has never been much of a runner and she is no match for January, fleet even in her damaged state. She plods and pants, her glasses jerking up and down on the bridge of her nose so that the world shakes on its moorings and she has to hold them steady with one hand. January skims to the corner and rounds it like the wind. Desperately Prue whips herself up to do more than lumber; she, too, gallops round the bend.

'Wait for me,' she calls.

January puts on speed. She sprints up Montgomery Drive and down Passchendaele Terrace. Rounding this bend in her wake and almost at her last, hot gasp, Prue is in time to see January appropriating a boy's bike propped against a wall. It is Roger Whittaker's bike and is snatched from right under his mother's nose, where it leans under the kitchen window at which Mrs Whittaker is to be seen open-mouthed with a potato in one hand and a peeler in the other, dangling a long, looping tail of peel. January trots the bike to the road and swings her left leg out behind her to traverse the cross-bar. She shoots off, standing on the pedals to give herself momentum. Carrot-haired Roger Whittaker makes a forlorn effort to pursue her, shouting 'Hoi!' and beating the air with his fists.

Prue takes off her innocent white cardigan and sits down by the wayside amongst the daisies and the dog-piss. Her head and heart pulse painfully and she streams with sweat. Tears prick the back of her eyes. Something in her chest and guts – a kind of swirling and tickling feeling you can't rub away – testifies to the unease she cannot begin to analyse in herself. It is a sense of implication for which she cannot afford to atone by turning it into guilt. She is on Dad's side, she has to be on Dad's side, she wants to survive and she doesn't want to be hurt or maimed. She is on January's side because she could not be otherwise, like a Siamese twin that fights the horror of an insuperable bond, flesh of her sister's flesh. If one twin dies, she will have to be cut away from the carcase.

With both hands Prue tears out clumps of clover and grass by the roots and scatters them out upon the partly melted tarmac of the baking road. At the sight of Mrs Whittaker in her slippers making swiftly towards her, she rises to her feet and makes circuitously for home.

*

Out of the Married Quarters and across the camp perimeter, through the village, past the Manse and the school and towards the Carse, January races on her stolen bike, lord of the cross-bar. She freewheels to a halt beside a little grove of pines and firs where the Scouts have a hut and practise their techniques of constructing shelters without the use of rope; building camp-fires in the rain, singing 'Ging-gang-goolie' and stalking non-existent animals; all the survival techniques recommended by Lord Baden Powell should they happen to find themselves stranded in a jungle. The hut is deserted and the wood silent save for birdsong and the occasional rustle of a scampering squirrel. January ditches the bike and covers it with bracken – she never needed Baden Powell's advice to equip her for survival. The ground is fibrous and spongy, it sinks with each footfall, being composed of generations of pine-needles, pulped bark and rusted shards of the brittle ferns of many outlived winters. Seagulls from the estuary perch on the trees and there is salt on the air. It is a place January has often haunted, flitting like an isolated shadow from tree to tree, sucking aniseed balls in a little sandy hollow which acts as a sun-trap and a spy-hole at the centre of the copse. Here January has on many visits secreted little hoards of imperishables – jackdawtroves of filched brooches, foreign coins, coloured pebbles and a Parker pen, as well as a tin of Victory Vs removed from her father's jacket-pocket (he sucks them compulsively against his smoker's cough) and a heap of small, smooth pine-cones which for some reason it gives her pleasure to hold in the palm of her hand one by one.

January ducks down into the hollow and crouches there, cradling her body in her arms. From head to foot she is one mass of hot, pulsing pain, in her back and thighs and chest and face. Indeed so hard has he pounded her this time that it's a wonder she isn't smashed and shattered. Unfamiliar tears bleed from her eyes. The tears gather from some bursting place in her breast, they knot in her throat, they well from eyes and pour through her nose, her mouth seems full of salt. Rage and hurt, hurt and rage, struggle in her brain, and are indistinguishable from one another, discharging themselves in a vortex of violent tension, at the centre of a deafening loneliness.

'God rot him, Got rot him,' she incants over and over again, and 'I hate them, I *hate* them,' and that seems to help, so that by and by the uncontrollable tears abate, giving her the power to curse him and curse them more vehemently, and the more she curses the better she is. Hatred squirts out tiny jets of adrenalin in the pit of her stomach, temporarily anaesthetising the huge and steady pain which she seems less to bear than to be.

But as her hurt converts to rage, so the rage is balked of any adequate aim and sets up a contrary tension of unexpressed need. There is no one here to pay back or take it out on: only herself. She grabs up her treasures and begins to hurl them in all directions. With an explosion of energy and screaming at the top of her voice, she pitches coins, pebbles, pen, brooch and other valuables from her hoard in all directions. She stamps with her heel on a clutch of pale-blue speckled eggs she's kept for three months pillowed on cotton wool in a scraped-out hole under the turfy rim of the dell.

On and on and on she stamps and howls and pitches out everything she can lay hands on, until only handfuls of sandy earth are left to throw, so she sprays that out like a dog burrowing in a ditch.

The ear-splitting cries suddenly cease. She sinks down beside the shattered eggs. All her lovely things, her comforting things, are gone. All gone. All. Gone. A gilt necklace swings faintly in her eye-line from the pendant bough of a fir-tree, glinting in the sunlight. Tears come again, not the violent storm that racked her before, but tears of utter sadness and incommunicable mourning.

She kneels and kneads her wet, swollen eyes with the heels of her coal-stained hands; she rocks herself in her own arms, to-and-fro, to-and-fro; she lays her head against the side of the dell, just under the parapet, and huddles to the sandy wall, like a soldier in a trench when the shells are falling.

The tears have subsided. She feels nothing now except her body's affliction and a sort of addled, stupid incoherence. Queer, disconnected images work their way across the inside of her closed eyelid, images without words – an enamel egg-pan running on legs, a man with one tiny eye where his nose should be, a kite in the shape of an eagle dropping bombs on the child who holds the string – they chase one another's tail inanely, one after the other. Quite suddenly, her body gives a convulsive jerk and she falls fast asleep, sprawling out across the bottom of the hole with her head and shoulders in the hot sunlight and one arm thrown forward, as if she had been shot.

Half an hour passes, during which space the sun shifts fractionally across the sky, angling more light and heat upon the sleeper in the sandy hole. She does not move at all. Beads of sweat break out on her forehead and upper lip, through the dried, caked mess of soot and tears. On the distant road occasional lorries rumble past unheard and an aeroplane from RAF Lossiemouth flies in low over the Carse. She lies so still that squirrels loiter nearby without detecting anything human in the hole. A magpie, attracted by the glitter of the scattered Woolworth's jewellery, alights momentarily on the fir branch and deftly removes the hanging necklace. With a thrash of black and white wings he lifts off with his spoils. The bough bounces for a moment and is still.

Gleaming black beetles navigate the mountains and valleys of the dell, and ants go about their community's business in proximity to her eyes and slightly open mouth. Where their paths intersect with her body, the black beetles journey round the obstruction, but the ants toil fanatically on, over hand and leg, stinging as they go.

A dun female thrush pecks about the turf, then hops into the hole. January's eye starts open. It is confronted by the soft and serene eye of the bird. January's eye closes again non-committally; she was not really awake.

The heat becomes torrid and thick in the hole. Her unprotected face is flushed with sunburn, even through the mask of salt and dust. She dreams. She dreams he has crammed her into a brazier under an iron grid and is burning her alive. The fire crackles.

Twigs crack under the bounding feet of a mangy stray cat from the camp which leaps at the thrush, but the thrush gets away. January wakes up, a shout in her throat which never achieves release. In her hot terror she thinks he is here, coming for her. She staggers out of the hole, spitting sand from her dry mouth and starts to run for it.

The copse peters out, the Carse begins. The great

expanse of fenny wasteland runs for miles in every direction. Pearl-grey at its horizon is the river-estuary and above it the sky is an iridescent white-grey gauzy net, for clouds are coming up fast from the north-west. Rays of sun pierce the cloud-layer to strike singly or in pairs upon the distant waters. She pitches forward toward the estuary. Her tongue is huge and bitter-tasting in the dry cavity of her mouth, her eyes unfocused, her mind unhinged with the shock of this violent waking and the absolute conviction that he is there behind her, following her, hounding her down. She daren't look back, but through her own panting she can hear his panting; the squelch of her own footsteps on the spongy grass covers the sound of his. Save for this pursuit of the panic-stricken child by her own fear, there is quiet that spreads in every direction, hardly interrupted by the mew of inland seagulls and the faint bubble of the intersecting streams that criss-cross the whole Carse in a network of waterways. In this wilderness, taboo to the children of the area because of the bogs and deep hidden ditches into which it's easy to tumble and be drowned, she runs wildly, frequently slipping and turning an ankle or losing her foot suddenly in one of the water-logged holes that increase in frequency and depth the further out she travels. Reedbeds and livid sphagnum mosses advertise the danger-spots. She tries to ensure safety by leaping from hummock to hummock. Ditches suddenly yawn at her feet, with tall, sheer banks of slimy grass; she follows them until they narrow and she can with great effort jump over and claw her way up the other side. As she toils onwards, the darkening cloud-bank keeps travelling in to meet her.

Turns round, all of a sudden. Turns round to meet him and the world whirls on its axis, unsteadily and decelerating like a teetering top which doesn't know which way to fall – and, boo, he isn't there. There's no one there. Her burning eyes squint back over the empty gap she's travelled, and there's nothing. Her mouth is full of gall and ash, her dry tongue tries to lick her lips.

No one there. Safe.

No. He's hiding. Down one of the steep-sided concealed burns, he's lurking there and he'll shoot out like a violent jack-in-the-box on the spring of his hate.

What's the time, Mr Wolf? What's the time, Mr Wolf?, chorus the children of Passchendaele Terrace, stalking the wolf in a chanting bunch and he turns like lightning, and if they don't freeze in time they're eaten up.

All fall down, all fall down, sing the children, and they all flop down dead.

The shadow of January's father suddenly emerges from behind a tussock and launches himself at her; she whips round and charges off with the momentum of new panic.

An hour has gone by. She is a dark fleck on the convex of the huge green eye of the Carse. It would need a telescope to make a human being of her from the mainland of the solid ground.

The smell of the place is pungent, filling her nostrils with an odour of wet silt and decomposition, salt and minerals: clean putrefaction. Her lungs wheeze and ache with exhaustion but she keeps on going, just about. One plimsolled foot vanishes in an ooze of black mud like oil. She drags up the foot, hanging on to a clump of reeds. The quicksand grips the ankle with cold, determined fingers. She can't budge it. She yanks, and swears, and up comes the foot with a slapping noise as the sucking mud closes upon a vacuum.

After this tussle, she involuntarily turns again. There's no father to be seen, only an eternal emptiness, and the toy trees and the scaled-down hills and miniature telegraph poles like needles linked with thread. He would have got her by now if he'd been there. He was not there. There is nothing and there is no one. And that too is terrifying, though less so.

What's this in her skirt-pocket? Her fingers fiddling in the debris down there come upon two elderly mint humbugs, half out of their wrappers, stickily dusty. The beauty of it; the sweet flush of pleasure; the rush of saliva to refresh her parched mouth and aching soul.

She pauses, closing her eyes, to relish the taste.

Hail Mary full of grace . . .

Beautiful, beautiful.

She sucks on it lingeringly, letting the sweetness suffuse her mouth, only swallowing reluctantly when she has to. Fastidiously, she conserves her store. When the humbug is about half eaten, she withdraws it and restores it to the wrapping paper. She wishes she had more. Should have come better prepared. And with that characteristically practical thought of self-preservation she is more herself. The pandemonium of alarm has almost completely gone off. She looks round to assess her circumstances and for the first time in her full retreat it strikes her as very odd that she should have come to be out here, in this deliquescent world, the soft, saline wind buffeting her face and body, the unseen water gurgling and the susurration of the reeds.

Once at the pictures she saw a bog-man, two thousand years old, preserved in acid peat, whose pickled hide was being disinterred, complete with stomach contents and the marks round his neck where he's been strangled. His tribe throttled him and bunged him in the bog as a malefactor, so the expert in a white coat with a fancy accent thought, or in a ritual to appease the goddess, no one would ever really know for sure. She liked looking at that film, it fascinated her. *Bunged him in the bog*, she thinks now, making her way ruminatively forward from one hummock to the next, *bunged him in the bog, they did, ee ai addy-o, they bunged him in the bog*.

Suddenly there is an efflorescence of water at her feet; she almost topples in, it comes upon her so unexpectedly. Not the river itself – that keeps its distance, darkened beneath banks of charcoal cloud, in dramatic and ominous contrast to the brilliant turquoise sky elsewhere prevailing – but a waterway of considerable size, running out into a channel guarded by armouries of spiky reeds.

That's her face in the water, that dark, tear-stained, muck-stained chimney-sweep staring up with the eyes of someone who's been a long time hopelessly drowned. She kneels on the edge, scooping up water in both hands to wash her face, and the cold water is absolute balm on her throbbing forehead and stickily sweating neck and arms. Waves pleat the water over the complex geometry of reversed reeds traversed by the arc of gull or tern. The waves ruffle her face, restlessly distressing the contours of its image. The reeds sigh and sough, and when the breeze stiffens they sizzle like rashers in a great fry-up. January stares at the forsaken January. *Bunged him in the bog they did, bunged him in the bog*.

Not yet they damn well haven't.

She's not beat yet.

Not nohow. Not in any way. Not by a long chalk.

Once in Egypt as a very little girl she saw the soldiers pick up an Arab terrorist. It was in the bazaar, the turbaned vendors were crying their wares: PRI – EE – MUS! sang the sellers of primus stoves and paraffin, BOT-BOT-BOT-BOT-DEE-LEE-AY! chanted the vendors of bottled water and fizzy drinks, and CAR-A-PETS! sang the dealers in beautiful crimson or green patterned carpets laid out in the sun. They let the little white girl fondle the soft pile, in the hopes that her parents might be near with wherewithall to buy. She was crouching in the hurlyburly by a stall covered in small brass replicas of the pyramids and cheap plaster reproductions of Queen Nefertiti when all of a sudden four military policemen appeared out of nowhere and wrestled a young man to the ground at her very feet. One's khaki buttock and holster were right up against her eye. The market-crowd dissolved away but January stayed exactly where she was in shock and fascination. The English soldiers beat and kicked the young man to set an example to the population. But as they dragged him away, he turned his head and shouted, 'Death to the Infidel! Egypt for the Arabs!' And that face, with its defiance and certainty, always stayed with January. He would fight, he would never give up. And lately she knew he'd won – she understands nothing about politics but she knows we had to hand Suez back to General Nasser. She heard her father fulminating about that devil Nasser and them filthy A-rabs, and she was glad the young man had won, in token of which she painted UP WITH NASSER on the NAAFI wall.

She will fight and she will never give up. She turns for home, sucking the second half of the sweet. Storms have broken out from the bunched, black clouds over the estuary, she can see the slant of pouring rain and hear distant thunder. The Carse by the moment darkens as the storm streams in, and she hurries before it, stumbling through the pot-holed wetlands and leaping the dykes in the effort to race the rain. As she gains the copse the pursuing rain finally overtakes her. The air is livid green and the birds have all gone quiet as it hits, hammering everything in its path. It rattles out a martial tune on the corrugated roof of the scout hut where January tries to seek shelter but it's padlocked. In a very short time her hair is plastered to her head and her clothes glued coldly to her body, sharpening and then numbing the pain in the welts scored there by her father's belt. The baked-hard earth at first repels, then gobbles the water but cannot drink the rain as fast as it falls, so that it collects in standing pools between the trees. Lightning flashes and then the thunder comes, five or six heart-beats away. She fights the bracken off the bike and takes off, head-down, oblivious of the fact that its wet metal frame makes it a perfect conductor to the home-bound lightning.

*

Prue lingers at her bedroom window looking into the bile-green twilight that has settled on the camp. The storm has passed over but the rain steadily continues. January never came home. Prue hid under the bed with Damian in her arms for comfort – her comfort, not his. The lino was dusty under there and they both coughed, reminding Prue of the morning, and the coal-hole. Dad came back in the thick of the storm, wet through but in one of his rip-roaring good moods. Jimmie Wood and 'Archie' Andrews were with him. 'Archie's' real name was Lennie but they nicknamed him after the radio puppet which he could mimic. Jimmie and Archie waited for Hugh at the front door while he ran upstairs two at a time to change his wet clothes and fetch his lighter.

'Nice weather,' remarked Jimmie to the bunch of Hugh's kids standing gazing at them, some with thumbs in their mouths.

'Nice for ducks,' added Archie Andrews, winking.

'Where?' cried three-year-old Francis, rushing to the door and looking out excitedly. 'Where ducks?' In his mind's eye several fine ducks and drakes trailing a family of ducklings were waddling two by two round from Somme Road into Verdun Terrace.

Leaning down, Archie hooked him back by the collar to stop him careering out into the duck-filled world.

'No real ducks,' he explained, squatting to the child's level. Prue smelt his beery breath. 'But if there *was* ducks,' he went on, with plodding logic, *basso profundo*, 'them ducks would be having a whale of a time out there. Splashing and cackling.'

'No ducks? No whales?' asked Francis, still hopefully craning.

'Gor blimey, why did I open my great mouth?' muttered Archie to Jimmie, straightening and scratching his head.

He went on to execute some bird-impressions until Hugh came crashing downstairs, merry and tiddly as hell. He wedged his cloth-cap down over his eyes and raised the collar of his mackintosh with both hands. He beamed round. His great fur-covered hand descended upon the heads of his two youngest and rumpled their curls fiercely. Prue saw the wiry hairs sprouting from his nose.

'Rascals.' said Hugh. 'Tykes and tartars, the whole blessed blooming lot of you. God bless you now, God bless,' he pronounced benignly, with a priestly gesture, and went off into the sloshing rain, rattling his keys and loose change in his pocket. Prue heard his explosive laugh as the Morris Minor door slammed, and the car drew off with its lights on in the murk.

The raindrops streak slightly askance down the window-pane in parallel lines, leaving traces like the testaments of snails or the smoke-tail of an aeroplane. Prue's eyes urge on the more sluggish and discourage the favourites. The new drops eternally cancel out the old. That baleful, ashen world out there has a terribly ominous quality. She breathes on the window and draws a heart in the patch of condensation. That heart is for Paul Cox, a pale, soft-voiced boy with eczema, whose father is a Warrant Officer Class Two; she looks at him sidelong in class and though he takes no notice of her, he does not deride her as Fatty or Goggle-eyes like the other boys.

Did he just forget he left her there buried in the coal-hole?

He went out murderous and he came in all charm and affability. What is the link? How to understand? Did he not care if he killed her? Was he two people, Hugh and Hugh, who never had a chance to meet and compare notes?

Is that how all men are, when you lift the lid? Father Friend and Duncan Macintosh and Paul Cox and Archie Andrews – would they go home and lock you in the coal-hole? Or are they all normal and just her Dad a madman?

Where are you Jan, where are you?

Once in Egypt they shared a room in a flat in Ismaelia on the edge of a desert. They were little girls of four and five. Sometimes they got locked into their rooms for whole afternoons for some piece of villainy such as the inscription with a needle of pictures of mountaineers all over the Marconi. January beguiled the time by tunnelling a hole in the plaster just beneath bed-level, with a view to making an escape like the intrepid inmates of German POW camps in the war films. This is Prue's first vivid memory – of her sister industriously gouging her escape-route with a screw-driver while Prue just stands passively looking out of the window. Through the grid of close-meshed wire-netting which covers it she sees the solitary figure of an Arab walking out into the desert. That is the full extent of the memory: the Arab in his flowing robes and head-dress so dignified and upright, just walking and walking out into that immensity of silence, the empty yellow space beneath the blazing turquoise sky, alone. She watched till he shrunk to a dot. Why was he out there in the full heat of the afternoon siesta, where was he going in such a straight line? She saw him through a frame, through a grid, through the fuzzy blur of her own already deteriorating vision, and she would never know. It is at once the most wonderful and the loneliest of memories. It seems she has been passively looking out ever since and never rightly understanding, and January has been fanatically tunnelling for freedom and getting thrashed black and blue for it.

She closes the curtains, turns her back on whatever is outside them and, perching cross-legged on the bed, opens her book at the bookmark. Gulliver is visiting the land of the Brobdingnagians who are sixty foot high and understandably inclined to regard him as an insect or a doll. In that precipitous world you walk on a perpetual cliff-edge and are always liable to be squashed flat by an unseeing boot.

*

Always before, January went home. She let herself in at the back door and slid upstairs; would open the door on Prue and Charity playing, say, cat's cradle or jacks. Gobstopper in cheek, never-say-die, she would saunter up and say 'Can I play too?' She would make nothing of her wounds, although the welts made by his belt, on her back or bottom, might, if he had used the buckle end, be caked with blood. She let Prue bathe them with salt water and would not flinch. Once or twice Columba saw what they were doing. 'Merciful God,' she said, and fetched the iodine. That hurt. January shouted out, with the shock of pain. 'Dear God, dear God,' Columba kept saying as she dabbed the welt. 'What are you thinking of to provoke

114

him to this?', she asked taking the child's bare thin shoulder between her hands. 'Don't you know he's got no control if you make him lose his temper?'

Why did they always make it out to be her fault when it was his, his, his?

'I don't make him,' she protested. 'I don't do *nothing*, Columba. It's not fair, he picks on me for nothing; he just has to see me and he goes berserk.'

Columba shook her head, for she saw what her father saw and could not love it – an unsavoury, vindictive, sly face like a little weasel's, a hating, hateful child.

'Well, keep out of his way. Then he won't notice you. You won't get hurt. Will you?'

'*He* can't hurt *me*.' January made not a murmur as the vest was carefully drawn down over her raised arms and the bruised, cut flesh of her back. The little breasts budding over the whippet-thin ribcage were desperately poignant. Columba looked, felt sick and looked away. She couldn't face up to the enormity of January's suffering and her father's crime. His violence had passed her by almost completely. She got only chucks under the chin, tickles and giggling games on the hearth-rug, and the odd slap on the behind. She has successfully guarded Prue against the evil, and that in itself seems vindication of the feeling it's hard to resist, that January brings it upon herself, somehow tempts him, almost as if she liked it. Columba hates the deep unease stirred by these considerations, and by the sense of guilt January awakens in her when these mutilations come to the surface. She rejects January still more for stirring up this nausea of self-distaste. And yet the pity wrings her. Sometimes the wounds fester, seeping with yellow pus. Columba wonders cursorily whether she shouldn't take the child to the doctor, or tell the teacher, or the Father. But what would happen to them then – what if Dad were taken away and put in prison, what would become of them? The young ones would go into care, wouldn't they? Columba reached for the cotton wool and TCP and dabbed the sore places none too tenderly. She usually ended by hectoring, 'And don't do it again,' as if January had reached round to flagellate her own back in unholy parody of the mortifications practised by the church martyrs.

Once January asked Columba in a small, hollow voice, out of the blue, 'Why? Why does he do it to me?'

'Because you've got no redeeming features,' Columba heard herself reply.

'Where can I get redeeming features?'

'By praying to Jesus and . . . and by . . .'

Columba paused, secretly doubting whether redeeming features were purchasable by January on any terms. She went on to specify a whole list of courses of action, both spiritual and secular, varying from repeating three decades of the rosary to washing thoroughly under the armpits with soap and water.

Sheltering in a draughty bus-shelter on the Forres road, January keeps her distance from a leak in the roof through which rain funnels in, spattering dismally. Her teeth chatter with cold, her mind is fuddled. Habit and the instinct for self-preservation urge her to turn for home. There's a bed for her, a place at the table, a gang of other Cahills, all in more or less the same boat. A roof over your head, something in your belly. A chance to shove the smaller ones aside to get in nearer the fire. January never underestimated the value of animal comforts. The foxcub instinctively ran for its lair, so did she.

But today, like the rat in the laboratory experiment, to think of going home is to step on the wrong pedal which discharges a flash of electricity through its nervous system.

The instinct has been thrown into reverse. The roof over her head is a coal-hole lid slammed down so that all she can see is four lines of light between the slats, and all she can hear is his boot stamping on the lid and his booming voice with the grating laughter in it, and *Let me out for pity's sake* she called and called, but no one came. *Mam, Mam*, she cried, but Mam turned her back. Prue helped, but Prue is no one. And Prue's got Columba, and Columba is the worst two-faced hard-hearted butter-wouldn't-melt shit of them all. Prue in Columba's arms, comforted, that's how it's always been, the two of them turning away from the one of her. She won't go back to that.

But she must go somewhere. She picks up the stolen bike, dumped in a gorse-bush by the roadside. The car-lights swoosh by through the torrential rain as the men head home. She rides against the traffic towards the Manse.

6

The Aberdeen train has been marooned outside
Elgin for over half an hour: there's flooding on the track,
the guard says, and some lines down, hit by lightning.
Isabel, sitting with her ankles crossed between her mother
and father, has gone into a state of trance. Neither of her
parents shares in their fellow-passengers' voluble
impatience or anxiety. Each framing parent seems deep in
a book, held up close to the eyes, for the light from the
tiny lamps above their seats burns a rather dim and bleary
yellow. Neither parent is ever observed to turn a page.
Either they are reading very slowly, chewing the cud of
every word, or not reading at all. Neither do they change
position, appearing to remain permanently in a state of
galvanised attention to the printed matter passing before
their eyes. Isabel knows well this barricade of shyness
and self-consciousness which the family erects before the
public eye. They have some cheese sandwiches with them,
wrapped in greaseproof paper. Isabel doesn't suppose the
packet will ever be opened while the carriage is full with an
audience. It isn't easy dealing with crumbs and problems
caused by one's having taken too large a bite in front of
that audience of swerving eyes. But she likes the train-
smell – sulphurous like hard-boiled eggs – and she enjoys
the lulling tācatacā rhythm when the train gets going, if

it ever does get going. The air is close and muggy from the rain-soaked passengers, whose umbrellas and macs had to be shaken in the corridor and whose folded brollies now spout small rivers on the floor. Isabel looks away when anyone catches her eye. She studies the criss-cross netting of the luggage-rack and the map of the Scottish railway system, also the framed pictures of Beautiful Loch Lomond and Majestic Braemar Castle. She gleans furtive information about her fellow-passengers from dangling case-labels and the state of their shoe-leather. When they nod off or read a newspaper, you can pin them on your gaze like a fly on fly-paper.

It's very hard to like people, she's observed. You notice the wart or mole on their hand, their wrinkles and the sagging places under tired eyes, or jowls and double chins; you say to yourself that they are too small or too big, or ugly, coarse, ridiculous or common. You keep busily comparing them unfavourably with the things you admire or would like others to find admirable in yourself. Then every so often you remember that to them you are nobody – a gangling girl twisted up with shyness sitting in a railway carriage wedged between her two grey, bony parents – and you blush scarlet and look away. Love thy neighbour? No; easier by far to love a dog.

'Poor naked wretches, wheresoe'er you are,' Isla murmurs inwardly, turning from her unread book to view her own multiple reflection casting the shadows of infinite Islas one behind the other in the black pane of the window, 'Poor naked wretches. . . .' *how does it go on?* 'That bide the pelting of this pitiless storm . . .' The rain batters insistently on the grimy pane and streams down obliquely now that they are underway, like a mnemonic of the many, many homeless and vagrants still (to our shame, it is deplorable, unforgiveable) roaming the streets of Scottish cities, sleeping under cardboard or newspapers.

> How shall your houseless heads and unfed sides,
> Your looped and windowed raggedness, defend you
> From seasons such as this?

Yes, that's how it goes, houseless heads and unfed sides – but if Shakespeare knew it and said it then, how come we have not dealt with it yet? It ought not to be, she thinks, in our day and age, with the Welfare State and a far greater sense of social justice after the War Years (ironically, *because* of the War – the men coming back insisting on a fairer, better world). It ought not to be tolerated, she thinks fiercely, but what can one do, she queries limply. And, secretly, isn't one glad to be a nice, dry insider, albeit on an uncomfortable train, with a flask of hot coffee, a packet of sandwiches and a good home to go to? She wonders about the eye of the needle; shall she finally squeeze through, justified, at the end of it all when the reckoning's made? Are good works, private charity, self-denial and voting Labour against one's husband's express wishes, enough to pay for a place in Heaven? *O I have ta'en, O I have ta'en, O I have ta'en*, advises the dreary obligato of the train-rhythms to the bored passengers, *too little care of this*.

Donald watches Isla pull down the blind to exclude the black desolation of the world outside. How fine her hand is but how worryingly thin it has become. The Aberdeen consultant will, he hopes, diagnose the symptoms she described to him in such a neutral tone for the first time five days ago; perhaps it will require a simple operation, or some tonic may be recommended. Perhaps it is something to do, as she vaguely suggested, with her time of life. It was a subject difficult to discuss without euphemisms or a wincing enunciation of anatomical names which neither he nor she could speak without feeling pain on her behalf. They have never had a language of the body. Her dear body is a silence, desperately naked because they know no words to cover it. Her breast, her womb, the place between her legs. These were the reserved, dark parts of her being he touched fugitively and rarely, by night with the light switched off. To name them would be to threaten her wholeness and to bruise her shyness, the deep, chaste privacy in which she maintained her identity as Isla. She always dressed and undressed when he was out of the room, and if he came upon her by accident in her petticoat, he would back out apologetically as if he had intruded upon a stranger. This was not a false pudency in her but represented something he respected, a deep part of her that was withheld and belonged to her alone. So, when she said, 'I bleed continuously, Donald, and I have lumps *there*', he winced with shock on her behalf, not only at the facts but somehow at the very words she must use to convey them.

Then there was the sudden scything blade of fear and alarm on his own behalf. He was familiar with death, presiding at parishioners' deathbeds, burying them, comforting relatives. But it had never once occurred to him that Isla could die. How could he live without her? She, not God or the church, was his cornerstone, the moral core of his existence. He loved her, he loved her. But he was ludicrously incapable of communicating any of this. He cleared his throat and blinked back his tears. He became even more rigid and dictatorial than usual and blustered, why had she said nothing before now? Why? – it was the height of irresponsibility. To preserve her health was her obvious duty, not only to herself but to her husband and child. His eyebrows beetled at her. He stalked off and rang his cousin's friend, the Aberdeen gynaecologist, who fitted her in for a consultation. Which is why they are sitting here on the Aberdeen train (which has now gone slowly into reverse) on their way to a visit he could do without to his cousin Rachel and her husband David, a man of whom he theoretically disapproves as being one of these liberal Catholics, probably a Communist, and a conscientious objector during the War. But a decent, quiet sort of man when you get close to him, modest, difficult to dislike. As long as he doesn't seek to influence the susceptible Isabel, who's at an unstable age and has somehow got hold of enough claptrap of her own without having her hot-headedness fuelled by ageing idealists who ought to know better.

As he fumes to himself, he casts a glance of angry worry at Isabel. She catches the look and resents it. Lately she has taught herself sign language from a system printed in the *Encyclopaedia Britannica*.

'There – is – no – God,' she signs, with great deliberation, looking her father in the face and smiling with her eyes.

'What are you doing?' he whispers.

'Deaf and dumb language,' she replies, folding her hands in her lap.

*

Uncle David is a nobody; any normal person can tell that. You scarcely notice him when you come into a room, especially when his wife Rachel is there, nervously brilliant and colourfully interesting, a person altogether outside Isabel's ken, who makes the world of the Manse and Kinleven look humdrum and staid. Even in middle age she is a powerfully lovely woman, and a sculptor of unique talent but small output who has made a name for herself in the circles of the cognoscenti but acquired no public fame. Her house is an Edwardian three-storey semi in the suburbs of Aberdeen, messy and chaotic, each room having something of the aspect of a studio and stacked with unhung pictures, ceramics and half-finished models.

'The junk of a lifetime,' says Rachel shrugging. Isabel lingers round her like a bee at a stamen voluptuous with nectar. She sips at her thirstily with questions that set off more questions. Shyness and reticence have to be set aside for this urgent interrogation of the sort of person who does not come one's way very often. Rachel is keen to talk about herself, in a sort of proudly self-deprecating way, so that it is hard to tell whether arrogance or diffidence comes out on top. Isabel's anxiety about her mother, who spends two full days at the Infirmary having 'tests', is much allayed by the fascination exerted over her by her second cousin.

'Isn't it pathetic?' asked Rachel, not looking for an answer, 'For all the hard work I put in, I can only manage to come up with two or three pieces a year worth keeping.' Isabel is enthralled by the hands that shape the clay and deftly crack the casts off the bronze; strong, tapered hands with bitten or broken nails, that flutter, never still, from one nervous, expressive gesture to another. 'It's not even as if I produced something massive and monumental like Henry Moore or Barbara Hepworth. I leave behind me a mingy little trail of miniature heads the size of an orange and inconspicuous reclining women no bigger than an average-sized water-melon. Honestly! So little to show for all my teeming big ideas.'

She gestures with her hand at a row of three terracotta children's heads and abstract bronzes, triangular but curved and undulant, shapes with dimpled textures you instantly want to touch.

'Yes, go on, pick them up and touch them – you're supposed to. That's the whole idea. From my hands I give it into your hands: we share it. Shut your eyes and touch, that's right.'

'It's lovely.' Isabel turns the ponderous, cold smoothness over and over in her palms. 'I would really love to be able to do something like this. But I can't draw at all or make things – never could.'

'That's a fallacy if ever I heard one. It's all in there, locked up, waiting to get out,' says Rachel with an air of agitation and regret, tucking a long wisp of stray hair behind one ear. Her pale blue eyes are penetrating and rather odd – they stare as if sizing you up; they are at once tender, vulnerable and somewhat sharp, almost unkind. 'I shrivel up, Isabel, I do, when I hear that kind of negative talk. It's such a waste – a waste of life. *Life!*' She almost shouts the word, as if to waken sleepers from decades of coma. 'Anyone can draw and model. Anyone. Any *child* can do it. It's not a special gift. Society takes it from us as it conventionalises us. It processes us at the same dead level of uniformity. I'm not special except that somehow I've kept hold of my gift.'

But Isabel can see she *does* think she's special; is indeed vitally committed to the idea of her own exclusive specialness – with gnawing doubts that make her dump most of what she creates. Isabel is partly daunted but far more aroused by the flamboyant figure of her second cousin, with her mannish baggy trousers and her dazzling purple and blue shirt. She eclipses everyone she's ever met. Isabel covetously imagines being her; putting on her personality like a brilliant suit of finery, putting off her own shabbiness. And yet there's something painful and a bit repellent

in that nervous, scintillating vibrancy, something so peculiar in the way she shrieked out the word '*Life!*' like that,
as if it could suddenly change pitch to become a cry of pain.

'Isabel has, no doubt, her own special gifts; and she will
show us what they are in her own good time,' intervenes
a voice.

Isabel had taken little notice of Rachel's husband, smoking his pipe in the window-seat. David is as conventional
in appearance as Rachel is out-of-order; all done up in
tweedy jacket, collar and tie and well-shone shoes, he is
a study in self-apologetic browns and duns, vanishing into
the background. It's impossible to imagine what Rachel
sees in him or how they fit together. He is a teacher of
history at the local academy.

Turning to her uncle, she finds that he is knitting. Pipe
clamped between his teeth, one knee crossed over the
other, he is transferring the row from one needle to the
other at a considerable pace, working what seems to be a
very complex pattern with rust and green four-ply wools.
Isabel has never seen a man knit.

'You're knitting!'

'True.' He knows what she is thinking and why she
wants to laugh. 'Can you knit, Isabel?'

'Not really.'

'Then that is not likely to be your forte.' He methodically counts the stitches, nudging them along the needle
with one nicotine-stained finger. Curiously, Isabel goes
over to sit beside him in the bay of the window and
watches in silence as he briskly fetches the wool over each
stitch with his index finger. She inspects his bent head, a
mass of dark corkscrew curls with a few streaks of grey,
and his very slight, gaunt figure. He is gentle, she sees,
extraordinarily gentle, and that is beautiful.

'Men don't generally knit,' she observes. 'Why is that?'

'Nobody taught them, I doubt. And they're too busy laying down the law and ruling the world.'

'Don't you agree with that, Uncle David?'

'No I do not,' he replies shortly. Turning the needles at the end of a row, he proceeds back the way he has come. 'If men would just have consented to sit quietly at home getting on with their knitting twenty years ago, there would never have been the Second World War.'

'A simplified view,' says Rachel, drinking her coffee and drumming her fingers on the table.

'Not at all. A simple fact. Prohibit cowboys-and-Indians and enforce mothers-and-fathers amongst the young and you'd eradicate war within a generation. As the Jesuits say, "Just catch the child before he's seven and I'll make a Catholic of him" – the same goes for peaceableness.'

'No, no, it's in the blood, the drive for power. It's in the genes, as strong as the sex-drive; we are a violent animal,' Rachel objects.

'I don't believe it.'

'Idealist.'

'Cynic.'

This is a novel view Isabel will take to her heart: knitting the remedy for the world's ills.

'I agree with you, Uncle David,' she says.

'Wonderful – that makes two of us; only another hundred million to convert. Just think of it, Isabel: Hitler, Stalin and Churchill all sitting down together knitting baby-bootees and discussing patterns for matinee jackets.'

'Crocheting doilies.'

'Sewing on hooks and eyes. Why are we laughing though? It's the world we're used to that's mad, surely, where dominating and killing people is considered more important than feeding and sheltering them. If you're

126

interested, I'll show you my Library of Conscientious Objection – do you want to browse round?'

The walls of his study are lined with Gandhi, Bertie Russell, Krishna Mennon, Pacifist commentaries on the Gospels, the Trench Poets.

He refused to fight in the War, he tells her. When the call-up papers came in 1944, he realised at once that Jesus would never have dreamt of bayoneting his fellow-man or exploding him with a grenade. If Jesus could not, he could not. It was as obvious and simple as that. He did subsequently allow himself to be persuaded into being drafted into the Army Medical Service and ended up at the Military Hospital at Ismaelia; then one evening he quite distinctly heard Jesus telling him in a quiet but firm voice to stop prevaricating. He went to his Commanding Officer at HQ and handed in his uniform.

'And what happened to you?'

'Oh, he was a decent, genuine man: he patiently tried to talk me round. When he found he couldn't, he naturally had no option but to have me court-martialled. I went to prison until the end of the War, which wasn't long. I had it very easy. No heroics at all. Quite prosaic, really.'

'I have a friend who was out in Egypt. She's an Army girl. Prue. She told me about the sand-storms and hail-stones as big as your fist.'

'Poor wee lass.'

'Why?'

'Oh – the Army life, it's no good for children. Sensitive bairns it harms or hardens. Women it scourges.'

Which will Prue be – harmed or hardened? Isabel sits down at David's desk with a copy of Siegfried Sassoon:

I knew a simple soldier-boy
Who grinned at life with empty joy,

Slept soundly through the lonesome dark
And whistled early with the lark.

In winter trenches, cowed and glum,
With crumps and lice and lack of rum,
He put a bullet through his brain,
No one spoke of him again.

*

You smug-faced crowds with kindling eye
Who cheer when soldier-boys march by –
Sneak home and pray you'll never know
The hell where youth and laughter go.

Yes, but how was Hitler to be stopped if we didn't take arms against him? Isabel is just about to go and ask her uncle for light on this subject when she hears her mother and father coming in at the front door. From the top of the stairs she sees Rachel embracing her mother and hears her mother's radiant voice:

'Tests all clear! He says I'm all right – just a touch of anaemia.'

Isabel shoots downstairs into her mother's tight hug; there are tears in everyone's eyes. So everything's all right. David pours sherry to celebrate, and Isabel gets a small token glass. All is calm and amiable between them, and nobody makes heretical remarks likely to offend the ears of the dour Donald.

If only her father would enter into the mood and stop looking so poker-faced and solemn; turning away, looking out of the window as if the communal outbreak of relief embarrassed him. Her father: he's awful. An awful man. How much more eligible and suitable for a father of Isabel is David; she's already begun to substitute him in her mind for the dreary, dogmatic bully she's stuck with. Now if only her father would (painlessly) die, and Rachel run off with a fellow-sculptor to Florence, David could marry Isla, and Isabel would be sure of the comforting presence of the first person she's ever known who reinforces her perceptions and sees as she sees, dissidently.

She can't sleep, awash with muddled emotions; and it's a turbulent night for everyone in the household. Rachel awakens, as she often does, with a terrible dream. Isla lies quietly on her pillow looking at the moonlight through the open curtains, acclimatising to her reprieve. Donald waits till he thinks she's asleep, then gets up and creaks his way to the bathroom where he has the huge relief of giving way to tears at last. Love of his wife and terror of losing her bear him down in the one tide.

*

Although Dr Fuller admired the clinical judgement of the senior consultant, Mr Macky, and could rarely fault either his diagnoses or prognoses, he was seriously inclined to question the ethics and, come to that, the psychology, of his dealings with patients on the human level. Macky was, of course, of the older generation, distrusting the new-fangled fad for telling the terminally ill the brutal facts of their disease and its likely progress. What did it matter, he snorted, if the dying person lived in illusion as long as it was a benign illusion which increased his portion of hope and the general quality of his life? And prognosis was not an exact science – anything could happen, remission, even unpredictable cure. Fuller muttered about patients' rights, human dignity, value of truth and so on, but obviously he was in no position to affect his superior's condescending policy. Playing God, abdicating painful responsibility. But there were obvious cases, so astound-

ingly obvious that you would have thought even a geri-
atric old fool like Macky could have seen, of patients
whose strength and sense entitled them to nothing less
than the direct truth so that they could set their house in
order and prepare for death. The woman with only weeks
left to live yesterday was a crowning example. He could
not look her in the eyes as she left the room; oh well,
things will be different in the future when Macky and his
ilk have been retired.

*

With a brick, January smashes the small upper window
of the pantry and heaves herself up, left foot on the sill,
right hand gripping the drainpipes; she scrabbles down
inside for the catch of the main window. Breathing in
hard, she squeezes her body in sideways through the nar-
rowness of the aperture and alights inside the pantry. She
has broken in.

It's hers, the Manse. Huge and stale as if its occupants
absconded long ago and left only odour of dog, odour of
Vim on scoured marble and wooden surfaces, the chill
breathed out by flagstones even in high summer, dead ash
in the range and mansion polish from the lofty panelling
of the hall.

'Hello!' she shouts into the empty silence. 'Anyone
there?' And she yodels and halloos and ululates to the
echoing ghosts of the place, none of whom bothers to
manifest.

Christ she's cold, Christ she's bloody freezing. Her
saturated clothes cling to her body and her hair is plastered
down to the dome of her head. As she runs upstairs, her
plimsolls squelch on the varnished boards.

Jettisoning her clothes into the massive six-foot bath,
January dries herself on strange towels, not Army issue.

She bursts into Isabel's room and ransacks her fanatically neat drawers for underwear, trousers, shirt and sweater. Her shivering is convulsive, even in the usurped outfit.

Fire. Food.

As she slides down the carved oak bannister, the grandfather clock on the landing sounds the half-hour with great portentousness, then stops in mid-tick, its works unwound. Downstairs she scrabbles for a torch or candle in the drawers of an immense oak dresser in the kitchen. There's everything there but a torch – loose ballbearings, sugar-tongs, nut-crackers, curtain-rings, a pot of glue, a puppet in the shape of a clown, Brasso, a bike-repair kit and a fat spider that scuttles into a tea-towel.

Come on, come on. She locates a torch in a drawer full of electric light-bulbs; rifles the larder for food and brings away the biscuit-tin and the cake-tin. In the old geyser's study she finds an electric fire but, shit, the power's not on and she doesn't know how you turn it on. And the taps don't work. She doesn't know about that, either. She fiddles with a wheel under the sink and somehow that makes the water come on. She puts her mouth to the running tap and drinks.

The darkness thickens as she sits in Mrs Gordon's armchair by the hearth and works her way through the biscuits. The shivering subsides. Outside on the landing there is a slight noise, a creaking and pattering – then silence. She stops crunching to listen. She switches off the torch. The pattering comes again, nearer now.

'Who's there?'

Into the wide eye of the sudden torchbeam the cat passes, soft-foot round the open door, tail arched high. Another life, another warm concurrent life, makes wary approach to her life.

'Come on, pussy . . . come on here.'

January woos it with kissing-noises of her lips and unfurled finger-tips. The yellow-green furtive eyes prowl nearer: then it springs into her lap, dumping itself on her undoubted mercy. Her arms wrap compulsively round its body and clutch the beating warmth of its black pelt against her chest where it purrs with a sonorous, pulsating engine-sound.

'Noisy little bugger, aren't you, aren't you,' says January. She fondles the whiskered complacency of its face and repeatedly strokes it all down its rippling spine and sleek sides. 'Lovely noisy bugger aren't you?' It came to her. It knew to come. It is her cat. If anyone tried to take it away from her she'd bite and scratch like the feline mother for its young. The cat shows no inclination to wander; it had been squatting on a pile of sheets in the cooled-down airing cupboard and anyone's warm lap is to be preferred. Upstairs she lugs it, crooning away, into the parents' room, where she deposits it on the nearer of the twin beds, separated one from the other by a bedside cabinet.

'Stop there now. Don't go, or else,' she threatens. The cat obliges, curling into a ball. 'Lovely, beautiful pussy.'

She sets up and lights two wax candles on saucers on the bedside cabinet, then draws the curtains on their flickering intimate privacy, she and the cat and her own reflection in the elliptical mirror on the wardrobe door, looking like an eccentric variation on the theme of Isabel in the captured baggy trousers and the V-necked chunky sweater. It's warm and it's kind in here. It's where she ought to be and has a right to be. Lifting a pillow, she divulges what must be the old geyser's pyjamas, striped flannel, neatly folded. So that's his bed and this is hers. Under this pillow is discovered a comprehensive cream-coloured night-gown, sprigged with faded roses, high at the collar and frilled at the cuffs, and also a hair-net. January gets into the mother's bed and coaxes the cat in with her. She burrows her nose down into its fur and its smell, its creaturely, so very living smell. Instantly it breaks out into its snoring purr. Lying on her side so as to avoid putting pressure on the welts from her father's beating, she easily sleeps.

*

In her dream, January dislodges Isabel from the sycamore tree. She does it quite calculatingly, and with relish. Her victim is swinging from her hands, high up. January lunges at her. Isabel, with a look of shock and puzzlement, loses hold and is hanging on by one hand alone, above an immense drop. January gets a big stick and batters the remaining hand, again and again and again. Isabel will not let go. It seems to be taking forever. But January has the infinite advantage that she seems adapted to treading air; she doesn't need handholds or footholds, she's free and doesn't require to be attached to anything solid. She brings the stick down with an almighty crash on Isabel's slackening fingers. Isabel sails down slowly to the ground, her full skirts ballooning. She lies splayed on the turf, with her arms above her head. Cuckoo January shins down the tree and streaks across the lawn to where the wren parents are standing looking at Michaelmas daisies. But the wren parents don't want to know her, they shoo her off with horror, the fratricidal intruder, they clang the Manse gates to (the gates that are never shut) against her, and through the bars she sees them go indoors with their daughter, who shoots January a wicked look out of one sidelong, grey eye, for she wasn't dead, only shamming.

*

The hot-water-bottle cat lies with its spine against her spine, in the grip of predatory dreams. Two hours pass. First light pricks pin-holes in the fabric of the curtains and the morning chorus strikes up. The cat, imagining blood on its palate, slides from the crook of her arm, and lopes out fast to cruise its hunting-ground.

★

Someone comes for January and takes her to Heaven. Heaven is a great place. There are no thin communion wafers doled out to a long queue by Brylcreemed blathering priests in Heaven; the altar there is a table stacked with satisfaction. In Heaven the guests wear party-hats and pull giant crackers, they let off streamers and tell jokes, they guzzle freely on mince-pies and trifles. You help yourself to as much as you want, and you never get bloated. January helps herself to her entitlement. There is nothing holy about Heaven, she discovers, there are no Holy Joes or Holier-than-Thous. It is an absolutely profane place where all are 'haves' and none 'have-nots'. Everybody is whooping it up. The Pope is jiving lustily with the Virgin Mary. God offers January a glass of dandelion and burdock. 'It's damn good stuff,' says God. 'Put hairs on your chest.' God is somewhere between Santa and their American uncle O'Neill who sometimes sends over parcels containing peanut butter and rich fruit-cakes in tins. Beatific feelings suffuse the sleeping child.

★

Her breakfast is a can of sardines and a can of cold baked beans, eaten straight from the tin with a teaspoon. After this she fiddles with the knobs by the electricity meter. By trial and error she gets the lights to work. She and the

134

cat prowl the house, buoyantly asserting the boundaries of their joint territory.

All this space. She cranes her neck. They have all this space around them, all to themselves. There isn't the forced friction, the rubbing up against your brother or sister so that you get a close-up on their every wart and pimple and freckle, jampacked like the sardines she's just wolfed. They don't have to hate each other.

In every corner, niche, shelf and cupboard she traces signs of Mrs Gordon. She is so real that she half expects her to materialise suddenly in the bay of the window or soft-foot in padding slippers from the hall in her dress that is dark as cloudbanks over the estuary. She is lovely, Mrs Gordon; she offers you things and doesn't look down her nose. She brushed January's hair that time till her scalp tingled, and tied it back with a rubber band; she took them down to the chilly cellar and showed them where she kept the apples all winter in crates, individually packed in newspaper so they didn't rot. They sniffed the pure cider smell, each polishing an apple on her sleeve and biting into the russet flesh. Once Mrs Gordon came into the attic where they were playing, carrying a jamjar.

'I doubt you know what this is,' she said to January and Prue. 'Don't you tell them, Isabel.'

Inside the jar was a fizzing liquid, the colour of dandelion and burdock. January had never in her life seen such a fierce fizz. Its bubbles chased each other in whirling circles as if on the boil, up to the surface from a core of bubbles at the base. It looked like a jar of life itself.

'It's lemonade, that,' said Prue. Mrs Gordon shook her head.

'There's something live in there,' said January.

'Good girl,' said Mrs Gordon. 'Well said.' She held up

the jar to the sunny skylight window and the golden bubbles scintillated in January's eye.

'I love it,' she said earnestly. 'I love it. What is it?'

'It's a ginger beer plant.'

'I've never heard of no such thing. Is it a real plant, like?'

'Yes, in a way. It grows like yeast. You can decant it and decant it to make gallons of ginger beer.'

January held the jar of effervescence and listened to its busy murmur through her fingers. She felt a passionate curiosity and covetousness. She would have nicked it there and then but there was only the one, and Mrs Gordon bore it away with her. She has no idea where it is kept, and her present researches have failed to uncover it.

She delves and sifts with forensic dedication. Mrs Gordon's winter under-wear folded in a heavy Victorian chest-of-drawers, with mothballs and lavender's musty freshness. She holds the outlandish long-johns up against herself and wiggles her hips in the mirror. Mrs Gordon's half-used jar of Vick and a box of Zubes in her cabinet drawer. She unscrews the Vick and sniffs; she eats a Zube. Mrs Gordon's tortoiseshell comb stuck at a 45 degree angle into her hairbrush, not a stray hair left in it. January pries and prowls, handling all the cold things Mrs Gordon daily makes warm by touching; sniffing up the expiring scents of a life she can't get near enough to. There is a sharp, turbulent feeling.

I want to love you but you don't need me.

With a pair of pinking shears January systematically slashes Mrs Gordon's nightgown into ribbons, with which she festoons the bed.

That will show her.

She quits the room and stomps round the hall and spare rooms, randomly knocking down anything she takes a dislike to – vases with dried grasses, family photographs. A few minutes later she drags back, deflated and remorseful.

Why did I do that?

She hastily gathers up the remains, which she stuffs in a brown paper bag and hides under the bed.

I didn't do that. It never happened.

She runs up and down the echoing staircases calling the cat. The high-ceilinged rooms tower haughtily away from the riff-raff that has got in, the *hoi polloi*, the rough Cahill brat. The colossal stair-well, through which one sees up three storeys to the skylight, is a vast well of vertigo, full of absence and disapproval. The cat is found on a smelly old cushion in the dog's usurped manger. Is rudely grabbed and forced to do duty as a source of *ersatz* affection. It's all one to the promiscuous, exploitative cat, which has just caught and half-consumed a mouse and will drowsily allow its satisfied body to be pawed.

'Nice moggy, good moggy.' For an anodyne hour, January does nothing but pet the cat.

*

Isabel's away but Prue comes to the Manse anyway, drawn by an inner magnet. She even rings the doorbell but of course there's no answer. She walks round the front and side, looking up with reverence at the ivied, red-brick frontage, the dark panes of the windows reflecting back the grey day with studious reserve. January didn't come home last night, but nobody except Prue noticed – and Prue said nothing. Dad didn't return from his boozing until four in the morning, singing so loud he'd wake the dead: LLOYD GEORGE KNEW HIS FATHER, he bawled, and ROLL ME OVER IN THE CLOVER, he implored, lumbering up the stairs, DO IT AGAIN, he demanded, practically falling in through the door to the parents' bedroom. Prue heard a ferocious crashing of bed-springs, accompanied by grunts, snorts and thumps, then, after about five minutes of such seismic manifestations, total silence. She knows that when she hears these sounds, Dad's doing sex to Mam. Jacko Jackson told her about the facts of life behind the shed at school, much against her will.

'The man shoves his dick in the woman's bum', he explained, 'and shoots in his germs. The germs infect her with a baby.'

Prue hates it when she hears her dad making that rumpus. She covers her ears but listens through her hands. It's horrible and it's fascinating and she can't help feeling a hot, pleasurable disgust. Sometimes after this she cries when it's quiet, without understanding why she's crying – but it's as if she mourned the future loss to herself of the quiet integrity she has so far preserved, by tricking them into thinking she's not really there. She mourns the end of her own maidenhood, when she'll be violently invaded in her turn and have to have the germs pumped into her; and want it too. She would like to ask Columba about these matters, but Columba is not Columba any longer. She looks right through you to where the walls are pasted with ogled polyphotos of Duncan, nothing but Duncan, in whom Prue sees no beauty at all, but notes dandruff all over his shoulders, and that he fingers a weedy little moustache designed, no doubt, to divert attention from his baby-face.

This morning she has slipped out early, before any shouting-matches have had a chance to break out, carrying a satchel packed with books, notebooks and pens, and taking a slice of bread and jam to eat along the way. She climbs up on to the lap of the beech-tree and, leaning against the central trunk, settles back and opens her book. Soon they will be back at school again, soon she can start working in order to go to university with Isabel. Though she has no clear idea of what university entails, she gathers from the almost religious fervour with which the Scots view education, that this is the way to equality with them. Miss Slorach said she was bright for an Army child. Miss Slorach who's so frugal with praise, said she was not far below the standard of the Scottish children, not far at all, keep it up; though she winces at Prue's pronunciation of their great national poet. All summer long, Prue, coached by Isabel, has been practising 'Wee sleekit cowerin' timorous beastie', which she is now capable of declaiming in private with a real lilt and swagger, but might lose hold of for public purposes under the onset of her incapacitating shyness. Now, lolling back in the crook of the tree, she reads the story of the Massacre of Glencoe, and how the Campbells hunted down the women and children of the Macdonalds, stabbing those who had not frozen or hungered to death in the snow.

These painful matters she contemplates from the vantage of quiet aloneness and compensatory security. The peace of the garden embraces her wholly. She feels the over-arching trees and high boundary walls blocking out threats as a mother encircles a child. No one can spy on her. No one knows she's here. She sits so still the birds and squirrels virtually ignore her.

The Gordons' cat approaches; pauses with one forepaw off the ground, but though she calls it, it will not come to her.

Was that a face in the high window? Someone seemed to tweak a curtain; flash a glance, then vanish. The blank eye of the pane returns Prue's fluttered stare. Was it real, was it a ghost? Prue knows well that ghosts can walk, for she has read true accounts made by people who have seen them. She knows you can have visions in broad daylight, as for instance the Blessed Virgin who appeared to a girl in Birkenhead when they were visiting their gran in 1957, and hundreds of people flocked to the bend in the Mersey where she had been spotted floating inches above the water, and saw her too. On the whole Prue had rather not be smitten by visions, even devout ones, so she tells herself it was just the shadow of a bird on the pane. Law-abiding, yearning Prue, in her lemon-yellow cardigan and neat white socks up to the knees, reads on, under the leaden sky.

Can you love a place in the way you love a person, Prue wonders, later in the morning, gathering her things together, throwing the satchel overboard and letting herself down from the tree-lair? If so you will never be let down or left out because you can always come back and it will always be the same. She feels as she does when she has drunk a glass of cold, fresh milk after being particularly thirsty.

The nocent, dark-haired sister indoors inspects the inno-cent sister out of doors, with a baleful glare. *Aren't you never going?* January's silent eyes demand. She itches for Prue to leave. *Bugger off, can't you. This is my place, not yours. That's right, off you go, good riddance.*

She turns on the wireless and listens in to the Goon Show. This is her world, her home, and she has no inten-tion of sharing it with anyone. In the evening, she heats up the water with the immersion heater and runs a bath: deep water right up to the outflow hole, not the miserable three inches she has to share with Prue in that other place, knees bent up, your head rammed up against the taps. The bath here is built for a giant. She tries out the anti-quated sponge and a long loofah. Getting out, she catches sight of the scars on her back in the steamed-up cabinet-mirror; she had pretty well forgotten them. They are healing with unusual rapidity and hardly hurt at all, or if they do it is with a muffled, far-away twinging, easily endured.

7

The heat; nothing to do but booze and get hung over; falling out with Chalky White over a bet; wife and kids on top of him, driving him mad; the beginnings of a head-cold and a crop of mosquito bites on his beam end all conspire to exacerbate Hugh Cahill's temper past bearing. He finds plenty of reasons to hand for doling out punishments to his aggravating slag of a wife (one black eye, one bruised shin), his sons Peter and Paul (two major thrashings over his knee each on Sunday) and his daughter Catherine whose head he repeatedly banged against the wall for cheeking him. No let-up to the heat. You could fry an egg on the bonnet of next-door's Ford. No improvement in his streaming nose. Just let anyone, but *anyone*, cross his will and he won't answer for the consequences. They're well-warned; they all tiptoe around like ghosts, and even get out of the window when they hear him approaching. At least they know who's master.

He lounges sweating in the sitting room, with his braces over his vest for the sake of getting a bit of cool, in the cross-draught between the open window and the open door. He blows his nose trumpetingly, to advertise his self-pity and his righteous indignation that is spoiling for a fight. Snatching up the *Daily Mail*, he shakes it open at a page where Archbastard Makarios is photographed blandly smiling from an open car and waving one beringed, soft-skinned hand to a cheering mob shrieking ENOSIS. If there is one man that really gets Hugh's goat, that man is Makarios. Why he was ever let out of the Seychelles where we wisely deported him to keep company with his fellow baboons, Hugh has never known. He only has to see Makarios' picture to get red-hot fighting-mad. Out there in Cyprus (where he was sent in 1956 on a short posting) there was literally no one and nothing to fight. Grivas' guerillas came like cowards tiptoeing in the night and blew up our planes and depots, and vanished without trace into the Troodos Mountains; the platoon scoured the woods for weeks and came up with nothing. Up the skirts of Makarios. Hugh hungrily feeds his already frenzied eye on that sleek snake, then flings the newspaper across the room. Any minute now his tether will break and he'll go for someone. He scratches the itching mosquito bites vindictively. Any – minute – now.

The anger of the riled tyrant breeds an exact ratio of retributive violence in his subjects: this political commonplace is borne out in the Cahill household by an access of bullying all the way down the hierarchy. The older children gun for the younger, the stronger for the weaker. Vicious quarrels have been breaking out as soon as Hugh has left the premises, and blows exchanged. The vulnerable youngest, whose suffering holds up the whole pyramid of pain, seek satisfaction either by banging their own heads against the cot-bars, pounding a mangy teddy-bear or lapsing into deadly indifference, as if containing and amassing their quota of grief and rage for some later occasion.

Even Mary Cahill's long-suffering temper has gone. She is just about to administer a slap to Damian for some minor offence when January comes in after a three-day absence and she can let fly at her instead.

'Oh so it's you is it, my girl. You've done it now. You're going to cop it right and proper when he gets hold of you. Where've you been?'

'Nowhere.'

'Don't you talk back to me. Where've you been?'

'Mind your own business.'

'How dare you say "Mind your own business!" How dare you! What do you mean by running off like that? Answer me. We thought you was gone for good.'

'You wouldn't care', says January, looking her straight in the eyes, 'if I had've gone for good.'

The undoubted truth of this observation takes the wind out of Mary's sails for a moment. Instead of replying, she aims a swipe at the belligerent, pinched face of her accuser – which, however, misses. There's something different about January, now that she comes to inspect her closely. Her hair is glossy and sleek, tied back in an elastic band; the habitual stoop of her thin shoulders has straightened out. *I care for myself*, she seems to be saying, from behind her customary screen of mutinous defiance.

'How dare you say such a thing to your own mother!' Mary counters weakly. 'Your own mother what bore you,' she adds on a rising cadence.

'Oh get lost. You may have borned me but you don't give a monkey's about me and I don't give a monkey's about you; you're the one what left me in the coal-hole.' Her voice is quite calm and neutral, as if going over finished business. 'So don't give me that crap, for God's sake.'

Most of Mary Cahill's children have been hard to love; this one has been impossible. But it was not that she didn't care. No, it was not for lack of wanting to care and cope that made for this mess and wholesale failure of affection. They were too many, cash and space were too little, Hugh was too much – and she herself, with or without the succour of the Blessed Virgin, was never enough. And it makes her mad to have it thrust in her face.

'I've always been a good mother to you,' she replies with rage, giving January a good push with both hands. 'Ungrateful, thankless girl that you are.'

'Get your filthy hands off of me,' growls January. 'I hate you, anyway. You're a toothless old slag.'

'Do you hear that, Hughie? Do you hear what she's calling her mother?'

'Where the hell do you think you've been?' Hugh advances, quiet-voiced, narrow-eyed, grinding out his cigarette in the ashtray. January backs round the table. Several siblings appear in doorways, inquisitive, concupiscent.

'Nowhere.'

'I said, where have you been.'

'A good place – a gentle place – somewhere you don't know about and you'll never go.'

'I'll thrash the living daylights out of you.'

'Oh no you won't, you animal – not never again you won't.'

'Oh won't I though? Won't I? Sure about that, are you?' He has her by one arm, which he now twists round behind her back.

'I'll call the police. You haven't got no right. You're evil, you're a murderer, you're a Nazi.'

Her whole scalp shrieks where he yanks her head back by a swag of hair, again and again.

'Hitler – Hitler – Hitler.'

'Don't you fucking call me that you fucking bitch.' It outrages Hugh to be called by that name. Did he fight the fucking Krauts in the fucking Western fucking Desert to have his own fucking daughter call him a fucking Nazi? A storm of moral indignation seethes in Hugh, it floods his skull with a kind of vile sweetness; he flushes through with electric anger. How dare she? How dare they? They're going to pay. 'I fought Hitler in the bleeding Desert for you. For another man's filthy bastard.'

He tightens his hand on the swathe of hair and drags her head right over backwards, so that she is looking at him open-mouthed, upside-down; he sees the rise of her small breasts pushed out against the sweater. That maddens him. Sweat breaks out from beneath his arm-pits. He knees her forward round the table, her arm still held behind her back, her head still pinioned. His knee-bone shoves against her arse as he propels her forward, out of the door and up the stairs.

She is still hoarsely shouting insults but you can't tell what they are, she gasps for breath. In her bedroom he drags a chest-of-drawers across the door. She has to be punished. Now. She has to be stopped. Once and for all. Now, this minute. It can't go on. He can't let it. She has to be made to see right from wrong if it kills him.

She is silent, breathing hard, like a cornered animal. Brings her knee up in his groin hard but he sees it coming and whacks it down. Claws his face with her nails and draws blood. Thumbs him in the eye. Kicks and screams and bites and will not lie down and take her punishment. That arouses him. He likes a fight. Rips her skirt off and tears at her pants. Plays with his flies, holding her thrashing body with the other hand. Loses her; she scampers across the pattering room with one hand shielding her crotch. Like a shy, nude little toddler but flaunting a pubescent body. (He plays with the babies after their baths, he pats their chubby bottoms with his great hands, innocent fun.)

'Dad, no, no, Dad, please, please.'

She begs now, in a loud whisper, too late; his great purple dick sprouts up from his dropped pants, he wades over to her with the light of God in his eyes, trousers round his ankles.

'I'm sorry, Dad – Dad, I'm sorry – I'll never do it again – Dad, for the love of God – Mam, Mam!'

*

Prue has never in her life heard such terrible screaming. It puts such fright and anxiety into her, she doesn't know what to do with herself, her tummy flutters and tickles, she wants to run round in circles.

'Mam, stop him, Mam.'

'She's got to learn,' says Mary, with glazed eyes. She puts the kettle on for when he's done with the child. He'll want a cup of tea. With a couple of custard creams. She puts them out on a plate. Her mouth is completely dry. The God-awful row goes on and on but now the staccato shrieking has turned to a pandemonium of sobbing.

She inspects the palms of her hands minutely. There is something ingrained; it is coal-dust or ash, or what is it? She lathers them and holds them under the tap.

Please God, stop it, she prays.

'Out to play, the whole lot of you,' she orders the children.

Prue goes out. Bees have got into her stomach. They crawl about and seethe all over its surface. They cannot get out. She holds on to her stomach and, sitting on the back doorstep, rocks to and fro. Damian and Paul begin to swat each other with sticks by a bramble-patch. Each child is sucking the thumb of his left hand whilst swatting

147

aimlessly with his right. The overgrown lawn is strewn with old cans and bottles, bricks and papers. The inhuman noise from upstairs goes on and on. The washing tumbles on the line; sun and wind litter the earth with a casualty of shadows.

The chest-of-drawers screeches as it's heaved across the lino. Hugh shambles downstairs, fatigued, out of breath, doing up the buckle on his belt. He accepts the tea from Mary with something of a shame-faced look, but not altogether displeased with himself, like a naughty boy who is hoping to get away with it.

'I didn't mean to hit her quite so hard like, but she has to learn.'

'What else can you do?' she bleats.

'God knows, Mary, I'm not a patient man, I know my faults, but this one would tempt a saint.'

He dips his biscuit in the hot tea, sucks, and grins boyishly at Mary, slipping her a placating smile. Then he yawns and stretches. Upstairs the unearthly noise is beginning to abate. Soon the house is so silent you could hear a pin drop.

*

Hugh doesn't feel so good. There is something uneasy in him he would give a lot to expel. The silence gets on his nerves. When he looks out of the window four stationary children are out there doing damn all at the end of the garden amongst the builders' litter. Two are sucking their thumbs, one is sitting crouched with its head on its knees, twining a handkerchief round and round its hand. Another is just standing with its back to the house, ramrod straight, as if to attention. They give him the creeps, the motion-less, expressionless, staring children, like effigies, like traumatised disaster victims in stockstill shock. He drums his fingers on the sill. He seems to itch all over his body, or in his body, or something.

Mary smiles at him like a ghost. She agrees with everything he says. She shrinks back from him as he passes. They all shrink as he passes. They all hate him. Are there some amends he could make?

'Let me wash up them cups,' he offers feebly. The unaccustomed gesture makes no difference. Mary thanks him fulsomely and her face becomes ever more obsequiously false.

He badly needs a drink. Thank Christ his leave's over tomorrow. Back to the real world.

'I'll be off to the mess then.'

'Right then.' She's relieved. She's glad to get rid of him. Nobody wants him. Nobody gives a tinker's curse whether he lives or dies. Nobody ever has, it's always been the same. 'You'll be glad to get shut on me. Under your feet all the time.'

'No, Hughie,' a wan, limp disclaimer from her hangdog mouth, deceiving no one.

He runs upstairs to have a pee. It's unnaturally quiet up there on the landing; he feels spooked. He'll go to confession, get things off his chest.

What if she's dead? What if he's killed her?

No. Don't be daft.

She had it coming. She practically asked for it. She waved her tits at him. She made it happen. She tempted him. He's only a man, he's only human after all.

All women are sluts. Except the nuns.

She had to be taught a lesson. Who's master. Now she knows.

What if she tells them?

She won't dare. Not after what he luridly threatened. In any case who'd believe the lying, thieving bitch? She's been suspended from two schools. The teachers at Mönchen Gladbach said, *Disturbed*. Known for it.

That drink. He needs that drink.

Hugh catches sight of his face in the bathroom cabinet mirror, two claw-marks from eye to ear. The vixen, the little cat.

He pees and fastens his flies. Goes to wash his hands. Christ, there's a smear of blood on the thumb and fingers of his right hand. Stares at the blood in horror. Christ, she's made his prick bleed. What has she done to him, the castrating bitch? The blood rushes in his ears. He takes down his pants fumblingly and examines his prick anxiously. Nothing wrong there.

No, of course it's not him that's bleeding.

Hugh washes January's hymeneal blood off his penis and hand. Scrubs the hand and fingernails with a nail-brush. Is it all off? He sluices both hands vigorously under the cold tap.

He is out on the street, striding fast, faster. Something huge and tumid is there inside him, some vile growth unbearably full and tight, it will burst, it will rupture. He is almost running, the loose change jingles in his pocket as he races to outstrip himself. *Jingle bells, jingle bells, jingle all the way*. The aortas pump blood, the glands adrenalin, and he takes to his heels as if all hell were after him. *Oh what fun it is to run*. The drink, the drink is what he needs. Start with a double whisky and go on from there. *On a five-horse open sleigh*.

He slows down, at the fringe of the Married Quarters, in a sweat, but things are calming down, getting more distant, less real. This kind of thing is a flash in the pan, it's soon over and forgotten. No real harm done. He'll go to the confessional box and say 'Bless me Father for I have sinned', and explain to the Father how he went a bit far, he'll tone it down a bit, the priests don't know a lot about family life, they're protected from the temptations and the pressures.

At the mess Hugh has a few too many. On this occasion he doesn't get merry and rowdy, he gets maudlin and lachrymose. Tells Taf Watkins, who's pissed as a newt and hence stupefied into the semblance of a very good listener, the story of his childhood. 'Oh aye,' says Taf Watkins, nodding blearily, at every natural break in Hugh's monologue, 'Oh aye.'

Sodden Hugh can see her now, his widowed Mam, fighting her way through privation and tuberculosis, shutting the door on them, locking them in for she had to go out as a char, and then all hell broke loose, they ran wildly round the panic-stricken house like rats in a trap, and he hung out of the window, hollering, 'Mam! come back!', and she didn't come. They hated each other, they hit each other, they fought over the loaf. They waited at the door panting like dogs for her to come home and then they pounced on her in a pack, they fought over possession of their Mam. What could she do? he asks Taf Watkins, and Taf Watkins fatuously answers 'Oh aye.' And yet he felt betrayed. To be left like that. Defenceless, with nobody to turn to. Not knowing if she would ever come back. He still to this day cannot think of it without his heart hammering, a dark screen coming down in his mind which blanks him off so that everything and everyone is a total stranger.

'It weren't my fault,' he insists to Taf Watkins. 'You know that, don't you? It were none of my fault.'

'Course not. Not you fault, boy. Nobody's blinking fault.' Taf's moist eyes seem to weep in sympathy through the fog of cigarette smoke. 'How about another round then?'

'She made me do it. I were forced to it,' Hugh pleads before the insanely lenient tribunal of his fellow soldier.

'Course you was.'

'*Oh my darling, oh my darling, oh my darling Clementine.*' Some of the lads, nice and tiddly, arms around one another's shoulders in brotherly embrace, are foghorning round the piano. Taf can't resist a song; lurches off to join them.

Hugh is sweating like a pig and flatulent. Headcold turning into 'flu? Feels bloody awful. He rubs at his ears to get rid of the buzzing in there, like a dentist's drill, a metallic resonance of tintinnabulation.

'*Thou art lost and gone forever, dreadful sorry Clementine.*'

A seething roar of sheer horror flushes right over him. He sees a girl who seems all gaping holes, the orifices of the shrieking mouth, the bloody hole of her sex between splayed thighs, no face at all, the face skinned over.

Oh.

The vileness, the trespass, the stink of crime to high heaven.

Oh no.

He pours the whisky neat down his throat, it scalds his stomach, it dissolves the white, violated child in the fire of alcohol. He is all burning. Begins to shout and stagger round the mess. Picks a fight with some ugly mug of a nigger-loving Socialist bastard and is thrown out on his head.

*

Mary is saying her prayers under her favourite icon of Our Blessed Saviour on his Cross. *Oh thou that takest away the sins of the world, receive our prayers.* It helps, oh yes it does help. She loves the gentle Christ with a passion at once maternal and filial. He is the protector, the shelter.

He is also the child and fellow-victim. He understands how hard it is because he knows how it feels to have the nails penetrate your vulnerable, soft person; the shaft of the lance jabbed in his side, the nails perforating the delicate sinews and tendons of his beautiful feet. He is there for her.

Oh thou that takest away. She asks him now to take away this burden of guilt for handing the child over to Hugh like that, casually and without mercy delivering her up as scapegoat to his violence.

Oh Lord in thy mercy. She doesn't know what Hugh did to her and she doesn't dare to go and see. And it was the child's own fault. Even so, even *so* . . . The far-away wooden Christ looks down from the peeling plaster where he hangs in the light, to the shadow where she kneels, with an expression of distaste. He looks through her rather than at her, implying that atonement requires something more practical than feeling bad about something.

Pardon and deliver us. Mary beseeches him with anguish, but how can he forgive her if she can't forgive herself. How can she forgive herself if she won't intervene?

Mary gets up off her knees. She goes into the kitchen and, taking off her wedding ring, begins to peel potatoes. There is a feeling of unease in her marrow, in her bowels. Then, when the baby flutters in her womb, it gives her a shock, like a jack-in-the-box, like a booby trap.

She ought to go upstairs and see to that child.

No.

She can't stand that child, she is afraid of that child, that child is a monster.

If she hates the child, she hates herself.

All right then, she will hate herself. Any road up, she will not go, that's flat.

But.

No.

January has only herself to blame. It's to be hoped she'll have learnt her lesson from this and will become a different child. Hasn't she got enough to think about? Sick as a dog with this fourteenth baby, her seventeenth pregnancy, counting the three miscarriages God was pleased to bestow. If you're bad, you have to be beaten, that's just how it is. It's right, it's normal. Anyhow, it's Hugh's fault, not hers. *Not my fault, not my fault.*

Perhaps she ought to just go upstairs and put her head round the door. She will do that.

'Mam, Mam, Father Friend's here,' says Charity.

'Oh God, where's me teeth? Run upstairs and fetch me teeth.'

She'll ask him to bless the house; sprinkle it with holy water. He's very obliging, is Father Friend. (Woe betide anyone who sits or tramples in the areas where the holy water fell, for several days afterwards.) But she can't see him with her curlers in and her teeth out. She tears out the curlers, dropping them on the kitchen table; combs through the resultant parallel lines of corkscrew curls with both hands. Beckons Prue indoors to go and see to January, hissing, 'And be quiet about it.'

*

Prue has taken off her glasses and folded them in her lap, keeping one hand lightly in touch with them, for if you lose them or they break, you're totally stranded and adrift – the thing she's most scared of and would do anything to avoid. When Prue awakens in the night, the first thing she does is to reach out and touch her glasses with her fingertips. Then she knows she's all right. But if you deliberately take your glasses off, always depending you know they're safe, the world becomes a better place. All its wicked cutting-edges soften and blur, colours flood into one another, the dark rim round vision is withdrawn, so that you are not isolated on one side of a wall of glass but drawn into the world's embrace. Your self is whole, and a part of the whole world.

Prue, sitting on the steps, took off her glasses and exposed her naked, vulnerable eyes to the unmediated light. She felt the air gently buffeting her lids and eyebrows. Now the regiments of army-quarters, with their concrete rendering and squared windows, have marched away off the periphery of vision; the fences that demarcate the limit of each family's tenancy have been broken down, and the notice, 'No ball-games here', in the patch of ground just beyond the gardens has been erased. Prue's vandalising vision permits the world to pour across the borders and barriers that circumscribe each person and thing as finite: you shall be that and no more. Her weak eyesight paints a wash on creation, through whose merciful blur the swimming light winks oddly, freely. Once in a while a drop of fine rain falls, catching on her lens and forming a momentary convex which reveals to her a normalised focus, then returns her to the womb-like blur of her myopia. Sitting there in her warm trance she saw nothing, thought nothing, distinct.

Then Mam said, 'Go up to your sister and make sure she's all right. And be quiet about it. The Father's here.'

'Oh Mam,' whined Prue, 'Must I?' She doesn't budge; hunches her shoulders.

'Go on this minute. Get on with you.'

'Oh Mam, I don't want to. Why me anyhow? It's always me.' Uncharacteristically, Prue breaks cover by showing resistance for she doesn't want anything to do with January. January's hurt is flagrant, rabid, horrible.

'Can I sleep in with Damian and Paul, Mam? I don't want to be in with her no more.'

'No you cannot. Just do what you are told.'

Prue replaces her glasses. She lags indoors, scuffing her sandals. Father Friend is being effusively offered a cup of tea, and remarking that he wouldn't say no to just the one. His mottled, bald head can be observed above the chair-cover like a huge speckled egg. His fine, fastidious hands play with Damian's curls. He has a kind word for all and knows each child by name. He suffers the little children to come unto him and forbids them not. Each one is a soul for the church. Father Friend is not one of these priests who ignores or makes little of the bodily distresses of his flock; he flinches when he enters some of these Army houses, the stench of misery assails and offends him like an accusation. He emphasises to these tired, used-up women and hungry, angry, ignorant children whose address is the end of the world, the Christ-like status of their suffering, and that Jesus and His Mother not only have suffered but are – every minute of the day – suffering with us. But it does not atone, it is no panacea. What can he do but his best? He washes his sensitive hands with Wright's coal tar soap and dries the fingers carefully, one by one, on an immaculate white towel.

'Now, Mary my dear, how are you going along? Did the little one get over his nasty germ?'

Prue, listening to the pleasant, plangent tones of his baritone voice, meditates shooting out of the front door and disappearing for the day. But something – not her mother's injunction, something in herself – drags the inertia of her reluctant legs to climb the stairs, some call of magnet to heavy, torpid iron.

Nothing moves in the bedroom but you always know if there is a breathing presence in a room and there is someone in here for sure. The room is in a state of havoc – hairbrushes, clothes-hangers, shoes scattered, as if they had done duty as missiles. The two beds skewed out of line, touching at the foot, and the biscuits of Prue's mattress have parted company with one another, a grey mound of blankets all bunched at the centre. Prue sees blood on the mattress of her bed. The papers from her bedside cabinet, which she keeps in methodical order, lie strewn on the lino. She automatically stoops to pick up a jettisoned *Gulliver*; its spine has broken, she will have to pay a fine on it. The book weighs more than the blood to Prue in this extremity. How dare they touch her precious books, how dare they?

'Jan.' No answer, but she suddenly knows where to look.

Half in, half out of the wardrobe, Prue's sister lies curled foetally tight, amongst the Wellington boots, the mothballs and a water-pistol, swaddled in a blanket. She is sucking her thumb. Her eyes are tight shut. When Prue puts her hand on January's shoulder, there is no response. Perhaps she's asleep. Prue crouches hesitantly. There's a horrible smell in the room, a disgusting bloody reek, she almost retches. It's a smell like when they're sick but worse; it's mingled with stale sweat, old shoes, sex and rancid pain.

'Jan, are you all right?' she whispers. 'Jan, it's Prue.'

Shouldn't she run downstairs now and fetch Father Friend and fetch Mam and fetch the police and demand that they confront this, insist, bring them face-to-face with it and force them to cope. She can't, she can't move; why can't she? Prue begins to cry as she puts one hand under January's head and pulls it up, still sucking the thumb even harder, cheeks working; the hair is matted to the scalp with cold sweat. She pulls strongly, the child comes up as if from drowning; her left cheek and eye are a mass of bruises and there is blood and vomit all down the left-hand side of the blanket. Prue chokes; retches; nearly lets go of the head and lets it crash back down into the debris on the floor of the wardrobe. But holds on because to let go and run away would somehow be more awful than to stay.

'Get up, Jan, get up,' she sobs. 'I can't lift you.'

January is docile. She would, if she could, do anything she was bade to do. She gropes for Prue's shoulders, eyes still closed, and the blanket falls away. She is wearing only a vest.

'Open your eyes, Jan. Come on, get up now.'

The child opens one eye; the other has closed over under its swollen bruise. Her one eye gets a view of the top of a face, the forehead and hair but not the whole face, and a perspective of towering wall and soaring ceiling. Neither wall nor ceiling is still, they tilt backwards and bend away like light refracted through water. As she pulls herself to standing, the floor beneath her feet, soft as hot tarmac-adam, has a treacherous doughy consistency; she sinks into it up to the ankles, up to the knees, and is sucked down into a furore of black pitch.

Prue stands at the top of the stairs and hollers, 'Mam! Father Friend! January's fainted!'

The mother is there, standing over January's body.

'Oh my God, oh my God. Shut the door. Shut it, I said.'

She stares pop-eyed. She doesn't seem to know how to react. She sees the blood dried on the child's thighs and knows, but doesn't know. She witnesses the bruises and the wounds, but doesn't see.

'Mam, do something. Tell him. Tell the Father,' Prue pushes against her mother's arm with both hands.

'No,' says Mary faintly. 'No. Stay here – I'll get rid of him – don't you move from this room.' She rushes downstairs and the priest is confusedly ejected.

January is bathed, anointed with ointment and put to bed, semi-conscious.

'What did he do to her?' ask Peter and Paul.

'He . . . I don't know,' says Prue, aghast. She doesn't know, and yet she does know.

'She's had it coming,' ventures Peter.

'No, she didn't, she did not so,' says Prue. She is shaking all over her body, she can't stop. She doesn't want to stay in the same room as her sister any more. What if January died in the night and she was sleeping next to a corpse? What if he comes in again and does it again, and sees Prue lying there and does it to her too?

'She's a slut,' says Paul. 'I know. Our dad said so.'

'You don't know nothing,' says Prue. 'You're only a child, you.'

She is no longer a child, but has been propelled by force and against her will over the line into the brutal world of the adults, where the fruit of the tree of knowledge of good and evil is devoured at every meal. She knows January suffers this obscenity for them all. They are all sheltering behind that frail shield of her sister's body, elbowing it forward to take the blows while they crouch and cower with their heads well down.

Mary gives Prue hot, sweet tea. She sits her down on the father's chair in front of the fire. Prue's head lolls back against the chair-back, covered with an embroidered cloth depicting a bonneted and crinolined lady with a basket of flowers, greasy with her father's hair-oil. Prue can't stop herself trembling and crying. The tears rise from way deep down within her and wash over her, wave after wave.

'You must never never tell anyone about this,' Mary repeats, half cajoling, half threatening. 'If you do, it will all get worse. Promise me now, Prue, promise your Mam on the Holy Bible never to tell.'

She produces a Bible and coaxes Prue's hand on to its cover.

'Say after me, *I, Prudence Cahill, swear . . .*'

'*I, Prudence Cahill, swear . . .*'

'*That I will never breathe one word . . .*'

'*That I will never breathe one word . . .*'

'*To no one never in my life . . .*'

'*To no one never in my life . . .*'

'*So help me God.*'

'*So help me God.*'

'Mind, that's a holy vow you've made. If you break it Prue, that's a mortal sin; you'll go to hell.'

'Will our dad go to hell?' The question dies unanswered. Will Hell be worse than this? Could anything be? Is a vow still valid if you raised your hand craftily to hover just above the Bible so as not to touch its dark binding, and if you mentally deleted the word *never* from the form of the oath, thus internally committing yourself to reveal all to somebody as some future, unspecified date? Why is our mam on our dad's side?

'I want Columba,' she bursts out, 'I want Columba.' The tea-cup trembles violently in her hand and the contents slop out over the arm of the chair and her own lap. 'I want to sleep in Columba's room with her, I don't want to stay in with Jan no more.'

Mary puts her arms round the hysterical child; it is her wisest move yet. Prue is lulled and comforted. She passively allows her mother to hold her, relaxing in the novelty of this closeness. Her face is up against her mother's surprisingly soft cheek; she receives words of sympathy and endearment that fall, drop by drop, into a fathomless pit of need. In the beginning everything was like this, secure and warm and wanted, in the beginning; and then the centre was lost, the lull and hush broke apart, something necessary went missing like a coin that rolls away undetectably into the darkness under a sofa. Prue lets herself be tucked up in bed beside her sister. She will say no word to a living soul so help her God and that's God's own truth.

*

Things look different in the morning to Hugh; don't they always? He came in paralytic and went out like a light, snoring stertorously. When Mary rouses him at 6.30 with a cup of tea, he feels quite lively and cheerful. As she sets his carefully-pressed uniform over a chair-back, he remarks:

'Well Mary me darling, leave's over. I'll be out from under your feet.'

She vouchsafes no reply.

Whistling, he does up the buttons of his battle-dress, rubs the brass buckle of his belt on his sleeve and fastens it, methodically knots the laces of his gleaming, black boots. Back to the real, the men's, world. Eats a bit of toast and marmalade on the wing. Sets his forage-cap at an angle and winks at his cocky image in the mirror. His boots crunch down the path and he is away. Mary runs up to the lavatory and vomits up her breakfast.

The house begins to stir, first the small ones' whinings, explosions of laughter and rude noises, drummings of heels, the clank of the cistern, demands for this and complaints about that. Mary sluggishly pours six cups of tea and burns ten slices of toast. Pity they don't have one of those many spouted tea-pots such as they use at Toc-H.

Soon the kids will be mostly back to school and someone else will have the bother of them. Things will be better then. She feels so awful in the mornings, with the dire sickness that taints all perception.

Prue comes to reluctant consciousness. She feels for her glasses, with her eyes still closed. Yes, all right. Her hand braille-reads the surface of her locker. Everything there, all right, all safe. Book, biro, jar of Nivea, miniature cushion filled with herbs which Mrs Gordon made with her own hands to give her last Christmas. The scent has faded but not entirely; she sniffs it now, its faint, aromatic freshness penetrates her, healing and clean. These are all her precious, secret things, homely and solid to the touch: the book, the pen, the little muslin cushion.

Shrieking light pierces the gap between January's eyelids. Last night she awoke, or thought she awoke, into a strange silence. Barefoot she crossed to the window and drew aside the net curtain. A full moon shone from the blue-black velvet sky, a moon more huge than any she had ever seen, magnified by a film of gauzy cloud and blurred and softened at its circumference by a sort of aureole. It was like seeing through a telescope. The moon was very close to January, and she was close to it. She stared and stared in wonder. The constellations and galaxies stretched back infinitely far beyond the two of them, and the moon was like an eye, a kind eye that watched January as she watched it. The milk-pale tranquillity of its light suffused the silvered houses and the phosphorescent street; the lamppost pointed up at the moon like an indicating finger. Nothing moved. It was beautiful, it was reserved for her. At last she let fall the curtain and padded back to bed, and whether it was real or just a dream she had no idea.

Now daylight forces passage to her eye; she snaps to

attention. One eye will only open partially. There, sitting on her bed in her vest and pants, is Prue, with a foggy, gormless look, fiddling with her glasses.

'The lens went and fell out,' says Prue, red-faced with panic. 'I can't get it back in.' She fits it back so roughly that the arm breaks off. 'What am I going to do?' she wails. 'I can't see.' She goes off looking for sticky tape. She does not come back.

January gets out of bed and dresses. Her face and body throb and burn; it is hard to bear the pressure from the elastic of her pants on her swollen waist and thighs. Everything she looks at, the most familiar things, seem threatening and alien. The chair, the bed, the wardrobe, are all somehow distorted, tilted at the wrong angle, looming at her. She is afraid. She has been overpowered. The world has called her bluff. She must appease.

When Prue does come back she smiles at Prue from where she stands at the end of the world, cradling herself in her own arms. The smile is false and terrible, like a grimace. Prue is unnerved.

'What is it? What are you looking at me like that for?' she asks in a scowling, fending-off voice.

January continues to smile her ghoulish, freakish smile from her bruised and swollen face.

'Stop it. Why are you doing that?'

January says nothing, just rocks herself and hugs herself. Then she steps forward, putting her hands out, and Prue flinches, thinking she's going to be hit. The smile comes running at Prue, a gap-toothed smile – he knocked one tooth out last night – a smile that might have been dug up out of a graveyard.

'No,' says Prue. 'Get off, get away. I'm sorry for you, but . . .' She cruelly bats off the desperate embrace, with an air of exasperation as at some nuisance or irritant – an insect or unwelcome but familiar dog. 'No, I can't.' She doesn't know what it is that she can't do or give, but she knows absolutely that she can't.

January retreats to her bed, the appalling smile having faded to a blank stare. She begins to masturbate, right there and then, as if nobody else were present. Legs wide apart, skirt hitched up, she rubs the place between them with violent momentum, moaning and grunting. Prue turns and rushes blindly down the stairs. The moment she is out of January's sight and proximity, her mind closes over; she hums and saunters out of the front door, then walks and trots the two miles to the library at Forres, where she sits and reads all morning, endlessly feeling with apprehensive fingers for the wad of sticky tape which is holding her view of the world together. Columba should take her to the optician in Elgin to see about mending her specs, but Columba no longer cottonwools Prue's world or lullabies her to sleep. How do you make an appointment with an optician anyway? What do you have to do? Prue doesn't even know how you manipulate a public phone. Maybe the sticky tape will hold, maybe her eyes won't deteriorate any further, maybe she doesn't really need to go again.

If only Mrs Gordon would adopt her. Prue daydreams about being Isabel's sister, co-owning Iain, eating broth with a big spoon at the scrubbed kitchen table, as of privileged right. At the same time she is deep in her book, *Lorna Doone*, and galloping over the Doone country, that world of glamorising words which make distress delicious. Over the dark-oak bookshelves a notice orders TOTAL SILENCE PLEASE, and when her adult fellow-readers of *The Scotsman* and *The Times* rustle the pages in turning them, or clear their throats, it echoes through the formal, book-lined room. The elderly gentleman beside her 'tut-

tut's' over a picture of the bearded, combat-jacketed figure of the young Fidel Castro vehemently gesticulating as he delivers a five-hour speech to the revolutionary people of Cuba. 'Castro – Communist dictator – very bad lot,' the hook-nosed man confides in a whisper to Prue, as if he could contain the observation no longer.

'Did he really speak for five hours without stopping?' whispers Prue.

'Aye. But that's nothing. He's been known to speak for seven hours on the trot. *Seven hours*. Imagine that.'

'Did anyone listen all that time?'

'Certainly. Listen to the speech or face the firing squad. *There's* liberation for you, young lady. Mind that, now.'

'Silence please.' The librarian frowns and the old man subsides. Isabel has told Prue that Fidel is not as bad as people say; he wants food, health and shelter for his people so he must be quite decent. Prue does not know how you decide, seeing only a military uniform and a mouth from which streams of excited words proceed and into which a Havana cigar is inserted. She is not really interested. Obligingly she assents to both sides of such arguments.

Prue reads on, reads deeply. Time and space collapse around her, her breathing becomes slow and regular and every sinew relaxes. Only the unreal Lorna in the non-existent Valley of the Doones has meaning for her now. As the vigilance of self-consciousness slackens, her hand beneath the table creeps to the comfort of the forbidden place between her legs. *No, no. Wrong. Mustn't. Bad place, horrible*. Blushing with shame, she looks round stealthily. Did anyone see? – Did that man? – She feels as if they must all know. Prue never does *that thing*. Prue wouldn't, she's nice, and God can see if you do; he writes it down in his notebook. All that nastiness of January floods into her memory but *no, no*, she beats it out and slams the door on it; sinks down into the deep-piled luxury of the cushioning pages and finds there as complete a rest as any she can know.

*

The maimed girl fawns upon her mother. She shadows her round the house, from room to room; she will not let go, will not let her be, and even waits outside the lavatory door when Mary pays a visit. Like a death's-head she is there grinning behind her whenever Mary turns, with her battered face and the profundity of her need.

Irritation seethes in Mary at the girl's refusal to put herself away somewhere, so that she doesn't have to see her. She'd send her outdoors, but how can she, bearing this evidence of ill-treatment – she'll have to be kept home from school, damn it, she can't be sent to school like that.

'You'll just have to tell them you was in a fight, that's all.'

January nods vehement agreement. 'Yes, Mammy.'

'What is it you want, why do you keep following me around all the blessed time?'

'Mammy. Love Janny, Mammy. Love Janny.' The child snakes her arm round Mary's waist and presses up upon her. Mary recoils.

'Stop it, you're not a baby.'

'Mammy. Janny want Mammy.' She grasps Mary hard and snuggles her head down upon her shoulder. She is slightly the stronger and taller. Though Mary struggles, the child limpets on tighter, grinding her head against Mary's collar-bone.

'Oh do get off, you're hurting.'

'Cuddle Janny, Mammy cuddle,' January insists.

Mary wrenches away but January cleaves to her, battling closer. With both arms she squeezes on her mother's

166

rib-cage, as if to squeeze love out, like meagre juice from a withered orange.

'Leave me alone, you're a bad girl, you. Bad. You're bad. From the day you was born you was nothing but trouble.'

'Not love Janny?' The child's grip loosens.

'Stop that baby-talk.' Mary is incensed with fear and revulsion. As she twists away, the tentacular grip is broken and both Mary and her daughter are free-standing, floating clear. 'How could *anyone* love *you*?' Mary hears herself shout.

January shrinks into herself. The longing to be held and hugged, to be gathered up and gathered in, to be tenderly soothed and told to *hush, it's all right, I'm here, you're all right now, all right* is so deep that it must be answered, it can't not. Always there was a hole, a gap, a nought, a big round O where this necessary embrace should have been. In her waking life she denies this need but her unconscious mind endlessly chases back to the time antecedent to Time to try to catch a wispy, fugitive memory of the fulfilment she now demands, at point-blank range, from her mother. Snaring the hem of a dream, she can sometimes know for sure that there was a time, earlier than the beginning, before Before, when she was completely safe and tucked out of harm's way, contained like the kernel in the nut-shell, the pip in the apple-flesh.

How could anyone love you? She is spat out, voided.

She sees the sharp vegetable knife, the kitchen-devil, glinting on the formica-topped table amongst a pile of half-chopped swede. She stares at the knife, whose yellowing bone handle and fine, serrated edge fascinate her eye. She can imagine the bone handle lying in the palm of her hand, and the blade, how she'd stick it in her, plunge it

167

in and out and kill, kill, kill, and then she'd be sorry. Picking up the knife, she weighs it in her hand.

'Got a knife here,' she remarks matter-of-factly.

'No – darling no – I didn't meant it, put that down.'

Mary backs toward the door, horrified. The girl just stands there, with her mouth hanging open, her shock of lank dark hair falling forward into her eyes. She tries out the knife-blade against the back of her hand, producing a fine, pink line. Having contemplated this in fascination, as if sleep-walking, she glances up into Mary's eyes, as if to indicate something they ought both of them to take into account,

'Sharp, innit?'

Outside a bedlam of boys' voices hails the arrival of the lorry selling fizzy pop which parks on the corner of Passchendaele and toots its horn. Peter spills into the kitchen, bawling 'Corona-man!' The tension breaks like an elastic-band. January suddenly yawns and puts the knife down. She forgets what she was saying. What was it? She doesn't know. The pressure cooker is hissing and spouting steam like a geyser on the stove; the potatoes jostle and thump around in it. With shaking hands, Mary adds the cubes of swede. Out of the corner of her eye she observes January who is vacantly preoccupied with the game of soldiers Peter and Paul have set up, having grizzled for fizzy pop to no effect. Has the child gone mad?

'What was you going to do with that thing anyway?' she asks January, nodding toward the knife.

'What with?'

'With the knife, of course.'

'Don't know. Nothing.'

'You picked it up. You threatened me with it.'

January shakes her head. She peers at her mother

through her expressionless eyes, dark as currants, as if she's sure she once met her but can't at present place her.

'No,' she insists. 'Didn't do nothing,' and begins to rock herself to and fro.

8

Isla Gordon sits at the living-room window
threading a needle. The eye of the needle seems to blink
whenever the black thread approaches it. She sucks the
thread between her lips and pinches the end; looks away
out of the window to refocus her addled eyes, and has
another go, screwing up her brow in concentration. Will
it? It won't; the needle definitely declines to be threaded,
as her mother used to say, years ago, but she can hear the
voice as clear as yesterday. That was a tough, durable
bond, for all its reticence, surviving the apparent terminus
of death with such tenacity that she often chats with her
mother in her mind as if she were really there. It is easy
to imagine what her mother would have thought upon
any issue; hence she can be reconstructed at will and
debated with – such a straight if narrow mind, never
conformist but full of Biblical certainty, blessedly free of
her own, uncomfortable awareness of Biblical contradiction. One last attempt. Part of the thread consents to be
introduced into the needle's eye; she nips it between finger
and thumb and pulls. The thread splits, one fine line
entering the needle and the other snagging as it coils down
over the remaining thread. Where is her mother now? Did
she get through the needle's eye? *Shall I?* The chestnut
leaves are just beginning, she notes, to turn yellow. They

kindle faintly at the tips under the cold, crisp sun and soon the children will be out there conkering. She recalls the pleasure of that, swinging her well-polished nut on a knotted string. She must do things with Isabel this autumn, lovely things, all sorts of excursions they'd either never thought of or never brought themselves to afford. The evergreens will soon be thick with cones. As children they used to hoard them in caches – under numbered and coded stones in drystone walls, between the roots at the base of secret trees. Years later at the appointed season they would excavate and bring to light these treasures. *Here, wasn't it here, Lizzie, that we buried the jet-black stone?* Their fingers delved the fibrous peat. *Look here's the long cone shaped like a carrot.* That is how life should be – a provident honeycomb of half-forgotten but ever-accessible memorials. We were here. We did no harm. This was our world. Her thoughts of early days are quiet and tranquil – and unbelievably consolatory. It's as if these things could never entirely die away. What they must do is to get hold of a car and go out more into the country; store up plentiful memories to last Isabel out through the coming years. At the hatching of this bright idea, she sits up straight on the window-seat and smiles to herself. The thread glides quite painlessly through the eye of the needle.

How on earth did the tramp get through the pantry window, though? she keeps asking herself. He must have been a decidedly thin man, to say the least – if a man it was, rather than a lad. Donald was convinced the culprit must have been one of those good-for-nothing, vandalising children of the camp. He was all for calling in the police and getting it investigated.

'But look', she pointed out, 'there's no damage done –

just a wee bit of food eaten and some superficial mess in the bedrooms.'

'And what about your nightgown? Slashed to ribbons and stuck back under the pillow. What about that?' asked Donald. 'Some pervert, evidently, who should not be roaming loose.'

'Some poor soul with his mind half gone,' she replied soothingly. 'Let it be now, Donald. There's no harm done – all's well.'

He could deny her little. Like a sorry bairn he rushed to do her bidding, as if in tender, belated attempt to remedy years of domineering and hectoring. He sighed deeply and bent his head. She put her hand over his great brow in momentary token of blessing, as if to brush away all his unspoken anxieties about her health and well-being.

'You're all right? You're sure you're all right?' he asked for the hundredth time.

'I'm fine – fine. Stop worrying. The doctor said so and I say so.'

'You're quite sure?'

'Donald! When I'm not I'll tell you so. Dinna *fash* yoursel.' Her irritation and the sudden little blurt of dialect from her childhood reassured him.

'Had we best put some window-locks on the accessible windows?' he enquired mildly. 'Of course most of the ground-floor sash-windows are jammed or painted in, so they should be quite secure.'

'Whatever you think best, dear.'

Donald went to work with his screw-driver and that settled his mind. After all, what was it but an episode out of Goldilocks and the Three Bears? Nevertheless, it was an odd feeling to know that a stranger had penetrated her world, using her bed and crockery, wearing her bath-hat, emptying Isabel's drawers, but with inexplicable scrupulosity, taking nothing at all away with him. It left you fractionally uneasy. She laundered all the bed-clothes and towels and hung them on the line in a goodish wind; they flapped and somersaulted and wound themselves round the line. When she fetched them in, she held the purified swathes of sheet in her arms and smelt the fresh air in them. The strangeness was washed away, leaving only a sense of querying compassion. There were so many people who needed help and had a right to help; who could wonder that they helped themselves?

That evening at supper, she confided to Donald, 'I don't believe there should be any such thing as private property. There cannot be, in all justice.'

He stopped chewing his lamb chop and stared.

'That is a Communist doctrine,' he replied in a clipped tone, as if this were in itself a repudiation that, properly speaking, clinched the matter.

'No, dear, it is a Christian opinion.'

He swallowed the mouthful of meat only with the help of a mouthful of water, to avoid choking. First his daughter declares herself a righteous atheist, now his wife is a saintly Red.

'So you are now a devotee of Karl Marx?' he enquired in a neutral tone, rolling the 'r's in a kind of skirl. 'Tell me, Isla, didn't he despise religion as the opiate of the masses?'

'Yes but I've often felt he said some genuinely Christian things: "From each according to his abilities, to each according to his needs". What's wrong with that? It is very close to the Sermon on the Mount, if you think about it.'

He stared at her for a long while, or so it seemed, absorbed in the perception of her, as if her complexity were something new to him entirely. Of course Isla is a very innocent person, and contact with the naive fanaticism of the Aberdeen kin was always likely to be inflammatory.

'How do you propose to implement this Christian Communism? It's a fallen world. We give to charity. We care for the sick and the distressed in our parish. We can scarcely be said to live in the lap of luxury. What do you propose?'

'Oh I don't know, I can't say. It's all words, isn't it, hollow words, and vanity and self-indulgence. And people go on suffering. And there's no help for them.' Her face worked with grief, ugly and distorting and naked.

'No, it's not vanity, beautiful Isla.'

On the impulse of the moment, he took her hand and kissed it repeatedly.

*

Prue pauses in the doorway. There is Mrs Gordon in the bay of the window sewing buttons on to shirts. It is a picture of such peace and stillness that Prue fears to disturb it by the merest ripple of her presence. She watches the figure, so private and solitary, drawing the thread up into the air and rhythmically returning it to the button and the cloth. Mrs Gordon is in silhouette against the high, broad window which tips in light upon her greying head and the earth-coloured cardigan sleeve which dips to pierce the cloth and rises to tauten the thread. But the mass of her face and body is deeply shadowed. Iain sleeps at her feet, head on paws, leonine in his bulk and goldenness. Prue is as aware of the double frame – the window-frame within the door-frame – as of the person; she is aware of a silence surrounding her, a remoteness. There is always the overwhelming urge to run to this woman, to beg pardon, to obtain counsel – if she had the words, which she has not. At the same time, there is a sense of awe and shame. If Mrs Gordon knew the horrible way she and her family lived, she would under no circumstances open the door to her, ever again.

'Is it Prue?' Isla has not looked up. Prue tentatively crosses the threshold.

'How did you know it were me – I mean, was me?'

'Oh, I have second sight. No. I can nearly always tell a person by the way he walks. It's rather a useful skill. I heard you coming – you have such a light tread, as if you tiptoed through life so as not to waken people – quite unlike any child I've known. Then you paused, and the floor gave a little squeak. When I heard the squeak I thought: Now she's going to creep away like a wee kelpie into nowhere. So I spoke. Was I right?'

'Yes.' Prue blushes and gives a shy, suppressed grin. She looks up into Mrs Gordon's face, biting her lower lip, and her eyes say, unmistakably, 'You are lovely. I love you.' Isla reads the worship and a pang goes through her.

'Let me say something to you. Now, while there is time, and we are on our own.'

Prue nods; an anxious frown puckers her forehead. It sounds serious; there is always the fear that she might have been found out and seen through.

'Some day, Prue, you will leave here. How do you put it, your father will be moved on to some new place – stationed . . . ?'

'Posted.' Tears spring to Prue's eyes. This is the word which above most others she can least bear to hear.

'Aye, posted. Well, Prue, when you find yourself in some new place, that place will not be the end of the world, as you now imagine.'

Prue says nothing. The welling tears spill down her

cheeks and she rubs them furtively away with the back of her hand. New tears gather, constricting her throat.

'You must remember all your life, you were loved and valued here. That does not simply go away, Prue, it is something you have for your life, you carry it with you. You cannot lose it. And the fact that you were valued here by all of us means that you can win that regard wherever you go. Because you are yourself. Because you are Prue.' She puts out a hand to the child, taking one of hers and gripping it firmly. 'Will you be able to remember this? Remember I spoke to you today and what I said?'

'Yes, Mrs Gordon,' says Prue quietly. She thought just then she saw tears in Mrs Gordon's own eyes; she retains the pressure from the hand even though it has now been withdrawn and is doing a business-like job finishing off the sewing of the button.

'That's a good girl.' Isla looks round for the scissors but can't find them and bites off the cotton. 'Did you know someone broke in while we were away?'

'Did he? Did he take any of your lovely things?' Prue looks round the room apprehensively.

'No, poor man, he just came in from the cold.'

Prue recalls how she had sat in the boughs of the beech reading about the Massacre of Glencoe, and how she thought she saw the ghost of a face flash in the window. She wonders if she ought to say anything; opens her mouth, closes it again and feels guilty. But reflects that if Mrs Gordon doesn't mind tramps and beggars and burglars poking around in her house, then why should she say anything?

Iain, awakening, gives a great yawn, his mouth stretching right back to bare his yellowish teeth. It makes Prue yawn too. She laughs and crouches down to fondle the dog's forehead and bronze coat.

176

'Dozy great creature,' says Mrs Gordon. 'He's becoming quite soft and sedentary in his old age.'

'Is he old?'

'Fifteen. Elderly for a dog this size.'

'Mrs Gordon, don't you honestly mind the burglar getting in? Not at all? Not even a little bit?' Prue looks up at Isla with timid curiosity. There is so much she does not comprehend. If it were possible to interrogate and cross-question Mrs Gordon exhaustively, answers might come, but she is never sure what the questions ought to be that would snare these answers like hooks and eyes done up in a row.

'Oh, Prue. One minds and then one questions the minding. Why should some have so much and others nothing at all? It cannot be fair. In that sense, he was welcome.'

Prue does not know if she can approve such indulgent hospitality. And once you let in one of the despised and rejected, how about all the rest?

'But what if there were fifteen tramps that all wanted to come in, Mrs Gordon? Or fifty? Or a hundred? What if they all crowded in and set up camp?' Prue's imagination crowds the Manse with dossing down-and-outs, all drunken, smelly and filthy, the alien men you get off the pavement to avoid when you see them coming. What if the Manse played open-house as a refuse for derelicts?: the have-nots would take over from the haves, and the space and amplitude of Mrs Gordon's benign world would choke on its own hospitable excess. The unbidden guests who'd all got in on the same ticket of universal charity would cram the place from wall to wall, edging even the personally invited Prue out of her privileged, if humble, corner.

'You're right,' Isla sighs. She knots a new thread and draws the needle carefully through the cloth. 'I can only

177

cope with one at a time. With what's to hand. Had you not noticed', she says, more to herself than to Prue, 'that there is a flaw right at the centre of things?'

A floor at the centre of things, thinks Prue. *A floor at the centre of things.* She will want to turn that one over in her mind. Beneath these unstable, shifting surfaces, a floor. A ground that holds firm, like the bare boards of this living room, with their nice knots and whorls and uneven patches that her eyes ruminatively play on, and the few mats hand-woven with designs inscrutable because fading. Yes, she can see it now, the floor at the centre of things, floating like a raft that holds steady in a weltering sea.

'Yes,' says Prue softly. 'Yes.' She plants her feet apart and looks down at her white-socked, thick ankles and the second-hand Clarks sandals that pinch her high instep, and which she has left off polishing since Columba went off with Duncan (that weed, that pimply weed). She stands sturdy and balanced on the floor at the centre of things.

'How would you like to take Iain for a walk?'

'Do you mean, on my own?'

'Yes, it would have to be. Isabel is practising her piano for her Grade Three examination, and then she must go to the dentist.'

'But would you trust me with him?'

'Of course I would. But you'll have to hang on tight, Prue – he's terribly strong, he'll pull you off your feet. But he's biddable. If he runs off, whistle and he'll come lolloping back. Will you be all right?'

'Oh *yes*.'

Electricity flows through Prue's veins and glitters in her eyes as Iain is fitted up with his lead. Her face burns fiery red with the excitement she tries to suppress and her heart bounds and bounces like a yoyo on a string.

178

'Go up the road to the Housty Estate, I should, and walk him through the wood. Keep to the path.'

Isla receives the signal of the child's hectic, secret joy through the tremble of her hands as she clasps the lead, and the almost painful ecstasy of the quick look she casts her as she turns away. An impression of Prue's gentle presence stays with her in the child's wake, a delicacy that is also somehow neediness – a neediness that blinks out silently through thick-paned spectacles, slightly cock-eyed and mended with sticky tape. A disquieting quietism. A blur of smoke signals drifts indecipherably from a distant hill, the semaphore of a match-stick figure almost out of focus. She turns her eyes away. She is weary, weary. The last button is stitched on; she puts away the workbox. A cynical feeling of futility all but overcomes her. What is the point of it all anyway? Other people's children, other people's problems – the endlessly harassing, tedious worry about the great bruise of the Creation, about which one is powerless to do anything significant, for what is not God's fault is man's fault (not hers, certainly), and no detailed intervention of hers can straighten what is out of true in the warp and weft of its fabric. Why bother? At this stage, why bother? She is like a visitor to a foreign country whose visa has almost expired and who now, shaking her head at the chaos indigenous to the place, prepares to board for the journey home.

*

Iain drags Prue down the long, straight white ribbon of a bridle path alongside which runs a high wall with rhododendron bushes and, at the end of the wall, one spectacular Scots pine, shrunk to a shrub in the vista of the large perspective. Iain flies her like a kite, she bobs and soars, her heart as high-flown as the few dunlins and

179

gulls the wind-currents chuck about the turbulent grey sky. She leans back against the drag of his shoulders that muscle forward, and alternately totters and pitches as he bears her toward the scents that tow him in their irresistible wake.

'Iain, slow down – heel, boy, heel!' But the dog ploughs on, panting ardently; the leather leash rasps her hand and wrenches her arm in its socket, for he wants his way so badly, and must have it, and will. In the midst of Prue's pride at having sole charge of the beautiful creature palpitates the fear that he will bolt and won't come back – she will have lost him and the trust she ached to engage.

'Don't run away, Iain – don't, *please.*' One mighty yank, and he's away, bounding down the white roadway and then cutting off at an angle to the little burn which runs alongside, keeping up a commentary of a suppressed gurgle and murmur. There he noses and ferrets excitedly, slithering about on the wet, overhanging grass of the bank and presenting only his great bronze hindquarters to Prue's anxious eye. She puts two fingers to her mouth and whistles piercingly; and again. Snuffling and scrambling up the bank, he trots obligingly back to Prue and looks up at her.

'Bad dog,' Prue rebukes him, fondling his cold, wet face. The countryside is so still and large around them as they continue outward bound; not a bird, not an animal, not a human being to be seen or heard. There is only the intensely felt reality of the creature's life journeying alongside Prue, and Prue's life bonded to it by the leash, as centred and confirmed as it will ever be. Their breath condenses and is chased away as, like whipped hoops, they bowl downhill toward the pine at the apex of the crossroads.

The autumnal wind soughs through its upper branches,

tossing the outer ones about but leaving stillness at the centre, in the lee of whose blue-green gloom Prue stands, braille-reading the scroll of its flaky bark with her finger-tips. When she looks around her, the countryside has a strangeness, an intense otherness which makes her shiver. *So here I am*, thinks Prue, and that seems strange too, as if she had just been put down at the centre of this scene and left to her own devices by someone unknown, out of nowhere. She overheard her own breathing as if she were as foreign to herself as the dog, as the respiring air that soughs in the pine; she sees the hand on the leash as if it belonged to another person, a person with plump, stubby fingers, nails very much bitten and none to clean. But *this is me*, thinks Prue, *not like any other person; just myself.* And knowing this, accepting it involuntarily, is like coming out of hiding. She has spent her whole life like the beetles and toads they sometimes unearth under stones (and she hates it when the boys stamp on the insects or pick up the unprotected green-brown mottled toads in their dry hands that must hurt the toads all over their delicate skins that need to be moist and chilly to be happy). She has pretended not to be there, as if you could curl up and disappear into yourself in eternal hibernation, and she has never affirmed *I am Prue* quite as she does now, to the flying slate-grey skies and the salty wind with the bitter edge and the running grasslands and the distant woods of the Laird's estate.

'Come on then, you.'

Prue steps out of the skirts of the pine and lets Iain drag her toward the forest.

*

The severely disorientated January squats by a hydrant on Passchendaele Terrace, hunkering down with her hurts beneath the lowering skies like a sad, savage animal that retires to lick its wounds. All her short life she has been a scavenger, a fighter, a never-say-die; when they knocked her down she bounced straight back up again, like one of those tiny magic balls they sold in Woolworth's which flew up ceiling-high if you so much as dropped it lightly – and, if you whacked it, it ricocheted madly between floor and ceiling, and gave you one in the eye if you got in the way. Now she has taken a fall and finds she can't get up. Whichever way she angles herself, she is lead-heavy; there is no fight in her; she is down. Shock makes havoc of her very guts. She couldn't stop shitting this morning, and even now there is the feeling she might shit her pants if she lets go. She shrinks back against the cold, bile-green metal of the hydrant, her navy gaberdine inadequate protection against the scything wind that penetrates cuffs and neck, and whips her legs, which she now pulls up to her chest, deriving some elementary satisfaction from picking at the scabs from old falls and collisions.

The ganging boys swagger insolently along the middle of the road, over the chalked hopscotch pitches, kicking cans. They are the crew-cutted jetsam of the Privates' children with whom January has often been tree-climbing, graffiti-daubing and Paki-baiting; one of them, yet not one of them. She's a bent girl, a bad apple, a clock wound up and ticking backwards, in their eyes – a freak. They jeer behind her back and to her face. She's fought with most of them, biting and clawing, aiming to kick them where it hurts. She gets hammered but she won't give up. She's as good as any boy, any day. Forever prowling the margins of the tribal hierarchy, she insists on her right to a place in the group. You prove your right in single combat. Like a dominant pack of male gorillas, they alternately tolerate and turn upon her with bared teeth. She has always asserted her rights head-on. Dived at their legs in a flying tackle when they're least expecting it; or, on a celebrated occasion which won her some short-lived respect, dropped down in ambush on Micky Drew, the 15-year-old bully at the apex of the pyramid as he lit a fag under a wall; cracked his head open against a stone and concussed him enough to require the attendance of the MO.

Her entire lack of physical fear meant that the gang could exploit her as an expendable vanguard or reconnoitring party. She stole from the NAAFI for the pack and led them against the Boy Scouts pow-wowing in the Housty Woods, singing *ging-gang-gooly* round their campfire while the gang sabotaged their wooden shelters, built so laboriously without the aid of string, out of woven sticks thatched with bracken and leafage. *Ging-gang-goo, ging-gang-goo*, chorused Lord Baden Powell's sterling citizens-to-be, baking potatoes in the red embers, which they prodded with sticks according to jungle lore. *Haila! haila shaila!* they warbled in half-broken voices, and their billy cans steamed in a row, hung from a metal rack of their own devising. January and the gang crept behind their black silhouetted backs and systematically dismantled their houses, depositing their sleeping bags and nightwear in a handy pool. *Haila shaila ging-gang-goo!* roared the Scouts, drunk with fresh air and invigorating activity, their faces scalded by the crackling fire. Archaila, the Latin master at the Academy, who on Monday would be administering to them their *hic haec hoc*, sat hot and relaxed from the fire and the whisky secreted in his sleeping-bag, and singing out boldly from under his moustaches in a magnificent bass, the morale-boosting message, *Shally wally, shally wally, shally wally, oompah oompah oompah oompah*; while the gang slunk off, camouflaging hoots of half-suppressed laughter as nocturnal bird-calls, and carrying with it a rich booty which included Archaila's stopwatch, his compasses and his ordnance survey map as well as the whisky bottle.

Now the gang struts past, in a state of rampant boredom, hands-in-pockets, whistling and discharging uncouth remarks at passers-by. Some are armed with sticks, with which they either fence among themselves or aimlessly wallop lampposts or the kerb. They are almost past the cowering girl before one of them spots her.

'Blimey, what's *she* doing there? Sun-bathing, are you? Counting ants? Waiting for a dog to pee on you?'

'Nah, she's wanking.'

'Wanker, wanker!'

January stares. She pulls a minimally energetic face, by raising the right side of her lip toward her nose, and replies automatically but in a voice that comes out thin and tremulous, 'Get lost.'

'Who give you the black eye then, Rat-face?'

She shrugs. The encircling boys hover at a little distance, making feints toward her, threatening her space.

'I can see her pants. She's got blood on her pants.'

She squints up at Jacko Jackson. January can normally take on Jacko and beat him one-handed. Jacko the monkey. Jacko the weed. Emaciated, feeble, greasy-haired, crafty in manner but without the necessary intelligence to inform it, he's right at the bottom of the pile of boys. Now he's asking to be punched. But this time his taunt seems to kindle a red pain in the place between her legs, an unholy, hot feeling of intense unease. She blushes scarlet and jumps to her feet, legs tight together. Jacko dances at her, feinting with his fists, head down in imbecile parody of a flyweight boxer.

'Let's see your spare parts,' pants Jacko, jabbing the air with his sharp knuckles. 'Go on, give us an eyeful.'

His eyes and his sparring fists dart in and out, his eyes that are prune-brown like her own, in a sickly white face like her own, and are mindlessly expressionless except when they register the brief, soon-curdling satisfaction of retaliatory malevolence. She is frightened of those mirroring eyes.

'Give it her, Jacko. Go on, give it her.'

As the eyes dance nearer, January quails before their invasiveness and doesn't know why. She winces back, bumping into the hydrant. Tears prick her eyes.

'No, Jacko,' she begs, never having begged before. 'Don't. Don't.'

'Say please.' He puffs out his pigeon-chest.

'Please,' she mutters.

'Okay,' he agrees, to his own surprise and hers. His aggressiveness sags and deflates like a balloon, almost with relief. It's not often that he scores a submission. 'Want a bit of licorice?'

January accepts the licorice. It doesn't taste of anything; it's like chewing a length of string, or rubber. Nothing tastes at all any more.

'Who done your eye?'

'Me dad.'

'What for?'

'Dunno. Just messing about.'

'Want to come and scrag the officers' kids?' He extends the invitation not as to a comrade-in-arms but as to a fool who can be left to carry the can at the end of the day. In their revolutionary raids on the small park for officers' children with its swings, slide and roundabout, January's assaults are rash to the point of frenzy. While the mass of the ruffians prudently scarpers at the first sign of parents, let alone military police, January courts sacrifice and notoriety by remaining at the fence of the tennis-court lobbing over stones, until the dogs are almost on them. *Street Arabs, riff-raff, dregs, plebs, gutter-children, the great unwashed*, the officers nominate them, in the high-pitched nasal singsong of a scarcely penetrable dialect of English such as is scarcely known in civilian life. Floribunda roses festoon their gardens, and ornamental shrubs straight from the nursery, still wearing their explanatory labels. By lamplight on summer evenings you hear the drawl of their voices as they sip sherry by the open windows. Chars visit their houses every other day, and the postman tips his cap to them.

'Come on,' Jacko encourages her. 'Let's go and give it them right up their arse.'

But she can't go, even if she wanted to. As she steps away from the hydrant, there suddenly seems too much space around her. There is nothing to cling on to, just the queasy emptiness of air in all directions, without bearings or anchor-points. Before her there is space, behind her there is space. She lists and sways at the kerbside, staring round in anxiety. If she looks forward she cannot defend her back. If she turns round her front is blind.

'No,' she says. 'I'm staying.'

'Suit yourself.'

The proletariat takes off, drumming its sticks against a parked grocery van and a Morris Minor, and emitting impolite noises.

The raw wind moans a meaningless dirge in the telegraph poles, as January crouches down. Once she climbed up one of them, three-quarters of the way up to the top, taking the idea from a native up a coconut tree she saw in a film; if he could do it, she could. She made herself a sling like his, and hitched her way right up there where the chilled sparrows gather now like ink-blots against the grey sky. How tiny people looked from up there. What a shock they got when they saw her; one woman nearly fainted. January waved. She did not feel scared. She looked down upon them all. Now she's afraid even of the German woman from Number 4, old *Sauerkraut*, fat Gertrud, in whose wake they are wont to hare along hollering 'Eva Braun! Eva Braun!' She cowers back against the hydrant as old *Sauerkraut* passes, and shuts her eyes as if this will prevent her being seen. In her weakened state even that helpless loner could haul her out and do for her.

Gertrud Binny passes on her way with stately slowness, pushing her baby in a second-hand, but refurbished pram, whose chrome she has polished to gleaming perfection. The baby, Elisabeth, is the pride and joy of her life; the pram perhaps the second. She has few other joys or vanities to sustain her in this standoffish, foreign wilderness, where her mother-tongue remains locked up in her mouth and her neighbours cross the road when they see her coming. She talks to herself and the baby *auf Deutsch, in der Muttersprache, der Heimatsprache*, never in English. The baby, like Moses in Egypt, may have no choice but to exist in this desolate prison-camp but will never belong to it, and one day will escape on both their behalfs to the land of Goethe and Schiller, of *Bratkartoffeln mit Wurst*, of kindness and kin. Meanwhile she parades the blessed child, to the undoubted envy of the feckless English housewives, with their catarrhal infants and their undisinfected doorsteps. Spotting the Cahill child lurking by the hydrant, she detours slightly on to the grass verge and gives a pre-emptive glare; is vaguely surprised that the hooligan girl abstains from her usual manic taunting – which, indeed, she does not blame on the child, for what can you expect when a human is brought up like a pig in a pigsty? You expect an *Untermensch*, and that is what you get.

January peers through the gap in the quarters at the

countryside beyond the camp, which thrusts its green slopes forward with an effect of foreshortening. Always that excites January's appetite – the sense of open spaces beyond this rat-trap. Some mornings the pang of appetite to be out there, to be in it, crazes her like new-baked crusty bread to watering taste-buds. It is the sense of Scotland all around, like a dazzling sea encircling their drab island of uniformity. Out there, the great Carse, the Glebe and meadowlands, the Housty Estate lie waiting, a licit roaming-ground where no one can keep track of you. Out there you get off scot-free. Only today the allure of the scene has been replaced by threat. Out there you are nobody. Nobody. Out there you are alone with the gunmetal skies and the unequal conflict of wind and beaten grasses cowering all one way.

*

Prue and Iain turn reluctantly for home, at the appointed place: the barred gates to the Laird's mansion, where the notice FORBIDDEN TO STRANGERS caps the series of discouraging messages lining the public way, each of which Prue has read with trepidation: TRESPASSERS PROSECUTED: GHILLY HAS GUN; BE WARNED, KEEP OFF PRIVATE PROPERTY. In the heart of the woods you scarcely feel the wind. You are screened and canopied by the great, still bodies of beech and rowan, pine and fir. A few shed leaves come drifting down through light thick and aqueous from the tarnished pewter skies and the shadowing trees. Prue catches them for luck, before they fall to earth. They spiral slowly, gilded with earliest autumn. Prue lingers beside the gate, in hopes to encounter the Laird himself. She has occasionally bumped into him in his plus-fours, his cloth cap, Wellingtons and hacking-jacket, like a dawdler from another era altogether. The game-keeper is gruff and off with you, but the Laird is sprucely courteous, even to children, his manner obscurely at variance with his hostile notices. Of course, the Laird would recognise the Manse's dog. He would recognise Prue as a somebody.

Prue idles along the path. Giant, slow bubbles of joy swell and rise to the surface of her mind and there grow exquisitely tense with the thought *here I am; this is me*, and then they burst with the pride of it all, the go of the dog that snuffles the trackside on its long leash, the imagining that she is admiringly observed by many eyes. What Mrs Gordon said about the floor at the centre of things was lovely; she will always remember that. Safe; safe and secure; safe as houses. Prue's broad, high-instepped feet step out now across the steadfastness of a world that holds itself wonderfully still so that she may pass over it in safety.

God is here, God is all around her. Stopping in her tracks, she sees it suddenly. Iain stops too, simultaneously, his head erect; he sniffs the air. Prue feels the angels cluster round them, between the pillars of the trees and the feathery, evergreen boughs pendant and still, legion upon legion, millions of see-through, airy presences. More strongly even than the crowding angels, Prue intuits the imminent closeness of the Blessed Virgin, mantling everything. The break in the clouds admitting a patch of blue air is the extreme edge of her cloak.

She is coming, she will come.

Prue holds her breath. Prue feels herself beckoned. The pent breath exhales in a series of little throbs. There, over there. She is led off the path into the arcane depths of the forest, past the notice reading TRESPASSERS BEWARE, through brambles and ladyfern, into the virgin depths. She knows exactly where to go; has dropped the tether but Iain follows, crashing along behind her through the undergrowth.

In a glade, between a charcoal-grey ash tree and the cinders of an old camp-fire, stands Our Lady, awaiting Prue. Our Lady is dressed in a blue cape, a white wimple like a nun's, and a pale, flowing robe. Her figure, whose back is turned to Prue, seems considerably larger than life, about eight foot tall perhaps, but whether the impression of height is caused by her levitation above the earth (she floats on air, she does not rest on soil) one could not say. At Prue's advent into the glade, the figure unhurriedly turns and ponders Prue with sad, reflective eyes. Iain whimpers, and backs to the nearest tree, precipitated by the forcefield of the living air, round which volts of static electricity seem to flow. The lady's face is a mild and compassionate oval, exactly as the picture-books represent her. Prue sinks to her knees in the soft humus, at the moment of recognition, and crosses herself with reverence. Her peace is charged with fear and her fear returns to peace: a complete circuit of emotion, beautiful and terrifying. Prue begins to pray:

> Hail Mary full of Grace
> The Lord is with thee
> Blessed art thou amongst women

The blessed Virgin waves the prayer aside; such formal words get in the way and cause her to fade. When Prue stops chanting, she appears more vivid, her gown phosphorescent as moonlight, her veil shimmering like violet mist. She is a person without distinct contour, her garments a radiant haze of white, blue and grey lights.

'Come closer, my child,' bids the Blessed Virgin.

Prue scrambles to her feet and moves closer, shamefacedly wiping the palms of her earthy hands on her gaberdine. The Blessed Virgin puts out one slender hand but Prue shrinks back and dare not take it. She stares up hypnotised into the maternal eyes that have compassed every human travail and sorrow. On Our Lady's cheeks two tears stand like the dew. Prue quivers and looks down. Our Lady bends over Prue's bent head; Prue is aware of the soft weight of her hand on the crown of her head and her breath upon her cheek.   ⊙

'Every hair of your head is numbered,' whispers the Blessed Virgin to Prue Cahill.

A shot is fired, a second: *crack, crack*, they echo through the timber, with a whiff of gunpowder. Prue, starting up, whirls round. Almost simultaneously, Iain bolts hell-bent through the glade and out the other side, dragging his leash and barking wildly. Prue looks right through the Blessed Virgin into the lumpy face of the Laird's gamekeeper. His rifle is over his left arm, still smoking.

'Whit did ye think ye were aboot?'

'Pardon?'

'I *said*, whitdidyethinkyewereaboot? Whit did ye think I said?'

'I were praying,' replies Prue simply.

'Praying? Holy Moses! Now I've heard it aw. Did ye nae ken ye were trespassing?'

Prue shakes her head.

'Can ye nae read, lass. Are ye no *literate*?'

'Yes, I can read.'

'So whit does yon notice say?'

'Pardon?' Prue's difficulty in following his excited dialect adds to his fury.

'The notice means get oot and keep oot and stay oot. Hae ye got it now? Ye could be shot or prosecuted in a court. That your dog?'

'No – a friend's.' She collars Iain and backs off. 'Can we go home now? I'm sorry we came into your wood.'

'It's no *my* wood, girrul. It's the Laird's.'

Prue hears it as *The Lord's*.

'Yes,' she repeats softly, and smiles as she turns away down the path. 'Yes it is. The Lord's wood.'

'Let that be a lesson to ye now.'

Prue waves back, benignly, all-forgivingly. For all is changed now, all. The Virgin Mary has appeared to her. She has been favoured of God. God has offered a safer hiding-place, a deeper camouflage. He has picked her up between finger and thumb with extraordinary care and put her away in his felt-lined pocket for all eternity. Singled her out. Her, Prue Cahill. She so unworthy. She who has sometimes come to the edge of disbelief in the past week in that hell at home, so much so that she heard Malachi call Father Friend 'that pseudy old queer' with an instinctive approval amounting to satisfaction. Now she has been vouchsafed a secret message from beyond the clouds, and she is transfigured, all life is transfigured. She has joined the ranks of the beatified.

Might I become a saint? thinks Prue headily. She imagines pilgrims coming from all over the world, to get a blessing or a cure, jostling for the chance to touch the hem of her cardigan: from Rome and Equador, from Cincinnati and France. After all, Saint Teresa of Lisieux and St Bernadette of Lourdes started out just ordinary girls and look what happened to them! Why not Prue too? She hopes it will not entail having to die young – martyrdom has no appeal, for all at once there seems so much reason to live; her world is lit through by a thrilling solace. Saint Prudence of Housty Woods. It doesn't sound quite right, not foreign enough to impress the ear. But if she's proud and stuck-up, the Blessed Virgin won't reveal herself again. She will withdraw her special attention and go elsewhere.

Mary Mother of God and mother of me, prays Prue in her silent heart. *I saw you. You came to me. I beg you now not to go away and leave me.*

They are out of the shelter of the woods. The wind bites and the pearl-grey skies pour down a piercing shine of Arctic light upon the unprotected eye. Iain races on before her toward the Scots pine at the junction of the ways, along the chalky track that curls on its downhill path through a long perspective of grasses and heathers. Prudence walks carefully, carrying her vision like a trophy she has won against all the odds, which must not be dropped or damaged in any way. Always there was the feeling, from the earliest days Prue can recall, of something or someone uncannily 'there': behind one's shoulder or round the next corner, a heartbeat away, a presence. If you could turn your head quickly enough (but you couldn't) or made a sharp enough dash (but Prue was never so nimble) you might catch a glimpse of whatever or whoever it was that sauntered just out of sight. The veil of the mundane fogged your eyes as you tried to peer through. You polished your glasses till every dust-speck vanished and you stared but you never quite saw. You constantly felt around for the edge of the colour-stained tissue that was laid on the surface of things to hide the something-else that lay on the other side, but the tissue was seamless. She always knew there was something underneath, something deeper than this veneer; it tickled irritatingly at her brain with provocative fingers, awakening her from bountiful dreams of great and plausible lucidity from which she started up saying to herself *I see*, but what it was she had seen she had forgotten. Now Prue has rounded the corner into that knowledge so secret she had thought it out of bounds to her, and seen what was there in broad daylight, on the other side.

What if I've grown a halo? She crouches over a puddle in a hollow of the path but there is only a homely, bespectacled face disturbed by wind-blown ripples.

She surrenders Iain at the door of the Manse to a strange woman, not Mrs Gordon but one of the elderly parishioners who help out with the flowers at church and prepare rose-hip jam and unfermented elderflower wine to be sold at bring-and-buy sales.

'Mrs Gordon is away to her bed, she is not so well this afternoon.'

9

Mrs Gertrud Binny stations her baby Elisabeth out in its pram for a regulation airing of one hour precisely. Everything has to be perfect and right for the little one, even to the organisation of its life on the almost military principles, gruelling alike for mother and child, advocated by the latest textbooks, which Gertrud has thoroughly studied. Fed on the hour every four hours, the infant is also exposed to trouncing blasts of fresh air on a potentially lethal basis. Its nappies are laundered to a fanatical cleanliness, ironed after a good blow on the line, and folded away with mathematical precision. Tirelessly knitting tiny bonnets and bootees for an offspring which already has an insane superfluity of such garments, Gertrud fulfils all the desiderata laid down by Trudy King and Dr Leary Benson for the Good Mother – all but one. She cannot bring herself to practise the required austerities with regard to holding back from excess cuddling, kissing and fondling her baby. She tries. Her breasts ache with milk that longs to be given; her arms reach out and she snatches them back. Baby must not be spoilt, Trudy King admonishes, Baby must not be given in to. Gertrud can't help herself breaking this rule, which, deep down, she doesn't really believe in, anyhow.

If it weren't for the baby, she couldn't bear it here; she

really couldn't. She'd get back on the ferry from Harwich to the Hoek and return to her native land, notwithstanding that all her family had died in the War. Even the gentle Eddie, her husband, with his idolising love and care, would not be enough to keep her here. Only the baby gets in between herself and her own entire dereliction, as if it had swollen morally to the status of a huge protector of her own small, dependent life. Elisabeth feeds and succours her, affording her identity from moment to moment. This morning she woke to find a swastika daubed on her wall, and she was *Heil Hitlered* in the NAAFI queue by a group of teenage youths, including Malachi Cahill from the worst family in their road. Several women in the queue had muttered sympathetically: 'It didn't ought to be allowed,' said one; 'Take no notice,' said another. But even so. And it angers her. How easily the boot might have been on the other foot, she often thinks – we might have won the War if a few things had gone our way that went against us, and then we'd have had an Army of Occupation over here. You'd be part of the Third Reich – no 'Great' in Britain then, just a province of Germany – and my God wouldn't you be licking our boots then! Well, it's been some comfort to see the contumely and arrogance of the British Empire crumbling in the last few years, beaten out of India, Egypt, Cyprus – the laughing stock of the world they were at Suez – and one day they'd be beaten out of Germany, too, not by force of arms maybe, but through economic decline. Maybe they'll be posted back to Germany next trip: Paderborn or Celle, Hildesheim or Mönchen Gladbach. She had married Eddie to get out of the ruins of Berlin at the end of the War; she'd waited ten years for this baby. The baby makes sense of it all. No one can rob her of the baby.

She parks Elisabeth a yard from the kitchen window at

1400 hours precisely. January watches. The pram is out of the lee of the house where the invigorating wind can fetch the infant a good, healthy swipe. Gusts spasmodically inflate the plastic hood and the canopy; they vehemently jingle the red and yellow rattle strung across the baby's line of vision. Three days have passed since Sauerkraut and her chariot passed January squatting at the hydrant – days of sick, pointless inertia, spent in part down an abandoned workmen's hole on the camp perimeter, sucking her thumb and fingering the bruise on her eye which has now changed from purple to livid green and yellow. She thought nothing and saw nothing, not even the clayey sides her eye was fixed on, or the grey wedge of sky she sometimes blinked at. Once in a while she went home to feed or sleep, and no person's eye met hers, they affected not to see her, they looked straight through her like a ghost. Now she sombrely observes Sauerkraut talking nonsense to the thing in the pram, *cutchy-coo*, she babbles, *ootchy-cutchy-coo*, reaching inside the hood with a smile; then flaps back indoors in her heelless pink carpet slippers and her capacious gingham apron. The pricy pram rocks on its silver frame at each buffet of the wind.

Sauerkraut's face peers out of the kitchen window to ascertain that all is in order, then disappears.

January approaches the pram and looks in. The baby stares back with an expression of mild reproof. Unhooking the rattles and canopy, January hoists the warmly swaddled bundle of baby out into the air and carries it away down the empty street, looking neither to left nor right.

In the moss-covered opening of an old wartime bomb-shelter at some distance from the quarters, she sits down with the baby and examines this imponderable weight of human life she has snatched up and appropriated to herself for no reason that she knows. She wedges the baby up against her bent knees so that it is facing her. The child seems to be made of knitting. A white woollen bonnet encloses its chubby face like a tight bandage; its jacket, leggings, bootees and mittens to match are Omo-bright, a launderer's dream. The child's uncanny eyes, violet-blue, stare at January from beneath an elderly, frowning forehead, as if seeking to frame some opinion about this turn of events. Its hands bat aimlessly, tied up with pink ribbons in their mittens. It whimpers but does not cry.

January begins to strip the baby. Under the bonnet, its head is downed with a pale brown fluff of hair. It is very soft. She strokes the hair again and again; pulls the infant forward and lays her cheek against it, rubbing it gently to and fro. The baby is a surrogate cat to pet, comforting January.

She encloses with the palm of her whole hand the skull of the baby. There are soft places in the bone which haven't closed over. If you pressed hard with your thumb, it would go right through the brain. The spongy, coiled-up beating brain, like the tripe the butcher displays on his slab. (She is fascinated by his eviscerations and disem-bowellings: the offal, giblets, collops, livers, kidneys and hearts that are the product of his trade. An honest trade, more honest than most, it appears to January. For we are no different to the animals, just a more successful kind of predator. A stronger species would hang our carcases on meat-hooks; slice and gut us; and serve us up as corned human hash or roast leg of man.)

The fontanelle pulses under her thumb. The vulner-ability of the creature panics her; its capacity to be hurt, its precariousness in her hold. If she dropped it now, the brittle baby would smash to bits. It depends on her to stay together; it needs her in order to go on breathing. January lets go her hold somewhat and the baby wobbles, its head a top-heavy fruit on a slender stem. She catches hold of it just as it's about to collapse sideways, and jounces it. The baby smiles, uncertainly. January smiles back.

But she hates the baby.

The baby is a German.

Germans are enemies.

The baby is an enemy.

'Bad baby,' accuses January fiercely. 'Bad. Bad baby.' The baby crows with laughter at the funny face before it. January takes off its mittens and slaps the back of both dimpled hands.

The baby's cry bursts from its lungs in one long, out-raged roar. January's heart has twisted to a knot of smarting pity and burning animosity. She doesn't know what she's doing but she watches herself doing it with fascination. The baby's clothing is entirely peeled off, layer after layer, to see what's inside.

It screams and struggles but it must be punished. It has done wrong.

Upending it over her knees, she begins to pat its bottom, saying 'No – no – no', in an admonitory voice. She taps with the flat of her hand. She likes doing it, it feels nice, horribly nice, to smack harder and harder the round quivering cheeks of the little bottom in its helpless nudity. She kisses between smacks; kisses as the bee stings, a dying act of retribution.

The child pees all over her skirt. Filthy. Filthy thing. Now it must be punished, punished good and proper.

Happy shall he be that taketh and dasheth thy little ones against the stones.

So the priest read with gusto from the Sacred Word.

January is as happy as the Psalmist fantasising over the brats of Babylon. She brandishes the Germany baby high above her head, charged with power; wheels about and about, the baby whirling too. She hears a blood-curdling scream and it is hers as well as the baby's. She stops and the turntable world goes on spinning. The body is lying beside her on the turf, spread-eagled and silent, on its back, where it fell. She stares at it in terror, the curdled, polluted feeling that boils in her throat being the taste of her self. She takes to her heels, speeds round the corner, then peers back.

'Elisabeth! Elisabeth! *Wo bist du*?' Gertrud Binny races up the hill from the empty pram, then turns and runs madly down. '*Jemand hat mein Baby gestohlen*!' Lost and gone forever, lost and gone. One slipper has fallen off, now the other one and she runs barefoot on the slippery mud, her milk-filled breasts bouncing painfully, fair hair streaming out behind her. The child lies casually splayed like a pink china doll someone happened to drop on the windswept turf beside the air-raid shelter, amongst a white scatter of garments.

She swoops and gathers her daughter up, bundling the chilled body inside her cardigan. The mildly concussed and traumatised baby whimpers, opens one eye and comes back to life in Gertrud's arms; she rushes it home, weeping a storm of relieved tears. Never, never again will she leave Elisabeth out for the vicious English to steal and maltreat.

Who would do a thing like that? Who? she asks herself, she asks the MO, she asks her husband. Someone sick, who ought to be put away, they all concur: a monster, an aberration, a nutcase, not one of us.

*

Daddy is the life and soul of the party. He is having a

grand old rollicking time in the bosom of his family. A great bunch of children, bless them, each and all. He surveys with pride the bright faces of his offspring, all loving Daddy, all in a howl of laughter at Daddy's jokes and his funny ways.

'Again! Again!' roars Paul, banging with his spoon on the table-cloth. Daddy repeats the gorilla impression, tongue stuck between his lower lip and his gums, jaw thrust out, hands under armpits. Solemnly beating his chest, he stertorously bellows, glaring down upon little Catherine who sits at his left and is nearly sick with giggling.

'Don't, Dad!' she shrieks.

'Yes! Again, Dad, again!' shrieks Paul, louder.

Even Columba, with her faraway look and her growing detachment from the coarseness of her home-life, has to smile. Dad can be so disarming, so winning, when he's in a good mood. You forgive his weaknesses and forget his cruelties in the fun of the moment.

'Oh Dad, do King Kong,' says Peter. 'When he puts his nose up against the skyscraper window and puts his paw in and gets hold of the girl, you know – do that.'

'I can't do it until you eat up your bread pudding – come on, Pete-boy, lovely bread pud your Mam's made for you.' Peter doesn't like the cold, glutinous slabs of the penitential dish their Mam cooks up out of stale bread and sultanas and a squirt of lemon juice when the week's money is running low, but to please Dad he swallows two big mouthfuls.

'Now who shall we choose for King Kong's victim?' Hugh looks round the table.

'Me, Dad! – Me! Do it to me!' Charity and Peter compete for pride of place.

'Well, you can't be, Pete, you're not a girl.'

The gigantic black gorilla beetles his brow at an imaginary window, where little white Charity lies asleep. He emits grunts expressive of gorilla excitement and covetousness. Skyscraper Daddy towers over shrieking Charity with his hairy hands and unshaven chin. He whisks her up bodily and carries her out of the room over his shoulder. Her long, fair hair trails all down his back like a maiden in a fairy-story. He plants her carefully on her feet in the hall, where she hugs him delightedly.

'There, my pet, you're Daddy's best girl.' He hugs her back, basking in the warmth of their united affection. 'And here is little Prue come in from her paper round. Daddy's other girl.' He reaches out an arm for her, but Charity, mortified at the thought of being unsurped, tugs her father's hand – 'We haven't finished tea, Dad' – and he lets himself be dragged back into the hubbub of the dining room. So Prue escapes the hug. She wipes her feet fastidiously on the mud-encrusted doormat and tries to hold on to the internal quiet, fragile as crystal, which she has lately acquired. Finding a place at the tea-table, she fixes her eyes on the icons of Our Saviour on his Cross and Our Lady, whose gentleness and forbearance are as rooted as the wood out of which they were carved. Her eyes are careful to avoid those of Columba, whose smile over her teacup solicits Prue's attention and pardon (though if it is withheld, it won't make much difference) for her defection. She avoids looking at Dad, who is horsing about, gay and seductive, and also solicitous of pardon as a lovable rascal everyone indulges. She avoids especially the ghastly look on January's disfigured face as she hovers in the doorway with a greenish-yellow bruise and the gap in her teeth showing as she looks round open-mouthed for a place at the table. January shivers from the cold, grey outdoors she has roamed like a wraith all day.

For a moment Hugh looks as if he'd seen a ghost. But then, smiling with all the charm he can conjure – a wry, rueful grin executed with one half of his mouth only – he makes a sudden act of negotiation. His hand is extended. January stares uncertainly at the hand, offered palm-uppermost.

'Come on me darling girl, come here and get your tea,' he blarneys. 'Let's make friends now. Daddy was naughty to your sister the other day', he announces to the suddenly frozen, silenced waxworks around the table, 'because *she* was naughty to *Daddy* and that made him lose his temper and hit her a shade too hard. So everyone smack Daddy. Come on, all smack bad old Daddy.'

Small fists rain feather-blows on Hugh's head and shoulders; his back is pummelled, he is whacked by a rolled-up copy of *The People*, with relish and energy.

'Come on Jannie-girl, you join in.'

She won't, she can't. She swallows painfully as if trying to keep from being sick.

'Right, that's enough now, that's enough. Paul, I said *enough*. That's right. Columba, brew a fresh cup of tea for your sister, will you?'

January has never known such civility; she passively allows herself to be seated on his right hand and watches him scoop out a tablespoon from the ruins of the strawberry blancmange, making sure that she gets a portion without skin.

'Yes – eat now, drink.' He nods approvingly, with every difficult mouthful. The tea scalds her tongue, comforts her chilled body as it slides down. She gazes up at her father when his eyes are off her, with a complex look mingling longing and dread, distrust and utter heartbroken need.

'There's a good girl,' says Hugh, flushed with relief.

He remembers now the white, panting timidity of her thin body, fluttering, pattering away from him across the linoleum. He sees in his mind's eye the tender breasts like little apples not quite ripe. He recalls the ramrod stiffness of his prick and how it ploughed and ploughed into the tight softness of her flesh. And Christ, the almighty explosion when he came.

She licks the spoon clean of pink blancmange and looks up from her wounded eyes into his face, betrayed by drowsy warmth and well-being into an expression that is tender with the need to be loved, wishful-to-please. *Don't tell me you didn't egg me on, Miss, don't tell me you didn't enjoy it.*

It was a sin, of course, but how bad a sin? She wanted it all right; and she wants it again, look at her, putting her face up to him with her eyes half shut, her chest thrust out.

He helps her to bread pudding.

'What might you be staring at, Prudence?' he asks, glowering, rattled, as if the child could have read his thoughts.

'Nothing, Dad.' Her eyes swivel away. See-no-evil, she fastens her attention on the plaster Virgin on the sideboard, gazing so fixedly that the statue seems to vibrate very slightly, where it rests between the Marconi and the lamp.

'It's rude to stare,' says Dad.

'Sorry,' mutters Prue.

'Dad, do King Kong again,' demands Paul.

'No, that's it for now. Go off and have your baths. Come on, your Mam's calling.'

All disperse, save Dad, January and Columba, who wants to go and put on her make-up for the evening with Duncan but somehow can't bring herself to go; the atmosphere's so peculiar and disturbing. She pours herself a cup of tea which she doesn't want: it's stewed and tepid. The other girls at work did her a perm today, and the lacquered curls feel like a helmet on a warrior, or a busby on a horseguard. She keeps patting it with her finger-tips, neurotically wondering what Duncan will say when he goes to put his hands through it and comes up against an impregnable wall. Probably nothing – he's so polite. She'll have to explain to him it's the height of fashion. Her mind, never intellectually wide-ranging, now concentrates all its energies inwards on considerations of Duncan. The Russians may overrun as many Hungaries as they like, ban-the-bombers may march to Aldermaston with blistered feet and babies riding piggy-back, the cost of living may soar, but the state of Columba's hairdo and its likely impact on her fiancé is a far more crucial reality. The rest of the world is merely a reel of Pathé news: the cock crows and the spool runs out. (If only, if *only*, she hadn't been born a redhead with freckles – *Carrot-top* from earliest days, it's always been a sore point.)

But through the closing aperture in this bliss of self-absorption (for Duncan says her hair's a glory, a film star might envy its auburn beauty) Columba sees there is something terribly wrong in the house she is preparing to vacate. Why is January looking at Dad in that weird way; what did our Dad do to her that makes him fawn on her? These questions uncurl like smoke at the far horizon of her mind. The bruised eye stares like a Cyclops. The child, she suddenly sees as if it hit her for the first time, is sick, disturbed, abused.

'Dad,' she says, clearing her throat. 'Let Jan alone. Leave her be.'

'Well, maybe I were a bit hard on her,' he admits, not taking offence at all. 'Bad-tempered, me, from a child.'

205

He sits back flaccid in the chair, a gesture of placating submission. 'Hasty, like. But I've said I'm sorry and Jan understands it's my temperament and to keep on my good side.'

Columba leaves it at that. Hugh looks her up and down as she leaves the room; *a nice, plump bird*, he thinks rather proudly, observing her outline in the tight black skirt as she walks out of the door; *what a chassis*, he thinks, *but a decent modest Catholic girl too*, as witness the silver crucifix round her neck and the neat way she arranges her lambswool sweater over her skirt as she gets up. She does him credit, does Columba. All his girls do him credit. There's Prue, for instance, with her book-learning. There's Teresa at the convent. But Teresa is an uncomfortable thought; her hawk-eyes look you through and through. She saw him for what he was from early days. She's better at a distance, to be bragged about to your pals: 'my daughter who's a nun'.

Columba applies her lipstick in front of the mirror, a very subdued and subtle pink so as not to clash with her fiery hair. She dusts her nose with powder from a compact. Father and sisters are already fading from her mind like the background of a dreary picture she is privileged to step out of altogether. She gave Dad a piece of her mind; she did her best. But that was easier to do because she is on her way, she is getting out and putting it all behind her. She has chosen Duncan because he is everything Dad is not: sweet and gentle, meek and worshipping. It can never happen to her. Never.

Dad sits with his elbows on the table, smoking a cigarette with his last cup of tea. He holds the butt between nicotine-stained thumb and finger. His eye still gleams with fun and geniality. He tells January tall tales of how he hammered Hitler in the Western Desert, more-or-less single-handed, one Briton pitted against a massed Panzer division and half the Luftwaffe. She seems as quiet as a broken horse that only asks to be ridden; a beaten spaniel lying low at its master's feet.

'You know,' he confides, blowing out a cloud of smoke. 'You and me have always been close, like. And that's why there's the antagonism.' So garrulous and voluble does he become in these melting moods that he has not the least idea what he is going to say next, and when it is said it's as if the words assumed an authority and inaugurated a new reality, simply from having been uttered so convincingly. He believes every word he has heard himself say. 'But we'll put it all behind us, my girl – we will, won't we? I'll be good to you – you be good to me. You could make something of yourself if you just took a bit of trouble. Smarten yourself up, do your hair. Will you do that for your old Dad now? Will you darling?'

She writhes like a charmed snake to his crooning voice. Yes, she will do anything. Withhold nothing. This isn't the same Dad who shut her in the coal-hole and did things to her three days ago. Not the same; opposite. His identical twin brother. She would lay down her life for this Dad; she would kill the other, kill him, kill him, kill him. Her blood roars in her ears.

'I were just saying, Mary', blares Hugh, raising his voice from its intimate half-whisper, to Mam who has come in to clear the table, 'I were just saying to our January, she should make more of herself, tidy herself up a bit.'

Mary, clattering, mutters non-commitally. She has had enough. Doesn't want to see, doesn't want to know. Wants to be left alone. Wants cash for necessary food and wonders if now he's in one of his sleazy moods he might break into his drinking-money. Wishes they had a tele-vision.

'Can you let us have a quid?' she asks.

He rifles in his pocket and slaps two down on the table.

'That do you?' he asks magnanimously.

'Ta.' She snatches the money up, in case the offer should be rescinded.

'And here's another. I tell you what, take yourselves off to the pictures. Go on, it's time you had a treat. Go on now, I insist. And here's something for ice-cream and popcorn while you're there.'

* * *

Jolly Dad tickles Damian and Paul, the smallest of the children who have been left at home as being unlikely to benefit from viewing 'The Dambusters', on the hearthrug after their bath. The boys roll round hooting with excitement, warm, pink and glowing from the tub. First Daddy pretends to be a wolf, then a jackal, then a roaring lion. The wolf, the jackal and the lion all have the same intention in relation to the boys: to eat them up for dinner. Vulpine Daddy stalks his gambolling prey. He pats their chubby behinds with his paws and blows raspberries on their bare stomachs. The boys fight for his attention. They wriggle between his hands and kick off from his chest with the tender soles of their feet. Curious Daddy feels for their little willies under the flannel of pyjama trousers. 'What's this I've found?' enquires Daddy the clown with a look of astonishment. 'Have you grown a tail, Paulie?' Daddy shall chop it off. Daddy bares his teeth and clacks his snarling jaws, amidst huge, complicit howls of laugh-ter, all-boys-together laughter, nervous exhibitionistic laughter. The little nuance of fear is necessary to make the game good.

Will Jannie join in? he woos. No, no, don't want boring sisters, the boys maintain, they want the taboo-threatening willie-games. But what Daddy says goes, Daddy's boss, they know that. Daddy wrestles January down on to the squirming hearth-rug, which writhes with knots of limbs like pale worms the spade has excavated. Daddy tickles, Daddy paddles his hand between thighs and under armpits. January plays with violent energy, a guerilla collaboration. Thrusts and punches. Daddy tickles till she screams. Daddy tickles the soles of her feet, bunching both ankles in one hand; he draws his thumbnail softly down her sole from heel to toe. And again. No no Daddy leave off. *And* again. Daddy tortures with feather-touches, strokes their ticklish places with exquisite villainy.

Hate, hate, we hate each other. Vile Damian kicks foul Paul in the guts where he lies in Daddy's arms. Vile Paul punches foul Damian. Both lunge at their shrieking sister.

Enough. That's enough now. Hugh carts the boys upstairs and dumps them on their beds decisively, threatening. They are commanded to go to sleep at the double. That's them out of the way.

Hugh crashes down the stairs two at a time.

Something has given in him, some spring that was always held back in a state of quivering tension has been released, the loaded gun is cocked and ready to fire. He could do anything to anyone.

Come here, January. He strips her, casts her in the bath. He plays with her, on her, kneeling at the tub, fiddling, squeezing, lathering slick skin. His prick is a burning rock-hard ramrod. Her cry of laughter is the Auschwitz scream God never hears. Hauls her out and her shocked eyes are wide, mad, mute, but he must, he must and will, and consequently she must, and he grips her hand on his root and makes her rub it backwards and forwards, fast and faster, accelerating to hell-brink, grunting and snorting, and then he's over the edge; it's over, he's done with her.

Disgusted, he turns away.

'Wash yourself,' he says brutally. 'And if you ever tell I will carve you up. I will slit your face open so that your own mother won't know you. Dirty little bitch. Wash yourself and say your prayers and get to your bed.'

She made him do that. She *made* him. Fondling and ogling with her eyes, inviting *Come on, do it to me*. He quits the bathroom, dives downstairs and drinks whisky straight from the bottle.

And anyway she's not his daughter. He knows Mary had it off with half a dozen randy blokes while he was away in 1946. She's some creep's bastard he's kept, much against the grain, like a cuckoo in the nest, and look where it's got him. He swallows another swig. It travels neat into his veins, anaesthetising, tranquillising. He forgives himself his human weakness. He can't help himself. He dozes in the armchair, in a pleasant if low-spirited haze of post-coital torpor.

*

January washes herself but it won't come off, the horrible white stain he's put on her. The bath-water's slapping, gurgling noises are magnified in her ear. She scrubs with a pumice stone till the skin is red. She hears, as if the sounds vibrated in her ear, a dog barking, a baby crying from somewhere across the camp. An aeroplane from Kinloss breaks the sound barrier far out across the sea with a remote crash. These sounds are all desolate, beyond anything she can imagine. She towels dry, madly rubbing the harsh fibres against her scoured skin, then covers up the indelible stain with her pyjamas and dressing-gown, knotting the cord tight. Her flesh crawls. There are insects seething all over it; she scratches till she's raw.

Passes her father's snoring body, spreadeagled in his chair. Her father's body is a monstrous thing. Hairs sprout from the dark orifice of its nostrils. Its greasy facial skin reveals large pores with blackheads, several small moles and other deformities. Stubble greys his chin. Hair thick as wire, crinkled and grizzled, covers his head. The obscene bulk of him seems to swell to fill the room. She sidles past.

She picks up the kitchen devil from the draining board. It makes itself at home in the palm of her right hand. She examines the white, transparent skin of the inside of her left wrist. The lace of fine-spun veins lies very near the surface. With a sudden movement she slashes the blade along the wrist. Blood wells out. A biting line of pain. The shocking pain collects all other pain to itself, draining the consciousness of all grievous recollection prior to this moment. She observes the blood in fascination. So much. It pools in her outstretched palm; it pours between the fingers and drips on to the bread-board. Like meat. Like bloody liver. The bloody mess of what we are. And that's *all* we are – that bloody mess, as she has long perceived. The world spins round upon the axis of January, first slow, then faster. The light disintegrates into vertiginous splinters which whirl like atomic particles and are extinguished, one by one. Blacking out, she hears the baby's riven cry, oh the poor baby hurled into the toppling dark.

*

Hugh awakens with the sense that he's been having a rather sordid dream. He feels unclean, as if with sweat dried on his skin after gross exertion. There's a curdled taste in his mouth. He passes one hand over his forehead, massaging his temples between finger and thumb. Yawns and stretches.

Christ crucified looks down from the wall at Hugh.

He has been watching in silence all the time.

He can read Hugh like a book.

Momentarily Hugh meets Christ's eyes, the austere eyes in the quiet face that generates in him an unease as unpleasant as the childhood comfort it once inspired. Hugh shifts his eyes away. But he is still being watched. The figure on the cross hangs with skewed legs and bent arms in surrogate agony, pinned there by the nails Hugh is daily employed in hammering in. Hugh's mother was devout, as Mary is devout. But her helpless incapacity to meet Hugh's needs on the most elementary level made God seem, as he grew up, more a matter of guilt on the one hand and formality on the other than a living help. In the soft, golden lamplight, the crucifix casts a deep shadow on the wall down its left side; the light picks out the Atoner's features and throws them into relief.

'Whosoever does it unto the least of these my children does it unto me.'

I won't never do it again, Hugh promises himself, hastily pulling himself to his feet and turning his back on the icon. *Honest-to-God. Never again*. It's not worth it. It's wrong. He knows that. There's no fun in it. He doesn't know why he has done it, anyway. It's not him that does it. Almost as if something gets into him; someone takes him over and acts through him. That's really how it feels. A force, a current passes through him. One of his brothers had epileptic fits. Spasming and bellowing. A devil in him; possessed. Then when it was over, John would just be lying there like a limp rag; bewildered, amnesiac. 'What happened? – What did I do?' So it seems to Hugh now, running for shelter from the X-ray eyes of the icon, that

212

he's had some sort of seizure in the last few days. It's not his fault, he's not responsible. He hurriedly leaves the room lest this defence be disallowed by the conscience on the wall that probes you through and through.

He should confess, and when he has confessed that will be the end of it; he'll breathe freely again. But what amends will be required of him? And how can a priest in his celibacy, almost a eunuch, possibly understand the story he is chary of telling, even to himself. No, better let it die quietly and be given a private burial. He drags himself heavily upstairs, pulling the body up by the banister, the heavy body of him, the unlovable mass of gross matter that is Hugh. He won't go near January again. He won't let himself speak to her. He won't let the anger rise that somehow activates his prick and gives him his biggest thrills. He can stop it if he takes thought in time before the red-hot stiffening has had a chance to set in hard.

Damian, the sweet child, sleeps in his cot. He sucks his thumb, lying on his back, his head turned sideways, face warm and rosy with sleep. His father brushes the tender cheek with the back of his fingers.

Paul can't sleep properly, he complains, he wants a drink of water, he keeps thinking of sad things. What things? He doesn't know. The dim walls are peopled with rustling shadows, whispering spirits; he can't make out what they are saying and he wants them to go away. Will it help if we turn the light on? Yes, he thinks it will. The spirits flee before the artificial dawn. But if the light is on, he can't sleep, he points out, sitting up.

'Well, it's either one or the other,' his father advises patiently. 'And anyway there's nothing to be afraid of. Your Dad's in the house and he won't let anything happen to you.'

Dad will sit and hold Paul's hand until Paul is asleep.

Yes, it's all right, he won't go away. Paul hangs on tight, eyes shut, battling the lassitude that drifts him down beneath the surface and will loosen his hold on this unheard-of privilege.

Hugh is content to sit on in the dimness of the bedroom, holding the thin, lax hand that comforts him more than he comforts it. His sons breathe deeply; they sleep well. The whole room respires with their guiltless innocence. He envies them their oblivion and tries to enter in to the rhythm of their breathing repose. The muscles at his neck are knotted with tension; he sighs and seeks to ease them. As he exhales he smells his own bad breath. His breath is vile. He never smelt it before.

At the doorway a figure hovers. Staring at or into him it mutely thrusts out a blood-drenched arm. Hugh's hair stands on end, he seems to shriek through all his body, the rich stink of his breath thickens and fills the room, like a leak of gas from an unlit stove.

After he has tremblingly bandaged the slit wrist tight, staring at the child who will not speak and will not respond to any question, even with the flickering of an eyelid, he bundles her into her room and shuts the door. Puts her away out of sight. Her mindless eyes were dead in their sockets; her mouth lolled open. She has left her blood all over the kitchen. He must clean it up before anyone sees. The blood is everywhere and will not go away. He swabs around with a wet rag and disinfectant; he wrings it out, he swabs again; it dilutes to a rust-coloured stain that will not entirely disappear. He has seen blood before and shed blood, but there was never any horror like this. He retches. Nearly faints. He does not know what the child is doing; he will not go and look. A cretin, her, a zombie, she should be put away.

He brushes his teeth and swills out with mouthwash.

The mirrored face to which he raises his face has staring, red-rimmed eyes, nicotine-yellowed canines and incisors. He would like to tear that face off like a rubber mask, but the face is Hugh, and Hugh must love Hugh and choose to be Hugh, and Hugh must conform to Hugh's nature, though he cannot account for and will not answer for what Hugh has done and is condemned to do.

*

Gertrud and Eddie Binny lie on their bed with their sleeping daughter safely between them. The police cursorily questioned neighbours about Elisabeth's abduction, but came up with nothing. Gertrud, who has been hysterical, has since calmed down. Eddie put his own grief and alarm aside to take the weight of hers. A plain, home-spun man, gentle and diffident in manner and uxorious to an effeminate degree as his mates allege, he can hardly bear to see his wife in this condition, knowing as he does the everyday hardship of her existence. And the child is the apple of his eye, the pride of his life.

'It is because I am German that they have done this to us,' says Gertrud for the tenth time. 'I know it; I know it. They call me 'Kraut' and 'Schweinhund', they spit in my face, and you do nothing about it.' It eases her to accuse her husband, the only being in this alien world over whom she has the slightest power, and who in the constancy and clemency of his disposition forgives her wildest accusations.

'What can I do? I stick up for you whenever I can. I won't hear a word against you, you know that Trudy. Be fair.'

'You should have gone into civilian life after the War, that was the mistake. And now it is too late, we cannot afford to buy you out, we must live in this slum amongst these animals – *diese Tieren, schmutzigen Tieren*. How are we going to feel safe? How is Elisabeth going to be safe?'

Eddie's arms embrace her and the baby, which lies with its sleeping face against both their breasts. He strokes his wife's long, blonde hair with delicate, caressing movements and wills her to be calm and comforted. He's never been much of a one for expressing himself in words but his hands, sensitive and tender, have known a language which transcends the strife of tongues. He shouldn't have stayed on in the Army, he knows, but he likes his trade and gets on OK with the lads. And he was told there were no jobs back home in Stafford when the time came for demob. It's been a hundred times easier for him than for Trudy, hauled round from one rootless billet to another, with himself her only friend.

'I'm sorry, Trudy. But I love you, if it makes any difference. I'll take care of you both, honest I will. We won't put Lizzie out at the front again, we'll always keep her under our eyes.'

'I will be a prisoner in my own home – which is not my own home because I do not a home of my own possess – I am like a refugee in a transit camp. And what will Elisabeth do for fresh air, tell me that?'

'Perhaps', he suggests timidly, 'she can manage with a bit less. She'll thrive fine.' Eddie has always harboured private scepticism over the merits of high gales.

'So you are a child-expert now, are you? You know nothing whatsoever about the true principles of child-care.'

'Oh darling – *Liebchen* – don't let's quarrel.'

Weak you are, weak, a weak man, Gertrud thinks, but she does not say, accepting the asylum of his ready embrace.

10

Breakneck north-easterly winds come streaming in from the North Sea, down from beyond the Arctic Circle, between Iceland and Norway, across Shetland and Orkney, through the Moray Firth, to hit land at Findhorn and flow south across the land-mass of the Scottish mainland. They beat up against the standing figures of Isla and Isabel Gordon, Prue and Iain, slamming into their bodies with breath-taking force, and hurling all Prue's hair upright where it remains, up on end as if she'd seen a ghost. The girls stagger over the shingle down toward the far-ebbed tide, tottering and grasping each other round the waist, howling with laughter that the wind tosses casually away out of earshot. Isabel puts a sheepskin mitten across her mouth to protect her fillings from the twinging cold, and grasps her pigtails which have been whipping her face like ropes, poking them down inside the collar of her duffel coat. The tide seethes and foams at their feet. Tiny and insignificant on the margins of the sea, Isabel feels the jelly-softness of her eye against the lancing of the wind; the aching openness of her ear to invasion. But nothing matters, she is buoyant, her heart coming floating up high and light, shrugging off all the hard questions which stream away like a row of bubbles on the gale and pop inconsequentially out of sight. With scalding face, she puts on a balaclava, draws her hood over it and shouts to Prue to come on.

Isla watches the two diminish. Their dark figures stagger along the shale, navy duffel coats belling; occasionally she sees them stoop for some treasure, crabshell perhaps or golden pebble, the jingling lucre of the shore. The sea's detritus is scattered all around her: bladder-wrack, spars of smoothly eroded wood, glass, the scoured remains of creatures, legs, tentacles, bleached bones and shells that once lived out there in the unpolluted waters. The wind booms in her ears under the flapping headscarf and the waves crash and crash monotonously. She is heavy with fatigue, a fatigue not only corporeal but as it were with life itself, and the cold burden of life, her faith a faint, scarcely credible warmth like a tepid hot-water-bottle clasped without conviction in the early hours of the morning. At the same time her eye-beam seems to seek for something, sweeping like a search-light toward the invisible Faroes, Iceland, Greenland and the Norwegian Sea, and beyond that again, to the heart-stopping white silences of the Pole. Beyond this relentless noise, beyond the gull's effort to breast the gale, out away over the churning waters, that desirable silence, that remoteness.

Of course she shouldn't have come out – she was in no fit state – but she had promised the girls and it's not in her character to give up. She turns from the view and makes for the car, the skirts of her camel coat blown out, her scarf sailing between the horizontal and the vertical. Huddled into herself, she hobbles up the pebbly embankment to the roadway. Detritus of creaturely life, sheddings, shards, meet her eye wherever she plants her foot: moulted feathers, hollow carapaces, the incomplete skeleton of a gull. Through her rheumy eye she sees a shore-line which is a great reliquary, strewings of mortality in every direction.

But there is the car, the wonderful vintage Ford. There it stands, monumental, black and fanatically polished, on the sandy road above the bay. The mechanical wonder appears as utterly out of place in its arrogance as a nobleman's crenellated folly on an ancient hilltop. She has to salute it for the splendour of its vanity and illusion – her vanity and illusions, rather, which have kept her afloat through this eery autumn, when she has not known how to evaluate the doctor's reassurance on her health which is evidently deteriorating from week to week. She has been living in a twilight world of great solitude and inner conflict, between the need to believe she'll live and the need to know for sure she'll die; to make her peace one way or the other. Meanwhile there is the car. The ineffable pomposity of its expression, looking out to sea with silver carburettor and lofty, curving mudguards like sneering lips, is matched by the supreme indifference of the unpeopled scene to any such piffling invasion. She lets herself in to the warmth and shelter of its interior and unscrews the lid of the thermos. The coffee comforts. Two matchstick children and one matchstick dog cavort at the water's edge, the sea tranquillised by distance to a sheen, smooth and safe as a postcard.

How they polished up the car with dusters and beeswax: Isabel, Prue, the two Margarets, Urquhart and Gillespie. So much elbow-grease and concentration, breathing on the wing-mirror, rubbing the paintwork till it shone like a black, ghostly mirror, giving back her own image, subtly distorted, to each of the painstaking girls posted north, south, east and west. In their sedulous rubbing they exchanged hardly a word, eradicating from the pre-War bodywork of the Ford every fleck and mote, both real and imaginary, with a kind of desperate earnestness. The car is of purely antiquarian interest, with an engine that does not bear close inspection, but it goes – if with judderings and back-firings – and it is hers, the product of most of their savings. The joy-riding began at once; she would not brook a day's delay.

'Prue, it's clean as can be.'

'No, I can still see some little bits. Here, look. But don't worry, Mrs Gordon, I'll get them all off for you.' She rubbed with zeal, her face close up to the black surface; a black Prue within staring out fixedly.

'Can you not see unless you put your face up close, Prue?'

Isla crouched beside her. Evidently the child's eyes needed testing. The glasses were fixed in two places by elastoplast and sat slightly askew, giving Prue a curious, lop-sided aspect. It struck Isla that this autumn the child seemed less well cared-for, less focused somehow; and the sister January had deteriorated severely. She did not come now to visit with Prue, but was occasionally glimpsed loping along the road to the Carse or, once, in the lee of the Manse wall, talking to herself. When Isla approached and softly spoke her name, she sheered off like a wild animal.

'Yes, I can see fine,' said Prue, screwing up her eyes. It was not true. The world was becoming blurred and fuzzy, but she did not mind.

'It's my belief you need an eye-test.'

'No, honest, I don't. I can see great.'

'You shall come with us on outings, Prue, if you would like to and your parents approve.'

'Oh they won't mind, they don't care what we do.'

It was not uttered as a criticism; yet the reproach of that

indifference stuck in to one at sharp angle and was difficult to extract.

Off they motored to Glencoe where the blue-grey mist came down in swathes between the cold, stark shoulders of the mountains, and the girls shrieked at the precipitous drop that fell away beside the narrow, sinuous road; to Randolph's Leap, where the legendary horseman vaulted the far-fetched gulf between boulder and boulder over the boiling current in the ravine.

'I do not believe that,' asserted Isabel. 'No horse could or would make such a leap. It stands to reason.'

There she stood in the sun, arrogant and vulnerable, with the light in her braided hair, from which a few, bright singular strands escaped and floated upward on the breeze. All around them the world was a bonfire of amber, ochre, rust and scarlet – the dying leafage of the old year – and at the centre of it all, it seemed to Isla, with the heightened senses that haunted her that autumn by investing all experiences with a painful intensity, stood the child saying 'I do not believe.' The world was becoming a vast catalogue of propositions in which Isabel could not believe. Isla's heart twisted and contracted at the bare-faced candour of her daughter's dissident integrity; that naive and potentially cruel faith that mere faith is unjustified and ought to be disproved. What will become of you? Isla wondered. Have I given you enough strength for the road? There was no knowing. Something was forever tugging at her sleeve, reminding her to let go of earthly things and turn away.

She turned away.

'Anyhow I think Randolph's horse *did* make the leap,' piped up Prue. 'It definitely did. Otherwise why is it called Randolph's Leap?'

'You can't argue from *words*,' riposted Isabel wither-ingly.

'I can. Why not? They wouldn't just make it up.'

'They would because they wanted to believe it. They wanted to imagine that the victim got away – the loser won – it was a miracle in their minds.'

'I believe in miracles,' muttered Prue. 'I do. They can happen. I know they can.'

She stood precariously on the grey boulder from which the putative Lord Randolph allegedly leapt, purple heather all around her, the bottled-up current below her feet, challenging its narrow conditions. She swayed unstably at the brink and Isla plucked her back.

'Hey be careful, you'll fall in.'

'No, I wouldn't – I couldn't.' The Virgin would never let it happen but Prue didn't share this information which derived strength from its taboo privacy. And she was canny enough to know that the visions which had kept her company and solaced her heartache in the past weeks would be unlikely to impress Mrs Gordon and Isabel. The Protestant mind had a barren literality, like a hollow box booming with its own emptiness. Like a crucifix without a body. Like a bare wall with no pictures.

'Miracles are just illusions,' Isabel explained in a superior tone.

'How do you know?'

'Cause and effect.'

'Each person has her own truth,' cut in Isla. 'And people may need illusions to survive. We all may. Had you thought about that?'

Isabel said nothing. Even if her mother urged her, Isabel would not yield one inch to the pressure of consensus, that lay everywhere, soft like a fungus that crumbled if

222

you so much as poked it – not one inch, and her mother was the best person she knew.

'My faith is not illusion,' said Prue suddenly, objecting both to Isla and Isabel, neither of whom had ever seen or would ever see the Blessed Virgin in the Housty Woods and sundry times and in sundry places subsequently; whose beautiful, reposeful presence Prue could occasionally solicit just by closing her eyes and calling her to come. First the blue haze of her mantle, then the delicate shining of hands and face, then the intervention of the whole person between Prue's eyeline and the barbed and betraying world. 'My faith is absolutely real.'

'Yes, of course it is,' said Isla quickly and with wistfulness. She knew something of what the child was guarding. From the beginning there had been the fastness of her own faith. Safety there, security. She came home to certain steady and unshakable truths which were never submitted to scrutiny. That nothing was meaningless. That pain and injustice were apparent only, and temporary. That a God of Love presided. That the body at the end of time shall resurrect. Faith was still there when she could resurrect it. But faith had never before been so hard-come-by. She was reduced to groping round for it as in a game of blind-man's buff, awkwardly stumbling around in defamiliarised inner space. When she prayed in the silence of her heart last thing at night, lying in bed on her left side, shading her eye with her right hand, all she could hear was the ticking of the clock, metronomically amplified so that its pointless tattoo seemed to fill the room with marching heart-beats; only after much searching could she come through to the quiet, recessed place within her mind where God had always, till now, been found. She felt his love then, after the struggle; he spoke to her, reminding her of comforting passages in the Bible, which she told over and over till sleep took her in mid-sentence:

The Lord is my shepherd, I shall not . . .
Yea though I walk through the Valley of the Shadow of . . .
Thy rod and thy staff they . . .

But she would awaken in the early hours of the morning, full of pain and nausea, with the same words jingling through her mind, drained of significance, inane as the fancies of a nursery rhyme: far-fetched promises, pap of make-believe. Then faith would be probed by violent doubts, thrusting their tampering fingers deep into the most intimate places of her spirit, so that she would sit up in anxiety and look round the curtained room as if some intruder had entered there. But there was only the huddled body under the dark quilt of the parallel bed: her husband to whom she felt able to confide neither these transgressive thoughts nor the crescendo of physical suffering. She swallowed a pain-killer and waited for relief to come, as it did. She was her own person, and so she would remain until the door was shut upon her final privacy.

*

Isabel traipses the shore-line in Prue's wake, and the weird, eery question surfaces yet again, *What is it, this being me?* The strangeness of it sweeps over her every so often, sitting pensively at the window with the dog's dear head in her lap or standing alone at the bus-stop on cold clear nights when all the stars come out. How peculiar to be looking out of your self, from eyes whose almond-sort-of shape you intuit, whose blurred lashes flicker on

224

the field of vision – to be condemned to occupy an obser-
vation-post in this black unknown and unknowable box
of self and never to be able to look back in. To be pointed
like a vigilant cine-camera at the world out there, with
your reel always running, except at night when you are
switched off and the film continues to whirl by fits and
starts automatically in your dreaming mind, odd or lurid
stories of what you dread or greatly want. To be a walking
microphone or loud-hailer through which some voice
recognisable as your own sounds off at the world, asking,
proclaiming, desiderating, greeting – but you listen to
yourself speaking and sometimes it seems like another
person. You are acting your self, ventriloquising your
part, a puppet entitled 'Isabel' – but what is really there
behind it? Isabel, staring up at the stars, comprehends the
answer to this less clearly than she can discern the present
reality of these galaxies light-years away and possibly now
extinct. For she reads about the universe in the *New Scien-
tist* and has come away with some amateurish general
point of view about the quantum and waves that are also
particles. But what waves and what particles account for
Isabel, she cannot conceive. She looks at herself looking
and thinks about herself thinking, so that there seem two
of her, and often one Isabel debates with a disputatious
other Isabel in her mind. They sometimes resolve the
issue, at other times agree to differ, often remain at logger-
heads for days on end. Is everyone split and obscured like
this or is it just her? And why are there no words to
communicate this fugitive dilemma that seethes like the
sea and is never still for long? Though at many times the
interrogation of herself and her world falls away and she
wakes up in the morning a child again, and the rough and
tumble is enough, the intuitive and ruffianly life of tree-

climbing, swinging on ropes or running with the dog along the deserted, wintry shore at Findhorn.

But then there is the problem of other people. What can be known about them? This question, too, brings an uncanny sense of isolation. Owlish Prue, sweet and earnest, pottering along the shell-strewn shore with her hands in her pockets, ahead of Isabel, looking out to sea with frowning eyes that are always trying to peer beyond the object. *Who are you really?* she asks that sauntering, turned back. *What is the Prueness of Prue which gives her that uniqueness? For you alone are Prue and because of that you are lonely. Just as I, Isabel, having no double or counterpart, am known by no one else and can never be known.* Her knowledge of Prue is of someone with a secret, who hoards that secret and dedicates her whole life to the retention of that secret; so much of Prue resides in the not-said. Evasions and silences, pauses and little oblique laughs, the ready blush and apologetic cough behind her hand. *What is it, Prue?* she wants to demand of her, straight-out. But Prue, like everyone else, is serving a life-sentence under house arrest – a house without doors and windows. You know there is someone trapped in the house and you busily post messages through the letter-box; you wait outside and get polite or cryptic messages back, but you will never actually see the prisoner in the sealed building. (She has never even been to Prue's house in the camp – how odd. Prue has never asked her. Why not? She will go anyway and see for herself.)

The tide sucks back strongly, and the pebbles grind and rasp with the pressure. Then the next legion of waves pounds in, and a boom is repeated all around the shore like the echo of artillery-fire. Isabel lets Prue wander on by herself; she stands still at the water's edge, looking out. If you open your mouth the cold wind streams right in

226

to the cavity and even tries to rush down your throat. The world is always seeking to get into you and it is your job to keep it out. Maintaining your perpetually besieged difference from everything out there, you have to pit yourself against people, there's no option. *Opinionated*, they call her; *a prodigy*, commented Dr Urquhart in her hearing; but *precocious in the extreme; very difficult; won't go to the kirk, you know; imagine Donald's chagrin*, said Mrs Gillespie when she thought Isabel was out of her hearing; and Mrs Harty came quickly in with the asseveration that Isabel was *a most wayward girrul, too certain of herself by half, wants bringing down a peg or two*. And even though Dr Urquhart snorted this down, insisting that Isabel Gordon was just an intelligent lass who thought for herself, the bad things they said hurt Isabel; the tears pricked the back of her eyes. For no, she does not feel certain – not inside, she doesn't. Except of opinions. But opinions were a sort of protective carapace like the exoskeleton of the crab worn outside the body to defend the mushy innards. Right at the centre there is uncentredness, a sac of shapeless water flowing and shifting around, so diffuse it could just flow away into the sand if it were spilt.

And then there is her body. What should she think or feel about her body? She can come to no accommodation with this budding and blossoming of soft tissue on the lithe, boyish body which used to be her rather than hers – but which now she apprehends as something separate which has become attached to her. Her instinctive response to her ripening body is to deny it; wish it away. How much more satisfactory to be mind solely – a travelling mind, free of burdensome gravity, which might at will vault or pass through all obstacles. Puberty brought a mixture of sorrow and shock, as if something were lost for ever which had never been appreciated at the time: a wholeness, a bounce and joy. Now there is the tingling shyness of tender breasts, the bother and pain of menstruation and the frequent feeling of something impersonal – Nature, biology, a nameless force – having laid claim to her raffish singleness and compelled it to join up in some mindless exercise of generation larger than her individual self and disdainfully negligent of it. There are no words for this, just surges of apprehension that seem to spread throughout her whole body from womb to brain. But she will fight, she will not be swallowed up in the race, there's more to it and more to her than that. She sees in magazines in the dentist's waiting room pictures of bleached albino women who are all voluptuous bosom and waggling hip and pouting mouth: Diana Dors, Marilyn Monroe. These are real women, the essence of woman, the text tells her. She gazes with furtive, scared fascination at the globular breasts and deep cleavages, her breath coming shallow and thin. She knows that she could never compete with that pulchritudinous abundance of fatty tissue, and to the virginal shame that she should so preposterously be asked to is added a kind of pity for these people who have assented to be displayed as meat on a slab. *Horrible men* they must be, *horrible*, who want to use you like that. Isabel will stay single, like Queen Elizabeth I and Florence Nightingale, awaiting the call to a life wider and deeper than the common female average.

Look at my mother, thinks Isabel, glancing up from the pile of shells she is sorting, crouched down with Prue with their backs turned to the wind and the roaring tide. *How small she looks from here.*

The far-away figure is recessed into the view, no bigger than the scallop-shell in the palm of Isabel's hand. Shrunk in the grey haze of the encircling bay, she could be anyone; she has no particular features and nothing to say for herself. Her familiar camel coat fades into the cold khaki and beige of the shingle. Yet she sees it is Isla, that straight-backed posture of stern withholding. It couldn't actually be anyone else. Isabel watches her turn and retreat toward the car.

Tension like an unseen elastic band tweaks at her breast, tugging her forward as her mother retreats, the needful bonding that constrains her, guaranteeing her stability like a guy-rope to a tent in a high wind.

'What is it?' asks Prue, straightening up, wiping her wet, numb hands on her duffel coat.

'My mother,' says Isabel vaguely.

'Where? She's gone.'

They pick their way between rock-pools slippery with seaweed. Premature twilight flattens and occludes the view. Isabel keeps her eyes glued to where her mother stood, tracing a guide-line toward her absence.

*

Isla stands in the hall looking at the picture that hangs there against the panelled wall: Honthorst's great sombre *Christ Before The High Priest*, a six-foot high reproduction. There sits the High Priest, the open Torah on the table before him, his bony finger raised authoritatively. The Torah, the Book of the Law, the law that condemns us to death. The face of the High Priest is in no way malign: it is wise, earnest and grave, not without benevolence. Parallel to the raised finger stands the candle, its slender flame the optical centre of the picture, from which all that is seen emanates and to which the eye eternally recurs. On the right of the table stands Christ, his face in grave dialogue with his seated adversary. Gentle, severe, austere, feminine, the attitude of his body makes Isla's heart contract, its crossed wrists accepting the invisible bonds

229

decreed by the Book the two interpret. The act of looking is entirely peaceful; for the thousandth time she is visited with wonder at the man before her, so real that one would swear he breathed or swayed slightly as he stood. Out of the umber obscurity that makes up two-thirds of the picture, the other observers' faces dimly peer. These people can hardly be made out, lubberly faces, burghers, Pharisees, odd bods, nothing out of the ordinary, still and watching and listening in with her, to the life-and-death debate at the centre.

Donald watches her through the framing doorway of his study. The grey, cloudy folds of her skirt and long cardigan hang as still as the drapery of the pictured figures. The impression of her remote dignity is so strong that he backs away before it. Retreating into his study, he draws the door softly to, without latching it.

I am dying, yes, I am dying, Isla says to herself, turning from the picture and seeing the line of light between door and jamb of her husband's study. She almost laughs aloud at the quaint absurdity of the notion: but it is true and it simplifies everything extraordinarily, clearing the mind of ballast. She can say to herself: *I have done very little good in the world, made hardly a particle of difference to the suffering out there from which, unjustly lucky, I was exempted* – and forgive herself that debt. It is possible to lay the debt at the door of God, without rancour, in the hope, if not the trust, that he could clear it. To look at the child she must imminently leave and speak the right words, afford the useful counsels, for that child's lonely road ahead.

Pushing open his door, she crosses to the desk where he sits in the light of the Anglepoise, one half of his face brilliantly alive in the glowing light, the other dead and shadowed. Taking his hand in both her own, she passes her new certainty across to him in a steady, neutral voice, as much as to say, 'It's raining outside' or 'It's dinner-time'. His face crumples like a child's as the helpful tears stream down; he stumbles up and takes her in his arms, the dammed-up love of years finding eventual expression.

*

In the end, it's very quick, mercifully quick, the work of less than a month. The last remaining leaves are dashed from the beech and sycamore by violent November gales; only the thick-skinned holly, rhododendron and fir hold out. The migrant birds have long since departed. Slates dislodge from the roof and shatter on the drive. Torn-off boughs and twigs litter the stormy garden. Nothing of these intimations obtrudes into the new-found, short-lived peace of the nights in which Isla and Donald lie face-to-face, their backs turned on the storm-damaged world. Not until the last week do morphine twilight and incontinence set in, placing Isla beyond communication, and even then Donald continues to lie beside her most of the day and night, murmuring words of love. Nothing direct is said to Isabel, who is fobbed off with vagueness and barred access to her mother's room. She sleeps poorly and has bad dreams. Messages of deep unease and presage are passed her from her father's red-rimmed eyes, his som-nambulist's inability to register her presence as he stumbles about the house, the secretive coming and going of Dr Urquhart, and – one hair-raising midnight – a sort of rushing-sound and whimpering in the hallway, where she spied her father dashing her mother over to the bath-room, waltzing her over, as it seemed, in an old-fashioned three-step. Creeping back to bed, she blocked it out; but distress is coded in the irregular soughings of the trees outside her window like a ghostly Morse. She goes off her food and complains of stomach-pains. 'Colic,' says Dr

Urquhart and recommends bran. She quarrels with the two Margarets, one on the grounds of being Dr Urquhart's daughter, and clings to Prue with a new air of desperation and dependency. The odd sense of affinity with Prue has greatly deepened.

'Prue, can I come to your house?'

'Oh, *Isabel*.' Prue shrugs and blushes. They are playing ping-pong on the dining table in the book-lined room where the deacons meet. She bends to pick up the ball.

'But why not, Prue? You never invite me – I've never even seen your mother.'

'Your father doesn't let you come into the camp.'

'That's no reason. I can't help it if he's prejudiced. I *want* to come to your house,' she proceeds relentlessly. 'Why can't I? Don't you want me to come?'

'Oh *Isabel*. You wouldn't like it. It's not like here, you know. It's not . . . nice, like here.'

'All right then – if you don't want me to come.'

She serves a stingingly accurate ball low over the net, which Prue doesn't even bother to try to hit. Isabel is hurt but she is decided. She *will* come and she *will* see what it is that Prue is hiding, whether invited or prohibited. She serves another ace. Prue wildly snatches for it; sprawls, and the bat travels out of her hand and skids across the table.

'I can't hit those. I do want you to come, Isabel, but . . .'.

'But what?'

'It isn't your sort of world. It isn't the sort of thing you're used to.'

Isabel serves Prue a slow, bouncing ball she can hit. Prue misses.

'Come on, you idle Sassenach.' She targets right on the

232

centre of Prue's forlorn bat; Prue cannot help but return it. 'So when can I come?'

'I'll ask my Mam,' mumbles Prue. She lives by evading and avoiding the escalating madness and terror of that house. Even the Blessed Virgin will not appear to Prue there, but only manifests herself at a decent distance from that scene of wholesale crucifixion. Even the books which were the life-blood of Prue's inner world have failed her in that house. She can read for an hour together and not take in a word of it. Her sister haunts that house like a spectre, speaking insane words and obscene jokes, alternately fawning and violent, and their father creeps in to their shared bedroom and does horrible things to January or with January or on January, with grunts and twanging bed-springs and peculiar shrieking laughs from January; and Prue puts her head right under her blankets and lies dead still. Paralysed. Frozen. Lest he should do it to her. He passes by the bottom of her bed barefoot on the way out, ridiculously tiptoeing with many squeaks of the sole of his foot on the linoleum. She holds her breath until she can hold it no longer; until his body is gone, out of the door, along the corridor. In the morning there are teeth-marks on her hand where she bit it in her petrified silent frenzy.

That house is a place where Isabel ought not to come. Isabel is sheltered, free, perfect. Isabel is as if over-arched by the outspread arms of the great, patient beech. Nothing should happen to her, neither should she guess the grossness of evil which surrounds Prue's life. Isabel is like a talisman Prue can come and touch, and be restored by contact with that vigorous immunity. Hale and whole, Isabel does not know and must not know.

Head-down, Isabel cycles through the first snow of the year into the camp, and makes her way through the strange labyrinth of drearily identical streets, where soldiers in greatcoats are the only men you see and whose streets memorialise battles and Army commanders. All the Imperial Wars of history (those which the British won, at any rate) seem replicated here. Isabel freewheels from Malplaquet to El Alamein and wobbles uphill over impacted snow to where Lord Nelson abuts on to Fieldmarshal Montgomery to the left and Earl Haig to the right, in the form of a barren avenue in which a few, scrawny saplings have been planted, each surrounded by a vandalised cage of wire netting. Gang warfare seems the rule wherever she goes, with batches of roaring boys of every age lobbing snowballs at other groups or cramming it down the necks of shrieking girls. By trial and error, Isabel locates Prue's street and comes to a halt at the kerb a block away from her house. The red-brick houses in this most derelict part of the camp seem to have been dumped and left on an uncleared building site, surrounded by debris and swarming with small, excited children.

A youth is leaning against the drainpipe of Prue's house, one hand in the pocket of his leather jacket with its upturned collar, the other flicking back the quiff of his elaborate Elvis hairdo. A cigarette hangs from the corner of his mouth, unlit but half-smoked and trembles slightly, as does the quiff – for the youth appears to be dancing to some tune in his own head. *It must be her brother Malachi*; his insolent maleness alarms Isabel, as does his extraordinary beauty as he catches her staring eye. Through long-lashed, pale-blue eyes and over-full, sensuous lips from which the fag still dangles, he coolly looks her up and down, giving her to understand that he is assessing the figure of the pale, pig-tailed girl standing astraddle her bike. *Not much there, you scrawny chicken*, his raised eyebrow seems to say. And the face has vestiges of Prue's face, but beautified and empowered. Ambling back indoors, he leaves a trail of winkle-picker foot-prints in the snow, like some grotesque bird's trail. *How tight his trousers were*; hot-faced she sees the angle of his hips quite distinctly, and the bulge under the skin-tight leather, even when he has gone.

In and out of the twin front doors of Prue's house, the teeming children run: in and out. However many? Squealing and hooting, and treading the snow in. They slide down the hill on tea-trays. They bombard a fair-haired woman pushing a pram and wearing a moth-eaten fur coat. 'E-va Braun, E-va Braun', and when she's lugged the pram indoors they bombard the door instead. A man in a greatcoat comes lurching down the street and fetches one of the children a terrific swipe on the ear. Isabel flinches; the children scatter; the man lets himself in to Prue's house and begins to bellow. Suddenly the left-hand front door opens and the dark figure of January comes sprinting out; dead-eyed it hares straight past Isabel, ducks under the perimeter fence and disappears. The man reappears at the right-hand doorway and shouts something about a bitch. He looks round vaguely and then disappears, slamming the door. In an upstairs window, a girl's bespectacled face momentarily appears through a gap in the net curtain; it looks out blindly at the black-and-white world, then it begins to breathe on the pane until a misty screen blocks Isabel's eyeline – and when it clears, the face has gone.

The thickening snowfall comes down in fragments as big as cornflakes as Isabel plods back up Passchendaele pushing her bike. What was it Prue said about the freak storms in Egypt when she ran out with an umbrella over her head and a bucket to catch the hailstones big as ping-pong balls? A little girl in the sand on the edge of a desert wearing only a pair of knickers and carrying a brolly, catching the clattering ping-pong balls that rain down from the sky. That picture conveys the violent strangeness of this world, the foreignness of everything. The incredible *why*? of it all. The bellowing khaki man – her father – the aggressive beauty of the boy – her brother – her sister running out of the door – the blind, lost face of Prue behind the pane – the shock of this vision has been like turning up one of those nice, peaceful stones at the bottom of the Manse garden and uncovering a welter of coiling, slimy bodies below.

Down Passchendaele, along Aarnhem and Auchinleck Roads, up Trafalgar Parade. Violent names commemorating the licensed acts of destruction which (Uncle David said) have made England what she is. What would come next: Hiroshima Crescent, Nagasaki Boulevard? Home now, where it's safe and known.

January shadows her all the way.

*

Isabel felt nothing whatever at the news of her mother's death. She just said, 'Oh,' and turned away. Through the window, the anaesthetic, blank brightness of the lawn on which the snow had fallen steadily throughout the night met her eye like irradiation. All the birds had stopped dead in mid-flight and round their black forms the dazzling whiteness of the foreshortened snowscape rushed forward in a silent howl.

'But what are we going to do with the car?' she objected. 'She won't want it now.'

A white phantasmagorical limousine fabricated all of snow preserved its form in the mute fixity of the garden forecourt. On the wing-mirror a thrush perched, surveying its crystalline territory. The mirror and the perching bird cast a single, brittle, complex shadow.

'I don't know,' said Donald, laboriously articulating with a tongue which seemed too big for his mouth. 'I don't know at all.'

'We'd better sell it.'

'Yes.'

She pulled on the sash window and it travelled up with a crash, letting in an icy rush of air.

She felt nothing except a desire to laugh, which she suppressed.

The disfigured hawthorn raised its spikes like handfuls of knives pointed in all directions.

Individual snow crystals sparkled in the X-ray sun. Such immaculate whiteness had a hospital air of pathological hygiene.

The rooks bolted up from their headquarters in the sycamore with a sudden, ear-splitting outcry; they hung in the sky like ink-marks and didn't come down again.

11

'Columba, take me with you,' Prue whispers, although there is no one to overhear – as if rejection would be easier to sustain if one had asked tacitly, beneath one's breath; hardly asked at all. With soft fingers she brushes the lambswool sleeve of Columba's pink Marks and Spencer cardigan. 'Please – Columba, *please*.'

Columba's cases stand in a neat row of three beside the door, corded round and labelled with her new name and new address. From the dark bondage of that chrysalis, Columba Cahill, emerges a butterfly-self, light-hearted and jubilant, ready to take wing into identity as Mrs Duncan Macintosh.

'Oh Prue, pet, I can't – you know quite well I can't. We're living in one room at my in-laws. How could I take you? Sleep you under our bed? Pack you away in the wardrobe?'

Tears stand in Prue's eyes. She sits on Columba's bed looking straight ahead, her hands flat on her knees. It is especially wounding that Columba seems to take her desertion so easily, almost with flippancy. How can a person change like this? It is not the same Columba who used to carry her up to bed at night on her back when she was 10 and Prue was 3, toiling up the stairs under the leaden weight of the burden she had assumed and tucking the bedclothes in around Prue's neck so that no wandering draught could find its way down.

'I'd be no trouble, honest, Columba,' Prue whispers. 'You wouldn't hardly know I were there.'

'But there just isn't room.'

'Tell Duncan you won't marry him without *me* coming too.'

'Prue, it isn't like that.' Columba sighs at her sister's blinkered naïveté. 'Men don't go and marry girls plus their little sisters. It's ridiculous what you're saying.'

'Please, Columba, please.' Prue is remorseless. It is her last chance. 'Columba, ever since I were a baby, you done everything for me. You taught me to read. You kept me clean. You made sure I grew up decent . . . .'. She doesn't know how to go on. There is so much that cannot be said. So much that's foul and filthy, and which she would be ashamed to say, even to Columba. Last week their father penetrated their bedroom as he had been doing for several months which seem like several years, a life-time. Prue had dropped off, it was late, one in the morning. She was awoken by the smell of his breath, or so it seemed: the reek of alcohol from a hard-breathing mouth which panted like a dog and filled the whole room with sour exhalations. Turning over and opening her eyes, Prue saw the dark shape of her father looming over her – over her, not January, *over her*, Prue, coming for *her* as she knew he would.

Then he put his face down to hers and seemed to breathe on her as you do a mirror prior to cleaning the pane, with a slight sound of air – 'Hah!' – something like that. The drink lying on his bilious stomach gave out its acid fume in her face. He was addled, fuddled. Didn't know one bed from the other, one daughter from the other.

Her heart stampeded; a scream burst out but took no

sound with it. He hoisted himself up. He towered, swaying. Then his bulky shadow seemed to reel away. He stood for a while making little popping and sucking noises with his teeth and lips. Then he lurched out of the door, down the corridor to his own bedroom.

Prue sat up in bed shaking convulsively. It was all black, all menacing round her, like an appalling dream; she needed to, but dared not, switch on the light. To switch on the light would mean seeing January. Cannibalised, maddened January who would willingly throw her in her own place as bleeding offal to that sick animal, their father.

Since then she has only fitfully been able to eat or sleep. Fits of ungovernable jitters alternate with long spells of torpor, in which she seems to switch off her identity as Prue, and sits staring at the wall as if it were a blank screen at the cinema waiting for images to be thrown upon it. Last night, before the snows came down, Columba packed her cases. Prue watched her silently from the doorway, neatly folding her clothes, smoothing down the dove-grey nylon petticoats with their silky sheen, folding her stockings, holding up to the mirror her wedding night-gown, with its thin straps and froth of lace and ribbons at the bosom. When Columba went out of the room, Prue came in and unpacked the lot, tidily replacing it in the drawers of the dressing-table exactly where it had been. All smelt mistily of Woolworth's essence of hyacinth talcum powder and Columba. That must be kept, that fragrance of safety, more sacred than the incense in the Church hut. She would not let Columba go. Reverently she disinterred and laid out Columba's fancy little jars of make-up, her eau de Cologne and her brush and comb on the dressing-table top, having dusted it with her handkerchief. Columba, wafting back in dreamily, saw to her exasperation and with some unease that she would have to repeat her packing from scratch.

'Stupid little brat,' she said, stomping over to the empty case. 'What did you do that for?'

Prue said nothing. She went to the window and watched the first snowflakes eddying down from the spreading blue-black bruise of the sky.

'Columba,' says Prue in a very low but charged and urgent voice. 'It's Dad.'

'What about him?'

'I don't like it – what he does.'

'What are you talking about?'

'I can't tell you. Just, he does – nasty things. I don't want to stay in the house with him.'

'I don't know what you mean.' Columba puts a reluctant arm round her sister and gazes at her with a troubled expression. 'He's rough all right, I know he's rough, but if you just keep out of his way, Prue, you don't get into trouble. Do you? He never bothered me in my life because I knew how to handle him like. It's just common sense and using your loaf. Isn't it?'

Prue can't look Columba in the face. She blushes fiercely, twisting the handkerchief in her hands into a tight coil. Now is the time to speak. There is a long pause. Something weighs down Prue's tongue. The silence is frenzied in its denial of the compulsion to speak.

'Well, what, Prue?' Columba, shifting position, reflects that it's uncomfortable sitting here on the bed, with Prue obstinately saying nothing. She crosses one plump nyloned leg over the other and notes with some irritation that one stocking is slightly snagged. 'Oh come on, Prue. I've got a hundred and one things to do.'

Prue's agitation uncoils the handkerchief and twists it up in a new shape.

'Our dad . . .'

'Our dad *what*?'

Prue swivels her head to try to pass Columba through her eyes the tongue-tied necessary message, but as she does so she catches sight of her sister's boredom, her aversion and evasion, her wish to be gone. Something twangs in her head like a plucked elastic band. It's no good. She has been thrown out like the paper wrappings of a sucked sweet. There is only the sore and angry hurt, the poignantly focused pain of Columba's snapping of the bond. The desire to hurt Columba back, and the chagrin of perceiving Columba's immunity.

'Well, if you won't tell me, I can't make you.' Columba bounces up from the bed, whose springs creak at their release from her weight. 'Can I?'

'No,' says Prue.

'You'll be all right, Prue, if you're a good girl.'

So the Blessed Virgin has also assured Prue in their hazy meetings out on the Glebe or under the skirts of the rhododendron bushes at the Manse. Evil would not be able to touch a good girl; it would be physically prevented. Obstacles would be placed in its way, trip-wires insinuated. Evil would sprawl flat on its face with its legs in the air if Prue genuinely was, and could remain, a good girl. Prue has in some measure, and against her better judgment or vital instinct, acquiesced in the common view that because January was a bad girl, she had it coming – whatever 'it' turned out to be. A bad lot, a bad egg, a bad character. So she, Prue, would be – surely? – all right.

But what if something evil did happen, was allowed to happen, to Prue? Columba stands by the mirror, filing her oval nails with an emery board. Prue watches the two Columbas studiously filing their impeccable nails in perfect unison. As she watches, her mind whirrs like a dynamo on the problem of evil.

If evil gets to Prue, then Prue can't be a good girl; she must be bad, like January.

Or:

If evil gets to Prue, she might be a saint or martyr. Look what God allowed to happen to St Catherine, strapped to the burning wheel, to St Lucia, eyes gouged out and served up on a plate, to white-robed St Bianca, gang-raped by Infidel Turks and spiked through the heart. Prue has studied pictures of these virgins with expressions cheerful and composed as they proffered tokens of the damage sustained by their flesh for the infrangible Faith.

Prue does not want to keep company with such impaled, mutilated or incinerated persons. The electrifying horror and repulsion she feels at such sacrifice brings her on to the third and final equation, that:

If evil gets to Prue, that proves that God is weak or uncaring or bad or just not there.

No, *no*.

Prue shoots away from this suspicion as if she'd caught her finger in the flame of the Bunsen burner at school. Better be bad oneself than God be bad. She cannot look down that hole. It would put a void at the centre of all things, it would disprove the beautiful thing Mrs Gordon once said to her which she cherished and will never forget as long as she lives: *There is a floor at the centre*. She has not seen Mrs Gordon for a while (she has been ill) but the very thought of her brings a little alleviation of her tension, perhaps the ability to speak out. Mrs Gordon lets you take your time. She looks at you with grave, patient eyes.

'I do try to be a good girl,' she begins. 'I do, Columba. But Dad . . . comes into our room, and. . .'.

The two Columbas look up rather sharply, startled like rabbits that have caught a whiff of fox, and turn away from one another. The back of the auburn lacquered head in the mirror seems to refuse the knowledge reluctantly sought by the face that now confronts Prue with wide and anxious eyes.

'Does he hit you, Prue?'

'No.'

'What then?'

'He don't do nothing to *me*.'

'He hits January?'

'No. Not hits.'

'Something else?'

'Yes,' says Prue breathlessly. 'Yes, that's it – *something else*.' She infers from the tone and nuance that Columba has cottoned on.

There is a considerable ensuing pause, during which Columba averts her gaze. Her eyes wander around the room she is now to quit for good, as though to inventory and assess each negligible article. At length she turns her back on Prue and examines herself in the mirror again. Unscrewing the cap of her nail varnish, she dips in the brush. Now she begins to paint the nail of her index finger, with fastidious care, brushing evenly from the cuticle toward the tip.

'Prue, you'd better have this room of mine when I've gone. Cath were going to come in here but I think it'd be a lot better if you did. You'll be better off here, won't you, pet?'

Prue's mind darts forward along the eyeline of this prospect. It doesn't tackle the root of the question but, yes, it gets her away from the dangerous proximity of January, ensuring shelter, space and privacy. To sleep where Columba has slept, to catch echoes and vestiges of the peace that breathed for her wherever Columba was or had been, and was associated by her with her first inti- mation of the holy – that bequest would bring intense and daily comfort.

'Oh yes, I would – but Columba, would my Mam let me?'

Prue can hardly breathe for eagerness. In her imagin- ation she has already moved in, bag and baggage. The disappointment will be intense if she's not allowed. But in an over-crowded household, on what grounds can the insignificant Prue be accorded the unheard-of privilege of a room to herself?

'She'll blinking well have to let you,' says Columba. 'I'll make her.' And she will, if it's the last thing she does. For months she has held Prue at arm's length, defending herself from her grief and need which assault her with mercilessly empty hands but point the finger of a legit- imate accusation. She has tended to see Prue differently – as a nuisance, a pest, marked by growing untidiness and a gormless look that partly comes of the lop-sided specs through which Prue squints. In an obscure corner of Col- umba's mind is stowed the revolting suspicion of her father's nameless brutality to the younger girls: it lodges there like a message she has written to herself, of which she does not intend to accept delivery – stuffed down between the arm and the cushion of a chair, amongst the dust and crumbs which are at once out of sight and too objectionable to clean away. The knowledge has no status in Columba's consciousness. It is a question mark only; a blank or a dash in the sentence. Amongst other mental debris it lies buried and unexplored, expressing itself only as an occasional shiver down her spine or moment of turbulent silence in her brain. And yet now it's as if this knowledge of Prue's predicament has dominated her life, so profound is the relief, the release, at being able after all to leave Prue better off and safer. And when she says, 'She'll have to let you – I'll make her', there is a sense of energy and empowering, like the release of a long-coiled spring.

'Will you, Columba – honest?'

'Did I ever break my promise to you, Prue?' she asks, adding the saving clause, 'if I could help it?' She puts her arms out for Prue, and Prue rushes in. They rock in one another's arms; Prue's eyes are closed, her head on Columba's pillowing shoulder. 'Tell you what – I won't go if you aren't allowed the room.'

*

'Well of course she can't,' says Mary dismissively. 'Cath's going in there as soon as you're out. You know that perfectly well.'

Anemoned headscarf round her curlers, she is up to her elbows in suds, scrubbing at the grimy collars of the boys's school shirts. Damian is sitting on a high kitchen stool beside her, eating a banana and cranking the handle of the empty mangle with violent momentum. The kitchen sweats with wash-day steam, which condenses on the windows' frozen panes and runs down the wall.

'No, Mam. Our Prue's to go in. Not Cath – *Prue*.'

'Don't be daft. Wring these out for me, will you – I'm gasping.' Columba, dressed up in her finery, remains aloof to the pile of steaming washing which her mother has dumped on the draining board. Mary fishes her Woodbines from her apron pocket and lights up, inhaling deeply. The smoke mingles in with the soapy steam and the steam from the boiling haddock on the oven.

'I'm not having that, Mam. What *I* say goes here. It were my room – now it's Prue's; I've promised her.'

246

'You little madam. I don't know what you think give you the right to tell your own Mam what to do all of a sudden, but I can tell you your airs and graces don't cut no ice with me here, my girl. Don't you come it with *me*.'

These tough words are belied by their pleading tone, as Mary looks up at Columba, the previously dove-like and pacific Columba who lived up to her name best of any of the children and was always such a good, docile Catholic girl, with genuine astonishment and alarm. Life has been *so* much better for Mary lately. She simply couldn't believe her luck. The pregnancy has settled down, no more sickness, and there are spurts of elation, euphoria almost, for nothing at all. Tiredness, yes, but not too bad. None of the children off ill all term. She won £5 on the Bingo. But most of all, it's Hugh – he's pretended to turn over a new leaf, he's pretending (by and large) to be a new man, and Mary is faking to believe him. It's by his shifty eyes she knows he's trying it on, by the blood-curdling way he flatters and wheedles. It's by her occasional razor-sharp looks that he knows she is not beguiled. But he rarely hits her by day and never bothers her at night. He leaves her at peace, lying there in her curlers and hairnet, hot-water-bottle clasped to her stomach. He drinks more but he troubles her less; and that's a bargain she's prepared to go along with, even if it does mean that they're so short of cash by the end of the week they're down to bread and dripping for tea and have to cancel the milk.

Sometimes she's awoken at night by indeterminate noises: cut-off shrieks that might be a child crying out or just the human-sounding yowling of a cat on heat from next-door's garden, thumps and creaks as of bed-springs, but maybe it's just something she dreamt. She makes no effort to verify it one way or the other. 'Them Three Wise Monkeys', her mother used to remark, 'had plenty and a bit to be said for them.' One of Mary's ears being slightly deaf, she tries to sleep on the other side. She visits the confessional on a weekly basis and there acquits herself of her sinfulness. Hugh's he must answer for himself – if he can – but that's not her business.

Columba takes her mother under the elbow, propels her out of the humid kitchen, into the living room, and shuts the door. In five minutes Mary returns to her work. She sucks at her toothless gums with her lips. She rebukes Damian absent-mindedly for putting his banana-skin through the mangle. She has agreed whole-heartedly with Columba's proposal, on very little persuasion.

*

Prue is installed. *A room of her own!* She can't believe it, can't take it in. She hums as she methodically sets out her books, her pencils, her little horde of shells and pebbles from Findhorn Bay, Mrs Gordon's herb cushion, a small clock her Nan gave her for Christmas, her glasses' case. The humming turns to singing: *Vairmeo rovano . . .* Mrs Gordon's favourite air. They sang it together once when Mrs Gordon asked her to hold the wool while she wound it in a ball. She held her hands up and shuttled them to and fro like a loom, the thread travelled off the skein in a regular rhythm from one hand to the other and Mrs Gordon's hands whirled round the steadily accreting ball, and as they worked they sang. Mrs Gordon told her that so the women sang over their work all around Scotland, the weavers and the fisherwomen gutting the herring at the harbour-side, the bakers as they slapped and punched the dough, the factory-hands and the housewives over their cooking. They had always been singing, she said, and they passed the songs down by word of mouth from one generation to the next so that they would never be lost. Prue viewed in her mind's eye the dark figures of the women keeping the working songs going from coast to coast, bound together in the one poverty; and she and Mrs Gordon with her tremulous, rather self-apologetic voice were one with that choir as the skein wound off Prue's hand completely, and 'Catch!' said Mrs Gordon, throwing the completed cream-coloured ball, perfectly round like a globe, into Prue's pleased fingers.

Maybe now she's got a room of her own, Prue could invite Isabel – when they're all out at the cinema, perhaps, and the young ones asleep. When Dad's at the mess or away on manoeuvres. She could bring Isabel up here, with the electric fire, and tea and biscuits for her. Everything is possible when you have a room of your own.

Prue rearranges all the items she has just carefully laid out. The room is scarcely bigger than a sizeable cupboard, built in an L-shape, with a bedside cabinet made of an old box and the battered utility dressing-table in whose mirror Columba presented herself with her own image morning by morning, seated at the end of the bed. Prue sits there too, and congratulates her own radiant reflection in the same mirror. The image being blurred, as is Prue's whole range of vision nowadays, she cranes forward to eye herself at closer quarters. *You are all right, Prudence Cahill*, the grinning image assures her. *It's safe now – safe and secure.* The door even has a sliding bolt. She can lock herself in at night. Columba tightened the screws for her last night with the blade of a knife. Each twist of the screw-driver was performed with exaggerated emphasis, to make sure Prue was aware of how secure she was; then she made Prue slide the bolt across for herself, to check that she could do it properly.

'And do it every night without fail as soon as you come to bed,' she chivvied. 'Don't undress with the door unlocked. Don't forget. Now let's sort out your things – what a mess your drawers are, it's awful Prue. I never brought you up like this.' She shook her head and nagged; Prue loved it. 'I brought you up to be neat and tidy, Prue – now don't let me down.'

'No, I won't. Sorry, Columba.'

Columba had stopped prinking herself and drooling over Duncan. The future stretched out forever. Its promised bliss could be left to take care of itself for this last unmarried evening, while she sorted Prue out. Rolling up her sleeves, she washed her hair for her, as in old times, and got Prue to bend her head down in front of the electric fire while she brushed it dry, all falling forward from the nape of her neck, with its little, hidden mole, and the clean electric strands sailing up in pursuit of the brush. When Prue sat up and shook her head, it crackled. She laughed right out, joyously, and shook it again. Every hair of her head, Our Lady had declared to be numbered. It had taken a lot of believing, but she believed it now.

January wasn't there. That was a vast relief – to evade confrontation with those betrayed eyes as she made her escape.

*

Hugh has been hauled up before his Company Officer to be reprimanded for being drunk on duty. It is not the first time, and it seems to be getting worse. Hence, juvenile Lieutenant Frye felt bound to administer a warning to the quarrelsome old soak. *Demotion*, he mentioned, *rather unpleasant*. Hugh stood rigidly to attention, chin up, eyes trained on the young man's raised eyebrows, pale and blond (nancy-boy, poufter), working nervously as he ventriloquised the British Army's point of view about Corporal J H Cahill, 27659001, in a fancy accent (Public School git), from behind his hand, which kept hovering defensively over his mouth as if to stick back in the words it was obliged to emit.

'Not really on, I'd say, this sort of thing. Wouldn't you say? Not playing the game, letting the team down. No option but to . . . unless you can assure me . . . ?' He coughed politely into his hand.

'Sah!' roared Hugh, face red, chest inflated. He looked down with contumely upon his suffering superior.

'Coming on parade drunk . . . just not on at all. Setting an example to the lower ranks, and your juniors in point of age, after all . . .'

'Sah!'

'I say now, make some response to what I'm saying. That little shindig the other night at the Corporals' Mess – we can't be seen to tolerate that kind of indiscipline, you can see that,' he pleaded. 'What do you say, Corporal? Feel free to speak.'

Hugh meditates shouting another ear-splitting 'Sah!' but desists. He looks narrowly at the hot-faced, inexperienced officer.

'What exactly was you doing in the last War, can I ask you, sir?' he enquires evilly.

'Well, naturally, I was just a boy . . . a schoolboy . . . not old enough to serve . . .'. Anger prickles the veneer of diffidence which covers the privileged arrogance of the young man. He should never have given the fellow a chance to speak; that was a mistake. Treat these people like human beings and the ungrateful beggars are on to you like a shot.

'Right. Well, while you was a schoolboy – *sir* – learning your posh speech and your fancy manners – *sir* – on the playing fields of bleeding Eton – I were doing my duty to king and country – *sir* – killing Krauts and wops with my own bleeding bayonet in the Western Bleeding Desert.' He addresses his righteous indignation, together with a condensed account of his military exploits, to the Young Queen, whose portrait, wearing the coronation dress and the sash of the Garter, presides serenely above the Lieutenant's cropped blond head.

'Entirely irrelevant. Be silent.'

Hugh won't be silent. He proceeds with a detailed and stertorous account of his single-handed action against Rommel, on a diet of corned beef and hard tack, his one Howitzer against their massed artillery, punctuated with imaginative reconstructions of Frye Minor scoffing crumpets by the fire with his fellow homosexuals at Eton College, Windsor.

Reinforcements crash in and manhandle Cahill from either side. The officer gets to his feet in helpless anger, his knuckles on the desk white, leaning forward with blushing face.

'Insubordination to an officer – compounding the original drunkenness – very serious charge – report to the Guard Room – See the Commanding Officer at 0900 hours tomorrow – dismissed . . .' he manages to bleat (and anyway he was a Shrewsbury man, not Eton).

'Sah!' Hugh crashes to attention and salutes ironically. Vacating the Command Block, he is marched away across the snowy parade ground to the Guard Room.

*

Columba is married. Before leaving, she came up with a pair of Teresa's old tortoiseshell-rimmed National Health issue, to tide Prue over until she sees the optician in Elgin. These are too strong for Prue, don't quite fit comfortably

252

on the ears and have to be bent and fiddled with. The world they reveal is disconcerting – much smaller and crisper than the one that washed over her old lenses; she recoils from its sharp outlines, its jagged, cutting edges which circumscribe and confine each object out there to an unalterable definition. *We are like this and only like this and you will not change us by imagining otherwise*, the cup, the cross, the pavement, her mother's face, seem to say.

She goes to the Manse and knocks but no one answers. The dark, blank windows stare out like eyes too long kept open and sleepless. The drive is a flurrying mass of impacted foot-marks and tyre-prints, as if a great crowd had congregated there and just decamped. A thaw having set in, gobbets of wet snow slide down from roof and tree, smashing on the grey-white earth. Prue dances out on to the still spectacular whiteness of the lawn, where not a bootmark registers. Where is Isabel? The iron trees ring her round like ribbed bars of a cage; a metal bird sits motionless on the singing beech. Prue, returning to the front door, fruitlessly rings again: its two-note dirge repeats and repeats until the last stifled resonance dies into the locked vault within – nothing, nobody. She hangs around a bit, hopping from foot to foot, punching the fist of one green mitten into the palm of the other. After half an hour of this desultory lingering, she reluctantly turns away, and as she does so, spots a wreath of frozen, yellow flowers – spring flowers – someone has dropped in the snow by the gate. Wonderingly, she picks up the refrigerated, perishable flowers; takes the wreath to the front door and props it there. Daffodils and freesia, primula and snowdrops.

She sits indoors at home with her door locked, to wile away the rest of Saturday with Emily Brontë's *Wuthering Heights*. She weeps when she reads that Heathcliff shot the lapwings. She doesn't know why he did. But she enjoys the tears, and re-reads the passage to repeat the effect. Outside the hollering boys of the neighbourhood pelt each other with slushy snowballs and toboggan on tea-trays down the middle of the road. A cart comes with sand and salt, to spoil their slope, at which they hoot and catcall until they are summoned indoors for bed. Prue sits up in her bed wearing her coat, scarf and woollen hat, and has to remove her mittens to turn the page.

*

Corporal Cahill, standing between two green-bereted guards in the Adjutant's court, is asked by the Commanding Officer, Colonel Monkton-Lamont, whether he has anything to say in his own defence. The Colonel, an imposing, beaky man, with a jutting jaw and craggy nose, is suffering from dyspepsia, after an evening of Madras curry and too many gins, followed six hours later by a breakfast of bacon, egg, sausage and mushroom eaten too fast. He plucks at his moustache and looks up irascibly from beneath his peaked cap. The RSM stands to attention to the left of the flatulent Colonel.

'Well, speak up, Corporal. Yes or no.'

Hugh, having dried out overnight in the Guard Room, and having in fact enjoyed an unusually sound night's sleep in the barracks bunk, has abdicated his belligerent self and reinhabited his persona as the hard-done-by rascal, placating, matey and out to flatter.

'Yes, sir, yes – but I don't rightly know how to put it.'

The Colonel represses a belch, turning it into a sigh.

'In your own words, Corporal, without undue embellishment.' He profoundly regrets the gastronomic excesses of last night and will (tactfully) advise Beatrice against serving curry in the future, whether Madras or Vindaloo.

Daughter of the Raj she may be but we were in India to govern the natives, not to connive at their mouth-burning, ulcer-provoking culinary horrors.

'Well, sir,' says Hugh, and pauses. A clerk at the Colonel's desk appears to take down the words 'Well, sir'; then sits with raised, expectant pen. 'It's a matter in confidence really like – my wife, sir. Trouble at home.' He sizes up his adjudicator with a sly, ingratiating expression not lost on the RSM, who snorts quietly. 'In fairness, sir, I can't say more, I don't *want* to go into no details, sir, but it's been hell, sir, hell – on – earth. I turn to the bottle for comfort like.'

'Write down, "Pleads extenuating circumstances – Marital Discord",' says the Colonel peremptorily to the clerk. Alka-Seltzer is the thing, or Eno's. He moves swiftly to sentencing, reminding the offender of his previous breaches of Queen's Regulations; the seriousness of the charge in view of Cahill's seniority – he means by that seniority *in years* of course, he would remind him, not in rank. Seven days in jankers on fatigues; report to the Guard Room at the double. Hugh is marched out between the two beefy soldiers; that evening after work, wearing a stiffly starched but grubby apron, he is stationed between two vast tureens peeling spuds for tomorrow's mess-meal. Bile seethes in his stomach as he plops each potato into the cauldron. Someone is going to pay for this humiliation and, by Christ, it isn't going to be Hugh Cahill.

*

Mr and Mrs Duncan Macintosh are in their seventh Heaven. The gentle, shy boy found the mechanics of the thing difficult and embarrassing at first, but Columba, without being at all knowing, was so understanding that the clumsiness didn't seem to matter; was all converted into tenderness and loving-kindness. The two make many excuses to retire to their bedroom, which they have rigged up as a little home within the home, an aberrant china teapot and tea service (with a tea-cosy like a pink and white knitted hat, topped with a pom-pom) standing proudly on the dressing table on a crocheted mat. They sit side by side on the bed, like children playing house, sipping tea, toasting their legs at the two-bar electric fire. Then they cuddle on their bed, loving the at once licit and illicit closeness, in the knowledge that Duncan's father is seated directly beneath their floor which is his ceiling, reading his *Scotsman*, and that the mother is bustling with the hoover and duster in the hall. They are careful to avoid making the bed creak. They talk and laugh non-stop, somewhat under their voices, saying nothing, saying everything.

In this remote retreat, far from the routine chaos and loveless proximity of her family, Columba's consciousness closes out their reality, so that they fade and diminish, forfeiting both credibility and urgency. Prue is a little wan ghost at the wistful margins of her mind. Central to her life is this new joy – this joy so huge she can hardly get the hang of it. The intimacy and privacy of each minute; the most humdrum event expanded in its sharing to a momentous preciousness. And, too, there are the anxieties of her new state to absorb her concentration. To be accepted as daughter-in-law (a Catholic who has converted their son from his Presbyterian loyalties; a low-class product of England and the Army) is all-important. She wants so much to be welcomed and even, eventually, loved for herself by these retiring, old-fashioned people whose ways are so different from her own; she recognises how earnestly they strive to accept her. She is all antennae, sensitive to each nuance of implied criticism; stressed, and at the same time lambent and flowing with reciprocated affection. There isn't room for other thoughts. Though she may – she will – have a word with Father Friend about the situation at home, when things settle down here; it isn't right for Dad to mess the children about, though it is probable that Prue (being of a somewhat imaginative disposition from all those books she's read) was making something out of nothing very much.

She and Duncan mean to have children, and they will be loved and cared-for children, given every opportunity in life, a good Scottish education and a decent, God-fearing upbringing.

★

Prue knocks on the Manse door, in contradiction to her usual policy of refraining on a Sunday, in view of the fact that the Reverend (she knows and partly sympathises with his attitude) cannot be reconciled to his only daughter's friendship with the Army girls. As a Reverend, he has to keep high standards, especially on the Sabbath. But she has not seen Isabel for a while, and her mother not for weeks; she is bursting to invite Isabel to her new room for tea.

'Oh, I'm sorry,' she mutters, shrinking back apologetically. 'I didn't mean to . . . interrupt you . . . sir.' It is the first time she has ever spoken directly to Isabel's terrible Calvinistic father. Though she has occasionally been in the room with him, he always gave the impression of being blind to the existence of foreigners. The bifocals over which he peers reinforce that impression, and his lofty height that has to bend its head to negotiate doorways.

'No, no – you come away in. It's Prudence, isn't it – Isabel's friend Prudence?' He holds the door open and

Prue goes in under his arm, to be grossly licked by Iain over her face and hands. The Reverend doesn't seem so frightening now, but distracted and unkempt. A strand of hair hangs loose which he keeps pushing back. His eyes are shadowed and swollen, and a day's stubble greys his chin.

'Did you know about Isabel's mother?'

'No.' She shakes her head. 'Except that she's been poorly-like.' Prue doesn't want him to unload whatever heavy news it is that he is about to pass across on to her already over-burdened heart. The lamp high on the ceiling burns with a dim, yellowish light, smeared as if in fog; the candle-light in the picture of Jesus on Prue's left casts at least as strong a light in the wood-panelled murk of the windowless hall.

'Isabel's mother . . . Isabel's mother . . . died . . . last Wednesday,' says the Reverend. 'We buried her yesterday.' He chokes on 'buried'.

The message seems to echo up the stair-well. Its resonance fades into the gloom of the hall which always seems to smell of age and mansion-polish and dog.

'Oh,' says Prue, and after a long pause adds, 'I'm sorry.' She has read books in which this phrase was spoken by polite persons in receipt of tragic news, as constituting a fitting response – as though one were personally responsible and needed to excuse oneself. Prue stares at the Jesus-picture, past the Reverend's harrowed, shadowed face. She feels nothing, absolutely nothing. She thinks: *So you're in Heaven now, Mrs Gordon, are you*? And that is meaningless and unemotive too. She wonders if there is anything else she ought to add, but nothing springs to mind.

'Go along up,' says the Reverend. 'She won't talk about it. You may be able to cheer her.'

'My mother's dead,' says Isabel, as a flat fact that must be transmitted with minimum fuss.

'I know. Your father told me,' Prue replies in the same business-like tone.

'She died on Wednesday and we buried her yesterday.'

'I came to see you yesterday but you wasn't here.'

'Well, that was where I was. So.'

'Why have your been tearing up your books, Isabel? Goodness . . .' Prue bends and picks up a handful of carefully shredded pages, thin and old, from two waste paper baskets which are crammed full of dismembered books. Their well-preserved leather bindings have been shorn through with Mrs Gordon's tailoring scissors, which lie on Isabel's desk, with a pile of further candidates for censorship.

'Why have you done this – awful thing?' Prue is really shocked. She would have given her eye-teeth to possess such books.

'I've only destroyed the books which tell downright lies,' explains Isabel. 'It's a shame but I had to do it. It's an awful lot of work. I'm having to go through them one by one, and there are loads left to work through.' She sighs self-pityingly, glancing at her bookshelves.

'But *what* lies?' Pop-eyed, Prue fills her lap with torn-up pages, some having the gold-leaf borders of sacred books. They lie dishevelled in her skirt like fallen petals.

'Oh, just the worst sort. About God-is-love and the Afterlife. You wouldn't understand.' The pig-tailed apostate turns away from Prue and looks out of the window on to the lawn, which has suffered the blight of a nearly-complete melt, so that the remaining snow composes a slushy film, pock-marked with corroded grass. Icicles drip with mechanical regularity from the drainpipe above her window and ping faintly in a puddle at the base.

'Isabel, could I take the books rather than you just tear them up? They wouldn't be lies to me.'

Isabel pauses, coerced against her will by the eagerly soliciting voice of Prue who never asks for anything. The books were all handed on from her mother and bear her mother's maiden name on the frontispiece: Isla Ferguson, with a date – St Augustine, Bunyan, Milton, George Herbert, Buchanan. The books are private, between herself and her mother – her inheritance. They are hers and hers only, to keep or throw away.

'A-lie-is-a-lie-is-a-lie,' says Isabel fretfully, unconsciously reiterating what her parents taught her in early infancy.

'*Please*, Isabel. I haven't got hardly any books of my own. And these are – special.' Prue hugs one to her breast with both hands.

'Oh all *right*. Take them. I don't care.'

'Only if you're sure.'

'Yes, take them, Prue, go on, I don't care, I don't want them, do I, so why shouldn't you have them? Take them now – go on. Take them away with you.' She sweeps the pile angrily from the desk into Prue's arms. She is sick of Prue, incredibly sick of her. She loads Prue with her ire: ice-cold barren rage from the Arctic reaches of her eyes. She knows neither why she is focusing this anger on Prue nor where it comes from. She pushes Prue toward the door with a little thrust of her fingers. She must be expelled, got rid of. Rivalrous feelings, long so deeply dormant as to be all but neutralised, stir and spring up, fully formed. Prue competed for her mother's love. Prue wormed her way in to the Manse and made a bid for Isla with that lost look, that winning look, which touched her mother (*her* mother, not Prue's mother, *hers*) to the quick. Took her in. Took her away.

Thief; Sassenach; Papist; Army-child; fat girl; goggle-eyes.

Quailing before that look of wry contempt, Prue removes herself fast. She'd rather have had Isabel than the books; but at least, she thinks, (scurrying down the staircase past the stained glass window depicting the Marriage of the Lamb and the Horsemen of the Apocalypse) *I've got the books.*

★

Isabel plumps down on her bed as soon as Prue has latched the front door and Iain ceased his frantic barking. The anger has all drained away; indeed she does not recall being angry. The world is almost entirely blank and flat, on two dimensions. There is only this dull condition of estrangement, this boredom and inertia. The fit of energy which tore up the books has presented the only break in this cold tedium. Clock-watching. Observing her hand convey the cup to her mouth. Inserting into her mouth tasteless fragments of vegetable and dead animals and excreting the same in due course. Looking at the full moon from her window like a single peep-hole of light in a uniformly black world. She cannot cry. She cannot register sadness.

Her cousins Rachel and David are staying; they care for her father in his fits of violent grief, which alarms and disgusts Isabel when it comes on. She doesn't like it, doesn't want it, won't speak to him, though between attacks he's gentle and heedful of her at the distance she dictates. But 'Stop it! Be quiet!' she shouted at him when she saw his lip quiver, the eyes spouting tears – she hates it and hates him for threatening her frozen calm. She won't stop in the same room with him. A grown man, her own father, and supposedly a Christian and a minister, to blubber and snivel like that. If she can control herself, why can't he? For above all she doesn't want to pity him; that pity would bring her own heartbroken tears welling up and spilling over, and then how would she ever put her self back together again? She must not melt and dissolve; she must be rigid and stiff, and not let anyone get close to thaw and threaten her.

David is a passive presence merely, yet more real to her in this bizarre, ghost-swarming world than anyone except poor old Iain, who scrabbles against her mother's door at twilight, when Isabel calls him off harshly. David sits there, apparently not bored, though doing nothing and saying little, his pipe clenched between his teeth, in a posture of listening intentness. When the endless acquaintances and parishioners come to condole, they take no notice of him at all. Yesterday he talked a bit to her about Aldermaston and the demonstrations at Edgbaston against the South African cricket team, at the wake amongst the black coven of elderly sepulchral relatives from Sutherland she'd never seen before, wearing hats with veils like spiders' webs and gobbling oatmeal biscuits and talking with many a sigh about how dear Isla was a 'vairy guid woman, God rest her soul'. David talked about the iniquities of apartheid, and she found herself listening, so that for a while she could forget the dolorous pantomime being enacted around her.

Rachel cried a lot at the funeral, which Isabel in her fierce reserve resented; the ostentation, the unstoical wearing of your heart upon your sleeve. On the other hand, Rachel wouldn't wear black, insisted on the rainbow colours of the Covenant, for, 'Oh no, we are *celebrating* Isla, not mourning her – do you honestly think she's gone?' Extravagant, histrionic hand-gestures: 'No, she's all about us – in all this – all of it' and her hand floated out to encompass the whole Manse, the gardens, the Glebe and

262

Carse and Estuary beyond, and, as it seemed, the cloudy skies, the whole abiding globe and the vast space in which it swam. Accordingly, the dour funeral procession included one peacock – waltzing up the aisle in a coat of many colours and a prismatic silk scarf that wafted as she walked – somewhat contradicting her own manifesto by bursting into tears when at the interment the earth was scattered into the clayey hole to rattle and echo upon the box in which the mother of Isabel lay. But Rachel saw no shame in genuine emotion: 'It shows you're *alive*' she (tactlessly) later said, and David said 'Shush!' and frowned, pressing her hand, but Isabel – to her own surprise – said 'That's all right', for at least it was honest, and there wasn't much of *that* around where Death was; she saw that quite clearly.

Rachel and David do not seek to trespass upon Isabel's refrigerated calm; they neither woo her with their eyes (as her father does, falling as he is through infinite space at hundreds of miles an hour) nor with words of invasive comfort or pesterings as to how she feels or fares. They respect her 'Keep out' notice, and only ask sensible, practical questions as to whether she'd like an egg boiled or poached, and if boiled, whether soft or hard? – such questions as she is able to answer briskly and factually. Only once Rachel said, 'I've something to show you. I've never shown anyone else, even David. Would you like to see?', and despite the impermeable dead rind which bound her emotions, Isabel couldn't help registering a smidgeon of curiosity.

'What is it?'

'Well, it's nothing very spectacular. It's something I made – in a time of great trouble – I couldn't concentrate to work properly. I was just fiddling with some wet clay and I suddenly realised I'd made this – thing – and I put it away to keep – never showed it to anybody. It became secret, it became, though it sounds daft, *me*. It lives in darkness – I take it out once in a while and handle it – then I put it back.'

Out of a nest of wood shavings in a cardboard box she drew a glazed clay egg which she placed in the palm of Isabel's hand. They looked at it mutely together.

'It's always there, you see,' said Rachel.

Isabel didn't know what to say. She nodded and gave it back.

All she knows is that it is necessary to carry on being Isabel – her real self, not a dummy dressed in other people's clothes, not a puppet dancing when they tweak her wires. Especially now, in this blank abeyance of any bearings, when she feels as you do when you've been ill and lie staring at a dreary slab of windowed sky, and listen to the mindless birdsong out there, now especially it is paramount that she go on being Isabel. To do this against all the recommendations of common sense and even good feeling – even if it would have hurt her living mother.

Tearing the books would indeed have wounded Mother. Nevertheless it is Mother who has given her the power to do so. *To say, I am Isabel, even with my tearless eyes and stony heart.*

*

Prue lingers sadly in the chilly, sodden garden, Mrs Gordon's books in her arms, as if she'd benefited from a will and wished to thank the absent giver. She loved Mrs Gordon as she has loved Columba, but with the addition of reverence and devotion, across a great gulf of age, class, religion and tribe. It was an unequal love, that of a petitioner to a judge; she hid her begging bowl and yet it was evident that she came with empty hands to one whose

264

hands were full, in every sense. She could prefer neither rights nor claims. And yet it was an equivalent love, a doing of justice on both sides.

'I shall always remember you, Mrs Gordon,' Prue mutely tells the garden which is all that is left of her friend's mother. The blackened holly and rhododendron shiver in a rough little wind which rises and dies in the same breath. The ivied house stands cold and sombre in the midday twilight. Dank pools distilled of melted snow churn briefly in the breeze and are again flat and still.

The weight of the books in Prue's arms reminds her that she must get home; there's nowhere dry to put them down and their edges dig into her chest. Added to that, one of her boots has a small leak the effects of which are beginning to tell uncomfortably. Hobbling so as to use only the left edge of her left foot, Prue shuffles out through the rusting iron gates.

12

On his way home from the glasshouse, Hugh stops off at the mess. A Christmas tree hung with tinsel and baubles winks through the smoke at Hugh's sour and jaded eye, as he edges his way through the press of khaki drinkers and lodges his elbow on the bar counter. Above his head is draped an elderly-looking paper-chain and a solitary yellow balloon. He downs his pint in two long swigs and wags the glass at the barman. The barman isn't noticing. Is deliberately not noticing.

'Oi!' Hugh solicits his attention with jutting chin and baleful eyes. 'What about some service? Out on strike, are you?'

'Coming, mate.' But the barman does not come. Turning his back slightly, he pursues a football conversation with a friendly customer; is washing glasses in a leisurely way under the counter.

'When, next bleeding year? . . . Hey, I were next, not him. I *said*, I were next.'

The barman replenishes Hugh's glass, with a shrug of the shoulders and a raised eyebrow.

'Okay, okay, mate – don't lose your rag.'

Hugh turns his back, leaning with both elbows on the counter, staring through the thick brew of smoke and noise at the knots of men swapping anecdotes and jokes;

playing snooker at the far end. He ambles from one group to another, but each time the group seems to seal him out from its ranks. He is acknowledged and then ignored. People don't want to know him; is that it?

'Been in the bloody glasshouse for a week,' he confides to Lofty Short.

'I heard. Bad luck,' says Lofty. 'Who put you on charge? Johnson, was it?'

'Nah – that nancy-boy Frye.'

'Oh – him. Well, I'm off. See you, mate.' Lofty pulls his forage-cap from his epaulet and fits it on his head. 'Mustn't keep Er waiting or I'll cop it.'

Hugh takes offence but says nothing.

The hubbub of fraternal conversation goes on all round him. But Hugh prowls on his own; left out. He downs a further pint and then another. Is soon squiffy for he hasn't eaten anything but a handful of peanuts; squiffy and sorry for himself and looking round for someone on whom to unburden his soul. Researches reveal Taf Watkins, sitting pickled in a corner by himself. Lachrymose, Hugh pens him in and seeks to explain to Taf how his mother didn't love him; his father died and she let him wander the streets of Salford without a crust of bread to call his own; she went off to hospital for months on end and left them to fend for themselves. But even Taf, it seems, doesn't want to know. His pale blue eyes stare at Hugh blankly for five minutes, then they begin to cast around for a line of escape; he suddenly drops his fag in the dregs of the beer, where it fizzes momentarily; gets up and sheers off.

'What's the matter you bastard, have I got bad breath or BO or something?' Hugh enquires loudly of Taf's broad beam end departing through the press. Eyes look but no one answers. 'Welsh git,' he mutters to himself. 'All the bloody same.' Soft, squashy, unreliable people. Always let you down. Nice as pie to your face, and hands feeling around in your back pocket. 'Never trust a Welshman!' he advises his fellow drinkers at the top of his voice.

'Who is it over there? Making that Godawful racket?'

'Bigmouth Cahill again. Pissed as a newt.'

'Oh Christ, that old soak.'

'SAY that again,' says Hugh, butting up with his shoulder. 'Go on, say that again, to my face – go on, you, just you say it.' His fist comes up.

'Oh lay off, can't you.'

'Get him out, for God's sake.'

'Not him again.'

Hugh points out that the barman's mother was a tart and that he is having it off with the barmaid amongst the kegs under the counter (in graphic detail). He accuses Corporal Saunders of being a filthy nigger in need of a scrub-down and advises him earnestly to go home to Jamaica, there to consume coconuts with his fellow monkeys. He tells everyone (just as he is being jettisoned) that nobody loves him; he is a misunderstood man with a sensitive heart; that it will not be his fault what happens next; it will be theirs and then they'll be sorry.

Outside the closed doors, the mess can be heard to hum like a hive full of convivial bees. Its communal life pulses with a generator's throbbing. In rectangles of warm light, the windows disclose the shapes of men with beer-glasses comfortably clasped against the breast-pockets of battle-dress, or aiming a dart at an invisible board. In there they are all comrades; you hear bursts of muffled laughter; a sentimental Scot starting up 'Ye banks and braes' on the piano; the soughing of many simultaneous private conversations.

Hugh stands in the sleety rain in black exile and feels a pain of lonely exclusion as piercing as anything he has ever known in his life. In his chest is a raw hole like a shot-gun wound. He struggles into his greatcoat. Rams his beret down on his head. They have thrown him out and left him in the company of his worst enemy: himself.

> Ye banks and braes o' bonny Doone
> How can ye bloom sae fresh and fair?

So sings the powerful tenor of the Scots soldier, with many a fancy flourish on the unreliable keys of the battered piano, some of which are fastened to the hammers with elastic bands. The thrum of conversation hushes, diminuendo, out of respect to the extraordinary voice.

> How can ye chaunt, ye little birds,
> When I'm sae weary, fu' o' care?

Hugh, standing with his back to the window, looking out down the black, sleek street glistening under the lampposts with rain, finds tears in his eyes, which then overflow, their warmth mingling with the cold raindrops. He begins to walk away at the double, but the voice seems to pursue him with uncanny pertinacity:

> Reminds me o' departed joys,
> Departed never to return.

Hugh stops in his tracks, his heart a raw ball of shuddering pain. Something has been lost, lost for ever, lost before he even knew it was there to have. And he wants his Mammy, oh he wants his Mammy, he wants her, wants her. *Wants her*.

★

Nowadays January never thinks that she is lacking anything, that she wants anything or anyone. She is a creature on the loose, a wild animal kept caged all her life, and now discharged from her containment into a life pursued without ties or bondings; not even with the sense that such bonds once existed and have been severed. The stub of the cord that had been shorn from source used to hurt; it used to throb hotly and crumple her at the waist with its burning twinges that were signals that her being was once secured to the world, and fed and nourished through a common circulation. That sharp awareness is now dead. Like the jab the dentist gave her to pull her rotten back teeth, the area is anaesthetised that used to root her life, and pulse with avid pain. Now there is no pain; she is aware of little distress save the insatiable desire to keep on the move. She scuds before the wind of aimless desires at high velocity, building a momentum of energy which cannot be discharged. Her nerves seem to conduct electricity; there are occasional odd physical manifestations such as an aura in her right eye, the spinning fragments of splintered light accompanied by a sort of roaring in her brain and pricklings all over her skin as if she had a jumpy sort of pins-and-needles.

She is seldom in the same place for long. She keeps on the move; truants; loiters; filches from shops and the officers' quarters, occasionally with Jacko and the gang, more often by herself. She pries and noses around in people's back yards, snooping round their sheds and sifting through their rubbish. It's amazing how much information you acquire about people through these investigations. Useless information, perhaps, but somehow the occult knowledge affords its own peculiar, tainted satisfaction, like a sort of tickling carried to the verge of pain. It's like when you see people's backsides, when you imagine them straining on the toilet or caught with their pants down, there's a kick in that. She hears her own laughter, high and whinnying: solitary laughter that dies in mirthless silence.

Once she killed a cat. The cat looked down at January from a garden wall. It was not much more than a kitten – a black, brown and white tabby with lustrous fur, well-kept, with a gold identity disc hung round its neck on a red leather collar. The cat did nothing to invite or incur its death, neither was January sensible of conceiving par-ticular animosity toward the cat. It sat pleasantly on the wall in the thinly radiating sunlight of a chilly afternoon. Stretching its jaws wide, it mewed in a civil fashion. January's hands shot out and grasped the cat round the throat; with incredible force she throttled it. Its eyes opened wide, as if about to pop out. Dead, it was a far heavier, dragging weight in her hands than when it lived. She laid it down on the wall where it had been sitting. She ran off and bought a bar of Cadbury's fruit and nut from the newsagent's in Kinleven Village, with money she had removed from the housekeeping tin. There was no memory of a killing; just a vague recollection of a cat on a wall. But she did not walk back by the same route.

Next day she stood outside the butcher's shop. The butcher, Mr Beith, was mild and gentle in inverse pro-portion to the violence with which he brought his cleaver whacking down into the carcases. She watched the rise and fall of the chopper: wham, wham, wham, three pork chops peeled off the joint. They were displayed by the butcher to his customer on a piece of grease-proof paper and wafted around in front of her nose on the palm of his hand with a genial flourish, as if the slabs of pink-grey meat had been so many large blooms whose fragrance she was kindly requested to savour. January stared through the pane at the butcher's blood-smeared apron; at his hovering face with its cordial expression indicative of being eager to serve and nothing being too much trouble. Her eyes roved round the cuts of meat in the window: slices of a cow's haunch, a lamb's shoulder, a pig's back. HAGGIS was advertised as available, in white letters on the window-pane. Haggis was a bag of blood. People came in and asked Mr Beith for a bag of blood, and Mr Beith obliged, deferentially, almost tenderly. Of course. Words cooked and dressed the meat into something palatable and digestible, but both January and Mr Beith knew the raw product. She met his eyes through the glass, stared and turned away.

Mrs Gordon died. She saw that. She kept an eye on all that was happening. She climbed up and saw Mrs Gordon lying in bed with her grey hair unbound all over the pillow. She was not dead then. She waved a hand to and fro above the sheets, as if conducting unseen music or signalling to persons unknown on the other side of an invisible barrier. A glass half full of water stood on the bedside cabinet – medicine bottles – a clock. The hand waved and gestured fraily. Shadows in motion on the wall above the bedhead fluttered and faded. It was not a cruel hand. January's arm-muscles burned with effort; she had to let herself down the drainpipe, shinning down hand over hand.

January saw when they carried the staggering coffin out into the snow. She observed from an aperture in the garden shed. Black, inky figures slid and slithered; the hearse revved its engine, spinning its wheels on the compacted ice of the drive. When the white silence had closed over their wake, she came running over the maelstrom of their footprints and tyre-prints and clambered in the pantry window. Up the dark staircase into the numb bedroom. Lay on the bed that had been stripped of its sheets and blankets and was covered now only by one rubber sheet. Sniffed in the queer, dead odour. The cat padded in. January was up in a great bound. Chased it round the echoing house but couldn't catch it for it shot out through the hole by which she'd got in. The house exuded damp and age. A layer of dust lay over everything. The teapot was full of the thick, cold dregs of tea. She poured it out and took a swig: sour and stewed. Mrs Gordon's knitting lay on a chair in the living room beside the bay window. The cushion bore an imprint, as if someone had just that minute got up and left the room. January picked up the knitting; it was a sock on three needles, dark grey. The heel had been in process of construction when the knitting was abandoned; the fourth needle, having been left in a stitch, fell out with a clatter when January picked it up. Dropping the unfinished work, she wandered restlessly round a bit, then cleared off.

Once she went back after dark. She heard the dog baying. She heard a man crying. Crying at the top of his voice. Then it went silent. A light went off. January roamed away in the moonlight.

All the mouths in the world are lying mouths. January does not credit a tithe of what she hears; the nice good people are just as bad as the vile ones, or worse because they pretend to be better. Mrs Gordon was also a liar. She pretended to herself she was not an animal. She could not call a fart a fart, a piss a piss. She spoke a high and mighty language. She prided herself on being a kind lady, better than the common run. But Mrs Gordon boiled toffee and baked gingerbread-men, which she offered on a plate in extenuation, saying, 'Take as much as you want. There's plenty for all.' And because of this, her many lies could be partially forgiven her.

273

He's been away; in the glasshouse. She prowled his belongings in the advantage yielded by his detention. She assessed the contents of his drawers. *So this is you?* she enquired, assembling the evidence which betokened him. One handleless hairbrush, tortoiseshell and oval, carrying traces of his wiry hair; in it a brown comb planted, with one tooth missing. Motley time-pieces that don't tick, you can't make them tick. A dog-eared photograph of his Mam on Blackpool Pier. A pen-knife with a corkscrew. A dingy wallet with bus-tickets and bills in its pockets. Old dentures and denture-cream; she made them clack together like a skull's teeth. In a box at the dusty rear of the drawer, his medals from the War, on multi-coloured ribbons, like newly-minted coins, bearing the silhouetted face of George VI. Amongst the debris and the leavings, this bright currency lurking. She picked up the medals and jingled them in her hand. He won these for killing Krauts and wops – for heroism.

How did he kill them? With a gun, with a bayonet?

How many did he kill?

Blood-red images exploded upon the screen of her mind: him in the desert or the Troodos mountains stalking EOKA terrorists with his bayonet and that look she knows on his face, plunging the blade in and in and in.

She pinned the line of medals on her own chest. Reaching down his best forage cap from the top of the wardrobe, the one he wears on parade when King Hussein or Princess Grace of Monaco visit to take the salute, she assessed her father's daughter in the mirror.

She saluted the soldier in the mirror, just as she has seen him salute his Commanding Officer in the march-past on the Parade Ground: with fingers straight and rigid; with face like a slab, scoured of human expression; chin in – head back – chest out – stomach in – legs together. Like

274

a zombie. Like a man pretending to be a machine. Like a man who is a gun.

She puts his face where hers is. His square jaw and shiny, greasy skin, with the large pores. His staring, pale-blue eyes, truculent or wooing. His heaviness of eyebrow, moustache, nose-hairs, ear-hairs, head-hair. She fades out; he blurs in.

She will surely kill him.

He has said many times – in threat or panic or punishment – that he will kill her.

'If you tell anyone about this, you bitch, I – will – kill – you. Understand? I will kill you. Got it? Open your mouth – just once – *once*, mind – and that's it: you're finished.'

Sometimes he elaborated. Throttling. Suffocating with a pillow. Break your legs and arms like sticks first. Throw you from the window. Drown you in the estuary. She believed it. There was no lying here – just the brutal truth, endorsing a fundamental rule she'd learnt: the more brutal and bestial, the more truthful.

Sometimes he kissed her. Said drunken words of love. Evil love-talk more lewd than acts of violence. He seemed to hit her, then, with the sick shock of his false tenderness. He called her his darling girl, his sweet, kind darling girl; his tongue was lickingly caressive. She let him use these words indecently on her. She let him flay her with this silk, she must let him.

She screwed her mouth and eyes into a coldly murderous smile, which she directed at the likeness in the mirror.

And I will kill you, she said as a matter of fact to the wearer of the soldier's cap above the hero's medals, which was his face and her face; which was one face.

*

275

He's back home. The front door slams with a reverberation so fierce that the picture of the Shrine at Lourdes quivers on its nail and a jamjar full of paint-water placed by some child on the bottom of the banister topples and smashes. Clumping boots invade the hall and the house. Three small Cahills hastily remove themselves via the back door, to enter the relative sanctuary of the adjoining house – although he has been known to give chase and hunt you from house to house when he was gunning for someone, like a lurid game of tig, played for life.

Mary Cahill's rosary goes flying out of her hands; her head seems to implode as it meets the edge of the sideboard and, from there, the wall behind it. She lies concussed, a stream of blood flowing from her right ear. High Cahill kicks her body twice. He roars something incoherent and sweeps all the ornaments from the sideboard with one flourish of his apocalyptic arm: the smirking china shepherdess, the ash-tray, St Sebastian and King Jesus are all tumbled together in one sacred and profane heap. Mary opens her stunned eyes a crack and peers out, but neither moves nor emits a sound. The unborn baby also feigns dead. The fluttering motions of the tender dance it executes every evening abruptly terminate, and it seems to crouch holding its breath in a tense mound.

'Nobody loves me!' howls Hugh at the top of his voice. 'Nobody – nobody – nobody!'

The fender sails across the room, followed by the coal-scuttle, which dislodges the paper chains, followed by a dining room chair, which smashes a window.

'Where are you? Where the hell are you anyway?'

He doesn't know who he means but, by God, he is going to get them and then they'll know who's boss. Hugh pounds up the stairs. He'll find them all right. Make no mistake. Nobody puts one over on Hugh Cahill and gets away with it. Electric volts discharge in his brain.

Prue has locked her door and hidden in the wardrobe, where she huddles shaking from head to foot. Damian cowers in his cot, into which Paul has also climbed. Hugh bursts in. He beats Paul across the head, one-two, one-two. He picks Damian up and hurls him back down into the cot on his face; he does it again; and then again. Each time, the child's screaming dies the moment his face whacks down on the mattress.

Even Hugh's children don't love him. But they will be made to love him, if it kills them.

'I'm your *father*, do you hear, your *father*.'

'Yes Dad, yes Dad, yes Dad.' Paul protests his thorough and hysterical agreement with this proposition. He wets himself, he can't help it. 'Don't Da, no, please.'

'Your *father*, do you hear?' He grasps the small face in his right hand, under the chin, crumpling the features in till the cheeks bulge and the eyes half close.

Through squashed-up lips the boy manages to reassure him:

'I – know – you – are – Dad – *I know*.'

Hugh throws the face from him. Paul immediately scuttles away like a spider under Damian's cot and kneels there with his head in his arms.

Hugh rockets from the room. His rage is reaching crisis-point; it craves consummation. Kicking January's door open, he confronts her still figure, standing at the window with her hands behind her back. She appears bored and nonchalant. She is not afraid. This disconcerts him.

'Hello, Dad. Let you out, did they?'

The thin, sallow face, with its eczema scars and its battle-scars, confronts Hugh as if through a mask. It is caked in make-up, the eyebrows inexpertly pencilled so as to fly like wings somewhat beyond their natural arc, the cheeks unsubtly rouged, the thin mouth incarnadined.

'You little whore. What have you tarted yourself up like that for?'

'For you, Dad. Thought it would give you a thrill.' One corner of her mouth smiles, the other is still. Her legs are planted apart and she sways from hip to hip. The strange flying eyebrows like a beetle's wings give an odd effect to the low forehead of a studied air of ironic disbelief. 'Don't it turn you on then? Don't you go for it, you filthy old bag of guts?'

He goes for her but she is waiting. Side-steps neatly and he runs his head into the window-frame. When he recovers she is at the other side of the room, hands behind her back, sneering.

'Missed,' she comments. 'Try again.'

Hugh blunders after her, panting heavily. As he comes at her, he gets a whiff of the alcohol on his own breath and thinks he might be going to throw up. She leaps lightly on to the bed and there gently trampolines.

'Getting a bit past it, fat-guts,' she remarks pleasantly.

Out of her pocket comes his forage cap, which she fits on to her own head at a waggish angle. Now for the first time he registers that she's wearing his war medals on her chest.

'Hey, where d'you get them?' he asks stupidly. 'You been in my drawers haven't you? You been going through my bleeding things while I were away?'

He feels naked, abashed suddenly, as if he were caught marching on parade with his underpants down.

'Don't you think I've earned these medals, living with you – being messed about by you – beaten and hit and smashed by you – for nothing, all for nothing – you'll go to Hell, you will. I've told Father Friend on you, everything you done, I've told him the whole bally lot. You, a war hero? – Don't make me laugh – you couldn't fight a rotten tomato. You're not a hero, you're not a man, you're scum, you're dregs you are – I'm the hero, *me – me – me*'.

Again he surges, the bull to the red flag of her parted lips. She leaps down and the kitchen knife in her hand catches a flash of light. He pauses. Laughs with a snort. She can't hurt him: he's a trained man, she's only a girl. He was pounding up to bayonet-sacks and sticking his blade into their guts of padded sand and straw when she was still playing with ragdolls (shout *Aaaaaaaaaargh*! then thrust, imagine the bastard raped your mother, they told him, so *Aaaaaaaargh*! he shouted obediently, and thrust, and has kept on thrusting ever since) . . .

'Now you've had it. I'll get that knife and I'll cut you up like plaited dough, so help me I will.'

Up on the bed again she leaps, dances; then down, and smartly nips under his arm; plunges the kitchen devil in his back, just at the joint of the shoulder and arm.

Hugh bellows; swings around and grabs her wrist; loses it. She's like an eel; she's everywhere, jabbing, slicing at him, slippery, lithe, flyweight.

The knife rips the calf of his leg, it scores his face from nose to ear. But he's got her, it was only a matter of time, grapples the knife from her fist.

He raises her entire body above her head, laughing, gripping her by the waist. He laughs, hee haw, hee haw, at her impotently flailing arms and legs, her mad brown eyes.

Then the pain gets him. He goes off balance, then crumples. January sails sideways, finds her feet and is off, streaking down the stairs like lightning; sprinting past Malachi who has just come in and, aghast, hoisted his mother on to a chair. Seizing a coat off the stand, she pelts out into the dark.

Hugh pounding down in pursuit meets Malachi pounding up.

'You evil crazy bastard,' yells Malachi to his fuddled, bleeding father. He grasps him by the collar of his battle-dress and heaves him down the stairs, where he lies still.

*

On the main southbound road the infrequent cars and lorries rumble past. No one in this blank dawn is looking to pick up a mangy girl in a duffel coat and plimsolls standing on the grass verge with her thumb stuck out. Rain has been falling for several hours and visibility is poor; most vehicles have their lights switched on, to cut a swathe of light through the greenish murk.

Her feet are soaked through, and very cold. She feels entirely comfortless. Hunger has exhausted the emotional energy that pitched her out of her father's house and carried her to the Manse, where she found the pantry window – to her intense distress and incomprehension – boarded over. It had become a right of way. She bedded down shivering in the shed.

The lorries plough their furrow through puddles, which threw up a cold spray she has to keep dodging by running up the verge. Eventually, becoming too tired and jaded to make the effort, she just lets herself be soaked, cursing mildly each time it happens.

A green Morris Minor slows and pulls in twenty yards ahead. January dashes toward it, sloshing through the wet; she already has her hand on the door and is pressing the button to open it, when the driver, having leant across to assess her through the rainy window, changes his mind and shoots off instead.

So there's nothing for it but to get out there in the middle of the road and make them stop. The lorry, full of crates of whisky, has to jam on its brakes in order to avoid running her over. It screeches to a halt with a yard to spare. Ted Pimlott opens his window and addresses her in an inexplicably placid voice given the provocation.

'What are you playing at? I could have killed you.'

January comes round to the side of the cab and looks up, her raised head all awash with raindrops. The mascara has run and the lipstick smeared. She resembles a grotesque clown expatriated from the circus, of uncertain sanity.

'Give us a lift, mister.'

'Where are you going?' he asks doubtfully.

'South, England.'

'Where do you live?'

'In England. I ran away. Now I want to go home.'

'Well, where in England?'

'Liverpool. Are you going near there?'

'Get in then.'

The lorry is going all the way to Manchester. She climbs up beside the driver; eyes him sidelong as the rain souses the bonnet and roof, and the windscreen wipers toll their snail-slow heart-beat.

'You sure you're on your way home? Don't mess me about now.'

'Yes. Honest – no kidding.'

'Whereabouts in Liverpool?'

'Wallasey – Birkenhead-way.'

That's where her Nan lived, her mother's mother. She feeds him authentic details about Wallasey and the Birkenhead Ferry. He is not particularly convinced but now she's in, and wringing out her socks and warming her bare feet by the blast of the heater, he supposes he's saddled with her.

'Too soft by half, me. Can never say no, that's my problem.' She flashes him a look, cunning, business-like. Will he want payment, she wonders. Corpulent to the point of obesity, red-faced, balding. He wears an open, zippered jacket from which a tartan paunch protrudes. She is just about to offer payment in kind when he goes on, 'I'm Salford-born and bred myself. Not far from your way.'

'My dad's from Salford.'

'What part?'

'Crescent-way.'

'Oh, I know that well. Used to be a right nice, decent area in the old days – now it's proper run-down. Want a bar of chocolate? In there – that's right. You'll likely find a bag of humbugs there too – dig around a bit; you never know what you'll come up with.' Ted warms to the theme of Salford. Shows her pictures of his three children – Toni, 15; Mel, 11; Barbara, 8, the baby of the family and spoilt rotten. January chews, surveying the photographs in hostile silence.

'Get that muck off your face, eh?' He passes her a handkerchief. 'You don't need all that at your age. How old are you anyway?'

'Sixteen.'

'Pull the other one.'

'Honest, mister. I'm nearly 16 but I look young for my age, everybody says.'

'I'm going to pull in at the next caf – we'll get us some breakfast.'

January nods off in the warm, droning cab. Lolling there across the seat with her head near the gear-stick and her legs curled up, she looks like a child of six. The driver imagines his young one, his Barbara, say, out on the road in this downpour, far from home. He feels the burden of the girl and wishes he weren't such a sucker for hard-luck stories; but still, since she wants to go home, he'll take her home, and that will mean one less poor bugger out on the streets. He feeds her bacon, eggs and fried bread with tomato sauce, an enamel mug of steaming tea with four teaspoons of sugar. Sitting with his elbows on the green-and-white check plastic table cloth in the wooden hut, he enjoys the view of the small loch with rain dimpling its sleek surface, and taps the end of his cigarette on the table prior to lighting it. Queer-looking miserable stick of a girl; looks half-starved. He wonders what her story is.

'I'll do anything what you want,' she suddenly volunteers. Nobody does something for nothing in this world. Men are all out for what they can get. These things are axiomatic – the rules of the game which she does not bother to question. Her dark eyes are without expression as she takes the force of his stare.

'You what?'

She shrugs. 'You know. What you want. Doing it. *It*.'

He gets to his feet impatiently. 'I don't know what you're on about. Now I'm on my way. If you want to come, come; if you don't, don't.'

The cab revs up. It's a safe place, this high, warm sac way up above the other traffic. January looks down snootily on the puny cars as they overtake. The engine throbs with a mighty sound; the cab smells of battered leather, oil and tobacco. She puts on her dry socks and wishes the journey could go on forever. The nebulous countryside peels away at either side: hill and valley, pine forests whose overhanging branches graze the roof of the lorry with clattering echoes as they pass. Once a fogbound deer is caught in the headlights, a private, beautiful creature with huge eyes that leaps away into the brush. The road curves past a loch with a small, grey castle at one end. Far out over the hills you see the dark turbulence of rain-clouds and the bucketing rain pitching down aslant upon some sheep-grazed hillside or hidden tarn. They have come from nowhere and they are going nowhere. Nothing is real but motion – and then the eery stasis when they stop for a pee; the vibration of the engine ceases and the silence all around is large and strange. January stretches her stiff limbs by the lapping waters of a loch; crouches down in the fibrous, brackeny undergrowth to relieve herself, and hears the birds sing piercingly into the silence. Amnesiac and improvident, she glazes her eyes to all but the immediate journey.

'It's a grand country, all right,' says Ted. 'I'm all for settling here or hereabouts when I retire. Build a bungalow in the middle of nowhere. Up there for instance in that clearing with only the birds for neighbours, and the odd squirrel.'

Ted isn't driving flat out; he's ambling, cruising. He has time to spare and he enjoys this part of the country. They stop for the night at Braemar. The mountains in the clear evening air are heart-stoppingly beautiful. He sits in the cab with his arms folded and just stares. The girl is a good companion for she listens – or gives the appearance of listening – to his garrulous anecdotes of family and friends, and says little. After a Scottish high tea of malt-bread and fruit-cake, he has a few whiskys and beds down in the back of the lorry, with January in the cab. She awakens once in the night. The eyes of the stars are tiny pinpricks in the blue-black velvet sky. She sleeps again.

The second day, the countryside flattens and becomes less arresting. Ted puts on speed. *Slow down, slow down,* she inwardly begs him; she wills him to put the brake on; she presses herself into the back of the seat. The lowlands. Conurbations. Grey-green fields with drystone walls. Gretna Green where the love-birds flock. Over the edge into England.

'Bit of an unusual name, January. What made them call you that, then?'

'Don't know. I were born in January.'

'I were born in August but they don't call me August.'

'I suppose they ran out of names.'

'Many brothers and sisters?'

'Yeah.'

'How many?'

'Too many.'

'You mean, mind your own business. Don't give much away, do you? Want to put the wireless on?' The music blares Buddy Holly, then the Everley brothers. 'That your sort of thing?'

'It's all right.'

'Coming to the outskirts of Carlisle now – soon be home.'

January says nothing. She looks sullenly out of the window at the complacent, semi-detached houses of the suburbs, net-curtained and neat-hedged. She had faintly begun to trust Ted, to attach herself to him with little suckers of her mind, drawing in a sort of warmth from his beefy, unmolesting presence, accepting food at his hands. She had settled into this floating womb of the cab; for once in her life allowing herself to credit an illusion. He has asked nothing of her except to provide an ear to his boring stories of Sal and Toni and Mel and Barbara. Now, at the talk of *home, going home*, she recoils, scowling, and says no further word to him all the way to Newcastle, where she says she needs a pee.

Manchester. He stops to let her down near the Ducie Bridge. He has given her the money to cover a rail-ticket to Liverpool.

'Get your train at Victoria Station – just down there, turn right at the end here. Mind and go straight home now. Don't hang about. Your Mum and Dad'll have been eating their hearts out with worry. Good luck now, love.'

She pauses undecidedly at the open door, one foot out. One part of her wants to throw her arms around his neck and beg him to take her with him, then hang on tight and not let him go. But he does not want her and for that she hates him. She must throw him away like something that is used and valueless.

'Let you into a secret. I don't live in Wallasey. Never did. You've been had.'

She is off; scampers into the crowd pouring over the Ducie Bridge. Ted soon puts her out of his mind and only recollects her when he opens his wallet later in the day to find two pound notes lifted and the photographs of his children torn to shreds.

*

The women outside Victoria Station under the railway bridge have peroxided hair hanging down on their shoulders or piled on top of their heads and held in place with lacquer and multiple hair-clips. They are scantily clad, considering the punishing weather, and shiver as they stand under the soot-blackened arches that seep rain-water like oil. Their customers either pull up in cars or are taken off to a sheltered alley behind the bridge. One woman, Cath, plumply fleshy and middle-aged, with three teenage children of her own to keep (one other on the game already, another on remand), is quite maternal to January. A real relationship has sprung up between them over the fortnight the child has been hanging around the arches. At first she tried to talk January into going home, on the grounds that it can't have been as bad as all that; it can't have been as bad as *this*, for instance; there's nothing more important than food in your belly and shelter over your head. But on January's insisting that it *was* as bad, no, it was worse by *far*, with angry certainty, Cath left off nagging her. She was adequately acquainted with human cruelty.

Today she shows January what to say and how to behave with the punters. What to do if they turn nasty. Never to let the client kiss you, for that's obscene. What to say if the coppers book you. Clap, pregnancy, drugs, a complete run-down. She gives January a swig of beer from her can. A Ford draws up.

'Do you feel all right? Go on then – here comes one now. Looks okay. Have a go, chuck.'

'Want business?' asks January, as the door is opened to her. A sprucely dressed, youngish man with gold-rimmed spectacles cranes over to size her up. She is evidently not what he expected, this child with painted face and gym shoes, carrying a duffel coat over one arm and wearing her loose V-neck sweater off one shoulder.

'Too young. Hop it,' he says.

'I'm 16,' January assures him. 'And I'll suck.'

He gestures her in with his head; the door slams; the car pulls away.

*

When Dad gets out of hospital, he's not exactly the man he was. He sits for long periods staring into the fire as if a fuse had blown in his head and put him out of action. He easily becomes lugubrious; weeps copious tears when he's in drink, which is every night, and waxes lyrical on the subject of the distant past and sentimental on the subject of his little darlings, whom he takes on his knee and fondles. Malachi has left home, going south to work in Huddersfield at a meat-packing factory; to his mother's intense but stifled grief. The baby she was carrying survived its shock, and as Christmas approaches it cuts such alarming capers in her belly and swells to such a prodigious size that she begins to fear it might turn out to be twins. But for the moment – with Columba, Malachi and January all gone – the pressure on space in the house has been alleviated. January has been put on the Missing Persons list and (to no one's dismay) no news has been heard of her. The attack she made on her father before she left was, as both Hugh and Mary alleged to the police and social services, entirely unprovoked, the result of the girl's well-attested instability. They can't cope with her, they candidly admit. If she is ever located she will have to be taken into the care of the Council.

She hardly took up any space, she was so spare and lean. Her meagre, bony body seemed to hunker down into itself; her elbows gripped in to her waist as she walked, her head crouched down into her shoulders as if constantly vigilant for ambush. And yet even so there had been too much of her. She had focused all the turbulence of the group. Its violence deposited itself in her; they looked at her aghast, and side-stepped when they saw her coming. She was their creation and their sign, just as they were society's creation and its sign – for though they had the disease, she was its disfiguring rash. And those brilliant, hectic eyes had seemed not only to accuse them but to say with a kind of electric vengefulness, *Watch out, I'm free. I'm myself. You're none of you safe with me around.* Her speed, her agility and tough, punchy resourcefulness had been there amongst them like a nemesis. Her pain cried out as a denial of all rules; all rule. Now she is gone, there is not one heart in the household that knowingly mourns. The space she occupied seals over; her absence is neither inwardly rued nor outwardly alluded to.

Mary Cahill pinches down the memory of her seventh child to a little black ball, which she tries to flick away. But the pilulous residue refuses to be expelled. At night, in throes of guilt, the ball unfolds into the dark ghost of a girl who flies like a bat through the tenebrous regions of Mary's sleep: a bat with talons and a piercing inhuman shriek to which she can no longer turn a deaf ear. In the morning she reaches for a fag and lights up; she inhales deeply and wonders what she dreamt.

Hugh Cahill, on sick-leave, nursing his injured shoulder and back, is becoming so fuddled with drink that he frequently forgets where he is and gropes from bottle to bottle in a fog of incomprehension. His rage rises just as frequently, but turns almost instantaneously to tears. He sits in the best armchair and hears himself talking or hears himself snoring, and the one is just about as comprehensible as the other. The Army is threatening to discharge him on medical grounds, and what will Hugh do then for a living? Something has gone from his life: some frightful, sick satisfaction, through which he got his own back at everyone and everything. He recalls his daughter only as a vicious black sheep who gave nothing but trouble and got what she deserved, but his spirit – and his prick – wilt with a sort of superstitious dread that comes over him, especially at night. He cannot get over how she stood up to him like that, dressed up to kill, dressed up in his cap and medals as himself – a girl guerilla armed with a kitchen knife to carve him up, her own father – and how she danced around him like a nimble, flyweight boxer, and ducked, and flew, and neatly swerved, and swiftly stabbed, and mocked him like a demon. He is startled at the least noise. He rushes from the light-switch to the bed as if something might get him in between. He peers round fearfully in every spooked room with its shadowy corners and doors that slyly creak ajar, in case she should material-ise, waif, wraith, made of air and ire, raised by the vileness of his crime and the vileness of himself. This terror makes him booze more; and then the booze knocks him senseless; and then the terror comes up twice as bad and he dis-charges it by weeping; and he seems to himself the most pitiful and lonely thing in the whole of God's creation; so he takes another drink.

January has taken wing, but she has not been abolished from Prue Cahill. Prue would have to peel her very skin from her bones to divest herself of January. Something of herself would have to be excised and left for dead in the road – some organic part of her, which she splits off into an obscene double that demands more atoning compassion of her than she has it in her to bestow. Prue cannot deal with this dark identification, so she squashes it down like the coal buried in the coal-hole on delivery day, and tramples on the lid. Prue retires more deeply than before into the sanctuary of her mild and unforthcoming silence. Retreating into the pages of her books, she takes hands with the ancient dead, turning the gold-edged pages with reverencing fingers. She is careful and orderly. It bothers her if her toothbrush is not stood in the mug at a particular angle, just so; she washes her hands compulsively; all her clothes are folded in the drawers of Columba's old dressing-table with geometrical precision.

Dodging meals, she brings her plate upstairs, to eat with her head in a book, cross-legged on the bed. For the atmosphere downstairs at meal-times is weirdly oppress-ive, dominated by the hangdog lugubriousness of her father. He feeds himself as if putting food away under compulsion into the mouth of a creature of another species. He masticates long and without enjoyment, and seems to keep coming to his senses with a jerk and reminding himself to deposit another piece of meat or sprout into the creature's mouth. His eyes are often red and puffy; he makes no secret of the fact that he has been crying. While this operation horrifies Prue, it also fascinates her; and the the fascination alarms her. She flees upstairs to be out of range of the magnetic tug that twitches her heart along the radius of his need. He looks at her sorrowfully and almost with reproach, invading her with an uneasy sense of being accountable – but for what? He seems like a different man from the madman who did . . . those things. But then he always seemed different from himself. There were so many of him: the joker, the piper, the rascal, the sweetheart, the tyrant, the betrayer, the monster, the fraud. Now there is this sad man, this very sad, slumped man, shameful and shameless, with the fume of alcohol never off his breath.

Prue eats two mincepies, biting one and then the other, keeping them fraternally equal, making them last. In the paper-thin world that lies open on her knee, Little Nell is dying, page by lingering page, deliciously. Prue has a lump in her throat; she spins out the oozings Dickens pumps from her tear-ducts. Laying down the book at the end of a chapter, she thinks she will creep downstairs to secure another mincepie, and maybe a few cheese straws, still cooling on the tray.

She nips past *him*, sitting with his head in his hands at the fire-side, unmoving except for the slight shaking of his bulky shoulders, which indicates to her that he is crying again. He appears not to register her presence. Her mother is out at the front, shovelling coal; she hears the scraping of the shovel and the tinny clattering as the coals hit the scuttle. Prue places one still-warm mincepie and three cheese straws in the copious pocket of her skirt, and prepares to renegotiate the passage past her father. But this time he is sitting up, alert.

He winks. 'I won't tell,' he promises.

'Thanks, Dad,' Prue flushes. 'I only took one, anyway.'

'That's all right, my girl. Your Dad will keep your secret.' His complicitous voice drawls thick and slow. He pats his pockets and the arms of the chair. 'Seen me fags anywhere, darling? Blest if I know where they've got to.'

'Here, Dad,' Prue bends to pick up the packet of Players. 'And there's one stuck behind your ear.'

'So there is.' He strikes a match and lights up. 'That's better. Getting on with your studies, are you?'

'Yes, Dad.'

He sighs. 'You was always the clever one of the family, Prue. You and Teresa, but she were always more holy-like, from a little one. Always a one for reading and books, you was. And cornflake-packets and milkmen's bills and the paper round the fish-and-chips if you couldn't get hold of nothing else in the way of printed matter.'

Prue says nothing. She didn't know he'd ever noticed her as being a separate person, let alone her literacy. Some-times he'd muddle her identity with Charity's and seem genuinely confused as to which was which.

'Well, you stick to it, Prue. Don't let *nothing* get in your way – nothing at all. Life's over for me but you've got it all to come – don't throw your life away like I've thrown mine. I've made bad mistakes and I'm paying for them.'

She wants to go; she wants to stay. She doesn't like it that he is eyeing her so closely, as if awoken to the some-thing unique she's kept hidden so long, which is Prue's self, her private, inward, germinating self. She is detained as if by force by his interest in her, his gentleness.

'I've got to go now, Dad.'

'Don't go, Prue. Stay and talk to your Dad.'

Prue lingers. His attention is riveted on her, as if she were something very special and surprising that had just flowered into his view, an exotic orchid in a cabbage-patch. Then, as her mother comes in lugging the coal-scuttle, which she plonks down on the grate with a bang, Prue takes the opportunity to slip off. She can hear her mother riddling the fire with a poker, her father's voice droning. She hears him say her name – 'our Prue' – as she leaps upstairs two at a time. There is an ominous feeling. She slides the bolt across. She feels like a timid, nocturnal animal that has been flushed out of its burrow in broad daylight. She cannot now enjoy the cooled mincepies, which she places on her bedside cabinet for later. She longs and longs for Columba, for Mrs Gordon, for the visit of the Blessed Virgin.

Prue stands at the window, looking through the complex thread of the net curtains at the deepening twilight, the blue-grey dusk shot through with swathes of dusky pink as the bloodshot sun is swallowed into the horizon. Pinkish light smears the windows of the quarters and burnishes the red-brick to fiery auburn, dimming and darkening by the minute. The world of street-lamp, pavement, hydrant, houses and hopscotch-pitch is criss-crossed by the grid of netting; it is delimited by the frames of Teresa's glasses; it is distanced by the pane of glass that intervenes between herself and itself. She is always inside looking out or outside looking in. A child in a pale, gingham dress that glows in the strange light with a milky radiance plays on the chalked hopscotch pitch, a million miles away. She carefully throws her stone, then hops to the end, on the return journey picking up the stone, balanced on one foot balletically, then throws again – and it all takes place on another planet. Prue is never there, where it is happening, but outside, hovering on the margins, like an eternal spectator at a communal game. Does everyone nurse this sense of standing apart and alone and watching; a pair of eyes merely, looking out of something unknown on to something unknown?

Columba is married; Mrs Gordon has died; the Virgin Mary veils herself from sight. There is no one to whom she might apply for answers to these questions, or whose presence might annihilate the questions, so that she forgot she'd ever asked them.

The smaller children are chased into bed. Prue is required to bath Damian and Paul; she towels them dry, brushes their hair and cleans their teeth. From the bathroom door her father stands watching these ministrations. He leans on the doorframe, biting at a hangnail and smiling benignly.

'You're a good girl, Prue,' he says. 'You're a proper little mother to them.'

She doesn't like that. It is too huge a burden. And besides, she feels nothing for her young brothers except a vague aversion. She acts by rote, and because she will always seek to comply with what is asked of her, so as to remain inconspicuous, not to break cover. She doesn't like it that Dad is singling her out, loading her with this praise. She blenches and turns her hot face away.

'Stand still will you, Paul, and keep your mouth open. That's better.'

She says their prayers with them and blesses them for the night, just as Columba always did for her. But when she kisses them she feels nothing, even when Damian's

294

arms curl round her neck and he kisses her cheek repeatedly, with every appearance of warm affection.

He waylays her in the corridor.

'I'm going to bed now, Dad.'

'It's too early – much too early – a big girl like you. Come and keep me company, Prue-girl – come and sit on your dear old Daddy's sweet old knee.' His speech is slurred; his hand travels down her arm and closes over her wrist.

'No, Dad. Please don't.'

'Your poor Dad – so lonely. So lonely, Prue.'

'Someone's coming. Up the stairs.'

As he turns to look, Prue darts into her room and shoots the lock. Waits at the door in mounting panic. Has he gone? What does he want? Why her? She thinks she can hear him breathing on the other side of the door. Then discrepant noises take over: voices, the lavatory flushing, Charity and her friend Nidjah barging up the stairs. He must have gone. She allows herself to begin to calm down.

But he won't hurt her. He doesn't mean her any harm. He's changed, sorry, gentle. He's a wounded, broken man. *It's all right, it's all right, Prue*, she lullabies herself. *Nothing bad will happen, forget it.*

He needs her. He loves her. Oughtn't she to let him in? The Holy Virgin will protect her.

Will she?

Prue sits on her bed with her eyes closed and tries to summon the Queen of Heaven, the Mother of God, into her bedroom. But Mary has never suffered herself to be invoked into this house and she does not now change her policy. In Prue's hands, the little chipped plaster model of the Madonna takes warmth from her fingers. But the powerful, authoritative Mary, the real one, will not come to her – the one who has promised to safeguard every hair of Prue's head.

She is bursting to go to the lavatory. She hangs on as long as possible; then, listening to make sure that the coast is clear, she pulls the catch and hurries across into the bathroom, snapping the bolt across.

As Prue slips into the bathroom, Hugh emerges from his bedroom where he has been dozing, and shuffles into Prue's room.

Prue washes her face and cleans her teeth, replacing the toothbrush just so, at an angle in the turquoise mug at which it will not touch and be infected by germs from anyone else's. The horror has passed off to a considerable degree. Tomorrow is Christmas Eve: she will go round to Isabel with her present to her, and a bone for Iain.

Back in her own room, she immediately pulls the catch on the door and advances down the perpendicular of the 'L' to the end of the bed. In the lamplight her father reclines with his back against her pillows, his slippered feet on the bed; he has her book in his hands and is leafing the pages.

'Good book?' he asks.

'Please, Dad . . . leave me be,' she whispers.

'Don't you want your own Dad? Don't you love your Dad, Prue? Don't you want to comfort him when he's down?' Oh God it's true she doesn't love him. Nobody cares about him. He knew; he always knew. The old, dismal record begins to spin screechingly in his mind, round and round, faster and faster, hellbent, the same old tune winding him up and up till it's unbearable, something must explode.

Tears partly channel off the energy. 'Even you, Prue – turning against your father, your own father, your father what's been hurt and wounded – I can't believe that even you . . .'.

Aghast. 'No, Dad. It's not that.'

'Then put your arms round me Prue. I won't hurt you, my darling girl. I swear by my life.'

His face is huge upon her eye. It fills the whole horizon. It dilates so that she can see every pore and every lash, each stump of bristle on his chin, each mole and fleck. The face is a planet out of orbit, violating the elliptic of the earth. As it descends upon Prue, she is completely engulfed. She does not put up a fight. She screams neither for help nor mercy.

Sequel

For two further years, until January 1962, Hugh Cahill continued to molest his daughter Prudence, the abuse spreading to his youngest sons, Paul and Damian, during 1960. Prue was nearly 14 when she in her turn ran away from home to her eldest sister, Teresa, a nun at the Convent of the Sacred Heart just outside Stoke-on-Trent. She hitched a lift from the rented house in Salford where the family went to live shortly after her father was invalided out of the Army, uprooting her from the Scottish countryside to which she had so closely bonded herself. Presenting herself at the front door of the convent, which was opened by a novice of the order, she told her story to her sister behind the grille, showing her the bruises, contusions and scars which testified to her ordeal. Sister Michael (Teresa) obtained permission for leave of absence. She instituted proceedings against their father, who received a prison sentence of five years, with remission for good conduct. The boys went into a Barnardo's home and Damian was later adopted; as a much-loved only child, he grew up caring and gentle, but always slightly needy. He became a nurse in a mental hospital. Peter, Paul and Francis were disturbed and unruly as children: Peter joined the Army like his father, but Paul and Francis turned to petty crime and were frequently in and out of prison. All three men battered their wives and children as a matter of course.

Charity and Catherine married at 17 and 18, respectively, and each had two children by the age of 20. Whereas Catherine's marriage was a happy one, Charity and her babies lived in constant terror of her husband, whom they left in 1979 to live in squalid poverty. Malachi made a good life for himself in the record industry, wheeler-dealing till he was well-off enough to set himself up in the South of France, where he lived in the lap of luxury without a care in the world.

Mary Cahill kept her youngest son, Brendan, a victim of Downs syndrome, in her care. She went to live in her family home at Wallasey. She died of cervical cancer in 1971, having also suffered premature senile decay, in the course of which Brendan was removed into the care of a Council Home.

Hugh Cahill was at a loss when he got out of Strangeways: the dilating space, colour, traffic and bustle of the outside world bombarded his eye and unnerved him, so that he wanted to turn round and bolt straight back into the familiar control and confinement of the gaol, his mates and the screws. It had not been so different from the Army, really – a world of males, regulated and hierarchical, you knew where you were and who was who. Severely disorientated, he crept down the main road, keeping well in to the wall until he happened upon a pub. Once inside the womb-like safety of the beery, smoggy snug, he began to recover. He got chatting to some locals, he passed the time of day with the busty little barmaid, he swigged his pint and mellowed. Hugh made a kind of shambling life for himself, renting a sordid, damp bed-sit in Salford, eking out his dole by cleaning people's drains on a door-to-door basis. His circle of drinking-friends included a lad of 16 who had run away from his home in Ireland – a bit on the simple side but a strong fellow who could earn a good bit moonlighting as a brickie. Hugh took him under his wing, taking Collum into his home and bed. Once in a while Hugh liked to go off to an Air Show at Woodford, or an Arms Fair, or the Remembrance Day Parade past the Cenotaph. He'd talk big, to impress Collum, of his life in the military, and with a nostalgia for those good old days which would make his eyes brim with tears. He regretted being unable to show Collum his war-medals, which had been pinched from him years ago. In due course, Collum drifted off. Hugh took in Jake, a runaway from a good middle-class home in Sheffield. Jake was 12.

Prue Cahill went to live with her elder sister, Columba, but Prue's jealousy of Columba's babies made her a disturbing presence in the house. She was taken into care, in a Home near Stoke, where she withdrew totally into herself, neither speaking to anyone nor appearing to register what was said to her. She conversed in private with imaginary presences, whom she addressed variously as 'Mrs Gordon' or 'Our Lady'. She became angry with shadows, but she would tread carefully so as to avoid damaging an ant or a fly, inwardly agonising over the involuntary pain one must inflict on sentient organisms merely by existing. On these grounds she for some time refused to eat, neurotically convinced that even vegetable food felt pain when she chewed it. In December 1963, Teresa's efforts to locate a foster-family for Prue in the Catholic community bore fruit. Her new family, the Reeds, lived near Birmingham. They were able to give Prue the loving care she had always craved, and in some degree to remedy the evil she had sustained. Prue trained at Birmingham College of Commerce to qualify as a librarian, a post which, however, she was only intermittently able to hold down, as she suffered not only from a crippling shyness which made her unable to show her face in public without agitation, but also a guilt at her own existence which left her at best depressive, at worst suicidal. At the age of 26 she married John Saxon, a widower, Quaker, and retired teacher, considerably her senior. She shared with him the four happiest and most stable years of her life, until his death left her alone again in 1977. Although he had done everything in his power to strengthen her to bear and surmount this inevitable catastrophe, a total breakdown followed this bereavement, in which she made two suicide attempts and was committed to Rubery Mental Hospital to the south of Birmingham for psychiatric care; she remained an outpatient for the rest of her life, having become addicted to the high doses of valium with which they treated her affliction. Subsequent attempts to come off the tablets gave her severe withdrawal symptoms, during which she again attempted suicide.

In 1982, Prue went to live with her foster-sister, Jo, who supported her in her attempt to re-adjust to normal living. It was hard for Prue to believe that Jo or anyone else could truly love her for herself, but such trust – which her foster-parents and then her husband had sought to build – did, sporadically, stabilise her. All her life she heard voices and saw visions. They came to her at times of greatest loneliness. One night she sat bolt upright in bed, having been awoken by a woman's voice which told her, quite distinctly: 'There is a floor at the centre of the world.' The next day she told Jo she was going back to Scotland to visit a place where she once lived. This worried Jo, who knew the events that had occurred there, and she tried to dissuade her sister. But Prue would go; she must. There was no point in arguing. Prue took the night train to Elgin and disembarked on a bright, chilly morning in November 1984, rubbing her eyes at the brilliance of the light.

In twenty-two years, much had changed. Prue put up at a small guest house in Forres. She felt very quiet and easy, loving the lilt of the Scottish voices which surrounded her, especially that of the landlady who served her breakfast of coffee, warm rolls and blackcurrant jam. For once in her life, Prue felt no particular self-consciousness; she had little sense of being a stranger or foreigner. The woman was interested in her profession as a librarian: she prized book-learning above all accomplishments, she said. Prue told her it was frustrating to be surrounded by so many books and yet to be prohibited from reading them. 'Ah, but you will breathe them in,' the landlady observed. Prue nodded, appreciating this perception. 'I know just what you mean,' she said.

Prue made no attempt to visit the Army camp. Alighting from the bus, she turned her footsteps toward the village, and thence the Manse. Out to the north-west, the great Carse rolled greenly from the patch of pines and the school-house out to the estuary; all was as before, save that the school-house windows were boarded over. Gulls called through the salted air; they wheeled in the wind above Prue's head.

The walls of the Manse were down. The Manse itself had been converted into luxury flats; much of the vegetation in the garden had been cleared, and a block of further modern flats had been erected where the sycamore once stood and rhododendrons ran in wild abundance, with their secret corridors, at the most dense, most private end of the grounds.

Prue stood silently, seeing herself suddenly as middle-aged: greying at the temples, thickening at the waist.

There was nothing here to come home to. It had all perished.

What had she expected? She stared at the stone walls of the great house, cleared now of the riotous ivy, whose antiquity had given its runners the girth of the branches of a small tree, sucking the firmness out of the pointing. The windows were mostly fitted with blinds, drawn down, now, against the piercing sun. Beside the door stood a list of tenants' names with individual bells: Miss Brown-Forsyth, Dr Ryan, Mr and Mrs Eager.

Then Prue saw the singing beech. It had not been touched by the wholesale acts of demolition that stripped the present of its growth of the past – no, but had been left to stand with its arms spread wide, its base partially concealed amongst rhododendron and holly. Prue approached the tree and laid the flat of both hands upon its cross-bough. It all came back, the grazed, abraded back of your legs when you swung from the tree upside down with your thin, green cotton skirt belling over your head, a private tent through which the light poured, tinged with emerald. And as you hung you sang how Charlie was your darling, the young Chevalier; and you rocked a little, with your arms trailing beneath you, quite loose, just brushing the earthy roots. A wild desire swept over Prue to do it again, clamber up and hang upside down by the legs, letting the blood rush to her head. But of course she didn't. She laid her forehead briefly against the great, cool bough, between her hands; she sighed deeply and turned away. It was not that she had found something. It was that she had found there was not quite nothing.

Later at the church, she asked the curate if he had any knowledge of the Rector and Isabel. Donald Gordon retired, the young man told her, and went to live in Fife; Isabel had quarrelled bitterly with him in her late 'teens and left him to live in Aberdeen with her cousins, but was reconciled with him before she went up to Edinburgh University. She acquitted herself there with distinction, he believed – First Class Honours in Philosophy – could have taken up an academic post, but instead became something big in the UN. Third World problems, he understood. A very powerful woman, he remembered her; spoke her mind, and *what* a mind. Intolerant, arrogant, some might say – rubbed people up the wrong way, she had a real knack of it – and yet it was innocently done, she never meant to offend. He himself had not disliked her, he honoured her integrity – and integrity has always (wouldn't you say, Mrs Saxon?) a somewhat wolfish character. Whether she was a happy woman, he couldn't say. He imagined not. She never married, as far as he knew. Perhaps happiness would not satisfy a soul so burning. But remarkable she surely was – remarkable.

'So was her mother,' said Prue.

'Was she indeed? I never knew her, I'm afraid.'

Prue found she was eager, now, to get home – she had got what she came for, though goodness knows what that was, exactly – and she did not want to confront the ghosts that crowded on the road that forked from the village to the camp.

Her father.

Was it possible ever to forgive? She had sometimes got herself to the verge of such forgiveness, knowing him to have been an ignorant, damaged man. But never could she persuade herself over that edge into the act of forgiveness which would allow her to lay the past to rest. The evil was still alive in her, germane to her; she carried it with her as part of herself. The longing for peace and oblivion was always overwhelming; the pressing desire for sleep.

Her poor sister.

There could be no forgiveness for what had been done to January. None. No pardon, no indulgence, no excuse. What had been inflicted on Prue did not compare with the crucifixion of January. Since infancy, the murderous beatings, withdrawal of food, the lockings-up, the lockings-out, then the rapes, the sexual hate – he had sought to kill Christ in her. Yet she had scrambled down off the cross with her wounded hands and feet, the gash in her side, and fought him back; and that was her glory. She was lashed, mocked and derided, and the spirit nearly quelled in her, but she bounced right back up again and took him on, on his own terms. And she won, she broke him. For he was never the same again – more maudlin and coercively ingratiating than violent (though he was that too, oh yes, he was that too when the mood coincided with the alcohol-level). And that was one reason why Prue, unlike her husband, was confused and ambivalent about her commitment to pacifism. The colonised and oppressed must fight back – they *must*, she broke out; injustice must be resisted.

Yet she herself did not have it in her to fight back. Gentle as a lamb, she had meekly let him lead her to the shambles.

She remembered hunkering down with January as very little children. In some sunny spot at some indeterminate camp or other. They were playing fives; then they played marbles; then they ate peardrops out of a paper bag. They cast long shadows and the two shadows were one. The shadows joined inseparably at shoulder, elbow, foot or knee, however they moved.

And always and everywhere around the shadows of the girls, the towering shadows of the soldiers. Brute power and armed force ringed them round in their play-space.

Over them all the shadow of the nuclear bomb soared. These facts were the unquestioned foundation of their world. They sat in the dappled shade under a spike-leaved palm-tree in Ismaelia and shared a sherbet dab on the edge of the desert; each child wore a tasselled fez on her head; a soldier ambled by with his sleeves rolled up and a rifle over his arm, whistling. It was a companionable memory. It was before Dad started to lay into January. They must have been about 3 years old.

In the 1970s, the Salvation Army traced Prue's sister. She was dossing in a filthy squat in a squalid attic in Manchester's Whalley Range. She was in the terminal stages of heroin addiction. Teresa, who had left the enclosed order, tried to get January to come out of there and let herself be taken care of.

'Don't give me that crap,' said January. 'Don't bullshit me. Thanks for coming and now sod off. At least here I can be me.'

Prue, entirely uncertain as to whether she can claim the triumph of such a testament, gets on the minibus for Forres. She takes two valium and momentarily closes her lids over the contact lenses which ache on the dry, tearless membrane of her eye. Automatically she opens her book and begins to read.